THREE WARS

JOSEPH E. KAUFMANN

CHAPTER 1

I go back as far as I can remember It wasn't that I wanted to but sitting in prison I had time on my side Nothing but time The first thing I could remember was getting up one morning I was only about three years old My mother came and woke me She kissed me and said I was going to help my father today I still remember the feeling I had I couldn't wait for the day I could go out in the fields and help my father and my brothers do the work We had a farm We grow vegetables We also had some cows My father owned his land He made a good living off the land At lease that is what I trough I found out later he didn't own He just worked for the government He grow food for the soldiers.

My mother and sisters stayed home and did the cooking I had two brothers and two sisters. My brothers were all older then me My sisters to My mother said I wasn't to be She had her hands full with the rest of them But my father disagreed with her He said I was a strong boy and I could help out around the farm That was all I wait for The day I could go off with my brothers and father helping grow the vegetables I never know what the word hungry was We always had food on our table My brothers and sisters loved me I was the youngest I was like a new toy to them They played with me all the time I had a happy life at the start

That change a year later. Getting back to my first day in the fields my job was to help my father hit the horses.

"You had to make them move." He would say.

His plow wouldn't work if they didn't pull it. That is what he told me; so my job was to whip the horses. I like the way they jumped when I hit them. It made me laugh. I guess I did a good job my first day when my sister came out with the lunch she said my mother said; that was enough for one day I had to go back home with her." I didn't want to go but my father said I did go and I could come back out tomorrow with him." When I got back to the house my sister told my mother what my father said. She to said; I did good. She kissed me and gave me some cookies for doing so.

When my father and brothers came home that night to eat; all they talked about was how I whipped the horses and how good I did. I guess I was proud of myself; because I remember I went to bed feeling good. The next day I got up with the man and did everything they did. That was how I started off Half a day at first then longer and longer days more and more work. By the time I was four I was out in the fields all day long with my family. I went from whipping the horses to planting. That was hard I had to make a hole and drop seeds into the hole I made and then cover it back up with the dirt. That wasn't the hard part the hard part was keeping up to my brothers. They kept yelling for me to hurry. Some time I would lose sight of them I got so far behind. But my father said I was learning and I did a good job. That was what counted.

That went on day after day seven days a week. Once in a while I would hear my mother and father talk when they trough we all went to sleep. They were talking about something they called a WAR and a man named Hitler. My father worked for this man and so did my mother. My mother didn't like him, but my father stood up for him. He'd keep saying he was a good man, and how this man will free the world some day.

Day after day we would see more and more of these things flying over head. My father said they were air planes. This Mr. Hitler was building a lot of them for the war. My brothers said one day they will fly in one of them for this Hitler man. My father was getting excited watching them fly over. He would come home and tell my mother how many we saw that day.

"Good she would say." But wouldn't talk to him after that; he would talk to my brothers and tell them of what a great man this Hitler was. Then he would tell them about when he was in the war with America. He got a lot of medals he'd say and then he would go and get them.

My mother would always say,

"All for what? You lose the war."

That would get my father mad; he would start yelling at her "Hitler is different; he would say. With him leading us we will win this time you will see. My mother would keep quite again. She knew he would hit her if she said anything more about this Hitler man. I remember one day he did hit her. He took the whip from the wall and hit her hard. We all watched him. He said "That is the way you treated a woman that spoke out against her husband."

From that day on my mother never said anything about this Hitler man again. This Hitler man was my father's friend, and he let my mother know she shouldn't talk bad about him.

My work in the fields was getting better I was keeping up with my brothers; my father said Mr. Hitler would be proud of me."

One day I asked my father where this Mr. Hitler lived?"

"Oh he said He live in a big house and had a big army. That is where the food goes; we grow." he said. We feed Mr. Hitler's army.""

"You mean they eat all our food?" I asked. Boy there must be a lot of them? I remember thinking. We grow a lot of food.

"No, he said. We are only a small farm Mr. Hitler got bigger farms growing more and more food. His army is getting bigger and bigger all the time. Some day you will see my son.

"What for one day." I asked as we finished eating

"Ha "was all my mother said.

My father through his plate at her and told her to shout up. He came back to me and said "What for my son; for you and your brothers. You see my son People in the world are taking away everything we do. Mr. Hitler is going to stop that; Mr. Hilter said he is going to make Germany the father land the way it should be. No more Jews to take it way."

"Jews "I said "What are Jews?" That was the first time I had heard that word.

"Jews are dirty people;" my brother said.

They knew all about them and when the night was over with I knew this Mr. Hitler was a good man to help us. I could see why my father got mad at my mother for talking bad about him. He was going to get rid of all the Jew's for us.

One day when we were out in the fields we saw a cloud of dust coming up the road. My father saw it first; he stopped plowing; he got up on the horse and looked to see who was coming.

"Quick "he said to me and my brothers "We have to get back to the house we have a friend coming. This was pretty exciting for us. We never had anyone come visit us. My father unhitched the horse from the plow and hooked it up to the wagon. That meant we were finished for the day. We all climb in the wagon excited and headed for home. It must be pretty special for us to stop work in the middle of the day. All I can remember was no work for the rest of the day. That was fun. When we got to the house the cloud was getting closer.

"Mommy; "my father called; get dinner ready we got guest coming. Boys change into your best."

Boy was this something we never wear our best

Momma came and got me; all of us ran around like crazy.

Whoever it was he moved fast; I remember one day we saw my brother coming from that far way and it took him a long time to get home. This person was coming up to the front of our house already and he wasn't riding a horse; he was in some kind of wagon with no horse pulling it. Boy was this something. The man got out; he was covered with dust from head to toe. My father came running up to him and hugged him as if it was his brother. I found out it was his brother; one I never heard about. In fact I never heard about any one of our family back then. This was all new to me I just sat and listened to them talk.

He was driving what they called a motor car "Everyone had one;" he said.

"We didn't we were away from a lot of things. Like time was passing us by; my mother would say; all for this Hitler man.

My uncle Hans was in the army of this Mr. Hitler He said my father and brothers could join. My mother didn't like the idea about him talking to them about joining.

"She said we do enough for the man; he couldn't take her sons."

My father got mad at my mother again but his time he gave me the whip. He told me to beat her with it.

"No father; my brother said let me do it."

That was the first time I saw my mother cry.

"See my father said proud; what man Hitler will get from my boys."

"He would be proud;" my uncle said.

"Good then we will set out in the morning."

It's funny how you can remember every little detail when you think back.

"What about us?" My mother said.

"I will send for you; he said; as soon as I know where Mr. Hitler will have me.

"And what about our farm?" she asked

"Don't not worry furling; we will send some Jews to run it. My uncle said you will live in a big house now; he said your husband will be an officer of the third ricks; now nothing is too good for his men."

He stood up and did something I had never seen before. He clicked his hells together and stuck his arm and hand straight into the air a said the words "Hal Hitler.

My father stood and did the same. Then my brothers did it to. I tried but fell down trying my uncle picked me up and said "Some day my little German."

They all laugh at me except my mother she tried to hide her tears

My uncle stayed over the night. Him and my father talked till I fell asleep. I guess they talk all night when we woke up in the morning my father was gone and so was my uncle. They left at day break.

My mother had breakfast ready for us and said we had to work the fields by our self. My father would return soon to fetch us and we would be off to the big city. My brother's were happy and so were my sisters. They couldn't wait to go; no more farming for them. It was the army for them and a big house for my mother and sisters. For me I didn't know what was for me; I was too little for anything. So I just sat and listened to them talk. My mother came to hold me and try to tell me what was happening; but I didn't want to hear what she had to say. My father told me not to listen to her. And besides what did she know?

For days; me and my brothers worked the fields. They didn't get to much work done. We played soldiers all the time; shooting each other and marching up and down the fields. I played with them but they always made me be the Jew. I didn't know what that meant but I did know they were bad and they had to be killed or put to work. That is what my brothers said they did. On the eighth day they saw a cloud of dust coming. They said it was our father; I didn't see anything but I jumped and yell just like them. I wanted to be like them so much I did everything they did. My oldest brother Herman took the horse and hitched it to the wagon

"No more farm for us;" he said

Then we all went back home watching the cloud of dust coming closer.

My mother saw it to; her and the girls were watching it as we pulled up. My brother Herman told my mother to start dinner our father was coming. He sounded just like my father. My mother looked at him as to say something but stopped when he picked up the whip and showed her he had it. She went back into the house and didn't come back out again. I felt sorry for mother; but back then I thought that was the way she was treated. I didn't know better. The cloud was getting closer I could see this big thing coming. It was bigger then the Motor car I saw my uncle coming in.

"Look my brother said. It's a truck."

"What was that?" I asked

"A Big motor car; my brother said.

It came up the front gate and stopped at the bottom of the hill

"Why they stop." I asked.

"I don't know;" my brother said.

I was going to run down and see when my brother stopped me.

"Wait here." He said

Just then a motor car came from behind the truck and came up to the front of us. My father stepped out and stood on what they called a running board He just looked at us; I couldn't believe what he looked like; He had the same uniform on as my uncle had.

"Oh Mommy didn't he look rich and handsome;" my sisters said.

I don't know about that I will say he looked proud and strong. My brothers ran up to him and did that thing again with the arms and hands.

"Hail Hitler; they said. My father did the same thing. "My wonder full children I have returned. And I have good news for all."

"Come father. My older brother said I have mother fixing you dinner."

"Good; he said I have not eaten since last night.

"Poppa he asked "What is that truck waiting for?"

"Them my son he said Are Jews. They are going to farm our fields till we return. Then they will be ours to keep. No more work for an officer of the third ricks." He said.

"Hail Hitler; they all said. He got out and stood looking at us.

"Yes my sons he said you're going to make fine solders.

"Me to Papa." I said looking up at him.

"You to my son; he said picking me up and carrying me into the house.

"Hello Mother; he said Are you pack and ready to go?'He asked

"We are; my brothers said.

"Good; first we eat he said then we leave."

"Just like that?'My mother said.

"The war can't wait old woman like you; he said now either you come or you stay with the Jews; what will it be?"

"I go for my children;" she said.

"No more your children; he said Adolph's Children now. You will have more." he said.

I didn't know what he meant by that on till later my mother was having another baby. I didn't know it then but she was.

My father ate, and told my brothers to pack up and have everything out in front. He was going to get the Jews out of the truck.

"Can we come;" they asked him.

"No he said taking the whip and saying "Joseph will come with me."

That was me. From then on I felt bigger then my brothers; my father picked me over them I felt proud. He handed me the whip and said "You my son will help."

He walked out the door and down to the truck I had to run to keep up with him. I had the whip in one hand and holding up my pants with the other. You see I had my brothers pants on; I'd would grow into them;" my mother said.

When we got to the truck two solders jump out and did the thing with their hand to my father. My father did it to them and said "Get them out."

"Yes sir; the two solders said and ran to the back of the truck. I didn't know what was back there except they were called Jews. I didn't know what kind of animals they were but I did know from what my brothers told me about them; And the way my father talked about them I was scared to look; so I hide behind my father's lag watching.

The solders opened the back of the truck and started yelling.

My eyes almost fell out of my head when I saw what was coming out of the back of the truck. It was people. Man woman and children. The solders were pushing them out on to the ground and kicking them to move.

"Papa "I said holding on tight; it was scaring the hell out of me

"Now son he said you don't ever have to be afraid of them Jews they can't hurt you."

"Look "he said and went up and kicked one of them See they can't hurt you. He kicked another one. They didn't even cry when he did it. They were so dirty I couldn't see their faces. When they were all out on the ground. The solders lined them up and told them to stay that way. My father walked up to them and looked at each and every one of them in the face.

Then he said "You see I look at you in your face. This way I know you. This is my farm; he said You will run it. But if I hear of anyone of you destroying it I'll come back and have you shot. Do you understand me?" He said

One of the solders hit a man on the back of the head with his rifle and knocked him to the ground.

"Do you hear me?" My father said again.

"Yes;" they said together.

"Good "he said. Now when I leave I want you to work my farm and grow the biggest crop ever. Make my fury Proud; then you make me proud it came from my land."

"You; he said pointing at a little boy a little bigger then me "Get out here;" he said.

The solder pushed him to the ground in front of my father

"You my little Jew will be for my son "Joseph my father said Come here.

He looked at the Jews and then he said to the solders "watch this; this is a true German. He told me to whip the Jew boy like I whip the horse.

I trough it was a game of some kind so I took the whip and remembered what my brothers did to me what they said I was the Jews. I swung the whip around my head and let it land on the boys back. The solders and my father cheered me. I looked back at them; one of the solders said "More and harder." I did it again for them; the more I did it the louder they cheered me. I didn't see the boy I was whipping I just saw the glory in doing it.

"One of the soldier said "You had better stop him before he kills him.

"So my father said we can get more."

They all laughed; I stopped to laugh with them. That was when I noticed the other Jews looking at me. The woman had tears in her eyes. She didn't take her eyes off of me. She made me uncomfortable I hide behind my father and said "Make her stop."

My father stopped laughing and saw her looking at me "Oh my lady Jew; he said Looking at her. My son did he do something wrong?"

My father did something I'll never forget. He took out his gun and shot her in the head. She didn't say a word she just kept looking at me as she fell. Her eyes stayed open till I couldn't see them anymore.

"How my son does she still bather you?"

They all laugh again. The other Jews didn't move I turned around to run to the house. I had never saw a dead person before; I didn't like it; but as I started to run I tripped over the boy I had beating.

He looked up at me with tears in his eyes. The water washed his skin clean. He had two lines down his face; his eyes were big and all I could see was them.

"Get out of his way." One of the solders said kicking him across the dirt. He landed in front of his mother; at that time I didn't know it was his mother. That was on till he cried out.

"Mother "and went to her

"You see the soldier said. They cry like a pig; no German would cry like that. Look at your boy he said Good German."

My father picked me up and held me in the air. By this time my brothers had came down I guess they heard the shot

"Father they yelled What is it."

Oh he said laughing I killed a Jew for your brother.

My oldest brother said "Kill one for us to Papa."

"No "he said; if I do that then we will have no one to work the fields."

They all laugh again. This was funny I started to laugh again when I saw the little boy looking at me. I didn't want to tell my father. I didn't want him to kill him to; so I just looked the other way.

My father picked me up and said to the soldier's to take the truck to the house. The other soldier had the Jews take out the rest of the boxes from the truck then he took out some chains. I didn't know what they were use for, but again I found out. He started to chain the lags of the Jews together

"What is that for?" I asked.

"So they can't run away; he said you see we need all the soldier's at the fount. We can only leave one here with them. The chains make them know they can't go anywhere."

"The soldier said and they know it' so I can watch them all without worrying."

He gave the key to my father and said "I won't be needing this anymore."

My oldest brother asked.

"What if one of them die; how will you get him out of the chains?"

"You got smart sons "the other one said.

"Well "he said These Jews got a choice; Pick him up till he ruts out; or chop off his lag and leave him to the side. I had one work gang that kept them till they rotted. Man did they stink Most of them chop their lags off."

"But how could they use the horse." He asked

"Horse; my father said our horse is coming back with us; Adolf needs all the horse he can find. The Jews don't need a horse they do the work for the horse."

"That is a good idea my brother said. A horse works to hard."

Your older son is a smart boy." One said I got something for him."

My father looked at him and smiled

"Why not he is of age. Come Joseph he said picking me up and putting my on his shoulders. We go see what mother is doing."

I looked back to see what my brother was doing. Again I didn't know. The soldier had a woman on the ground and had her clothes off; My brother was climbing on top of her.

"Papa "I said I want to play to." He stopped and turned around to look.

"No; he said you're too young next year; he said I'll let you play not now."

"Put Papa I'm big now." I said.

"No, he said you got to be bigger to play that game."

We got back to the house again my mother didn't say a word she just looked at us I could tell she wasn't happy.

My father said to her "You had better get used to it, it was their way of living from now on."

My sisters were running around getting thing together Of course my other brother just watched out the window at what his brother was doing

"Come; my father said to me "You will help me pack."

I felt as big as my brothers when my father asked me to help not them.

He went into his room and took out this big trunk; he opened it. Inside were his old uniform and his guns "This he said will be yours some day." He held up a pistol My heart stop when he took it out of it's holster and handed it to me

"Can I kill Jews with it?" I asked

"That is what it is for my son. He told me; plus all the other bad people in the world;" he added

I took the gun and placed it in my hand so I got the feel of it, it was heavy and hard he took it off of me and said "Remember your gun should always be loaded you never know when your going to use it."

He took out what he called a clip and showed me some things he called bullets He showed me how to load the clip as he called Then show me how to put it back "This is the only way you will live he said

It was hard for me to understand what he was talking about but I listened to him and remembered what he was showing me.

My mother came into the room and told him she was ready. My father stood up I trough he was going to hit her again but he didn't. This was the first time and the last time I saw he do it. He took her in his arms and kissed her on the top of the head saying "This is what I've been waiting for. We live proud now."

She had tears in her eyes as she said "I hope for all of us it is true."

That was all she said and took his bags and went out side with them

"Your momma worries too much he said she will see."

He picked me up and carried me out to the truck

"My sons; he said as we all got in. "Look at this and remember how we lived. Tomorrow we will live like kings."

"But Papa; one of my sisters asked "We are coming back aren't we?"

"Yes my child; he said, when we conquered the world."

All of us got in the back and had a set' my father road in front with the drive. He told us to hold on tight the roads were bumpy. He drove down to the place where the Jews were waiting. He stopped the truck; we all looked out to see what he was doing. He got my older brother in the back with us Then he was talking to the soldier that was going to stay at our house He told him to look after it and he would send a truck back with supplies by next week "Have the cows and horse ready to return with it." My father was taking everything and giving it to this Mr. Hitler He said he needed it for his man. I remember looking at my brother as he got in the back with us. He just smiled and said

"The solder said I was a man now."

My mother told him it would take a lot more then a woman to make him a man."

He stood up and pointed his finger at her. He told her she didn't know anything about being a man and if she didn't shout up he would take the whip to her."

I never saw my brother act this mad before He looked at me and said. "Woman should learn to keep their mouths shout."

"Us to;" My sister said to him.

"You too; he said looking at them. Learn the new way;" he said Hail Hitler he said trying to click his heels like my uncle did. The truck started and he fell back of course we all laugh at him That got him mad; he jumped up and said "I'm a soldier of the German army no one laugh's at me." He went to swing at my mother but my other brother stopped him. He just stood up in front of him and let him hit him instead. That started them two fighting. They rolled on the floor of the truck fighting; they always forte; my mother just watched and didn't stop them. My sisters just played with their dolls they brought; me I looked out the back of the truck I never rode in one before and I was feeling proud as my father said.

As was went past the Jews I saw the Jew my father shot Her son was bending over her trying to get her up

For some reason I was waiting for her to stand. I didn't know what the word death was yet. As we passed the little boy he looked up at me with his big eyes. I waved to him as if I was saying good bye to him like I'd see him again tomorrow to play. He watched us go without moving. When he was almost out of sight I saw him wave back to me. That made me happy; he wasn't mad at me for playing the game to ruff. It was only a game all kids plays games.

We drove for days; in one town and out the other side. We didn't stop; people came to look at us. Lots of them cheered us; we waved at them as we drove by but we didn't stop; we kept on going. Once in a while we would pull over to the side of the road to go to the bathroom; or get something to eat; but we slept in the truck. Once my father took me in the front with him

He didn't let my brothers; just me. I sat on his lap; he would show me all the different thing I had never seen before. Motor cars and Trains. He said they were filled with soldiers going to the front. Big guns he pointed out. He said the army was moving Mr. Hitler was at war."

"Good papa I said we can shot Jews." I said

"Son he would say. You will have all the Jews you want; your father is going to be in charge of a prison camp filled with Jews."

"Yes comrade; the driver said And we are bring more and more in every day for you Mr. Hitler is making sure they don't get away. We need them to work our factories and farms. The men of Germany need to be free to fight."

"He is a smart man; my father said. This time we will win the war."

"Yes Captain he said to my father. This time we will win our factories are working around the clock making tanks guns and planes. We have a air force bigger than any other country; boys like your sons are even fighting. My own son just turned thirteen. He is in uniform."

"You see my two boys? They will make fine soldiers.

"Papa what about me?" I said

"You my little pumpkin are going to be the best I've made arrangement for you to go to school for officers. My other sons like to fight too much. Him, he said looking at me; is the one with the brains

Adolf will be proud of my bring him up. My son will serve me proud;" he said

I fell asleep in his arms It was like I was dreaming everything was going so fast. When I woke I could see a big river

"Papa what is that?" I asked.

"He said that is a water way; our boats are being built over there;" he said pointing at this big boat as he called it.

My father told the drive to stop. My father got out with me and looked at the big boat he told me about. "Look mother he said you see Mr. Hitler knows what he is doing. Did you ever see a finer ship in your life?"

My brothers all came out to looked. They asked if they could go on it?"

"No he said but some day maybe."

"Oh papa my brother said I want to go on the ship I want to be a sailor."

"You do, do you; he said. We will see about that."

My other brother said he wanted to drive a tank."

"And you he said picking me up. "What do you want to do?" he asked me

"Me I said I want to kill Jews."

"Ha; he said Hear him momma?" he said hugging me

I looked at my mother but she didn't look back She kept her eyes to the floor of the truck

"We are almost there; he said everyone back in the truck"

We drove into this big city; my father said it was Berlin the heart of the German army. I saw what he meant. Everyone was dressed in a uniform All different kinds. My father told me who was who Sailors soldiers' air man and officer's. I'd never saw so many people at one time; in fact I never saw any people till the other day. The Jews were the first people I saw. We pulled up in front of this big building and stopped. He said he was going in and he would be out soon.

"Papa, take me with you." I said

"No My son I have to report."

"Please Papa." I said crying

"Come; he said. He took me in his arms and walked inside I could see my brothers getting mad at me when I passed them. My older one held up his fist up to me As if he was going to punch me when I got back. I made a face at him showing him he didn't scare me."

Men stopped and did the arm thing to him as he walked into the building He went to a desk and said his name. The man at the desk told him something and pointed up stairs. He took my hand and we walked up the stairs and down a hall. This building was so big and shiny it took my breath away. Never before have I seen anything like it I just held on and looked. My father came to a door and stopped; he let me down.

"You wait here; he said I'll be out soon." He sat me on a set and went in the door. I just sat there looking at all the people walking by. They were so many of them, But no one even look at me They all had things to do. Before you know it I was getting tired I laid my head back and went to sleep."

The next thing I know someone was shacking me. I opened my eyes and saw this big man looking at me.

"What are you doing here?" He said

"My father is a soldier." I said standing up

"Oh; he said and where is your father?" He asked.

I pointed to the door he went in

"That is good;" he said and what do you do?"

I looked at him at his side was the same kind of gun my father told me I was going to get to kill the Jews with "Kill the Jews." I said with that gun;" I pointed at it.

"Oh he said but you're to small."

"No, I said standing up straight looking at him in the eyes. "I killed one all ready."

"Oh, he said laughing He reach over and picked me up. "You did, did you?"

"Yes ask my father." I said

"That we will;" he said taking me into the door My father went into

When he entered everyone jumped up and did that arm thing to him and yelled Hail Hitler

"Hail, the man said and looked around the room "Witch one is your father?" he asked

I looked but didn't see him "I can't see him." I said

"Well then I guess your going to have to come with me."

That got me scared I didn't want to leave my father. "No I said I wait for him."

"But you don't see him maybe he left you?"

"He is here." I said

"Show me." he said

"I can't see him." I said

"Then you come with me." he said

"No I said backing away from him; you touch me and I'll kill you."

"Oh he said laughing again "And with will you kill me with?"

"My father's gun." I told him

"But you don't have your father's gun."

"I will get it." I told him

"You are very brave for a little boy." he said With that he turned around to ask someone if they know who my father was; his gun came right even with my eyes.

I don't know what made me do what I did but I did I took the snap off it and pulled it out without him knowing. When he turned to look at me I had it pointed right at him.

"You leave me alone or I'll kill you." I told him

The look he gave me scared me. His eyes just looked right through me. He said "Go a head and do it you will be the most famous boy alive."

He wanted me to kill him. He reached down to take his gun back but I pulled the trigger; just as I pulled it someone grabbed me from behind. The gun went off up in the air. The person behind me hugged me. It was my father

He started yelling at me I didn't know what he was saying but the man I was going to kill was just laughing at him and me

"Come; he said and walked away

My father picked me up and followed him He walked pass all the doors on till he came to this big door with gold birds on it. Two solders opened the door for him and he went in. My father followed; he kept saying to me. "You're going to get it."

The man went behind this big desk he took off his hat and looked at me and my father.

"Your son almost killed me;" he said

"Sir I'm sorry I shouldn't have brought him I'll take him and whip him;" he said to the man

The man laugh and said "I don't think so;" he said He then looked at me and smiled His eyes hurt me I couldn't look at him I knew something was wrong My father was shaking as he held me; he did put me down.

"Well; the man asked standing "Who are you

My father snapped his heels together like my uncle and said his name. What he did in the army before in the other war.

Another man came over to his desk and said something in his ear. The man looked at my father and smiled

"Sir Gruber is it?"

"Yes sir."

"My officer tells me you were to be a prison guard at Doctow

"Yes sir; he said

"Well sir Gruber I have good news for you."

"Yes Sir Hitler."

That was the first time I heard the name of the man.

Hitler was the name everyone said was the man doing it all. Was this man Mr. Hitler?

"Sir Gruber being you was an officer in the Germany army before and you raised such a find son I'm making you in charge of the prison camp. I was looking for a good officer such as yourself."

"Thank you Sir Hitler; he said letting me down "Hail Hitler my father said and did the arm thing

"It is man like you that are going to make me win the war;" he said

"Thank you Furor."

It is told you have two more sons to join us?"

"Yes my furor."

"If they are anything like this one I'm proud to have you. Your work on your farm has made my soldiers not go hungry. So my good man I have decided to reward you and your son." He said looking at me "You are now a General in my army and your job is to make sure we do something with the Jews as we fight the war."

"Yes Furor." He said

"And you young man, you will see to it your father carries out my orders. Did he really kill a Jew?"

"Yes Furor." My father said proud

That was when I remembered I still had his gun

"Here;" I said holding it up to him

"Excuse him." my father said He doesn't understand yet."

"Oh he laughs. He does he killed his first Jew and almost killed me; with my own gun. This man has trough us all a lot." Meaning me. He called me a man

He came around from his desk. He stood right in front of me "Even a baby Jew could be dangerous you showed me that; Lucky for me you aren't a Jew." he said Laughing

"No sir; my father said "Tell the Furor about the Jews."

"I kill the Jews." I said they all laugh.

"No my son; he said that gun is yours you take it and kill some more Jews with it."

"Thank the Furor." My father said

I held out my hand to thank him but he didn't take it he stood up and clicked his heels saying "Hail" to me. I put the gun down and did it to him

"Would you look at this soldier? He can't even hold a gun but yet he knows how to salute me. Sir Gruber you have any problems you come see me. He said. Now Joseph you pick up your gun and you go help your father run the camp."

"Hail Hitler; they all said as we left. Mr. Hitler gave my father a paper telling anyone what Mr. Hitler told him. My father said it was his orders as we went back to the truck.

The driver asked "where to?"

"Doctow" I told him. He looked at me and said you're kidding?"

"No, my father said proudly and showed him his papers. He saw it said; "General" and jumped out of the truck. Hail Hitler; he said doing the arm thing to my father. My father smiled at him and said

"Eric you are going to be my driver from now on." That made the driver the happiest man around. He couldn't even drive he was so happy. I don't know what it was all about but I guess it was something good. My father told him to stop at a place to eat. He felt like celebrating.

The driver told him he know just the place. And off we went. My father kept hugging me and kissing me.

"You he said I know would be something." He told the driver all about what had happened. The drive couldn't believe it he kept saying "No No you kid me?"

My father took out the gun and showed him. The driver took it and smelt the hole in the front "Dos is true he said handling it back to him."

The drive looked at me and said.

"The furor's friend"; and kissed me. I don't know what the big deal was about but I eat it up. The driver pulled up and stopped in front of this place with a lot of tables and people eating in it. My father got out and went to the back and opened the curtain so my Brothers and sisters could come out.

"Come my family we eat and drink your brother is a great man from this day on."

He picked me up and walked into the door sat down at this big table. The driver was talking to the man behind the box. When he finished he came around and stood in front of me and gave me the Hail sign. He told my father the food was on him and we could eat all we wanted to."

Buy the time the food came everyone was standing around me watching us. My father told my family what I had done. All the people in the place clapped for me when he finished. My brothers didn't like it but they were to excited to be mad at me. My mother didn't change she kept looking at the floor. As we eat more people came and looked at me. Some of them asked if they could touch me.

"You'd had better watch out he will shot you;" my father said.

They all laugh.

My father took the gun Mr. Hitler gave me and stuck it in the rope I had to hold up my brothers pants. People just looked at it they didn't touch it for some reason; they just looked.

We finished and went back to the truck I was going to go in the back with my other brothers but my father said I should ride in front.

"No man a friends of the Furor should ever ride in the back."

"Hail" the drive said and started up We drove for another couple of hours. We came to a place to rest. It was called an Inn. It had beds for us to sleep in.

The drive said a "General doesn't sleep on the road." He got out and opened the door for my father then he ran in and got thing ready for us. This was the first time I had a taste of the good life. The beds were big they even had a wash tub in the room for us to bath in. My Brothers and sisters played on the beds I got ready for the first bath. That was an honor in it self I was always the last one to get a bath. The water was always cold.

My brother's didn't like it but they saw the way my father looked at them and didn't do anything. I liked doing it to them; they always did it to me. Now it as my turn.

We got dressed and went down to eat again. A lot of solders were sitting with us. They all know what happened and who my father was.

"My father looked so proud sitting at the head of the table. The driver said he out ranked everyone here so he was to sit at the head; and I sat right next to him. The food came out; my eyes opened wide; I had never seen anything like it before. It was a whole pig with an apple in its mouth. My father stood up and said "a meal fit for a king;" and pointed at me.

The whole table stood up and all of them said the word "Hail Hitler" and raised their steins to drink. Just the way they looked at me made me proud. This was to much for me I only finished half my meal and fell asleep in my set. My father picked me up and was carrying me to our room when the man that owned the Inn stopped him. "Sir please it would be an honor if you would do something for me."

"What?" my father asked

"The gun; he said could you have your son shot a hold in something for me; just to tell the people of the great son you have."

He set me down on the step and took out the gun He held me up and gave it to me

"Here, he said. Shot the man."

"Oh god no; the man said. Just the wall will do."

Everyone started laughing and saying "Shot the man Shot the man."

I pointed it at him and asked "You a Jew?"

"No; he said bragging. I'm German like you please don't shot me."

My father helped me with the gun and pointed it over the man's head and fired. The noise scared me but I didn't let them know it. He hit a plate he had on the wall and broke it into a lot of pieces. The whole place cheered me my father picked me up and put me on his shoulders and went up stairs. I looked back at the people; I like the feeling I was getting they were cheering for me. That was the first feeling of real power I guess you could say I had. My Father placed me in this big bed and pulled the covers over me.

"Good night my son;" he said and kissed me.

The next morning we got up dressed went down to eat Breakfast. No one was around, not like last night that is. We eat and went on our way

We drove for a couple of more hours with me in the front of course. We came to a road with solders blocking it. They stopped us but when they saw the paper my father had they back away and did the arm thing to us and let us pass. As we drove down the road we came up to people walking; it was Jews coming to the camp the driver said.

The solders were wiping them and pushing them to keep going.

"Papa; I said. Can't you kill them here?"

"No my son we need them to work."

"Pigs;" the drive said as we passed them.

"Soon;" my father said there will be no more pig to get in our way."

The driver said "Hail to that;" and kept driving

"There it is; he said as we came around a turn. You could see a lot of buildings and a big tall thing down the road ahead of us. My father said it was a smoke stack A chimney like the one we had at home but bigger.

We pulled up to the front gate and stopped. The driver showed the papers and again the solders jumped. One of the solders jumped on the truck; he was showing the drive where we were to go. We pulled up to this big house and stopped.

"Here; he said you will live."

My father got out and took me with him. He told my family to get out we were home. We all just looked at it; this place was big. This is what they called a prison camp. My father walked up to the front door the driver opened it for him.

"Welcome." he said as my father walked in

"Momma; he yelled get the children settled first. Joseph to get his own room;" he said looking at her.

Again my brothers didn't like it but my father set them straight at the dinner table that night. The driver got all the things in the house. The house was furnished already so we didn't need any of your things. My mother kept some thing and the rest was burnt out in the back. My father told her to burn it all he didn't want anything to remind him of the way we use to live. He was happy he was back in the army again. I saw a change coming over him. He was turning into a different man; no more farmer he was a General now And all because of me.

It wasn't that he wasn't a good soldier. He proved him self in the last war. He was an officer then also; so it was easy for him to order man around. He said it was what he was meant to be; A soldier not a farmer. Well we got our rooms and Like my father said; I got my own the others sured rooms; the house was big we had trouble getting use to it.

It was our way of life from that day on. The driver came up with a truck load of clotheses; he said he took it from the Jews they arrested."

My mother was to look at them to see if anything would fit. We didn't have much clotheses on the farm but we sure had them now. My mother had pretty dresses and I had suits and shoe and everything else. My sisters had dresses and coats and hats. It was as if we all had a birthday together. That night the Driver came with the other soldiers from the prison. They all sat in this big room and talked.

I guess they wanted to show him how things were run around the prison. I could tell they were talking about the Jews and what they did to them It was as if it was a game to them. My father walked them to the door when they left. Then he called all of us to sit down and hear what he had to say to us."

"Well we are home now and this is where we will stay. Now we are going to change our way of living. It may be hard at first but you'll get use to it in no time." He looked at my brothers and said "You two going to join the Navy I have word you are leaving for training camp tomorrow. I want to wish you all the best and come home safe."

Mother and sisters will act as host to the German army. Your mother will be in charge of the officers wife's at the camp. You young ladies; he said to my sisters; will have to go start school."

They didn't like it but they know what my father said went. Then he came to me "You my son who we all owe this to; you are going to be my right hand man till you can enter officer school.

"When Papa I asked

"With in the year; he said. But first you have to learn to read and write."

"Like us;" my brother said

"Like them, he said. We didn't teach you because you are still to young; so for now you will help me run the prison."

"And kill Jews." I asked

They all laugh It was good to here them all laughing again. It seemed as if everyone was happy except my mother; she just listened to what my father had to say and didn't say a word.

I didn't know how she was feeling because she never talked to me much. She was always busy doing things around the house. I was closer to my father he would take me on his knee and tell me all about the war he was in. I would listen to him falling asleep in his arms. My brothers would be tired of working in the fields and would go to sleep early; so did my sisters. I was at the age I didn't do much work but I could listen and that was what he wanted I guess someone to listen to what he had to say. He liked talking about what he did. I remember sitting on his knee and hearing the same war stories and how disappointed he was we lost the war.

I remember the first night we slept in our new house. It was kind of hard. Trains were coming back and forth with the Jews. Trucks were driving by all hours of the night. Lights were all over the place on all the time. Soldier's with whistles blowing all the time.

The next morning we got up my mother came in to wake me when I opened my eyes she smiled

"Well my son you ready for the day?" She would always say that to me. She had new clotheses put out for me.

"No she said looking at the pistol I had under my pillow. You can't sleep with this;" she said reaching for it

"No; I said and stopped her from taking it.

"Mr. Hitler gave it to me; you don't touch it." I told her. For some reason she didn't say a word she just looked at me. "Your, your fathers son." and walked out of the room.

I got dressed and was about to go look around at our new house when my Big brother came in. He pushed me to the ground and got on top of me.

"You are going to get the whip?" he said and slapped me across the face. He laughs and said I was too big for my pants and slapped me again.

I just looked at him and didn't say a word.

He slapped me again "Cry; he said and did it again. Cry baby cry."

But I didn't I just looked at him. He looked back at me and saw I wasn't crying the way I use to when he hit me. "I'll make you cry; he said and started pulling my hair. He hurt but I didn't cry I kept looking at him the way Mr. Hitler looked at me. He stopped and got up off of me "You think you're a man now?" he said I'll show you;" he said going over to my gun.

I jumped up and went over behind him. He bent down to take it from under my pillow. I saw a glass jar on my table; I picked it up and before he could get to my gun I hit him over the head with the jar. That was the first time I felt blood on me. The blood from his head came shooting out all over the place. I saw it running down his neck and over the sheets. He just laid there not moving. I took my gun and put it in my belt like my father did and walked out of the room; not caring what I did to him. He had hurt me to much for me to care. I got back at him for all the time's he beat me. That will show him I was a man and for him to leave me alone. I walked down stairs when I reached to the bottom my sister Gretdal saw me and started screaming. She saw the blood all over me.

My father came running out and stopped when he saw me "Joseph what happened?" he asked

I told him what I did and walked into the kitchen and sat down to eat. My father ran up stairs to get my brother; I heard he yell. "He is still alive."

Then my mother ran up. They all ran up to see. I stayed at the table I didn't want to see he was bad to me I just gave him what he gave me. My father carried him down and put him on the table He told my mother to get some water to wash him off and some bandages to stop the bleeding. He looked over at me and didn't say a word. He fixed my brother up and told him to go and rest. After my mother cleaned the table we eat. My sisters kept asking what happened?"

My father said "Not at the table; finish first. He said. Then help your mother with the dishes."

My father got up and told me to follow him. He walked into the big room he was in last night with the soldiers. It had a desk like Mr. Hitler and books on the wall. Over his desk was the picture of Mr. Hitler I like this room. He closed the door and told me to sit. I sat looking the room over.

"Joseph do you know what you did?"

"Yes father," I said. I didn't say anything more

"Son you can't go around hitting your brother over the head you could of killed him."

"So "I said

"But why?" He asked

"He tried to take my gun." "I said holding on to it.

"Oh I see he said He should know better than to do that."

"Yes father; I agree."

He just looked at me with out saying a word I could see he wasn't mad at what I did so I just looked around at the book

"It doesn't bother you?" He finely said.

"No father;" I said looking at the blood on the front of me

"Go change and wash the blood off you."

"Yes father I said getting up I went to my room and took off my shirt. My mother came in and cleaned me. She had another shirt for me to wear. She took me in her arms and told me to tell my brother I was sorry I hit him." I was going to tell her he hit me first but she stopped me."

"Go" she said

I went in to his room and looked at him He gave me the fist again meaning he was going to get me. I walked over to his bed and took out my gun. I put it to his head and said.

"You dye the next time."

"My brother didn't know what to do; he just looked at me. I saw that look before it was on the little Jewish Boy when I whipped him. I put the gun back in my belt and left his room. From that day on my brother didn't talk to me. He and my other brother left two days later for sea camp for the ships.

I was glad to see them go. I didn't like the way they use to beat up on me all the time I know they were my brothers but I never really know them. My father spent most of the time looking at books. He said he wanted to know how everything was run around here before he went out and had a look. Soldiers would come to the house all day long telling him of what they were doing. My father was a wise man he never did anything he didn't know about. He would always read about it first. Even at home he had books. My mother told us what a smart man he was and all the schools he went to. After the war he didn't want to do anything but farm.

The driver came in with a bunch of people. He had them lined up outside the door; my father came out and looked at them. They were to help my mother do cleaning. I remember looking out the window and watched them. There were ten woman and three little girls and two little boys older than me; but smaller then my brothers. I would say about ten or twelve. My father talked to them; he picked two women and one girl plus one boy. The rest were taking away. I ran to the other part of the house to where the drive took the ones my father picked.

He had them go to the cellar I went out the back to have a look at them. He had them take off all their clotheses. He had some soldier looking at them. They were checking them all over I don't know what they were looking for maybe that had some bugs? My mother would look in my brother's hair for bug some times. That is what it looked like he was doing

"Joseph my father said coming up behind me What are you looking at?

He saw what I was looking at and smiled at me

"I see your a ladies man already

"No Father What are they doing?

"They are going to work around the house I don't want them to have any bugs You don't want to catch any bugs from a Jew do you?

"No father

"That is why we are checking them You can go and watch if you want he said

"No father I saw

"Well then go help your mother

"Isn't that what they are to do? I asked

"God you are smart he said Yes son your right How would you like to come with me? I have to make my inspection of the prison

"Can I take my gun? I asked

"Only if you don't shot anyone he said

"No father only if you ask me to

Something was coming over me I didn't know what it was I guess I was acting the way my brothers acted when they said they were officers of the army and beat me because they said I was a Jew Who knew's what did it All I know I liked acting like the soldier Plus being I was a friend of Mr. Hitler it gave me the right to do so My father didn't mind He liked it I could tell He didn't tell me to stop So I kept it up I was playing the officer of the army

The next couple of hours were the worse of my life. At least I though they were back then. I don't know why my father showed me this but he did. Later on I know why I was his son and his son would be him. That is what my mother told me all the time. I was my father's son. We went from barrack to barrack; they were the houses that had the Jews sleeping in. The smell almost made me sick; I kept seeing my father looking at me out of the corner of his eyes; seeing what I would do, I guess. He would walk from one end to the other just looking at the Jews. They looked ugly skinny and sick. The other officer's that were coming along with us kept saying I should leave it was no place for a boy. My father kept walking He'd looked at me with that proud look.

From one place to the other we walked. They all looked the same. Then we went to this place they called the "Ovens". It was like a hot room Firers were burning all the time in these big brick holes.

One officer came to him and asked if he could take be back to the house?"

My father answer was "WHY?

The next building was the one the Jews were being cooked; it smelt; Plus they made a lot of noise burning.

"Something not for a boy to see." The soldier said again

"Oh? My father said why don't we ask him? "Joseph, are you getting sick?"

"No;" father I said

"Joseph do you want to see how the Jews are burnt?"

"Yes father." I said looking at the officer with us.

I didn't know what I was in for at the time; I still see and smell what I was about to see to this day.

"Good; my father said. Then let's go; he said to them.

We went to this last building I could smell something bad the closer we got the more it smelt.

"Sir the officer asked again you sure?"

"Yes captain;" he said "My son is strong and I want him to see what we do with the Jews. It's the young we look to train Captain remember that."

"Very well sir; he said this way."

I was sorry I went He opened the door the smell made me sick. I was about to throw up when my father picked me up in his arms and just looked at me. It stopped; he kept me in his arms as we entered He made sure I was looking He walked over to this hole and we looked in People were in there looking around They were Jews with no clotheses on

"Now "my father said

The whole room went on firer I could see the people trying to get out; their hair and skin starting to burn. My father held my face turn to look at them I could see him watching me.

I started to shake all over I couldn't hold it back anymore I throw up all over him. He put me down to wipe him self off. I ran I went out the door and kept on running

I don't know where I was going I didn't care; all I knew is I couldn't stay there and watch like my father wanted me to. I ran and I ran till I couldn't run no more. I stopped and fell to the ground and cried. I didn't think they were talking about what I just saw. That was when I know it wasn't a game anymore. The Jews were real people and really people were dying. I couldn't stop think of the looks on their faces when the flame came out and started burning them. The smell almost chocked me. I still smelt it in my nose today. I could never get the smell out; to this day I still smell it.

I stayed on the ground and cried. This wasn't fun any more I didn't want to play Kill the Jew's" anymore. I wanted to go home and be on my farm with my brothers the way we were before.

I heard soldiers calling my name. I didn't want to go back I couldn't go back I couldn't go back and watch what my father wanted me to watch. I kept hearing their scream's; it was making me sick all over again I got up and started to run again I remember saying to myself; I'm going to run home to my farm; this way my father and mother would have to come for me. I know they will stay once they see it again. I had to get back to my farm. I ran as hard as I could

I was in a woods now and still running. I saw it coming but I couldn't get out of the way fast enough. My head hit the branch of a tree I saw black I opened my eyes and saw nothing but black. I just sat and cried I was cold and I could hear nothing. Then I heard crickets I was still in the woods and it was dark out. I didn't want to move I was so afraid I just sat and cried till I saw the sun coming up. The birds started singing almost like on the farm. Maybe I ran far enough? I opened my eyes and looked around. Oh my head hurt I went to rub it that was when I felt blood I was dying I just curled myself up in a ball and cried some more Where was my father? I wanted my father; I cried

The sun was getting hotter I could feel the heat on my back. The birds were all over the place just looking at me and making noises. The bird's stop I could hear someone coming. He was running fast I didn't jump up to see who it was; I was afraid they would bring me back to watch the people burning again. I just kept my head down and cuddle myself tight; hoping they would run by me like my brothers would do when we would play soldier. I heard them coming closer I opened my eyes just in time to see this boy run right into me. He fell over me; he rolled and hit his head on a rock. He just laid there he didn't move. I was scared so I didn't move either I just look at him and stayed where I was.

I sat for an hour just looking at him. He was dead I said to myself. Then he moved I got up and hide behind the tree. I watched him get up and look around. He didn't see me he went over to the brook over by the tree; he bent down and took a drink. Why didn't I see that? I was so thirsty my mouth was sticking together. It was the way I felt out in the field working with my father. I always had water to drink then. My father always told us to drink plenty of water when working in the fields.

The boy was bigger than me. He looked like a Jew I didn't want to let him see me; he might kill me. I kept down and didn't move hoping he would go on his way.

"Arr "I yelled. The tree I was hiding behind A squirrel came out of a hole on the side of it He came right in front of my face. He almost bit my nose he was so close. I fell backwards to the ground I looked up to see if the boy was coming over to kill me. He wasn't He was gone

I must have scared him away. I got up and looked; he was nowhere in sight. He was gone; I went over to the brook and got my drink. As I was bending down to drink the boy jumped on me. He held me down and didn't let me up.

"Who are you he asked Tell me or I'll kill you he said

I could see he had a rock in his hands over his head. I saw it in the water.

I started to cry "Please don't kill me." I kept looking at him in the water. He didn't put down the rock he kept it over my head.

"Tell me who you are?" He said again.

"I come from the camp." I said

"You too?" He said letting me up

"I escaped to." he said. Do you know where we are?"

"No," I said I'm lost." I told him

"Me too;" he said

"We have to keep running the solders well find us and kill us." He said helping me up

"No, they won't kill me."

"Oh yes they will. He said they kill all Jews that escape."

"But I'm not a Jew." I told him

"No, he said then why are you running? Look I know you're a Jew I was told to say that to when they came for me. Look I have the star to prove it and the numbers." He rolled up his sleeve and showed me something on his skin.

"But I'm not a Jew." I said again

"Don't fool me your a Jew and so am I. We both have to get out of here before they come looking for us."

I was going to tell him who my father was when I heard dogs coming.

"Run; he said going across the brook "Stay in the brook the dogs can't smell us."

I followed I didn't want the dog to get me.

I didn't know the dogs were with the soldiers.

He said that they will let the dogs eat us if they caught us that made me move I didn't want any dogs biting me. We ran down the brook; I fell a couple of times tripping over rocks. He would came back and help me up.

"Please he said run they are going to eat us."

We kept on running till we saw a road

"Get down; he said and laid in the high grass Listen something is coming."

I looked up and down and couldn't see anything

"Look there; he said. Down the road."

It was a wagon with hey on it. Just like the one we had at home. A old man was in it. The horse that pulled it was moving slow. "I told the boy we could hide in the hey my brothers use to do it all the time."

"He will see us;" he said

"No, I said, follow me."

The wagon came past us; I got up and ran right into the hey. My brother told me how to do it. If you went to the side you could go right into it. I turned around to see if the boy was coming.

He ran and did what I did. The wagon hit a bump so the old man didn't know we were in it.

"Now just be quit." I told him.

I guess we must have fallen asleep the next ;think we know the wagon was stopping. We looked out to see where we were. We were on a farm. The old man unhitched the horse and left the wagon next to the barn. He but the horse way and went into the house.

"Now what?" The boy asked

"I don't know, I said. You're older."

"Great," he said

"Let's go in the barn to see if we can find something to eat." I said

"Good idea," he said

We both climb out and headed for the barn. It was starting getting dark.

"Look, I said. Corn."

"He looked at me and said that is for the cows."

"So it tastes good," I said picking up one and eating it "My father always use to eat it like this."

He looked at me and took one

"Good? I asked

"Good. "he said and we eat.

I guess we eat so much we fell asleep again. The next thing I remembered was the roasters crowing. It was sun up and we had to get out of there before the farmer came out.

"Come, he said lets go." He went out the door and started running for the woods; I followed him. We didn't stop till we were deep inside of them once again He stopped and fell to the ground

"This is far enough for now I have to get my breath."

"Me too;" I said sitting down on the ground beside's him

"Where do we go now?" I asked

"I don't know; he said do you?"

"No; I said but I do what to go home."

"Me too." He said

"Is your mother and father there"? I asked

"No; he said crying they were killed back at the camp; what about yours?"

I told him they still was at the camp I was about to tell him again who I was when he got up and said.

"We had better keep going." He started walking in front of me I got up and followed.

We didn't know where we were going but he knew we couldn't stop. As we walked he was talking

"Those Germans were killing all of us; one day it will turn around and we will kill them."

"But why?" I asked.

He told me about Hitler and he was a crazy man.

"All he wanted to do was kill Jew's.

"No "I said. Again I was going to tell him I meet Hitler but something stopped him.

He looked and didn't move; I stopped to. He sat down and didn't move; I did the same. Then I saw what he was looking at. There was a road behind the bushes; we almost walked right into it. We heard people talking; he held his hand over his mouth for me to do the same. It was Jews marching to the camp with soldiers.

The soldiers were whipping them to make them move faster. They were laughing at the Jews every time they would whip one. As they passed us we could see the pain the Jews were in. I was close to the ground all I could see was feet; No shoes and their feet were filled with blood.

I started to get up when the boy held me down Just then a Jew fell in front of us. The soldiers came over to him and started beating him with their rifles. He cried out for someone to help him but no one turned around. They all kept walking; after they beat him they left him at the side of the road.

"He is dead; one soldier said. Leave him he is no use to us now."

They kept going leaving the man on the side of the road. The mans face was right in front of me. The only thing between his face and mine was this grass. That is how close he was to us.

"That was close; the boy said as he got up "Come we have to get far away from here."

"What about the man?" I asked

"You hear them; he is dead."

I was still on the ground I parted the grass to get a better look at him.

"OOOh I yelled. His was looking right at me.

"The Jew wasn't dead. I said. He is looking at me."

The boy came running over and looked.

"He is dead his eyes aren't closed is all. Come we have to go or else we will look like him."

That I didn't want I got up and started running with him. Again we didn't know where we were going We followed the road

"If they were walking that way to the prison. We had to go the way;" he said and kept on running. I tried to tell him to stop put my mouth was dry I couldn't speak. He pointed to something "Water" he said

He ran over the hill and down to the brook. He went head first into it. He didn't come up till I got there. I did the same thing; did it feel good. The sun was going down and it hot and we didn't have anything to eat all day."

"I'm hungry." I said

"So we don't have any food just drink water."

"Look over there; Potatoes; I said and pointed to the fields.

"Where?" He asked

I went over the fence and started digging "Here; I told him picking up one out of the ground.

"How did you know they were there?" He asked

"We grow them."

"Oh;" he said digging for his own

We dug up a lot of them and went back to the brook to wash them off and eat By that time is was dark

So we crawled up together and went to sleep The next morning we woke and eat some more This time we went back and took all we could carry I packed them in every pocket and shirt I could

"Ha I laugh at him He had his pants tired at the bottom He started shoving them down his pants It made him look fat

"What's so funny?

"You' I told him; Your fat I said

He looked at his lags and started to laugh him self "Me fat he said Come he said we got to keep moving We don't want the dogs to get us.

"No we sure don't I said and followed

We couldn't move to fast because the potatoes were weighting us down But we need them for food so we just walked slow As we walked we talked He told me his father was a doctor and his mother was a school teacher One day the Germans came and took them away Then weeks later they came and took him and his sister's away That was where he saw his mother and father last at the camp He saw them going into the ovens to be burned

He started crying

"Why do they do this to us? he said asking me We don't hurt no buddy My father helped them and so did my mother she was a teacher She taught the Germans now to read he said and cried

I didn't know what to do so I just held him in my arm's

"Come we will rest I said sitting down

He looked at me and said "I'm sorry I wouldn't do it again

He said his father told him "Crying is for babies To smile is for God

I didn't know what he was talking about Who is this God person? But I didn't say anything I was scared to tell him who I was It was my father that killed his parents I knew this now I didn't want him to leave me so I didn't tell him anything We eat more and rested

We got up and walked some more My feet were hurting I couldn't go any more I told him that he stopped "Come he said We will rest in the woods

We went and found a good place for the night I guess we both missed our family Because the both of us cried ourselves to sleep The next morning he woke me and asked how my feet felt I told him sour He told me to take my shoes off and he would have a look at them He took some leaves off a tree and rapped my feet with them

"There That is the best I can do

"How did you know how to do that? I asked

"My father was a doctor remember

"He told me things like that I guess he was getting ready for this day

"Why didn't your father leave? I asked

"He said it will pass and he couldn't leave his patience He and my mother said someone had to teach the children "So they got killed for it What about yours? he asked

"I don't know I said I got up and started to walk "Good Meaning my feet felt better I said lets go

He got up and followed me

"Look a cow

"So "he said We can't eat it

"No But we can have some milk from it

"You know how to do that? he asked

"I do it all the time

"How? he asked

"Come I'll show you Put your mouth down here

I grabbed the tit and pulled It came out and went all over him I started to laugh "No silly you have got to catch it in your mouth as I squat it

"Oh "he said Like he never did it before

"Like this I pulled the nipple and held my mouth open to catch it as it came out "See That's how

"OK give me some He bent down

I did it again this time he got some

"That was good he said "More

We played with the cow till we had enough Then we went under a tree to rest

"Now where? I asked He pointed to a mountain and said We got to get over that one to be safe

I looked at what he was pointing at "Them? I asked

"Them he said He remembers his father telling him about another country on the other side of them

"How do you know they are the same ones?

"They look like the same ones he said

"They are far way

"Would you rather be dead !

"No I said

"So Lets go

We walked across the fields It was wheat I showed him how to eat it The only thing wrong with eating it it made us dry I forgot about that part We always had water to drink The sun was over head now It was getting hotter

"Suck on a potato get the juice I saw my father doing it once when the water bucket got a hole in it And we had no water It worked

"We should rest till the sun goes down I said "It getting to hot walk

"No tree's he said We will dehidrate if we don't get under some shade

I showed him how to make a hut for shade I took some wheat and laid it over the tops of the big ones I tired them together so they wouldn't fall from the wind

"Hey this is nice he said when we finished it We crawled under out of the sun and went to sleep The next thing that woke us up was the rain It started raining

"Now what? he asked

"I don't know I said

Neither one of us know what to do So we just cuddled up and tried to stay dry as much as we could It didn't work

"Lets see if we could find a better place We started walking We walked throw miles of wheat The rain stopped and the moon came out

"Look he said over there

I saw what he was looking at it looked like a watering station I remembering seeing one before The big farms had them The farm next to us had one My father used it once in a while

The rain started again "Run he said

It was a water tower We stayed the rest of the night under it Plus we had all the water we needed. The next morning he climbed on the roof of the tower to look out and see what he could see

"What do you see? I asked I was too small to get up there He kept looking around.

He pointed "I see smoke coming from over there he said

"Maybe it is the farm house." I said

"Maybe your right you're smart; he said coming down

"Can you see it?

"No; He picked me up to show me.

"I see it; It is a farm house I knew by the way the smoke is coming out. Someone is doing baking. See the smoke is white; if it was a firer it would be black. My father told me that

"He must have been a smart man too he said

"Come I said walking I didn't want to talk to him so I just walked

"Hey, wait for me you'll lose me in this wheat."

He was right it was why over our heads and if you walked too far in front of anyone you would get lost I waited for him

"Can you see anything?" I asked.

"No;" he said

"Lift me so we know we are going in the right direction He did "That way He let me down and we walked some more He picked me up about four times to make sure we didn't get lost The last time we were getting close We came to the end of the heat and there was the farm house

"Maybe we can spend the night here?" He said.

"No, wait;" I stopped him.

This farm was one like ours and it had a soldier in it to watch the Jews work.

"No the soldier will see us." I pointed to the farm house On the front pouch the soldier watching. I showed him what he was watching. It was the Jew works just coming in from the fields;

"Let's go he said getting up and ready to run back into the wheat."

"No I said He will go in the house as soon as the works go to sleep."

"How do you know? He asked

"That is what they did on my farm." I said He didn't ask if I was a worker. We kept still and waited

"Stop that." I said as I felt him pulling on my pants lag.

"Stop what? He asked.

If he wasn't doing it then who was? I looked at my lag.

"Oh god this dog was biting my lag. I jumped up and looked at him. The boy just started petting him.

"Look he said he's hurt."

"Get back down the soldier will see you."

I jumped back to the wheat. The dog just laid there without getting up.

"Look he's chained he's bleeding on the head. The boy took his head and looked at the cut.

"Will he live, it doesn't look that bad It's the chain he can't move; it is so short."

I rolled over and took it off him.

"Hold him don't let him run." "The dog was to skinny to run. He looks like he didn't eat for days. Let's get out of here he said the soldier is making me nervous. He picked the dog up and we ran back into the wheat. We stopped and rested "We will go back later when they go to sleep."

We sat and looked at the dog

"He looks like he is dying." I said

"He is; he said we have to get him some water."

"I'll get it. I said I know the way to the water."

"No you'll get lost." He said

"No, I'll just follow the tracks we left."

"Hurry; he said he needs it."

I ran and got the water I filled up the bucket that was there and ran back. I must of spilled most of it; it was heavy and hard to carry.

When I put it down the dog started to drink.

"See he needs it."

"Want me to get more?" I asked.

"No; he said I'll go this time I was to small to carry it full; so he would go. "You stay with the dog and keep him warm."

I told him to keep in the wheat trail I crushed down with my feet. If he didn't he would get lost

"I know; he said I'll be right back. He took the bucket and left. The poor dog was shacking I took him in my arms and kept him warm like the boy said. The moon was high it was like a big light. I just petted the dog waiting for the boy to return. Something must have gone wrong he wasn't coming back. I started getting scared I could never do it by myself I needed him. I had better go look for him. I put the dog down and went back to where the water was. I walked slow looking for him I stop when I heard something. I didn't move.

"There you are; I heard someone say "Stop or I'll shot."

I stop and didn't move; it was the soldier I know it was. "Please don't shoot me." I was going to say but I saw he wasn't talking to me.

I dropped on the ground and listen. He had the boy.

"You what are you doing here?"

"Nothing;" the boy said

"Oh nothing? Let me look at you come closer;" the soldier said. You're a Jew; he said laughing where do you think your going Jew boy? Get over here or I'll shot you."

I heard the boy tell him he was lost and didn't know where he was

"You all say that; the soldier said Get over here." Then I heard the boy scream.

"Oh you like to get hit;" the soldier said. The boy screamed again.

I crawled over to see what he was doing to him. I got to the road and saw the soldier beating the boy with his gun.

"No please. I yelled don't hit him;" and stood up.

"What is this? He said More of you's?"

He turned to look at me I don't know why I did it but I did; I started to run

"Stop; he yelled or I'll shot." I kept on running Bang I heard the gun go I fell to the ground

"Please don't shot me I said holding my hands over my head. That was when I heard the dog. I got up and looked. The dog was biting the soldier. He must have stopped him from shooting me. The soldier get back on his feet and picked up his gun to shot the dog.

"No; I yelled. Don't shot him." I ran straight for him. The soldier was pointing his rifle at me when I heard someone else tell him to drop his gun. I didn't see who it was I just kept running to save the boy and the dog. When I got to the soldier I ran right into him and tried to knock him down. The soldier just stood there and didn't do anything. I started to punch him. He still didn't move I stopped and looked up He was looking at the other people that told him to stop. He took hold of me and held me back from hitting him anymore. Then I felt another hand on me.

"Joseph what are you doing? Your father is worried about you."

It was my father's driver.

"What is going on here?" He asked

"These two; the soldier said were stealing water. And they let the dog go."

"Is that true?" He said me

"Yes sir." I said we were thirsty."

"Joseph you shouldn't have run away; your mother is crying she missies you so. Come we go home."

"No;" I said

"But Joseph your father wants you home "Come you have to go."

"Take my friend." I said

"Him? He said He is a Jew."

"Please take him." I said

"Your father will kill me; he said looking at the boy.

"Then I don't go." I said

"Joseph I have to take you back."

The other soldier asked "Did he come from your camp?" Looking at the boy.

"He isn't one of yours?" He asked.

"No the other soldier said. I have all mine."

"I'll take him back with me;" the drive said "Come Joseph he will come back with us."

"My dog." I said

"Oh no; the soldier said. He stays"

The driver looked at the dog "What did you do to him?" He asked the other soldier.

"I was teaching him not to bit me; he said

You don't treat a dog like that."

"Oh and what do you know;" the soldier said.

"I know I don't like anyone beating a dog;" the driver said

"So it isn't your dog. What are you going to do about it;" he said."

The driver took out his gun and pointed it at the soldier and said "I'll shot you; that is what I'll do."

"For a dog?" the soldier said

"For the dog I love dogs;' the driver said And to see what you did to this dog gets me mad I'll shot you over a dog; he said. I out rank you so don't get me mad. The dog is going with me. Joseph go get the dog."

I ran over to the dog. The boy was still on the ground I get the dog and went over to the boy.

"Joseph; he said leave him alone."

"But he is hurt to;" I said

"He is a Jew Don't touch him. Boy; he yelled get up or I'll leave you here. Joseph you had better go with the dog." He said

"But he is hurt." I said again

"He is a Jew Joseph; your father will kill me if he knows I let you touch a Jew to help him".

"No, I said and help the boy up.

"The soldier said He didn't know who I was but if he was the driver he'd take a stick to me."

The driver told him to go back to his business and he would take care of it He told him to have the car brought here. For that he would give a good report about him."

"Yes sir; the soldier said and ran back to the farm house.

The driver came over and looked at the boy. He is only going to die anyway; he said Leave him here."

"No; I said. He is my friend."

"Your father isn't going to stand for it; he said Let me kill him now."

"No; I said and started to run away again.

"Stop Joseph; he said and ran after me. He picked me up and carried me back to the car that was just pulling up.

"Now you sit and I'll get the dog for you." He put me in the back set and went over to get the dog. He told the other soldier that was driving the car to get the Jew. He got the dog and gave it to me. The other soldier picked the boy up and throws him over his shoulders. Then carried him to the back of the car.

He tired him to the back and got in.

"Let's go;" the driver said and off we went. I looked back at the boy. He was bleeding from the head his eyes weren't open. He must be dead I just took hold of the dog and cried.

"Joseph; the driver said You had us all scared Your mother has been crying for days How did you get this far?" He asked did this Jew kidnap you?"

"What do you mean Kidnap?" I asked.

I didn't know what the word meant

"Did he make you go with him?" He said

"No; I said I meet him just the other day."

"Where were you going?" He asked.

"Home." I said

"But you were home;" he said.

"No; I said; back to the farm."

"Why? He asked

I told him about the people burning up and screaming

"Oh that he said "You will get use to it we do it all the time. Joseph we don't have enough room for all of them so we have to get rid of some of them. You like to kill Jews don't you?" He asked

"No; I got sick." I told him

"You are young yet; he said You will see it's the only way you will get use to it. You like that dog?' he asked. He is a fine dog maybe your father will let you keep him; that is if you tell him you will never run away again."

"My father will hit me." I said

"No Joseph your father isn't going to hit you He loves you Your brothers all left for camp and he is lonely He has no sons home to help him

I looked at the boy and then at the dog and fell asleep I woke up the sun was up The boy was still on the back of the car And the dog was still next to me We were still driving We came to a stop It was a farm house

"Joseph come we will get something to eat." He got out and went to the door and started banged on it "Wake up he yelled I'm a German officer and we need food."

A old man came to the door.

"Get us some food and be quick about it."

The old man got his wife up While we went in side The drive carried the dog in He gave him water and food He looked at the cut on his head And the cuts around his neck from the chain.

"What did that bad man do to you?" he said to the dog. The dog liked him he sat up and his tail started to wag. "See he said he love me." The dog licked his face. Oh now he said you're going to be all right; see Joseph he is getting better already."

"Help the boy." I asked him

"He is a Jew;" he said

"Please "I asked him and started to cry.

"You're going to get me into big trouble Joseph."

"No I won't; please give him some water.

He looked at me and shook his head.

"Please."

He went back and untried the boy. He was still breathing I could see that.

I ran and got some water and gave it to him. I picked up his head and started to wipe the blood from around his face. It was hard and black I could see the hole in his head the blood was coming from.

"Please help him." I said looking at the driver "Joseph your going to be the death of me."

"Make him better like you did the dog."

He bent down and picked the boy up and put him on the pouch. He took some water and a rag and started to wipe his face.

"He is in bad shape; he said He won't live the day.

"No Please help him. I ran up to the boy and grabbed on to him. I started to cry "My friend I said I'm sorry."

""Joseph what are you saying He is a Jew If anyone see's you doing this they will think you're a Jew. Let him be;" he said taking me away from him.

"Please. I said he is my friend he saved my life."

The driver didn't know what to do. He looked at me; I could see a tear in his eye. I know then he would help me. He was a kind man he didn't want to hurt him.

"Please; was the only word I know to make people do things for me? I use it on my sister's father and mother. It always worked with some tears; Except on my brother's; they didn't fall for it.

I had to help the boy and I didn't know how little did I know; he was going to help me out later on. I just couldn't let him die. The driver did what he could for him. He placed him back on the car. We went into eat; the farmer and his wife gave us food and drink. The driver gave some more to the dog; I saved some for the boy. I eat and went out side to give it to him.

"No; the driver said; he doesn't eat."

"Please; I said again just a little?"

"Oh Joseph; he said looking at me. What am I going to do with you? Go ahead;" he said and went back inside.

"Boy; I said holding his head up Please eat I have food for you." He opened his eyes and looked at me.

I tried to put some food in his mouth but he didn't open it.

"Please you have to eat you will die if you don't eat." I said

The driver came back out "Come Joseph we must go now your father is waiting for you."

"Can he ride in the back with me?" I asked

"No," the soldier said

The driver looked at him and said; let him ride in the back."

"You're the one that is going to get in trouble for it; you do what you want;" he told him.

The driver got out and picked the boy up "Joseph you're going to get me into a lot of trouble for this."

"Thank you," I told him and held on to the boy's lag as he carried him the car.

"Joseph he asked how did you get the cut on your head?" I told him I ran into a branch and got knocked out the boy helped me.

"You sure he didn't do it to you?"

"No I didn't even see him then."

"Joseph you had better be telling me the truth If you're not both me and your father will beat you."

"Yes sir; I said. That is the truth."

I took the boy in my lap and kept wiping his head off with the wet rag. I looked down at him "Please don't die." His eyes opened and the tear came out. One in each eye; I was young But I could remember it like it was yesterday. I guess things like this stay in your mind forever. The driver said we were coming to the camp soon. He stopped the car and said he had to take the boy out and put him on the back again."

The dog was sleeping and so was the boy. He picked him up and put him back and tired him again. We went into the gate without stopping. My father was standing waiting for me

My mother came out of the house crying. She ran over and picked me up; my father went to get me but my mother took his hand and pushed them away from me. That was the first time and the last time I saw my mother stop my father. He didn't do anything to her he just looked at the drive and let her take me into the house. I looked over my mothers shoulders and saw my father talking to the driver.

"I hope he don't kill the boy." I said to my mother.

"Joseph what have you done?" She asked crying. She got me into the house and took off all my clothes. She had a bath waiting for me. She put me right in the tub; she cleaned me off. She was crying as she was doing it.

"Joseph; she said picking me up And holding me tight "Never do that again;" she said taking me to my room. She had some hot soup and milk waiting for me. She sat next to me looking at the cut on my head.

She cleaned it better and put a bandage on it

"You are lucky you didn't get killed she said OH my baby she said and cuddled me and cried.

I guess she missed me my father came into the room He just looked at me

"Joseph, my mother said looking at my father "Your father said you won't have to see the Jews burning anymore."

"Yes Joseph he said you are still to young when you get bigger He said

"I never wanted to get bigger I told him

"See my mother said you did it to him

My father just looked at her and left the room My mother stayed with me My sisters came in and sat on my bed. They just looked at me and didn't say a word; they were just as glad I was home and wanted to make sure it was me.

"Joseph; My oldest sister asked. You got a dog?"

I looked at her and said "It is my dog."

She asked me if she could play with it. My mother told them we will talk about it tomorrow.

"Momma, can I keep him?"

"We will talk about it tomorrow; she said you get to sleep your tired."

I guess she was right I closed my eyes and went to sleep

The next morning when I woke my sisters were standing in the door way

"Joseph we got something for you

I sat up and wiped my eyes then I heard the dog bake. My eyes opened wide I got out of bed to see where he was. He pulled away from them and came running for me. He was bigger than I was; he knocked me down jumping on me. He started licking me all over. I started laughing and couldn't stop. My mother came in and pulled him off of me.

"If that is what he is going to do; she said you can keep him." She meant about me laughing; she said she never heard me laugh so much; it did her heart good to hear me laugh." She said

I didn't know then her reason but I know now what she was thinking. She was worried that I would never laugh again from what I saw. I guess she told my father he did wrong by showing me. What ever the reason was I never saw the ovens again. Don't get me wrong I saw a lot of things they did to the Jews but I never went near the ovens again. Something kept me from even looking over at them. Most of the times my mother would be teaching me. She said she wanted me to be a leader with brains. My father know it scared me so much he didn't push me.

He had his hands full with his job. More and more Jews were coming. I could hear them screaming all night and day. I could hear gun shots all day long. I was kept away from the prison. The boy was put back to work my father said. I didn't see him again. I remember asking my mother how people could love a dog and hate Jew's?"

"That is one thing I can't teach you my son I don't know the answer myself."

CHAPTER 2

For years my father did his job my mother kept teaching me; I kept away from the cries and screams of the prison. My sister's were enjoying what they called the good life. My father stayed away from me; my mother said he was too busy; but I knew by the way he looked at me I hurt him I wasn't his son no more All he would talk about was my brother's. How proud he was of them

That was on till the day my mother came to me and told me we had to leave. Something was wrong I could tell, the whole prison was running around like crazy it was four years later. My mother had another baby; A Girl, I kept reading and studying it was my way of blocking out the screams. I kept the dog I named him Mike; he didn't leave my side He went where ever I went. No one could come near me If they did he would go to bit them; even my sisters. They didn't like it but after a while they started going out with soldiers. So they didn't care about me or my dog.

My mother told me the Americans were coming and we were losing the war. She feared for our lives. For days we saw and heard bombs going off all around us. Then planes started going over head. My father didn't come home most of the nights; he was burning as many Jews as he could. That is what my mother told me. "She said he wanted to make his Furor proud of him.

Trains were coming and going. Soldiers were passing the camp going to the front; my sisters said. The Americans were coming and we had to fight them.

"Hitler was going to stop them. My father said when we saw him. My mother kept asking him to let us go. He got mad and said we will stand a fight. "Our Furor is going to win over the Americans you wait and see."

Then one day the bombs were getting closer and closer; my father came home and told us to pack. He was putting us on the next train out of here. My mother got my little sister ready my oldest sister took her; then she got me. She told me the dog couldn't come."

I guess that was the reason I ran; I don't know what made me run but I did. Me and my dog.

Running to the main gate I don't know what made me turn around but I did. I guess to see if my mother was coming after me. But when I did a bomb hit my house; I could see my mother standing in the door way looking at me. All I could see was a plane coming over the house and dropping something. The whole house went up in flames. I stopped and started to run back when this soldier stopped me and picked me up. It was the driver he yelled for me to get back by the train my father was waiting for me."

I remember yelling "My mother"

He looked back at the house and said "There was nothing he could do about them they were all dead.

He picked me up and carried me off. He was heading for the train yard when more planes came over. He dropped me on the ground and fell on top of me. I heard the plane's shooting and dropping more bombs. Then I heard the bombs hit what was a ammo dump. The whole place went up trains and all.

My dog was still by my side; I felt him pulling my arm and barking. The driver was still on top of me he felt heavy. I screamed for him to get off but he couldn't he was dead. The plane's killed him my dog was trying to get him off of me.

"Please I screamed someone help me." I couldn't move his body off of me; he was lying across the top of me I couldn't move bombs were going off all around us. My dog kept trying you get me out.

'Help me "I kept yelling No one could hear me I felt my breath leaving me from his weight on top of me

"Oh please someone help me. Then I felt the driver being picked up off of me. I didn't know who it was he took my hand and we ran across the court yard into this building. He closed the door.

"We will be safe here;" he said to me.

"Thank you I told him not knowing who he was; "my Dog" I said getting up.

"Wait; he said I'll get him. The man opened the door and my dog came running in.

"There he is." he said and closed the door again.

"We will wait till the bombing has stopped and then we will run for it;" he said

"My father is down by the train." I said

"No; he said your father left; no one is left;" he said The Germans all left the prison they run like rats;" he said

It was dark in the room I couldn't see him. I didn't even know where we were. The bombs kept up for hours but none came near us. I didn't know why till we went out side after the bombing stopped. I looked at the building we were in; it was the ovens.

"Oh no; I said backing away. I must have went into shock because I don't remember what happened next

The next thing I remembered was the sun shining in my face and the man putting water over my face

"Joseph, he said "You feeling better?"

Who was this man? I opened my eyes and looked at him "Yes" I said sitting up

I looked around and saw flames coming from all over. The camp is burning

"My mother and sisters." I yelled

He held me down saying they were all dead. The bombs got them;" he said

"No" I screamed I remember him holding me down and me fighting to get up. The think that I couldn't understand was why my dog didn't bit him I could see him just looking at him and me and not doing anything to stop him.

"Please the man said don't do this your family is dead and we can't help them; now stop it or your going to hurt yourself."

"Who are you?" I asked when I realized he was right.

"You may not remember me; I was the boy that ran away with you years ago.

I looked at him and then at the dog. That was why he didn't bit him he remembered him.

"My dog knew you;" I said looking at him. He was so much older looking; he was so skinny and dirty. I put my hand to his head and lifted his hair. The scar was there the one the soldier in the field gave to him; I never did no his name.

"You save me once; he said now I save you."

"But you're a Jew." I said

"No; he said Remember what you said to the soldier that took us back. You told him I was your friend; you're my friend; he said Not a German."

He held his hand out for me to take. I looked at him and went into his arms I could feel his bones he was so skinny. What did they do to him

"Come; he said I know a way we can get out of here." He took my hand. We walked over bodies around burning buildings; the bombs did a lot of damage; nothing was standing but the ovens and the prison barrack's.

"The Americans didn't want to hurt the Jews;" he said. He went around more building's and out to the train yard.

"Look at all the trains burning. Soldiers all over the place Dead or wounded. Buildings were still blowing up.

Then we came to more prison barracks.

"We will be safe here; he said. My people said the Americans will come and save us."

Just as we were going to the barracks two Jew man stopped us.

"Stop You? Where are you going?"

The boy told them. "To wait for the Americans."

One of the men saw me and said "He is the Generals son;" and went to grab me. My dog jumped on him and started to bit his neck. The other man came for me the boy took a stick and hit him over the head with it. "Stop I said you'll kill him.

He looked at me and back away.

"Come; he said to many people know you they will kill you".

He ran back into the woods Me and Mike followed. We ran till we couldn't run any more and fell to the ground.

"You could kill your own people"? I said to him.

He just looked at me and said "He would of killed you."

That was all that was said about it I know from then on he was my friend.

We rested for a while and then started walking again Bombs were going off all over the place that didn't stop him; we kept walking they were far away but you could still heard them and see the light they made.

"The Americans were really coming! I asked him.

"Germany is finished; he said the war is over. The Germans have lost; he said the American's are to late my people are all dead; he said Hitler had them all killed; your father killed thousands in the last few days hoping he could get all of us before the Americans came."

"I'm sorry;" I said

"No; he said you didn't do it your father and Hitler did come here;" he said He took out this needle.

"See this; he said it is the numbers your father put on us to make it so people would know we were Jews. I must put one on you."

"Why;"? I asked

"My people know you and will kill you. If not my people the Americans will kill you; knowing you're a German. This way they will think your a Jew like me and leave you alone."

He took my arm then took some burnt wood from a tree. He stuck the needle in my arm over the burnt wood.

"Ouch; I said pulling away. You hurt me"

"Stop; he said and don't move. He kept jabbing the needle till the blood was running down my arm

"There; he said spitting on it; then wiping it off. He did it I had numbers on my arm just like his

"Now; he said they will leave you alone. Let's go and find the Americans."

"That wasn't easy we saw more German soldiers than ever. We had to keep hiding so they wouldn't see us. We walked for days and no Americans. Mike was good he'd let us know if anyone was coming. We both wondered if they were coming or maybe Hitler did beat them. I started to get scared the more we walked the more German soldiers we saw.

"What if Hitler did win?" I asked him

"Then he said I want you to kill me."

"I can't do that;" I told him.

"You must; he said I can't go on living."

One night we fell to the side of the road to sleep when we saw this car coming. The both of us jumped into the woods and hid. Mike heard things we didn't he didn't make a noise. The car stopped and the two soldiers got out; they were going to the bathroom.

We tried to hear what they were saying but we were to far away to hear. Just then another car came up the road and stopped. It had one driver Oh no he had a dog with him. My dog get up and looked at him. The dog in the car heard him and came running out of the car after him. The two dogs started fighting in the middle road; half way between us and the soldiers. The soldiers came over to watch them.

One of them said "Shot the dog we don't have time for this shit."

"No, I yelled and stood up without thinking.

"Who are you?" they asked pointing their guns at us. They saw me and the boy. "There Jews, shot them."

I don't remember how or where I got it. Later on I remembered when I was packing my things I took the gun Mr. Hitler gave me and put it in my pants I took it out and fired it at the three of them. I killed all three with just three shots. The boy just looked at me and said.

""They were your own people." He said

"You are my friend." I said the same thing he said to me. Then I turned it on the dog and shot him. He was killing my dog My dog was weak he didn't eat for days; that was the only reason the other dog got him.

I ran over to my dog to see how he was. Oh god he was ripped apart his neck was ripped open the blood was pouring out of the cut. I stood up and pointed the gun at Mike I pulled the trigger and shot him in the head. He closed his eye's and didn't move. I didn't want him to suffer any more for me. The boy took the gun off of me and held me tight. Just then another car came up. We didn't hear it; it was on top of us before we could run. The boy looked at me and then put the gun to his head and pulled the trigger to shot himself.

"No don't." I heard someone say in English; Were Americans."

I went to stop the boy from pulling the trigger but it was too late he pulled it.

"No Please; I said looking at him.

The gun was empty it had no more bullets in it. I jump on to him and hugged him to the ground I was so glad the gun was empty I couldn't let him kill himself. We both cried The American soldiers came and picked us up and took us to their Jeep.

"You crazy jerks; they said the war is over You don't have to do that."

The both of us just held each other and cried. They drove us back to their camp they took us out and feed us; then they put us with other Jews they found along the road

"We were saved;" the boy said

"Saved for what?" I asked him I had no family left and no place to go what was the sense of living?"

He looked at me and said "Maybe we should have killed ourselves."

We went to sleep in each others arms crying what tears we had left.

The next morning the Americans came and gave us food again. They treated us with care. They had doctors look at us being most of the Jew's were sick. When it came to me the doctor said I was the healthiest Jew he saw. My friend said they just captured me I was in hiding with the under ground for years."

Just as the doctor was taking a look at the numbers my friend put on me a soldier came over and pointed at us and said.

"Them two both;" the boy and me started to run. We didn't get too far they caught us.

"No, he kept saying; "Nin" In German. Then another soldier came over and spoke German to us. "He said they just wanted to talk to us It seems the three man I shot last night were Generals in civilian clothes. The Major wanted to thank us. They took us to his tent; inside we went. This man in uniform asked witch one of us killed the Germans?"

"I did." I said

He looked at me and held up Mr. Hitler's gun

'Where did you get this?" He asked

My friend said we took it off one of the Generals

I'm glad; he said that I was going to tell him Mr. Hitler gave it to me. That would have been something; he would of shot me right there.

I looked at the boy and smiled. The major said we did a good job and asked us what our names were?"

Again the boy answered for us.

"My name is Seymour Goldberg and this is my Brother Joel Goldberg."

"Goldberg; he asked again

"Yes sir we both said

"Goldberg? He asked again. He started to get me worried. He acted as if he knew the name.

"What was your father's Name?" he asked.

The boy Seymour answered I don't know if that was his real name I never asked him his name before

"Joel Goldberg."

"Was he a Doctor?" He asked

"Yes sir; I answered I Remembered what Seymour told me. Seymour looked at me and said. "Yes sir he was."

"And your mother was a school teacher?" He asked.

I answered again "Yes sir

"You know he said your father saved my daughter life many years ago.

We both looked at him and didn't say a word. Was he just saying that? Was he trying to make us give him information the way the German soldiers did?

He went on and told us about the time him and his wife were on vacation before the war. His daughter got sick "Your father saved her life. He operated on her and she lived;" he said

"Sir "Another soldier came in and said we are transporting the Jews back to the main base Are you finished with them?" He asked.

"No, he said I'll take care of them."

We both looked at each other we didn't know if it was good or bad. He saw the worried look we had on our faces.

"Don't worry your going home;" he said

"We have no home; Seymour said, our mother and Father are dead."

"You have a Uncle and Aunt living in America; he said. Your father asked me to look them up when we got back to the states. I kept in touch with them when the war broke out; your uncle asked me to try and find them for him. I'm sorry I didn't get here sooner I'm sure he will welcome the two of you and I'm going to see to it that you're on your way. That is the least I could do for your father."

Seymour looked at me he grabbed me and cried

"We are saved;" he said crying.

CHAPTER 3

That was the start of my new life Seymour didn't leave my side all the time we were getting ready to go to the United States. I was scared as hell and didn't know what to do. If they found out who my father was they would kill me and probable not let Seymour go. I told him that when we were a lone He said he didn't want to hear it I was his brother and that was that. He told me he wouldn't be here if it wasn't for me; so that was the end of it. He owed me and this was his way of paying me back.

I got a new brother but I was thinking about my two real brothers. Did they make it? Were they alive? I guess I'll never know for some reason I didn't care. Well our long trip started. We were off to America Seymour's uncle wrote to him just before we got on the ship. The Major stayed with us all the way. That was on till we boarded the ship; he handed Seymour the letter. The letter said he would be glad to have us and he couldn't wait to see us. He did ask when I was born Seymour's father didn't write to him that much; so he didn't know he didn't have a brother.

"See Seymour said it will work out for us."

All the way to America Seymour taught me about being a Jew. By the time we reached New York I was Jewish. What a sight when we pulled into the harbor.

"What a city; look at this," he said. The both of us were jumping up and down on the boat "We made it;" he said hugging me.

I guess something like this doesn't happen every day. I was Ten and Seymour was 16 He looked much older than that. He started putting on weight and his hair was growing.

"What if they don't like me?" I asked

"You got me; he said don't worry."

For some reason I didn't the boat docked we waited in line to get off. We didn't have much But we were alive."

"Would you look at this?" He would said And I would tell him the same thing if I saw something different." Together we both saw the Statue of Liberty.

"Look "we both said; was she beautiful."

From that day on we were an American.

His Uncle meet us at the immigration station Ellis Island it was called. He stayed with us all the way throw checking out. Then it was home. He took us by the hand not letting go of us. We got into his car and drove off. We couldn't believe what we were looking at. The streets and houses People and dogs the Birds and Flowers we went on and on; things were so pretty here and no sign of war. We asked him if all the cities were like this. The Germans didn't touch them?" We asked together.

"No;" he said

"Hitler said he was going to come and destroy the us." I said

Seymour kicked me to stop me from talking

"Oh he did, did he? Well he found out he made a big mistake by getting us mad didn't he?" He said

"Yes sir I said looking at Seymour and gave him a smile.

"What is this?" He asked about the three German Generals. Seymour told him it was nothing." And kicked me again. "Nothing;" he said

"Your hero's; he said. The papers want to talk to you about it."

Seymour looked at me I know what he was thinking

"No uncle; he said; we don't want to talk to reporters. Were afraid Mr. Hitler will come and get us."

"No, he laugh Mr. Hitler is dead. He killed himself. The war is over now you have nothing to worry about anymore.

We just looked at each other and then back out the windows. We pulled up to a house with a white fence around it.

"Will; he said we are home boys." He got out of the car and held the door open for us.

Both Seymour and I just looked; we didn't get out.

"Come he said your safe now. Momma he called. Come we are home." Out they came our new family two girls and a woman came out to meet us. "Come he said holding out his hand for us. Don't be afraid."

Seymour was the first to get out "Uncle you have a nice house;" he said

"It is yours; he said; Call it yours to. My brother was a brave man to do what he did. You two are the only living family we have left Hitler killed all of them."

"We are glad to have the both of you;" his wife said talking our little bag and holding both of ours hand's walking into the house.

For some reason I didn't feel scared any more. I could see Seymour didn't either. What a difference from there to here. No one shooting and running around worrying about the bombs coming. Children playing in the street's; Cars driving by with out Flags on them No soldiers anywhere.

"Where are the solders?" I asked

He smiled and said "They are around but they don't bother you."

"Hi "one of the girls said as we walked in "I'm Marsher and this is my sister Bee

'Hi," Seymour said Pleased to meet you." Then held out his hand for them I did the same.

They shock our hands and started to ran away

"Girls "Show the boys to their room."

"Come; bee said and she went up the stairs Seymour looked at me. The aunt said to go "It's OK we don't bit."

We followed them to this large room. It had bunk beds in it

"This is your room; she said the both of you can stay here."

Well that was how it started in America; Warm and friendly. The aunt came up and told us she would go and buy clothes for us tomorrow. She would have had them ready for us but she didn't know what size we were."

"Oh thank you Aunte; Seymour said it is nice of you."

"Girls make the boys feel comfortable supper will be ready soon." She left and the girl started talking. Boy did they talk just like my sisters. Seymour loved it; he didn't have any sisters or brother's I did and they were the same. Talk, talk, talk. They told us about the school and the kids they played with. They told us everything we should know.

Well life was turning around for us. I slipped a lot but Seymour would cover up for me by saying. "I wasn't around Jew's to long. The Germans took me first; it was luck he found me."

"Oh Boy's;" The uncle said after the dinner The news paper people will be around tomorrow Don't worry; he said; Nothing is going to happen to you. Just tell them what happened and they will go."

"But Uncle; Seymour said; we really don't want to talk about it."

"Son I know but they'll keep bothering us if you tell them everything you know they will leave us alone."Please." he said I won't let them ask too many questions."

"I'll ask them to leave; she said with him. What you two did was a hero. You should tell the world about it."

The reporters came and went and it wasn't as bad is we taught it would be. One of them even asked if the gun I shot them with was Mr. Hitler's." Seymour said we didn't know." And that ended it that was on till we saw the paper the next day. Our Uncle came and woke us up "See he said you two should be proud."

Seymour looked at me; I could see the look on his face. It read 'Jews fight back'. It had a picture of the both of us sitting together.

"This will stay in our lives forever." He told us. You are the talk of the Temple; Friday we go I show the two of you off." Again he hugged us and said how proud he was of us."

The girls said all the children in the neighborhood wanted to meet us."

Seymour looked at me and then said "Please we both are tired we would like to spend some time alone."

"Yes, the mother said they have been through a lot. We must give them time to them self's;" she said.

I was glad she said that I was getting scared they would find out I wasn't Seymour's brother.

When they left Seymour said "This is no good." He held up the picture of us.

"Hitler is dead." I said

"I'm not worried about him; he said It is the Jews that lived; they might remember your face and come and tell my uncle you're a Generals son."

He had me worry I didn't want to go back to Germany. He said that my father killed millions of Jews and it would be hard for his people to forget. So that is how I lived my life worrying about someone coming to the door and taking me away. To this day I still think about it. I found out later the Jewish people were just like us; there was nothing wrong with them. I didn't know why Mr. Hitler hated them so much they did a lot of thing differently but I got use to them and did what Seymour.

We started school; he both of us was ahead of the other kids in our class.

We learned English fast. Night and day we'd study together. I always like school Seymour wanted to be a doctor like his father; as for me I just wanted to be a soldier.

Don't ask my why I just did. Maybe it was because I remember the way my father felt ordering man around. He was a proud man or maybe it was the way I felt when I killed someone. I couldn't explain why but that was what I wanted to be. Our Uncle gave us anything we wanted; plus the Jewish Temple help out. They paid for our school; it was because of the Generals we killed. Later we found out that they were like my father; they too had Killed lots of Jews for Mr. Hitler. It was as if we saved all the Jew's that were still alive over there. They didn't let us forget it we were treated with the highest respect any where we went. Life was easy for us; his family accepted us. I learned to keep my mouth shout about who I was and Seymour just stayed by my side. We didn't go any where with out each other. People called us the twins. Seymour was in a higher grade then I was but we went to the same school. The Girls accepted us also; we all got a long together.

I remember the first time Seymour wasn't with me He had a date with some girl. I felt left out at first. Thinking back that was the start of our going our own way. His friend's were older and I made new friends. Little by little we parted. We still were the talk of the temple but even that was wearing out; I was glad of that. People use to ask us all kind of questions about the war and the Germans. It was had not to tell them about myself so I had to watch what I said at all times.

Seymour was off to College I started high school. That was a lot different in grade school the kids acted different. I kept much to myself Reading and studying. Girls didn't bother me at first but as the year went on I started talking to them. They mostly wanted to talk to me because I was the smartest in the class.

Then this soldier came to the school one day. He said he was going to set up this class for kids that wanted to go on into the service after school, ROTC it was called.

Of course I was the first one to join. Plus being what I've been through the sgt. made me in charge of it. This was what I really wanted. The rest of the school year went by fast I took control. By the end of the year I had a lot of Guys joining. I don't know if it was the uniform or me What ever it was the girls came around me like flies I had my pick.

Seymour came home once in a while from college we'd go out to a movies or something together.

One night when we were out We ended up in a part of town we never went to before. There was some movie playing there that we wanted to see. I guess you would say we shouldn't have gone. Being we were in a America now; who knew; I guess a lot of people still hated the Jews. But we didn't see it till then. Everyone around us was Jewish, School, stores, neighborhoods. Well to make a long story shout when the movies let out we found ourselves confronted with a gang of boys saying "Kike's "and bushing us. I guess it was because of the banes we had on our head.

I guess that was the time I learn if my training worked. I started kicking and punching and before you know it they were all on the ground. The cops came and locked us all up. My uncle came to the jail to get us out. He just smile at us; the other boys got what they called a JD card And their parents came and got them. They let us go with nothing but the cops told us not to come around that part of town anymore. Most of the people were German there."

From that day on I know life wasn't going to be easy being a Jew. I read about it in News paper it was happening all over the place. People hated Jews for what reason I couldn't understand; so from that day on I had to watch myself. I didn't want any more things like that happening to me even thou I enjoyed it; I really kicked some ass. The whole school heard about it. Again I was the talk of the school. It wasn't heard of a Jew fighting, I got chewed out from the school and my friends cheered me; so what do you do?

Each year I learned more and more; I got real good with my hands. Our class in ROTC held top honors in all classes. I guess you could say we were the best. But I still didn't have anyone I could call a good friend. I still kept to myself I still worried about them finding me out. So I kept studying and going to ROTC after school

Another war was starting It was In Korea Something about the north and south and the ninth eighth parallel. We had more and more kids joining the ROTC. By the time next year rolled around we had all we could handle. I was made Major; the rank was the highest I could go for that year that is. I had Officers coming down all the time to watch us. When they left they were impressed with what I had done. Our school went along with us; why shouldn't they; we gave then something to be proud of. Even the basket ball team was Proud of us. They would ask us to do Drills at half time.

This one girl kept asking me to take her out. I really didn't want to. I guess it was the way I saw my mother and sister burn; that kept me away from girls. I really didn't know why but they didn't mean anything to me. But like ever red blooded American Boy I fell into their trap. I went out with her and found out there was more to life then School. We went to a movie on our first date. When we sat to look at the show I saw a lot of other kids kissing. What did they pay to see the movies for if that all they were going to do? I found out why soon enough; she started with holding my arm then taking my arm and putting it around her shoulder. She did it I didn't want to but what the hell everyone was doing it. Then from there it was a look over my way and a quick kiss on the cheek The most exciting thing that happened was when I turned to kiss her; My hand slipped and went on her breast.

"Oh sorry "I said taking it off.

"That's OK; she said I got a bra on."

I didn't know what she meant by that so I asked. She said I could touch them as long as she kept her clothes on. Nothing could happen."

She was wrong; Boy was she wrong. I don't know who ever told her that but they were wrong.

At first I didn't know what to do so I just kept moving it out of the way. My dick that is It was getting hard and it was bothering me. She looked at me and asked if anything was wrong?"

I told her what was happening to me and she smiled."

"That is supposed to happen silly;" she said.

"Oh OK I went back to holding her breast and kissing her.

"Oh I said it was getting to hard I had to take it out it was hurting me.

"No "she said you can't do that."

"But it hurts; I said it is cutting into my pants. Look I'll cover it with my coat No one will see."

"OK she said but when it goes down put it back.

She said she didn't want the movie to end and me have it out of my pants.

I couldn't blame her I think it would have embarrassed me more if people saw my thing. So we went back to feeling and kissing. That only lasted a little while before I know it her hand was coming under my coat. "Hey I said what are you doing?"

She said she was just checking to see if it went down.

"No I said I still can feel it. I'll tell you when;" I told her.

"Oh "she said and stopped she didn't take her hand out she just left it there. She came over to me and started doing something to my ear.

'Hey what are you doing?"

She whispered SAYING "Look at the two in front of us; she is doing it to him."

"Oh "I said I guess it is OK I let her do it. My thing was getting harder and harder.

"Look "I said pulling away from her. "I think we had better stop."

"Oh please; she said "Why?

"My thing isn't going down." I said

"Maybe if I rub it;" she asked

"No I said I don't think that would help."

"Let me try;" she said

"No;" I said

"Oh please; she said again and went back to my ear. "What if I don't look at it?" she said

"What will that do? I said you will still be touching it. I don't remember what she said It sounded like "I feel so sorry for you I want to do something to stop it from hurting; Please; she said let me try."

"OK but don't look at it." I told her

"I won't she said I'll look at the movies; she said and looked straight ahead. I felt her hand coming along my lag till she came close to it. "You're not going to be mad at me?" she asked and stopped

"No I said you're only trying to help me."

"Good;" she said and took hold of it

"OOOOH I yelled and jumped almost out of my set. I guess I scared the hell out of the kids around us. They all jumped and looked around.

"Knock it off they yelled we want to watch the picture." they all said

Ha I said to my self none of them were watching it I sat back down and she whispered in my ear again.

"Did I hurt you? She asked. She had taken her hand away when I jumped.

"No I said.

"Then why did you jump?" She asked.

"Why did you?" I asked her

She came to me again and said "It felt awful."

"No it doesn't. I said I like the way it feels."

"Why did you jump? She asked me

I said her hand felt funny around it."

"My hand doesn't feel funny;" she said

"Look let's forget it It's starting to go down now. It was for whatever reason it was.

"Good; she said maybe my hand did it. Let me try again this time don't jump;" she said

"OK I said go ahead."

She did; Shit it was getting hard again."

"I don't think it is working." I said

"I know she said it's getting bigger and bigger. You want me to stop?" she asked

"If you want to;" I told her.

"No; she said I like holding on to it; do you like me doing it?" She asked

"Oh it's all right I guess; but don't look at it."

"Oh No; she said I won't."

We just sat and she played with it.

That was good for her but it was uncomfortable to me She was going up and down on it, it was doing something I never felt before. She felt me stiffen up.

"Am I hurting you?" She asked and stopped.

"I don't know I said I feel something different going on; do you?" I asked her

"Something is making you shake she said I feel all wet down there she said "You didn't go to the bathroom did you?

"No I laugh I would know it

"Then what is it she asked She said she didn't know It wasn't her friend

"Her what? I asked

"Oh nothing she said

What the hell did she mean by that? Where was her friend? I didn't see anyone This kept up most of the movie The first picture was almost over and we didn't know it The end came on the screen and the lights came on The both of us jumped She almost knocked my coat off my lap

"Hey be careful I said holding on to it

"Sorry she said I got to go to the bathroom Want to come?

"No I said looking down at my thing I can't stand up it will stick out

"Oh she said want something to eat?"

"Some pop corn; I said would be nice."

"OK be right back."

Most of the girls did the same thing; all the boys stayed in their seats; I wonder if they had the same thing wrong with them as I did? Everyone was looking around at each other and not moving. The next show started and all the girls started coming back to the seats. Mary was her name; she was almost the last one to come back. Oh my thing had gone down so I but it way and put my coat on the set to save it for her. When she came back she had her hands full. A big Pop corn and one soda

"Mind if we sheer;" she asked she had two straws It would of been too much to carry; she said with two."

"No I don't mind." I said

"Oh she said looking at my coat; what happened?"

I told her it went down.

"Oh sorry; she said acting as if she missed it. She handed me the pop corn and she took the soda we seat and eat. When we finished eating we started it again me holding her breast and her kissing me

"Oh shit here it comes again." I said

"Good; she said handing me my coat. Take it out."

"No I don't think so;" I said

"Why not? She said she was talking to her friend about it; her friend told her what to do."

"You did what?" I said aloud

"Quite someone;" yelled.

"You didn't."I whispered.

'It was all right; she said she won't tell anyone." She was doing the same thing to her boy friend.

"I guess it was catching."

"No silly; she said that is what everyone does when they come to the movie; look over there;" she pointed at this girl about four sets in front of us. "Watch her." The girl was looking at us. When she saw us she bent her head down; I didn't see her any more.

"Where did she go?" I asked

"She was helping her boyfriend make it go down;" she said.

"How is she doing that?" I asked

"Take your jacket and cover it I'll show you

"I don't know about this I said

"She said once I did it you will always like it "Really

"Really "that is what she said; and she knows She goes with a lot of boys." Her friend that is

"She can't date them all?"

"See she said pointing to her friend again she is with two of them right now."

"Oh I guess she knows then." I said.

"Good she said putting my coat over me and trying to take it out.

"Hold on Let me your making people look at us." I said

I took it out and waited for her to do what she was going to do. I wish she would hurry it was getting hard again. She bent down and started to stick her head under my coat.

"Hey I said whispering "Where are you going?"

"Just watch and make sure no one comes;" she said

OK I guess she know what she is doing. I'm glad she did because I didn't What she was doing I didn't think was right I tried to pull her head away from me but she didn't want anything to do with it. She kept it under the coat Then she did it. She kissed it.

"Hey I yelled Stop it

She came back up and sat in her seat "Why did you do that? She asked

"You don't kiss it." I said.

"Oh yes you do; she said you want it to go down don't you?" By this time everyone was yelling.

"Throw them out." Meaning us.

"Look she said; just leave me alone."

"Mary please I'm sorry." I said

"No she said you won't let me help you and my friend is going to laugh at me for not doing it."

"Oh so that is it. I said your friend is making you do it?"

"No; I like you and I want to help you; she said what is wrong with that?"

"Oh hell I said Go head."

"You mean it?" she said kissing me

"But "I said don't hurt me."

"No she said she told me not to use my teeth."

"You're what?" I said backing away.

"Now stop she said Give me your finger

"My what?

"Your finger; she said reaching for it. She took it and held two of them together; then put her mouth over them and started going up and down on them. "See she said that didn't hurt now did it?"

"No. I said why don't you just do it to my fingers?" I said

"That went stop the other thing;" she said I have to do it on it to make it stop."

"You sure?" I asked again.

"Look she said if you're a baby I'll just tell her you didn't want me to do it." Meaning her friend who was watching us.

"Oh go ahead but be careful." I said as she was going down again. I just watched the movies That was what I wanted everyone to think. I was waiting for her to do it. Here she goes her mouth was going over the top of it and then she was going up and down."

"Ohhhh "I heard myself say.

She just hit the side of my lag to make me stop making that noise. It was hard but I stopped I just watched my coat going up and down. The feeling she was giving me was like nothing I had ever felt before. At first I wanted to stop her. The more she did it the more I didn't want her to. The more she moved the better it felt. It was as if I was lifting off my seat and going into the air. My body was feeling good all over. What the hell was happening now? I felt myself getting tighter and tighter; then it was her turn to yell.

She jumped up and started spitting all over the place.

"What the hell was wrong?" I asked

"You she screamed you peed in my mouth."

"No I didn't." I said trying not to make noise. That was a laugh; the whole movie was looking at us.

"You "she yelled again running out of the isle and out the front

The girl that told her to do it ran after her Every one said for me to sit down and shout the hell up I sat down and remembered my thing was still out When I went to put my thing back in my pants I got the surprise of my life Not only was it down It was wet all over the place My pants my underwearmy coat It was all over the place I mean wet all over I jumped up and ran to the bath room Oh shit look at this I had water all over me; I must of peed. It didn't feel like pee it was sticky. What the hell did I do? Oh man look at this shit; it was sticky and white and still coming out. This wasn't pee it was something else; how stupid could I be; I read about this; it was SCUM. Scum the stuff that comes out of a man when he reaches his climax. Man I couldn't believe it I had it all over me; was I that stupid was I forgetting about the birds and bee's being the way I saw people getting killed making babies was the last thing on my mind.

She must have got it in her mouth that is why she was mad at me. Hey I didn't know; she was the one that knew everything. It was her girl friend that told her to do it. I didn't know this would happen. She was coming out of the bath room; Her and her friend that is. The friend just left her standing there looking at me.

"Want me to take you home?" I asked her.

She was looking at my pants. "You got it all over yourself." she said

"I know. I said looking; it will dry."

"I don't want to go back; she said I made a fool out of myself."

"No I said I was the one that should of known Blame me;" I told her.

"You're not mad at me?" She said.

"Why I said it did feel good." I didn't know if that was the right thing to say but I said it anyway she looked at me and said "Did it really?"

That was the start of my sex life. On the way home she wanted to do it again. I let her of course. I was a gentleman. We went in the park I stood up and she did it to me again. This time she told me to tell her when I was coming. How that I know what she was talking about I warned her. As she stood up I kissed her; She took my hand and press it up under her skirt. That was the feeling she wanted; she moved all over. That was the end of the sex for the night. She wouldn't let me do anything else.

When I went home I ran to my room and just thought about what we did. The next day I went and found a book about doing it from the library. I read up on it the next time we were going to do it I wanted to make sure I knew what I was doing.

I meet her in the hallway that day. She asked if I wanted to go out with her tonight?"

I was ready this time; I told her I would pick her up and we would go for a soda or something That something was full sex; I mean putting it into her and doing it all the way. At first it was hard; she didn't like it but she was to afraid to stop. She didn't want her friend to laugh at her. I guess the both of us had to prove a point that night. Her saying she did it and me knowing I did it right this time. I guess this was part of growing up. She asked me if I would marry her?" That snapped me right out of it I didn't know you had to get married once you did it to a girl. I found out later after reading some more about sex; you didn't. Good! I was glad for that; I wanted to go to College first before I got married.

That didn't work with her; she started with the baby thing.

"What if you got me pregnant?"

"I don't think so; I said I use a rubber this time.

"So she said her friend said that don't always work."

"Well my friends said it did."

We had our first fight and it was our last. She found out that once she had it other boys would go out with her. Just for sex that is. I felt bad for her but what could I do she started it.

So life went on I found out it was the same for a boy once you had it you wanted it again. So I went out with other girls to get it. Some were hard to get and a lot were easy. I guess it was the uniform that did it. I had them calling me up on the phone all the time. My Uncle just smiled.

Well it came time for me to graduate. At the top of my class of course. Seymour was almost a doctor by then. He didn't come home as much. I was leaving myself I thanked my uncle and Aunt for taking us in and off I went with the rank. I had ROTC program. I get right in the college ROTC program. The guy's at the College program were all races. None of them were Jewish I was the only one in my class so I dropped the act and became none Jewish. Life was different away from home. So that meant I kept to myself again; most of the time. At first it was hard the upper class man wouldn't let the lower class man alone. It was called motivation of some kind. I did what they said to do without much trouble. That was all right I would get my turn when they left and another class came in. I really didn't go for that kind of stuff but it was like a game to them.

One day this upper class man came in my room and told me to shine his boots. I told him to leave them and I would get to them later. He didn't like that so he came at me. By the time I got to college I was pretty big I lifted weights and worked out with the martial arts a lot. I heard he also was pretty good. That was the reason he was in my room. I guess some of the others told him I was better."

"Now; he said; lower class man."

"Sir it states when one lower classman is in study the upper classman should give him the respect and wait till he finishes. That is what I said I would do Sir; I said looking at him

"Look Jew boy I said now."

Oh I said I see you can tell I'm Jewish Does it show?" I asked. Well that was his mistake He came at me I didn't even move I just took my finger and poked his eye out with it. I couldn't see messing up my self or my room when a fight could be over in seconds.

The officer of the day came in and asked what was going on?"

I told him the upper classman was coming to give me his boots to shine. I stuck my finger up to show him where to leave them and he ran into it. I was sorry for that but accidents will happen; I said as they carried him out. Ever since then I was left alone. Guys would talk to me but most of the time I'd be by myself I didn't mind I rather liked it that way. The Navy didn't like it. They always wanted team work. I wasn't a team work kind of man. With my good grades they over looked it. I went into town once or twice a week to see a movie; from there I'd go have a drink at a bar and picked up a girl. I didn't over do it thou I didn't want to get stuck on anyone just yet.

One night as I was leaving a bar with this young lady these guys came up to me and called me a 'Jew' I didn't know it then but I found out later it was the same classman I had the fight with. I guess he didn't learn the first time. Will I had to work a little harder since there were five of them; but still it was no problem. I guess they wished they had stayed at home that night. When I went back to the young lady none of them were moving.

"She said; you killed them."

"Maybe, I said we will see when we come back; if they are still there."

"And if they are!" She asked.

"Then they are dead." I said

She looked at me I guess she didn't like the look I had on my face. I tried to get the same look Mr. Hitler gave me. I liked the way it mad me feel when I did it to other people.

The next year went by and the next I was the top of my class three years in a row. The forth year was a repeat of the last three so it wasn't hard. One day while I was taking a shower one of the Officers asked me what that tattoo was?" When I told him he just looked at me. "You're kind of young to have one of them." He said.

"Oh and how young did you have to be?" I asked. Him.

"He said he had fought over there and what the Germans did to you Jews was a crime."

"Did you see what they did?" I asked him.

"See; he said I was there when we took the prison camp."

"Which one?" I asked.

"Doctow;" he said.

I got this feeling down my back. Shit maybe he could tell me what happened there.

"That is the "he said.

"No sir I don't kid. I said and gave him my look.

"Could I buy a drink Sir? I said Just to thank you for what you did."

"He didn't do that much He was cleaning up and taking the prisoners back to the main line. Most of them couldn't even walk; he said. Just thinking about them still gave me nightmares."

"You;" I said Try living three years with it."

"I'll take that drink;" he said.

We got dressed and went to the club. He ordered drinks and we sat and talked. I tried to see if maybe one of my family got out alive. I couldn't go back because the Russians had taking over and closed most of it off. The west was still free but still had a lot of war damage to rebuild. I go didn't want to come right out and ask him so I played with him.

"Why you want to go back and finish them off." he said.

"The thought has entered my mind." I told him

"Well son since I spoke German it was my job to find out who was who. Most of the German soldiers didn't want their rank discovered so took dead soldiers I.D.so they wouldn't be caught."

"They had their Families living with them at the time." I said.

"We did get some woman and children but they were taking off fast for fear the Jews would kill them."

"So some lived?"

He looked at me. "That you can bet on but the Russians took them;" he said.

"So that means they were killed?" I said

"Who knows the Russians don't say anything about them and we don't ask."

"What about the General of the camp?"

"Him "he said "Him I know was killed. By what I couldn't say; if it was the Jews they made him look like a bomb did it. He was dead that I know I bet he is the one you would like to get your hands on;" he said laughing.

He knew I wasn't laughing so he changed the subject. "Where do you want to go after College?" he asked me

"To war. "I said still giving that look.

"You would think you had enough of it for a life time."

"No I said I guess it got to me I can't get it out of my blood."

"Some of us have it."

"And some don't." I finished it for him

"You got that right;" he said looking at me He said he was in the intelligence division. He could pull some strings to get me in there if I wanted to."

"Thanks anyway I said but I was thinking Of the Marines."

"Marine's; he said you may not like it."

"Why is that?" I asked

"No I take it back he said you might just fit in with them."

"Well if I don't like it the first four year I'll change over."

"You're making it your life?" he asked me.

"I think so I said What else is there?"

"That depends; he said you might meet some woman and change your mind;" he said

"I don't think so. I said I tried that way. Don't get me wrong I love woman but as far as living with them; that I could do without."

"I take it you don't like Kids?' He asked.

"No it's not that. I said when I feel I could bring them up with out the worry of war I might change my mind. Nothing is definite in this world." I said.

"Sun, Tide and taxes." He said other then that your guess is as good as mine."

I like him he was a kind of man that didn't push He was a captain at the time I felt honored talking to him.

The last year went by slow. The war had started; I guess we were lucky in one way they moved some of us up and sent us to advance training OCS officer Candidate School; with the Marines Since I picked to join them. They wanted man to lead and where else could they find them. Just out of college and went through ROTC with flying colors. I was getting my wish War and being a soldier I received my orders and was off to Paris Island for boot camp. It was just a quick course to get us use to the Non com as they called; the enlisted and draftees. I arrived at base camp and sign in. I had a Drill instructor he was called. He was from the Japanese war. The other side of the battle front. He knew what he was doing but he didn't have a lot of respect for Officers. He was from the hard corps as one would call him.{A leather neck with no Brains} The officers called men like him but ones you couldn't do with out They were the back bone of the corps.

Being I was an officer wasn't easy. They seemed to make us work harder. We had to get the respect of the man if we wanted to lead them. Boot camp was for another three month and then we were ready for the world. The day before we graduated we had one day of liberty That was to let off steam one would say And that we did We were all young and full of fight You put that into one bar and what do you have A fight that took the whole MP squad to break up. I mean we raised hell and then some. As the MP's took us out we looked back and saw we did a number on the bar The DI wasn't to happy when he came to the brig to get us out He looked at me and said one thing "Asshole" and left.

"He loves you;" my men said.

"You got that feeling to." I said.

Well the time was here; we all made it; our first duty station was Korea. This was what we all were waiting for. Most of us that is. Some looked scared but what the hell we were young. Only the salts saw more than me. But no one saw war the way I did. We boarded the ship and was out to sea I had time to write so I said down and wrote Seymour and his family a letter one to each. I wasn't much for writing but for some reason I wanted to this time. The days were short and the nights were long; the ship took forever. We made two stops. One in Hawaii the other in the Philippines. Then on to Soul that was where we were landing. The fighting had started and it was full scale by the time we arrived. We pulled in port at night you could see the gun fire on land. The ship we were on went right into battle. As we were disembarking

it was firing. The long gun's would make the ship tilt as they went off
The smell of gun power made me think of the time The planes were
dropping bombs over the prison

Well here we were on land; Ready to relieve the first company that
had arrived for the first shots fired. It was winter time boy was it cold.
It felt like home around this time of year; snow and gun fire; my kind of
place. We mounted into ten buys and headed out to the front. Most of
the men never saw combat before; it showed on their faces. Young kids
most of them not even shaving; all heading out to kill or be killed. "For
what?" Who knew? All we know is that the US needed us and off we
went. I had my own Platoon. They were mine I got my Lieutenant bars
and that meant I was an officer. The Gunny came with me I requested
him. He didn't like it but out off all of the officers he liked me the best.
He even asked me to kiss his ass. Now that was friend ship. It isn't
everyone you would ask to kiss your ass; now would you?"

We drove for a couple of days. It wasn't too far to reach where the
war was. The North had already started coming down into the south.
It was our job to push them back. I think they called it the thirty eighth
parallel. Some kind of line some one draw in the dirt and said "don't
cross If you do your ass is grass. We stopped at this road sign and the
driver got out to look around.

"Hey I yelled you lost?"

"No he said the sign is down

"So I said you got a map; use it."

He said he was but it didn't show the road on the map.

"So now what?" I asked.

The gunny came out and said "Take anyone they all go to war."

"Makes sense I said you heard the man Pick one." Little did we
know we were heading right for the enemies camp. It was turning night
when we stopped on this hill. I got out and went to have a look.

"Over there. I said see the lights; must be the base camp soldier. I
said Head for it."

I got my first medal for this one. We drove right smack into the
enemy camp. We took them by surprise. The gunny saw it first as we
were coming up the road; it was too late to turn around. They thought
it was one of their convoys coming; who would think the enemy would

drive right up into their camp. We all got ready for our first fight. We drove right throw them shooting anything that moved. We stopped turned around and went back and finished them off. We didn't leave the trucks. When the sun came up we couldn't believe what we did. We took out a whole company and not one of us got hurt.

"Shit "the gunny said "Lucky"

We radio it in ; of course the top brass started yelling we weren't suppose to be there; to get our ass's back down the road. Make a left at the cross roads not a right." They said

"We have got to tell them what we did. Meaning the company we just wiped out.

"Don't bother; the Gunny said they will hear about it soon enough."

Just then some jets fly over. I guess they were coming to hit them. We beat them to it. Then the radio started jumping. All kind of shit was going on I even heard one commander said."Fuck them; they shouldn't be there. Drop them on them any way;" he said

The pilot called back "Sir they are our man we can't do that."

"Just drop one; he said That is too let them know how close they came to getting there ass wiped."

"Will do; the pilot said."

On the next pass he let a napalm go. Holy shit you could feel the heat from it. It wasn't close to us at all but you could still feel it And jet's took off out of sight.

The gunny said "We just made a friend We had better get back where we ought to be."

"What's the rush?" I asked.

"Oh nothing he said looking over the mountain you'll see;" he said hitting the ground.

Just them; a mortar came about twenty feet in front of us

"The other company on the other hill;" he said. I took the radio and called the jets back. I told them we had guest on the other mountain. It took only ten seconds for them to return.

"Man where did they come from?"

He pointed at the other hill. White tents "They were there all the time; you just can't see them from the air with the white snow gear."

"Oh shit look at that. The whole top of the mounting was on firer from the napalm hitting

"Cooked gooks." he said and got back in the truck. We headed back down the road that took us here. The unit that we were sent to relieve was already packed up to pull out; as soon as we got there they couldn't wait to leave. The major came up to our truck and called me out."

"Lieutenant Where the hell were you?"

"Well sir you see we stop to enjoy the country side."

"Wise ass he said Get your men out of the trucks

My men want to go back."

"Gunny" was all I said.

"He yelled for the men to jump and they did. The other platoon was loaded and ready to move in a flash."

"What's the rush?" I asked the Major.

He smiled at me and said "You'll see wise ass." He looked at his watch and said "Tea will be served at noon. He jumped in the lead truck and took off."

"What did he mean by that?" I asked the Gunny.

The Gunny looked around and then at his watch and said "We got five minutes to get in the holes; Move it."

I guess he know what he was talking about. As it hit twelve noon all hell broke loose. Mortars came in from all over the place. My orders were to hold this hill at all cost. "Shit how can we fight if we can't see anyone to fight." I said

"We don't; he said keep your head down."

My ears were ringing the rounds were so close. Later for this I got on the radio and called for an air strike." I had the same pilot as before I told him what was happening. He said he would try but it would do no good. He said he tried hitting them yesterday they were dug in the side of the mountain and it was a hard to spot to reach."

"Shit" Was all I answered. I took out my field glasses and walked out of the bunker

"Where are you going?" The Gunny asked

"I'm going to tell them where they are."

"You nuts you'll get your head blown off out there."

"So we all got to go some time." I said and walked out. I had the radio with me I still had the pilot on telling him what I was going to do."

"Their they are." I said looking at the mountain to my left. "Pilot see the ridge on the second hill just below the first landing. Do you think you could drop one on the landing for me?"

He said he could put he didn't see what good it would do; they were inside the cave's. Even his mother couldn't throw one in there."

"Just give me what I want. I said and if you can't then send me back your mother, maybe she could."

I guess that got him pissed. I watched him fly over us and head right for the hill. Man was he low. Then he went straight up and came around so he could deliver it right where I wanted it. Man the mortars were coming like rain drops. One after another I almost got one. Stupid me I didn't want to duck I wanted to see if he hit the spot. I could see the bomb hit and nothing. Damn it I thought for sure it would work. Then about two minute's went by and the mortars stopped. It worked the whole mountain caved in and covered the cave entrance.

The pilot came back over the radio and said "That should hold them for a little while."

"Thanks' I said Thank your mother too."

He gave me a roll to let me know he heard me

"Gunny; Get your ass out here and have a squad get ready to pull out on the double."

He came out of his hole and looked around.

"You call sir."

"You heard me get your ass moving we don't have time.""

He yelled for the first squad to fall out. I told him I would be back soon."

He didn't say a word he just smiled at me and went back into his hole. I took the man and headed for the hill. We double time all the way till we reached the bottom. I looked up and saw where they were.

"Let's go man." I lead them up the hill to where the cave was. I could hear them digging their way out. They didn't expect to see us. We set a load of charges around the mouth of the cave. Then went back down the hill to wait. I had the men take cover so we weren't seen. The Gooks came out of the hole and looked around. There they go again I Could see them running like crazy to get the mortars set up again.

Now let's see what these charge's can do. Holy shit almost the whole mountain came down. "Mop up I yelled heading back up the mountain. When we reached to the hole they called a cave we stopped it looked as if they were all dead.

"Man would you look at this." I said going in. They had to be here for years. It went deep; far deeper than I thought. The ammo they had supplied here would last an army for a year's. We went around and checked for live ones. Twenty dead and five almost.

"Hey Louie; A Cpl. said. This one hasn't been hit." He pulled one out from behind the cases of ammo.

"Small aren't they;" he said. The cpl was about six 2 and growing. This gook was no bigger than 4,3 If that."

"Bring he here, anyone speak their shit?" I asked.

"No one to bad shot him."

They all looked at me.

"You can't do that;" the Cpl. said.

"Just joking." I said Take him with us."

"You shit" the gook said in good English. He was looking over my shoulder as he started to smile.

"You like me? I asked him smiling back at him

"You die;" he said

I looked around to see what he was smiling at. I almost shit from here you could see all over the place. No wonder they picked this spot you could see way back down the valley. I could see a convoy coming and I'd bet it wasn't ours. This is why this place was so stocked. It was a supply store and here comes the shoppers."

"Oh shit Man." the Cpl. said. We are out numbered sir let's get out of here. Call for the air; he said.

"No Cpl; we can't do that."

He looked at me like I was crazy. "Why Sir?"

"You see cpl they came all this way for this shit and you want to spoil it for them. No, I said we are going to let them have it."

"Sir have you flipped?" He asked

"No cpl Get me more charger's up here."

"Yes sir; he said running back to get them. I told him to set some into the ammo and have it set to go off with a timer."

"Could you do that." I asked

He smiled and said "They don't call me Banger for nothing Sir."

"OK Banger Show me."

We went to work

"Sir "cpl said I don't think they will go for it. When they see no one here and their own men dead. They will know something is up."

"Your right Banger what do you suggest?" I asked

"Call for the air strike."

"That would be hard. I said see the way the valley turns they could hold up forever in there."

"No we have to make them to come to us."

"But Sir We can't blow the mountain on top of us."

"No Cpl your right; but you're getting warm. What say we stay here till they see us? Then we run as if they think we were scared off by the size of them. "Do you think that would work?"

"Maybe; he said but it is going to be close. By the time they reach the top to see us it will be to later for us to run."

"Who said anything about running?' We are going to act as if we don't even know this place is here. We are just a patrol that came across them if we hold up say over there. I pointed. I would say they would head for the cave for protection wouldn't you say Cpl."

"It sounds good to me; he said but who is going to wait for them?" He asked

"Oh I think four of us will do. You me Banger and one more; you pick him out for me. Have the rest head back."

"Me?" The Cpl said

"You help with the idea I think you should stay around to see if it works."

"But sir they have over a two hundred man coming."

"And we have Four." I said Sounds even to me. Now go; I told him. I told Banger what we were going to do. His eyes lit up.

"You mean I get to watch them blow?" Sir!

"If you do it right." I said

"You just watch me sir."

"Oh I will."I told him and went back to the cpl "You got our man?"
I asked. He pointed at the big guy.

"Good." I told the rest to take the prisoner back with them. Tell the
gunnery to watch. If it doesn't get them; call for an air strike to finish
them.

"What about you sir?" He asked

"See that bunch of rocks over there."

"Yes sir; he said.

"Tell them we will be behind them. Try not to hit us."

"You're kidding sir;" he said

"I'll let you know when we get back; if I was kidding soldier. Now
go get your ass out of here."

They left the three that stayed I told them what I wanted to do. I
wanted them to think we were just out on patrol. I don't want them to
see us till they reach the mouth of the cave. From where we would be
they all could get into the cave with out being hit by us. But on the other
hand they can't come down the hill with us here."

"Why would they want to sir? The big guy asked. They got all the
mortars they could want. All they have to do is to set them up and blow
the shit out of us."

"Smart I said That means we are going to have to take a couple of
rounds to make sure they all are in the cave; then banger here will do
the rest."

Isn't that right Banger"! I said looking at him.

"If he doesn't then by the time we get the air strike it well be to
later for us sir."

"But the air boys will get them Cpl. You don't have to worry about
them getting away."

"That is nice of you sir; the big guy said but why can't we just go
back to our hill and call for air strike and watch it from there."

"Why! Good question soldier. They have been trying that for days
the pilot said he couldn't touch them in the cave. It is the way the
mountain and the valley run's, it is hard to get a bomb in there."

"So "The Cpl said are we going?"

I looked at them and smiled "Front row seats gentleman." I said and
walked down the hill.

They followed I heard the big guy tell Banger he had better make it work or else he was going to stick one up his ass and light it."

Bang just smiled and said; he should make him pay for the front row set."

We got in position and waited.

"There is the front guard. I said Let them go in."

The point came running out of the cave and went back and told the main troops what was happening

I know it would get to them. They need the ammo. The point made it sound like the air strike took it out. That is what they heard back an hour ago. They had to move in fast before we took it over. This is what I was hoping they were thinking.

"OK ready or not here we come." I told them let me take the first shot I know when I wanted it to go off and no one else. This was my baby."

The stage was set now for the action. We started walking as if we didn't know what was going on We were looking for the cave but didn't know where it was. I told my men not look at the cave I wanted them to see us first I was counting on them to duck not letting us see them till all their man were inside. Once inside they know it would be hard for us to hit them.

That is how it went Boy was I good I saw them looking down at us and ducking. I could see the whole line of them coming up from the back ducking. They were going for it.

"OK man When I firer the first shot head for them boulder's over they; they can't hit us with rifle firer

"But the mortars could;" the big guy said.

"That they could big guy but it will at least take three rounds to pin point us; then Banger does his thing, Right Bang?" I said. He just smiled.

"Remember what I told you Banger the big guy said

"I know up my ass

"OK ready." I said. I shot one round at the guy looking at us from the mouth of the cave that did it; five of them opened fire on us. We headed for the rocks.

OK so far so good." I said then we heard it Mortar Round one coming. It missed, Round two coming, It got closer.

"OK Banger I said get ready."

Round three was coming Oh shit it almost got us. That was close. The next one was going to be right on top of us.

"Banger, do your thing." He stood up and let it go. Man the whole top of the mountain lifted off. It lifted about ten feet in the air and came back down. We could see bodies flying out of the mouth of the cave. I guess the blast from the back of the cave acted like a cannon shooting anything in it's way out the mouth of the cave.

It was over in two minute; the ammo went up with Bang's charge all at once.

"Call and tell them to change the maps on this mountain; it's a hill now. We just took fifty feet off the top of it."

"Man you see that." they said.

"Bang you could kiss my ass;" the big guy said picking him up in the air.

Just then a jet flew over he was on the radio.

"Hey man, save some for me." he said

"Go home brother; I said. Your coffee is getting cold."

He gave me the roll over I know he was the same pilot as before. He must of went back to refuel and came right back out to help us. I had to meet this guy I liked his style.

"That's a Roger "he said then went out of sight

Well it worked; we took out a whole company without getting a scratch. This was easy I said to myself only here a couple of days and already we made history.

"Ok Guy's we did our job now let's go back to the hill and wait."

When we returned the Gunny was waiting of us. He had a big smile on his face along with the rest of the men. Shit and why not? The radio was jumping with officers wanting to know what was going on out there?"

The gunny didn't tell them anything; he waited for me to give them the news.

"Get over here; he said tell them what happened." He handed me the radio I ID myself; Lieutenant Goldberg here."

"What the hell is going on there soldier?" One said.

"First platoon Company G reporting sir; Hill 27 is taking with no casualties Sir." I looked at the Gunny and smiled.

"You did it "he said slapping me on the back.

"Who is this!" the voice on the radio said.

I repeated it and sign off.

"Now what?" I asked the Gunny?

"We go home; he said the war is over." He couldn't stop laughing.

"You kidding?" I said.

"I wish; he said we just begun to fight sonny boy; so let's go. They want us to take this hill over here; he said pointing to the map.

"What happened with this hill? They told us to hold at all cost."

He smiled and said "No reason to how."

So off we went to this other hill. It seemed as if there was nothing but hills here. The Gook's were on all of them. From what the Gunny was telling me it was a battle of King of the hill. First they would take it then we would take it back. Back and forth; the hills were the key to this war. The one that had it was King I could see why from the first one. You could see everything from them; no one could move without being seen. If you had the hill you controlled the valleys; and without the Valleys you couldn't go anywhere. One man could hold back a Battalion for weeks. There was no way around them. That was on less you wanted to take days going around. Well we got to hill 52 and it looked quite; nothing was moving.

"So now what?" I asked the Gunny.

He smiled at me and said "we take it."

"Just like that?" I said.

"No; he said pointing at something.

I got my field glasses and look where he was pointing.

"Oh shit they are waiting.

"You can bet on that; he said and you can bet they aren't going to give it up easy either."

I could see why it over looked the whole Valley to the north. It was the biggest mountain around.

"Shit they could see us coming."

"Not yet; he said just stick you head over the top of this ridge and you will see you."

"No thanks' later for that. Set up camp Gunny. This one isn't going to be that easy."

"There all not as easy as the last one." He said laughing. I guess he knew he was here before. The first one was just luck.

We set up camp; the Gunny and I looked over the hill on the maps.

"Man this is shit No way."

"What about air?" I asked.

"Ha, he said I read the report hey hit it with everything they had and nothing. They were so dug in it would take the H bomb to get them off."

"That isn't such a bad idea. I said we got any around?"

"No; he said we used them all In Japan."

"Funny, so now what?"

"You're the big shot; he said you tell me."

"We sit and wait." I said

"No good; he said while we are doing that they are moving more and more troops up. With out this hill they can't; so we got to take it."

"What about mortars?"

"That is all well and good; he said they have them to. Once they know we are here the fun begins.' Right now they don't let's leave it that way till we see what we are doing."

Just then I heard a jet coming over the radio

"Ground to air; I said on the radio could you give me a report."

"Report hell; the pilot said you are in big trouble you got a couple of thousand gooks coming straight at you. And I can't do much to stop them, Roger."

"Can you give me there location?" I asked.

"Coming down the valley of the Dead; he said Roger.

The Gunny pointed to it on the map.

"Time of arrival?' I asked.

"Oh let's see you got one maybe two day before you make eye contact. Roger." he said.

"What will give me the two days?" Roger.

"Oh about ten of us and about a couple of hundred bombs."

"That is a Roger. I said will get back." I said He flow over and went out of sight

"Shit and they want us to hold?" I said.

"That is what they said we have to hold till they bring up some more reinforcements. This is a foot soldiers war;" he said.

I went back to the map and looked at it.

"No way we can't stop them. Once they reach this hill it is all over with."

"That is what they have in mind."

"What if we stop them say here." I pointed at and deep valley and a small pass.

"That would be good; he said it might delay them some; a couple of day's at most. But how do we get there to stop them?" he said pointing at the Hill 52. They won't let us pass; to go around them would take days.

"OK We have to think it out." I got my nap sack and went into a corner where my bunk was set up I went to lay down

"Hey what the hell are you doing?" the Gunny asked.

"Thinking." I said and went to sleep. I could hear him saying things I didn't listen to him I closed my eye's and went to sleep.

"Sir "some one said you want to eat?".

It was the Gunny he had made some food.

"You think enough?" he asked can we get on with the war now?"

"Yes why not; I said anything happening?"

"No he said they are still coming and we are still sitting; the same."

"Good I said

"Good he looked at me and said we got only 12 hours before we get hit."

"Gee's I slept that long?"

He looked at me and smiled "No, we got put into a time machine. Look sir either we do something or we pull back it's got to be one or the other."

"Do we have any Indian's with us?" I asked.

'Any what?"

"You know Americans Indians?"

"What the hell does that have to do with it;" he asked

"Oh nothing it's just something I remembered in a movie I once saw; it may work."

"You crazy; he said you want some Indians With or without Tomahawks?"

"Knifes will do;" I said Do we."

"I think so; he said we have two."

"Good, get them for me and the Banger."

"Him to?" He said Any one else sir; I think we have a couple of clown's if you want."

"Not on less you want to come along."

"No thanks' sir some one has got to report your where abort's." He left He came back with the Indians and Banger.

"Men we have a job to do and it's going to take you three to do it."

They just looked at me and didn't say a word. "Gunny, get me air on the radio."

He did I got the same pilot as before.

"Hey good buddy; he said you still alive?"

"Alive and kicking I said did you ever see the movie Indian Joe?

"Did I what? He yelled over the radio

"The movie I repeated myself

"I did so what about it?

"Remember what the Indians did in the valley?

He trough a minute and then came back and said "They ran horses down it to distract the army."

"That is the one; you have any horses?"I asked him.

"Back home;" he said

"No good fly boy I need them now." I said I got the Indian's; you have to give me the horse's." I told him.

"How about napalm;" he asked?

"That is what I was thinking."

Man If I drop one of them down that valley It will run like a herd of wild horses on the ground. Who ever is in the way of it gets stampeded to a crisp."

"All I want is to give me that extra day;" I said can you do it?"

'He laughs and said. That is a Roger; One an hour will stop any one from walked. The only thing they could do is wait me out."

"That is what I was hoping you would say. No way around them?" I asked

"No way; he said not down "Dead man valley" there isn't."

"Good I said Give me them. Oh one other thing fly boy make sure you don't drop them at the mouth of the valley."

"Why? He asked

"Because we will be there." I said

"What? He asked

"You heard me. I said I'll be setting up a gate to close."

"You'll be doing what?" He asked.

"Oh nothing. I said Just don't drop to soon I didn't want anyone to know what I was planning I knew the gooks could hear everything we were saying."

"That is a Roger; he said and sign off.

The Gunny looked at me and asked "Now how are you going to get from here to there?" He said pointing at the map when they are here."

"Easy; I said we walk. Banger you think you can blow these two mountains One on each side enough to close the door for the gooks."

He looked and said with about two hundred lbs of good stuff?"

"How about fifty lbs that is all we can carry; 25 and 25."

"That is going to be hard that mountain was there a long time. We tried that by air;" the Gunny said the jets can't get in close to do it right."

"See "I said pointing to the map if this is right they both have over hangs with the right charge they should go."

Banger looked at me and said "Maps don't tell it all;" sir

"So I said then I guess we have to go see them for ourselves."

"What if you don't do it?" The Gunny asked.

"Then we are goners; I said looking at the Indians and Banger.

The Gunny smiled. You got that right once they know you have broken their line's they will be waiting for you to return."

"I know that; I said we have to do it Right men?"

The Indian said "You crazy."

"That he is;" the Gunny said all of us are; now get out of here and do what you got to do. I'll keep them busy at this end."

I told him I didn't want them to know we were here till we got over this ridge. Once we reached the other side then they should concentrate there fire on the hill. By that time we should be under them and on to the valley; I hope.

It was getting dark we didn't have time to waste. The jet flew over head and gave me the roll over. Good I felt better knowing it was him. The four of us head for the Valley once we reached the ridge all hell broke out. The jet was doing his thing from where we were we could see the flames of the napalm going off

Then the Gunny started with his attach; he was hitting them from all angles. The gooks were to busy shooting back at the Gunny to see us. Plus it was dark. So the only thing we had to worry about was some guards. The Indians were good; one took the point, keeping us in sight. He would slow us down when needed and give us the double sign when it was clear. One Indian was named Goat and the other one was named Snake. I found out why they were called them names. Snake moved like a snake; you couldn't hear or see him. The Goat I found out could climb anything. That came in handy later. We got past the hill the Snake took out three gooks with his knife. As we went along we saw his work. No sound just death. He was good. We headed for the valley; it took us most of the night. The sun was coming up the Jets were still holding them down. Like the pilot said one an hour. We got to the place in the valley I wanted to get to.

"Well can we do it?" I asked.

Banger looked and said "Yea; if we were birds. Sir I don't get you; he pointed at the over hangs and said "We have to have a charge under them in order to make it work; without them there it would be useless. I could have five hundred Lbs it would do nothing."

"Shit; all this way for nothing. We can't go back without trying." I said

Goat looked up and said Where do you want it?" he asked Banger.

We both looked at him and laugh "No one can get up there."

"Snake said "Goat can that was how he got his name." Snake said. "Mountain goat."

Goat asked Banger where Banger pointed. Goat started up the mountain he had 25 lbs of c3 on his back. He was climbing like a goat jumping from landing to landing till he was almost at the spot.

"This is going to be the hard one." I said. He had to climb almost on an angle upside down almost.

"Shit I'll be;" Banger said Look at him go

It is as if he was born on a mountain.

Snake smiled. "He was; he said; Goat's mother was on a cliff when she gave birth."

Goat came back down and took the other 25 lbs and started up the other side. We just watched him go He wasn't human; no one could do what he was doing. Snake said that was nothing he seen him do better. That I had to see what he was doing a spider couldn't do. But he did. On his way back down he stopped and was looking at something. He started again when he came down he handed me a flower.

"Put it in your helmet; he said Good luck."

I needed all we could get I stuck it in on the top of it like a feather.

"Me Indian now." I said

"Shit; the both of them said. No way."

"Well Banger do your thing. We back off and watched him at work.

"Where do you want it to fall"? He asked.

"Cut the shit I said Just block the pass so no one can pass."

"Will do; he said and came back with us."

Bang one side went. Man did it go the whole side of it just slid down and landed right where we wanted it to land. Now for the other side Banger set it and pushed nothing.

"Shit what is wrong?"

He said maybe the first disconnected the second; I got no contact;" he said.

"Goat could you?"

Goat had the wirer in his hand and was already going up the other side checking for a brake. Man did he go he was almost at the place when he stopped. He gave us the signal he found it. He fixed something and was coming back down. That was when I heard the one shot. I looked over to see where it came from.

Snake said the "Goat got it." I looked back up at the Goat and saw him taking a header off the side of the cliff and coming down. If the bullet didn't get him the fall will. He hit the bottom with a thud.

"That mother fucker I yelled and started shooting at the gook that was looking at us from the mountain top. Snake took his rifle and shot it once. The gook took his fall off the mountain

Banger yelled he was ready."

"No wait." I had to go get Goat. He would be covered if we didn't get him. I dropped my rifle and took off over to him. I couldn't see letting him be buried under the mountain. Snake kept firing at the other sniper's that started forming on the top. He was picking them off one my one but they kept coming. It must be the advance patrol. I reached Goat his eyes were still opened and he had a smile on his face."

"My mother said I was a goat not an eagle." He died in my arms. I picked him up over my shoulders and ran back. The gooks were shooting at me Snake kept firing; I guess they know once that other side came down they would be trapped. I guess I would have fought hard if that was the case. The bullets were bouncing all over the place; I got back and told Banger to let it go. He did Man did it go.

The gooks were all over the top of it when it came down.

"An extra bonus; he said as he saw about twenty gooks coming down with it. When the dust cleared we saw we did it. Nothing was getting through that pass. It would take them days to dig it out.

"Let's go we did what we came for." I picked Goat up and started back.

Banger yelled for me to stop He ran up to me and took The Goat off of me

"You're bleeding like a pig sir." I looked down and saw what he was talking about. Shit I was hit Where; I didn't know but it was coming out fast; where ever it was I couldn't feel anything. My hip it looked like I took off my jacket and saw where it was coming from. Shit I didn't even feel it.

Snake looked at Goat and showed me why the bullet would have got me in the back. Instead it hit Goat's hand and just ricocheted down my side. It was deep but the bullet just landed in the ground. Not in me. Banger took a look at it He put something on it and said. "I'll live." He picked Goat up and off we went.

When we got back to hill 52 it was quite the sun was going down so we waited. Banger looked at me again and said the bleeding had stopped.

Good I didn't have that much to lose. My pants and my boots were full.

"It must have hit something." He said it traveled almost half way down my body it looks as if someone tried to cut you in half. I still couldn't feel it I guess that was good.

"OK now we try to get back. The Gunny isn't going to know we are coming so we have to watch both sides; our men and the gooks."

Snake took the lead; again Banger took goat and I hopped along behind taking up the rear. Snake was having trouble it seems they had more guards this time. They know we had to come back this way so they wanted to repay us for what we did. Snake came back and said too many of them; they are waiting for us.

"Shit, how what?"

Snake looked over head.

"Don't even think of it;" I said. I knew there was no way I was going to get up and over the mountain he was looking at. I was starting to feel pain my whole side started to stiffen up.

Snake said he would go and bring back the Gunny. Well some one had to help us we weren't going to make it with out help from the other side."

"Snake" I said taking the flower out that Goat gave me. "Take this." I said putting it in his hand. He didn't answer he knew. He took it and off he went. Shit he was just as good as Goat. Before you know it he was out of sight. Banger put Goat down and came over to me.

"Lets get ready;" he said and pulled me over to some rocks "We could hold them off for a while; he said if we have to." He gave me my rifle then pulled Goat back with us; we waited. The sun was coming up everything was quite nothing was moving.

"I hope he made it. Banger said. How will we know he asked?

"I smiled. When you see my beard reach about here then we knew he didn't."

"Funny; he said Just then I looked down and saw the flower Goat gave to me. Shit Snake dropped it. He must of dropped it. I picked it up and was looking at it. Shit it was Snake; he throws it at me. He was up on the other side of the hill trying to get our attention. The flower did it He was right over the gooks.

He didn't want them to see him so the flower did it. He was giving us hand signals; he was telling us to cover up and get down. He didn't have to say it twice. I pulled Banger over to me with out telling him what I was doing. That's when it started. We must have been dumping mortars all over the gooks. Snake was acting as a spotter. He would direct them to where the gooks were. Lucky thing we took covered; the rocks and dirt started coming down on us like crazy. When it was over we couldn't move we were covered from head to toe with dirt. The first one we saw was Snake. He came down the mountain like he was on skies. My face was the only thing that wasn't covered. Banger started to get him self out of the dirt when he saw Snake coming.

"Would you look at that he said turning over and watching him slid.

"That looks like fun I have to try that."

"Later "I told him Get me out of here."

Snake went over and pulled Goat out from under the dirt. He picked him up he was taking him home. Banger finished digging me out. We started to walk the rest of the way. Snaked had them drop the mortars right where they did the most good. It was easy if you had someone telling you where you wanted them to land. No one could escape; them mortars could drop right into your hole if someone told you where your hole was. Snake did just that I could hear the Gunny yelling on the other side. He was having my man come and help us. No more gooks on this mountain.

I got back to the field hospital where they patched me up. I was in bad shape but not that bad. I just had to rest for a month. They sent me to the base hospital where I heard the good news. I received a promoted and of course some metals out of it. I was on my way this is what I was trained for. The rank meant more to me then the metals. That was what I wanted; Rank' I wanted to reach the top.

After I left the base hospital I was send back for R&R for a month. That was when I meet the captain. The one that I meet in college. He was still with intelligence. He was a Major now He got his rank for doing something. He came to see me the day I was going to head back to Korea. They wanted to send me home but I didn't want to hear it. I got my wish and I was going back War was what I wanted; not a desk job.

"Hi He said coming into my room "You remember me?" he said holding out his hand for me.

"You got to be kidding; sure I do. How are you Sir?"

"Great I hear you did a hell of a lot of damage over there."

"Oh you know now it is Sir; War is hell."

"Want to go have a drink?" He asked.

"Why not I could use one before I head back."

"That is what I want to talk to you about."

"Oh I hope you're not going to try and change my mine?"

"No he said you crazy! We need man like you. What I'm here for is to see if you would like to join up with me and do some real good?"

"Intelligence?" I said

"You got it son; just say the word and you're in."

"I need to know a little more about it before I do;" I said.

"That is why I'm here; he said To wine and dine you my boss likes the way you work. He gave me the orders not to come back on less your with us."

"He heard of me?" I asked.

"You kidding the whole Marines Corp's knows about you. What you did will go down in history books."

"That is what I want." I said

"I know; he said looking at me straight in the eyes. You did mean it when you said 'Forever.'"

"This is my life I want to do the best I can."

"Well son so far you're doing one hell of a job." That is why my boss wants you."

"Who is your boss?" I asked

"You'll find out soon enough but for now; he said you have to say yes."

"Do I have time to think about it?"

He looked at his watch and said. "You have 6 hours to let me know."

"Well what are we waiting for? I said I can't get drunk talking here."

Off we went to find a quite bar. We sat down and drank. I asked him all kind of questions about what he was doing and what I would be doing? I asked anything that came into my head.

"Man slow down "he said once I was going overboard with my questions.

"Most of our shit was top secret if I was in I would have higher clearance. Then he could tell me everything; but for now take his word for it He said It would fit my style."

For some reason I believed him.

"I'm in." I said

"Good he said and ordered another bottle.

Man could he drink I wasn't doing that bad myself. He looked at his watch and said "You ready."

"Let's go; I said the war is going to be over by the time we get there."

"One other thing; he said taking something out of his case. My boss said this is yours." He handed me a box.

"What the hell is this?" I asked.

He said he didn't know his boss said to give it to you."

"Even if I didn't take your offer?" I asked

"Even if you didn't take my offer; he said He told me it was yours."

Shit what the hell could it be? All of a sudden I started to get worried. Was this a trip to get me? Did they know who I really was? At first I wanted to get up and run. But that wouldn't do me any good he would shot me in the back He had a gun I didn't. I could kick his ass. No he probable had other man watching us. Shit I know it would come to this.

"Oh hell I said you got me. I took the box and opened it. "My gun." I said

"Good "he said we were looking for you a long time."

"How did you find out?" I asked him.

He said with my record we'd be crazy not to want you."

"Wait a minute something wasn't making sense, I said to myself. He didn't know about me he just wanted me for the job. Oh shit I almost blow it.

"You mean you wanted me before."

"Look he said I don't know the whole story about you but when we meet at the college I went and told my boss about you."

"That was why you were there?" I asked

"To find some good man; he said I picked you Well any way when I got back and handed in my report my boss took it and said he know you And he agreed he too wanted you. I was going to assign you after college but he said to let you get a taste of combat first. Well you did and you made him happy. You came out smelling like a rose. Now he wants you more than ever; now you got good recommendations I got my next rank for finding you.

"Who is this boss of yours?" I asked

He said again. You will find out soon enough. That is yours?" He said looking at Hitler's gun.

"Yes," was all I could say?

He was like a kid giving it to me. He said his boss said "You would know who he was by the gift."

He was more excited then I was. For all I know it was a trap to see how I would react. Oh hell here goes "Mother fucker I trough I would never see it again."

"What is it?' he asked trying to look over the cover. I took the cover off and showed him it.

"Man he said a German luger. Look at that he said I always wanted to get me one. Why is he giving it to you?" He asked.

"He is returning it." I said

"Hold on; he said taking a deep breath Your not the kid that killed the three Generals; are you?"

I just smiled and took it in my hand

"You are aren't you?"

I smiled again His boss must be the officer that found me and Seymour on the road. The one that saved us. Inside was a note; It read, Sorry it took me so long returning it. I lost contact with you. My friend Mr. Goldberg told me you had join us I knew one day I would run into you and return it. It is yours." He said

"Could I hold it?" he asked

I looked at him and handed it to him

"Oh mother; he said I wanted to bring one back with me but I never got the chance. Hey he said Look at this Do you know who owned this?" He said reading the writing on the side of it.

"Hitler." I said

"He looked at me and just looked at the luger.

"The man him self held it in his hand and you killed his Generals to get it. Man he said you were only how old?"

"10" I told him

"Mother fucker you are something; NO wonder he wants you."

"Your boss was the first one to find me and my brother. My brother was going to shot him self just before your boss came. We though he was the Germans coming back for us. He was the first American we saw and to this day I never thanked him for what he did."

"He did say something about him knowing your father."

"Yes; my father operated on his daughter just before the war broke out. My father gave him my uncle's address to have him look him up when he got back home to the US. Your boss sent me and my brother back to the States to my uncle who raised us. We had no one left but him; after Hitler finished with our kind. If your boss didn't send us when he did we would still be in Germany today; the Russian side. Alive or dead who ever would have got to us first." I said picking up the gun and holding it.

"Do you know how much you could get for that?" He said.

I laugh and said "Nothing, Because I will never sell it."

"I wouldn't either;" he said

"Man could I hold it one more time."

I let him he was as if he could feel the power it gave you when you know who owned it.

"Well, he said handing it back. If you ever want to sell it see me first."

I put it back in the box and stood up. "We ready? I said looking at him.

"Ready as we will ever be; he said we have a plane to catch."

"Where to?" I asked

"Washington; he said we have to retrain you."

CHAPTER 4

So off we went; I wanted to go back to the fighting but this was even better. I know I would see more fighting this way. I was right it took us two days to get back. We had a car waiting for us when we landed. This one had flags on it; Just like the Germans had on their cars. This one had American Flags on it and a two star Generals flag.

"He is a two star General now?" I asked

"That he is; he said and he has more pull then the president."

Funny I forgot his name. I said to myself. Oh well he will tell me soon enough. His name I forgot but I never forgot his face. I still had dream's about him and Seymour getting ready to shot himself.

Here I was at the white house I had only seen it in pictures never before in person. We drove in the front gate. The marines saluted us without stopping us. This was my dream I was a General like my father and people gave me respect. That was power; power you couldn't imagined you had to feel it for your self to know what I was talking about.

We stopped in front of a building that had a sign on the front. 'War department' this is where all the orders came from. That I knew but never thought I would be walking in throw the front door and having Marines Saluting me. I snapped my salute as we walked passed them. Man did I feel good. We walked through as if we owned it. The Major know everyone. He called them by their first name. Even officers over him; he told me I would get use to it. We went up to the second floor and down the hall. It was at the end of the hall; it was in Big gold letters. 'Intelligence' Marines guards at the door didn't even stop us. We didn't even have to show any ID. They just opened the door for him and let us in. 'POWER'

That was the first time I saw her. She was sitting behind a desk looking over some papers. The Major said something to her and she looked up. Our eyes meet; I think it was love at first sight if that is what they call it? At least for me it was she kept looking at me as she talked to him.

"He is waiting for you," she said. Then asked me what my name was; for some reason I said "Joseph Oh shit what was I doing I was going to say Joseph Kaufmann. That wouldn't of been to smart.

"Lieutenant Joel Goldberg." I said

"Hi she said holding out her hand and saying her name Nancy Staubitz."

"Oh I said Your German?"

"Yes she said does that make a difference?" She asked as she held my hand.

"Arr no." I said lost for words

"Let's go;" he said you can talk later, he pulling me.

She smiled and let me go "Later" she said and in we went

That was him; I said to myself. He was sitting behind a big desk.

"Joel; he said standing and coming around to meet us. I don't know what came over me but it did; I ran to him and put my arms around him and gave him a big hug. I felt a tear coming so I pulled back and said I was sorry."

"No, he said coming back into me. I've been waiting a long time to do this;" he said

"Me too; I said taking him into me again. The both of us had tears in our eyes.

"What the hell was this?" The Major said. Two big bad marines crying?"

"Hey "the General said. Go fuck yourself and kept holding me. I wanted to do this to this man for a long time and no one was going to take this moment away from me.

"Well he said pulling away from me. Would you look at you?" He held me at arms length and just looked at me. "My he said You'd make your father proud."

Then I thought witch one? If he only know who my real father was.

"Thank you sir." I said shacking his hand and saying how much I waited for this moment. "Sir I said I had you on my mind all the time I was sorry I never got to thank you."

"Hey he said so was I; you know he said I owe this all to you."

"No sir, I said I'm the one that owes."

"No, he said remember the night I found you and your brother?"

"Do I?" I said; I'll never forget it."

"Well son the Generals you shot I went over their car's I found information that was the key to us finding out everything about the German army and Hitler. You see they had records from the main head quarters and I was the one to head the investigation. From there on it was nothing but up for me. Now I run it and it's all do to you and your brother."

"Sir; the Major said. Would you like to tell him what he will be doing?"

"Major"he said. Get lost we got old times to go over and you tell that woman out there I don't want to be disturbed. You got me Major?"

He looked at me and smiled "You got it sir;" he said and did an about face and went out.

"Come Joel he said have a seat I want to hear about you and your brother. I missed a lot about you two. Oh he said stopping. You did get the gun? Didn't you?"

I pointed to my bag and smiled.

"Good he said I didn't know if I could trust him with it. But I know once you saw it you would come.

"I know; I said. He tried to get it off of me already."

"You have to watch out for him; he said He would steal the eyes out of a dead man if he liked what was in them."

"I felt that, I said. That is why I kept it on me all the way."

"Smart man, he said. Boy have you grown; man you're like the son I never had;" he said.

"Sorry sir I said I didn't know."

"Now could you;" he said.

"Well then how is your daughter?" I asked.

"Thanks to your father she is alive and doing very well thank you. She gave me my son I never had I have two grandsons; he said. Thanks to your father."

"I'm glad to hear that sir." I said.

"Look Joel You can call me by my first name, he said. When no one is around that is."

"Are sir I said. That is why I never got back to you. I know it sounded stupid but I didn't even know your name. To this day I never asked anyone."

He laughs and said.

"What is in a name?" he asked.

"Nothing, I said it was the feeling that counted."

"Your right son I couldn't have said it better myself. Well My name is Bill Greene."

"Bill; I said holding out my hand. My pleasure."

"What about Seymour?"

"Him he followed after his father."

Shit I slipped again.

"Oh he said and you didn't want to!"

Little did he know I was "No sir, I said. I didn't want to I found it felt better Killing then curing. He started to laugh and couldn't stop.

"You; he said got the taste of it and now your a war hero to boot. I like that, he said. You're up front and to the point. Well you ready to take on this job?"

"I would if I know what it was about sir." I said.

He looked at me and smiled. "That ass hole he said everything to him is top secret. I take a shit and it is top secret to him."

"Major Ward?" I asked

"Him, he said. He is a good man but man does he bug me."

"He does over act, I think." I said

"Over act, he said. He is crazy; you know what his problem is?"

"No sir I said.

"He watchers to many movies about spy's. One time he came in and had his uncle checked out. He thought he was a spy."

"No." I said

"Really, he said. The man is a nut I told him he could tell you what you would be doing."

"Well he did say it was top secret and you would tell me."

"I'll kill him," he said.

"He was right. I said. He didn't want to tell me anything, just encase I didn't take the job."

"You mean you took the job with out knowing what you would be doing?"

I looked at him and said "The gun answered it for me; I'd do anything for you sir." I said

"I'm proud of you son; he said. And glad you accepted. Now I'll tell you what you will be doing."

"It doesn't matter I said I'd clean heads for you sir."

"Good I'm glad to hear that, he said. You might just have to."

"Clean head's?" I asked.

"No; he laughs. Just take care of a lot of shit around here."

"Oh then that means I'll be stationed here?" I asked.

"You kidding he said. We go around the world. Shit he said I was to Korea Japan and to Germany in two days does that look like I was stationed here? He said

"No sir I said I think I'm going to like this job

"You know you will he said I'll see to that if it is action you want Action you'll get and plenty of it "Good I said Then I'm your man

He took out my orders and said "I got them cut already."

He knew I would take it; I'd be a fool not to.

"Well he said getting up. "Let's go."

"But sir I said I don't have a place to stay."

He went back to his desk and took out a set of keys "You do now."

"What is this?" I asked.

"Your own place." he said. I'll show it to you later; come; he said I want you to meet my wife. She has dinner waiting for us." He went out the door and throws the keys to the woman. See to it that his things get in his place. You can reach me at home; he told her.

"Yes sir; she said and looked at me "Welcome aboard," she said.

"Come, you'll have plenty of time to get to know each other." The Major was waiting out side talking to some man.

"Sir, he asked, is he staying?"

"Yes he said walking past him. No thanks to you." he said

I just looked at him and followed

"Sir where are you going?" He asked

"Home you ass, he said, where else?

"Should I come?" He asked

"No, he yelled going down the stairs. Do some work," he told him.

He gave me a look and went back to the man he was talking to; the General went out the door and down the stairs and into his car as if he had to go to the bathroom.

"Come, he said. Dinner is waiting."

I guess he was hungry I got in and off we went. His driver took off like a shot. "Home he told him and just sat back a smiled. "See he said this is what rank can do for you. I run this place, he said, thanks to you." He took my hand and smiled. "Now it is my turn to do for you," he said.

"Sir I said I want to earn my rank."

"Oh he said. You have already started that. You're making a name for yourself without me. You know you knocked off a battalion almost single handed."

"I had help." I said

"Oh that we know, he said. But it was you that did it. You're a born leader." he said.

We pulled into the drive way of this big house. I mean real big. It was a little smaller then the white house but it looked just like it.

"See, he said. This is what you did for me Someday, he said. It will be yours

"Really." I said

"No he said not this one but something like it; this one is mine." We got out and he ran in ahead of me.

"Honey were home," he said. He looked up at the top of the stairs. When I looked I almost lost my breath. At the top of the stairs was this young beautiful girl no older then me standing at the top landing.

"Honey come," he said and ran up to meet her.

That was his wife; Holy shit no wonder he ran home. Man did she keep her age. He was at least 45. Her she looked no older than 23 if that. He reached her and started kissing her. Man I think I should leave; he was almost doing it to her on the steps. She pulled away from him and looked at me.

"Joel, she said coming down the stairs "I'm Mrs. Greene." She held out her hand for me. I didn't know what to do with it; shack it or fuck it. She had on this thing that you could see throw. I mean right throw. Man did she look good.

"Sir I said. Maybe I should go; I didn't want to interrupt anything."

"No he said we are going to eat; he said isn't that right sugar?"

I was missing something here. Something was wrong she just didn't fit. I found out later over dinner why his first wife died and he just remarried. She was his maid when his wife was alive. He said he got use to her being around so he married her;" he said laughing.

Shit he was dicking her before the wife died. She was just after his money. She wouldn't take her eyes off of me all the time he was talking about her. She just smiled at me. She know I could see throw her but she didn't care. She got what she wanted; who the fuck was I to judge her?"

"Well I must say; you cooked a good meal Mrs. Greene."

That got a laugh out of her.

"Me, she said I don't do the cooking anymore."

"Oh sorry I said but it seems so much you."

"She tells them what we want; the General said cutting in "You can take the cook out of the kitchen but you can't take the kitchen out of the cook;" he said and started laughing.

She didn't find that funny but I did. Man was she good looking. I found myself wanting her. I know it was wrong but I couldn't help it. She looked good. Her nipples would peek out and looking at me. She knew what she was doing. Every once in a while she would catch me looking and smile. The General didn't stop talking about me and she just looked and listened to him. When he finely stopped talking she looked over at me and asked as I was taking a sip of my wine."

"You like what you see?" She asked me.

Well that did it; the wine went all over the place right out of my mouth and nose.

"Oh sorry I said I don't know what came over me." I got up and started to clean the table off.

"Don't worry, the General said, she does that to all my friends."

"She is a dream and she knows it, he said. That is why I married her; I couldn't see anyone else having her. Tell him honey who is your daddy?"

"You "she said coming over to him. He did something that made me chock again. He took her tit out and kissed it.

"You see son, he said. The first time was for love the second time is for sex and fun. Remember that, he said. You got to try it this here woman could fuck you silly and still have more in her."

"Stop she said your embarrassing him," she said looking at me.

"Embarrassing shit he said He is sitting over there with a hard on a mile long."

"Willy, she said now stop it."

"Joel he said Tell her you would like to fuck her. Go ahead, he said. I know you would everyone does; that is another reason why I have her. I enjoy making my friends squirm I've always wanted to do it so I did I got me one pretty woman here and I know the only reason she married me was for my money. So what the hell I would have to pay for a whore anyway. This way I stay out of trouble when I die she gets it all. So what the hell fuck till you can't fuck anymore and then you die."

He started laughing and couldn't stop. I guess she was use to it by now. She just stood there and let him play with her. She just looked at me and smiled.

"Oh hell I said getting up. Yes sir I said I got a hard on and if you don't mind I would like to beat it alone?"

That did it; he started chocking from laughing "See; he said to her. Didn't I tell you what he would be like? I was right, he said. Wasn't I?"

She looked at me and said "You were right he is all man," she said.

"Well Joel I have to say this for you; you tell it like it is."

"That is the way I was brought up. I said. So now if you don't have her on the menu sir I'll have to go."

She laughs at that.

"That is a good one, he said chocking, I got to remember that one. Not yet I still got plenty of life left in me my driver will take you home. And Joel he said I really need you. Welcome Home son."

I thanked him and said it would make me proud to serve under him and her." I added

"See he yelled. A man after my own heart, he tells it like it is."

"Good for you, she said some night when he can't get it up I can call you?" She asked.

"Hold on he said when that day comes Joel you can have her. All I want you to do it shot me first." He laughs again.

"With the luger," I said.

He rolled on the floor.

"With the luger," he said almost crying he was laughing so hard.

I had to get out of there before I took her myself on the floor. Man did she know how to use her body. I turned to shout the door he was on top of her already. I guess he was living out his dream. If I was him I would do the same thing. He was a good husband when his wife was alive, but now that she is dead what the hell. 'Live a little' Men was that living.

The driver knew where I lived. He just looked at me and smile.

"Man I said Is it like that all the time in there?"

He laughs and said. "She is something."

"Something, I said God he knows how to pick them. She could come home with me any time."

"He said she acted that way but she doesn't fool around. The Generals has her watched all the time and she is as good as gold. She just acts that way and he loves it. You should see when he has a party. Most of the women come out screaming at their husbands. He gets a kick out of it. He said he is getting back at all of them for when they use to bring different girl all the time cheating on their wife's. He never did he was a good husband but now he is making them eat their hearts out."

"I can see why, I said. Man was she good looking and her body was something else."

We drove up to what was to be my place. It was in a good part of town it looked good to me. The driver said good night and drove off.

"Hey wait, I yelled as I stood at the door I didn't have my key; just then the door opened.

"Welcome; she said it was the woman at the base Nancy Staubitz."

"Oh she said looking at my pants "I see you meet the Generals new wife."

I looked down and saw I was wet. The wine I spilled on myself.

"Oh I said you know her?"

She smiled and said, "You had better get in before you catch a cold."

"Oh yea." I said stepping in.

"So she said she do that to you?"

"Yes I said then, No I said I did it to myself."

"Was that before he sucked on her tit or after?"

I just looked at her "You mean he did it in front of you."

"He does it in front of everyone. He gets a kick out of it."

"I can see that. I said. A man after my own heart." I said.

"So he told you why he does it?"

"He did I said and I don't blame him. I'd do the same thing if it happened to me."

"That is what I said. She said I'm glad for him." He is finely having some fun out of life. He deserves it, she said. Now let's get your pants off."

"Hold on I said I just came from a house where a very pretty woman made me hard as a rock

"So." She said

"I've got to warn you I'm horny as hell. So if you don't intend to get laid I would advise you to leave right now."

She looked at me and said "He did say you were like him. She turned around and said over her shoulder. I'll show you the bed room."

I guess that meant she wanted to get laid I followed her up the stairs. "Man I said want a uniform does to one. She was in her uniform but this was the first time I guess she hear that saying that way."

"Oh she said my uniform. I was hoping it was me and not the uniform."

That did it I ran ahead of her and stood in front in front of her "The hell with the bedroom." I said and took her on the landing.

Man was she something. We did it on the railing on the floor in the chair that was in the hallway You name it we did it.

"Ho my;" she asked me how long has it been"? Meaning I didn't get laid for a long time. I know what I was about to say would get her.

"Oh I said it was only an hour ago."

"What? She said pulling away from me. You didn't."

"I didn't what?" I asked

"You didn't fuck the Generals wife; did you?"

I just looked at her and got up off the floor and asked. Where was the bath room?"

She pointed to a door and came up after me

"You didn't, did you?" She kept asking.

"I'll never tell." I told her and went into the shower

"You fuck she said. You did." She closed the door with a bang.

When I got out she was gone. Served her right for asking me how long has it been. Why did she care? It was for me to know and her not to ask. I got her back even thou she was good and I was expecting her to spend the night.

Was she the one to change my life around? She sure felt that way. I felt something for her I didn't feel before; was it love? That is the question. Did I blow it? Again that was the question. Well later for that I was tired and I needed some rest. She drained it out of me. She was good I didn't have any complaints with her and her love making. Did she feel the same way towards me? I guess I'll find out tomorrow. Hey look at this the bed room was something out of a book. The young Bachelor section. Wild but not to wild. I think I'm going to like it here I jump on the bed and went to sleep on top of the covers I still had just a towel on.

I was up at the crack of dawn I got dressed in my uniform. My dress blues that is. I guess that was the dress of the day. I went down and looked around, pretty nice place my first place of my own. I could get use to this kind of life. The door bell rang. Who was that? I went to the door and opened it; it was the Major. He pushed his way in and said. "He came to pick me up;" he was looking around.

"Lose something?" I asked

"Oh no he said nice place."

"Isn't it. I said getting myself coffee. Want some?" I asked.

"No thanks he said I had mine."

"Well I said we off?"

He looked at me and said "Blues are out."

"Oh I said then what?"

"Greens; he said. Winter Greens that is on till you get assigned then it's civilian."

"You mean we go around in civvies

"You're a spy now; he said. You don't advertise it he said. You got three weeks of training and then we are off."

"I'll go change." I said.

"No he said. You won't be doing that much the first day; Leave them on. You meet her?" He asked in the same breath.

"Meet who?" I asked

"The Generals wife.

"Yes I said.

"Yes "he said is that all you got to say is, Yes?"

"Oh I said she gave a good blow job if that is what you're looking for."

He almost chocked on the coffee he said she didn't, she did what?

"You heard me I said she got me in the corner and took it out and started sucking on it."

"Where was the General?" He asked.

"Oh him he had to go out for something."

"That fuck; he said she did it to you and she wouldn't let me touch her."

"I guess she wanted a man;" I said and walked out.

I could see me and him wasn't going to get a long after all.

At first I liked him but now that I know him he is just a brown nosier, a ass kisser if you know what I mean. A Browne, whatever you call them. I yelled back "Lock the door when you come out."

I could see it hit him. I got to her and he didn't. I was going to tell the General what I said this way he would know it came from me. Knowing him he would get a kick out of it He drove us to the office. He kept looking at me but didn't say a word. I guess he was deciding he didn't like me either. Tough shit I wasn't here for him I was here for myself and if he couldn't take a joke, fuck him.

Nancy was at her desk as we came in; she turned the other way I went up to her and the Major was right behind me. I wanted him to hear what I said to her.

"Hi you left in such a rush last night you forgot to give me my key. I hope you have it? If not I'm locked out for the night."

She turned around and said "Over on the desk, she said and pointed.

"Thanks if you want I'll get another set made for you?"

That did it both him and her acted like I stuck it to them. I didn't know then I found out later the Major was kind of going with her. Shit I didn't know; oh hell what the fuck; win some lose some. I picked them up and went to the Generals door."

"Is he in?" I asked turning around to look at them. If looks could kill I'd be dead twice. Once from him and once from her.

I knocked since they didn't answer.

"Come," he yelled.

I opened the door went in and closed it. He just looked at me and knew something was up.

"OK out with it." He said looking at me.

"Out with what?" I asked.

He smiled and said. "You look like a cat that just swelled the bird; let's have it."

I told him everything he couldn't stop laughing. I know he would act that way.

He said I was doing what he was doing but I was getting to them without knowing it."

"Oh I don't think so I said I know what you're doing it looked like fun so I'm giving it a try."

"You "he said be my guest Feel free".

"You don't mind if I used your wife for a joke?"

"No he said she will love it. I can't wait to tell her she tells me about the Major all the time. He is so hot for her he goes and beats his meat every time he sees her."

"I thought that; I said IT's just like me."

"Oh, he laugh She do that to you?"

"Sir if I ever had a wish I would wish for one just like her."

"I like that; he said you're going to make it here."

"Sir I said one thing?"

"Yes he asked.

"I'm no Brown nosier."

He looked at me and said. I know that I don't want to hear that again I have enough of them around here; that is why I know you'll bring life back to this department; like I said you tell it the way it is and if you don't like it tough."

"That is me sir; I said I'm not built any other way."

"Good stay that way. Oh by the way my wife said if I do let her fool around she wants it to be you."

"Thank you sir I'd be honored."

"Can I tell her that? Or do you want to?'

"You tell her sir I'm afraid I'll have to keep my distance; she does something to me I don't think I could trust myself."

"Oh don't worry you have nothing to worry about. If you did fool around I'd kill you."

"I know sir that is why I would rather stay away."

He got a laugh out of that.

"OK he said Down to business here is where you go. I want you to know everything there is to know about this operations. You have to have it down in three weeks. We are short handed with his war going on and we need everyone we can get. Men like you are hard to fine."

Again he told me he was glad to have you aboard.

"Yes sir, I said and about faced and left the both of them were waiting for me to come out.

The Major waiting to hear if the General found out about me screwing his wife; and her just wanting to throw something at me. Both of them didn't do anything so I looked at him and said.

"You were going to show me around?" I was just rubbing it in "Or may you would?" I asked Nancy.

"I'll show you; he said wanting me to get away from her.

We left the building and went to this other building. It said on the front Special training unit Top secret clearance only. He walked in the guard asked him for ID. He showed it and I showed him mine. He took mine and called someone on the phone.

"Thank you sir he said Welcome aboard Your entered in now sir there will be no me trouble coming in sir;" he said. The Major said he took my picture now the camera knows you." He pointed to the camera over head. That is the 'eye' we call it. If the eye doesn't like the way you look it closes up the whole place tight No one gets in and no one gets out."

"I like that I said Good security."

"The best "the Marine Guard said looking at me.

We went in to another check point Then one more into what looked like a gym and a work shop all in one.

"Men would you look at this."

"The Major smiled and said we have the latest in anything here. He went over to an instructor and was talking to him. I just looked around. Man one could like a place like this. It was like a big air plane hangar with people all over the place doing something. All busy. The Major came over with the instructor and introduced us. He said he would be my instructor for the three weeks. "Listen to what he has to say it could mean your life." The Major said and left.

The man took my hand for some reason I know he was up to something I just beat him to it; I took him and landed him on the floor first.

"Sorry old man; I said you gave yourself away."

He got up and just looked at me. The Major turned and came back. Oh shit here it comes I guess I did a no, no; the instructor came back at me. He had me down but not out. I came up with a kick from the ground up and caught him in the nuts he went down.

"Look I said I don't play you got something to teach me fine if not we go at it now."

The Major stepped in between us and said. "Tomorrow gentleman;" and took me out.

"Hey don't ever do that again. I said stopping at the door. "You want to play you got the right man for it but let me warn you Major I kill I don't play." I walked away and found my own way out He was getting to me I know I was going to have it out with him soon. I went back to the office when I walked in she was standing there.

"Well I said you want to play to?"

She just looked at me.

"Your car is down stairs and here are some maps with instructions. The General thinks it better if the two of you stay away from each other."

"Thank you; I said and took them. "Well I asked did you get an extra set made up?" And walked out the door I didn't turn around to see what she was doing If she did she would be over if she didn't then I guess it wasn't love at first sight.

I got in the car the guard said was mine. He said I should park it here it had my name on the spot.

"It looks dry." I said

He said the. "General had it painted weeks ago."

"He did! Did he? He knew I'd take the job; that old fuck." I got in and drove around; I wanted to get to know the town. I spent the whole day driving it was getting dark so I head back for my place. I stopped and got some food to go some beer to; I guess this was my night. Oh hell she was good. I pulled in and got out I opened the door and went in I took a plate out from the kitchen. This place had everything I didn't need to buy a thing. I took my beer and sat down in front of the TV; this was something I never watched. I didn't have time to; that is on till tonight what the hell. I started eating when I heard something. It wasn't loud but it was something. It may be just the house making the noise. No I'd better check it out anyway I didn't want anyone robbing me.

I went from the kitchen to the living room. Then to the other room I guess it was an office or study. I even and a office some set up. Nothing; as I was going for the up stairs I saw something standing at the top. Oh my word it was Nancy. She had this see throw thing on and she was just looking down at me.

"Is this how she looked?" She asked.

I know what she was getting at; The Generals wife.

"No I said hers was black."

"Go fuck yourself; she said and ran back away from the rail.

I guess I said the wrong thing. I ran to the top of the stairs; she was gone. I heard her in the bed room I went over and knocked. "Anyone in there?" I asked.

"Go away;" she said.

"O K I said and started to walk away. She came to the door and opened it.

"Your mean she said where are you going?"

"My food is getting cold I said and my beer is getting hot." That did it she came at me and almost took the both of us down the stairs. Oh hell we did it again in the hallway.

After we did it like animal's I stop and looked at her

"What how?" She asked.

"Would you mind if we used the bed for the rest of the night?" I said

"Oh you; she said jumping on to me. I carried her to the bed and there we stayed for the rest of the night making love Boy was she good.

The next morning we both got up together. She went down to make coffee I took a shower and got dressed. When I came down she had eggs ready. I looked at her and said.

"Doesn't he give you enough?"

"What?" She asked.

"The major don't he?"

Well the eggs came flying and so did the coffee.

"You she said jumping over the counter at me. She landed on me feet first. I fell back onto the floor with her on top of me.

"You; she said again getting ready to swing. I caught her hand and held it. "We are ever." I said.

She looked at me with a puzzled look.

"Even for what? You said last night about the Generals Wife."

"Can we start over again? Hi my name is Joel. I stood her up and held it out from her.

"You she said jumping on me wrapping her lag's around my waist."You; she said again taking my face in her hands and kissing the hell out of me.

"I take it that mean yes." I said between kisses.

"Look I said letting her down. I have to go; lock up when you leave I don't want any other woman here when I get home; you'll do just fine. You can tell the rest to leave their number just in case. I'll get back to them if you don't work out."

"You; she said again.

"Oh one other thing. I said as I was walking to the door. "Clean up your mess before you leave."

That did it she started throwing anything she could get her hands on. I ran for the door and closed it just in time a dish came crashing into the back of it. I walked down a got into my car and drove to the base. She was my kind of woman not like my mother. She let you know when you pissed her off; that I liked.

I pulled in my spot and went to the training center. I didn't want to start off on the wrong foot but the major sew to it I did. I don't know what he said to the instructor whatever it was I didn't like it. I was going to put an end to it now. I walked in and the guard took my ID and passed me through. I went in and looked around Bang a gun went off;

I hit the deck and rolled over to some cover; what the hell was that? I looked out over the cover and saw ten men looking at me. One of them was the instructor.

"See he said that is the way you do it." He was telling the other man. "Not stop and look at where it came from; your ass is more importune, then seeing who was shooting at you. Now you see who was doing the shooting. "Good; he said walking over to me sorry about that."

It sounded as if he meant it. I got to my feet and before I could reach him he pointed to where the gun shot came from; it was over at the work shop.

"They do that all the time; he said you have to get use to it."

"No I said you still have to duck."

"Again your right; you get use to it your dead;" he said.

"Look he said holding out his hand lets start over I'm Cocokelly."

I took it and said "I'm Joel."

"Glad to meet you he said now we forget what happened yesterday agreed?"

"No sweat off my back. I said I'm here to learn."

"Good then it would be a pleasure to teach you. That is if I can teach you anything you're pretty good; he said. I'm use to getting ones like them." he said pointing over at the nine men.

"I see what you mean if they were agents I was superman." He told me the Agency was doing a turn around. College was the in thing; 'Brains not brawn.' You he said seem to have both It is an honor to have you;" he said.

"Like wise;" I said. Good maybe you could help me get some sense in to their heads if not they won't last a day out there."

"No I said I don't think so. Nothing could help them I said I wouldn't want any of them watching my back. I'll pass I don't want anything to do with sending them out as agents."

"Thanks; he said I appreciate your honesty I only wish I could walk away from it."

"You could you know."

"But then who would train them? I've seen the list of instructors there just as bad as the trainees. What is this world coming to?"

"I guess it is changing like everything else around here."

"Well he said we can't do anything about it so let's get started and get it over with. Three weeks of what use to take six month."

I was top of the class I spent most of my time over at the work shop. You wouldn't believe the weapons they had here and the ones they were working on. This is where these guys should be working; not out in the field. But who was I to judge!

The General sent the Major off on some assignment letting Nancy and me got to know one and other. She moved in of course; I didn't mind that. Infect I like it she was like a new toy for me. This was the first time I had other thing on my mind other then getting a head, or worrying about my true identity being found out. Oh I still worried about them finding out I was a German Nazis as they started to call us. More and more Germans were being found and brought to trial for their war crimes; as the called them. The Jews had set up a world wide network to track so called Nazis. They were either killed or they would bring them to trail. All depending on who they were. Someone like my father they would lock him up and drag his name across every paper in the world. Someone like the drive; he would be found dead in the street in some out of the way country. That would be called an accident and no one would hear about him ever again.

The General was busy most of the time so I stayed away from his office. The last week of training was the best I was fitter for everything. From shoes to gun I had my Id up graded to top secret clearance. That meant I was ready for my first assignment. I went to the Generals office after everything was completed. Of course he was pleased with my marks. He said I had the highest score in a long time."

I told him it didn't surprise me seeing the type of people that were being assigned to the agency."

He knew what the story was; I guess. He had heard it before. He said they do my work on computers. The day of the foot soldier is almost past."

"Sorry I said they don't show me shit."

That got a laugh out of him. He was a different man behind the desk. One would never know about his home life if they didn't see it for them self's; I did.

"Well here is your first job. Take it read it and go get the son of a bitch."

I took the file and went out to see Nancy. She was at her desk going over papers.

"My first job." I said showing her the file.

"Oh she said I guess that means you're joining us?"

"I guess it does."

"Can we go out and celebrate;" she asked.

"I don't see why not; see you tonight. I said and left I knew why they had a study set up in my place. I found it relaxing to read the file sitting in my out chair behind my own desk. OK how let's see what kind of shit they got me doing?

is name was Sgt John P Smith and he is under investigation for miss use of government funds. He was a supply sgt. They have him from Germany to Korea taking his supplies and selling them. No one cared about it till how. Shit how could they not see? As I read the file I got more and more into it.

This guy must be rolling in dough. I checked the orders with the deliveries and came up with about three million dollars missing supplies. Didn't anyone run a stock check once in a while on his supplies?

Nancy came in and came to the study."

"Hi ready."

"No, something is bothering me."

"Oh what might that be?"

I held up the file and she looked.

"Oh business."

"Is there anything else?" I asked

"Well sex is on the top of my list;" she said.

I smiled and said. "You got it but only if you answer one thing for me?"

"One;" she said sitting down.

"This guy how could he get away with this for this long. Three Million in supplies missing.

"Oh that's easy before that is. Now since we are getting computers into do the work; we are finding out more. Look she said coming around the desk. See this? She pointed to a page with 'attacked' on the top of the page. That means he was attacked on that day. The list of items that got destroyed; were entered as lost."

And on and; and on;" she said turning the pages.

"Man where was he in the heart of the battle zone?"

"No, he was hundreds of miles from the fighting."

"So. "I said. How?"

"Will you see he was attached to the unit that was attacked? So he just put it in the record and no one said anything about it."

"Then what is this?"

"Oh that is 'weather'. They had a bad storm that day he lost a lot of paper goods. It said here that they couldn't be used."

"Three hundred cases of toilet paper Two hundred cases of light bulbs and look at this one. A hundred M1's rifles now how could rifles get damaged?"

"They didn't; she said. The officer in charge must of just sign the approval without looking. You will find that throughout his reports. Every time toilet paper appears on the head of the list Guns or high explosives show up some where down the list."

"So why don't you lock him up."

"We can't; she said. All the things are gone and there is no way of proving it. The officer in charge sign them off what your job is it's to find something they didn't lose yet."

"Oh is that all?"

"That's it now can we have sex?' She asked.

"But three million." I said

She looked at me and smiled. "A drop in the bucket when you're talking billions."

"Shit, give me the three." I said I'll leave the bucket for the next guy."

"That is what gets them caught all the time; she said they don't know when to quit. They always want more. Now if that was me; she said like you said take the three and leave, but they don't and that is where you the CID comes in."

I was beginning to see why the high tech boys were coming in. You could get them just by sitting down and going over their files."

"Now?" She asked.

"Oh sorry Dinner first."

"Maybe; she said "Where?"

"You pick;" I told her

"Then dinner it is; get your coat. She said Sex after.

She drove; of course I didn't know any places to eat. When she pulled up to this restaurant I just looked.

"Fancy." I said

"And so are the prices;" she said getting out.

Oh hell why not this gave me a chance to see how the other half lived. Man what a place it was like a castle I mean from main hall to ballrooms. She took her coat off some lady came and took it from her. Then this guy that walked funny came. He seated us then gave me the menu. He clapped for someone else to come over to take our order.

"Hey what is this going to cost?"

She smiled and said "You don't ask."

"The menu was in French I know how to read it. I know four languages and spoke them well. French, German, Japanese and English.

So when the waiter came over I did my thing. Nancy just looked at me and smiled

"I didn't know you spoke French

"You do now;" I said.

"Impressive; she said and handed him the menu. The gentleman will order for the both of us;" she said.

The dinner was good that was on till the bill came."

She covered it with her hand and said "Bill it to the General;" she told the waiter.

As we eat she would point out different people and what they did around the capitol. "Big shots she said.

"They all looked like people to me. Some louder then others but people all the same. We left and headed for home.

"Sex next;" she said.

"After that meal I could go for a hamburger."

"Get out of here; she said pushing me.

"Oh you want to play;" I started to tickle her.

"NO she screamed I can't drive with you doing that."

"So pull over."

She did and we did.

After we finished she looked at me and said. "I was an animal."

"I know, I said so are you." She smiled and drove off.

She went to bed and I went back to the file. This was getting to me. This sgt. was over in Korea now. He was doing the same thing there. I guess I had to go and find him and bring him back. That was my job. The next morning I kissed her good bye and left. I didn't know how long I would be away So I didn't say anything. She knew this and didn't say a word. I got to the base air port and jumped on a flight. I was going back to Korea With my ID I could go any where in the world I got fitted for civics and uniforms They paid for everything; I just had to get recipes for everything. So far I like my new job but lake everything I had to see.

I arrived at the base where this sgt. was stationed. I set myself up as a field Officer with some unit. I covered myself so he couldn't check me out. I doubt he would he didn't know anything was coming.

Then I found out about the black market. Man what shit it got me sick knowing what went on here. Well one thing at a time like they say; First things first.'

I walked in his office and handed him a order sheet.

"Sgt Smith I came to pick up some supplies." I said and showed him the orders."

"No he said shacking his head "No and no Sorry; he said we don't have any."

"You got to me kidding I came all the way down from the north and you tell me you don't have them. Now what?" I asked him.

"You can wait; they well be in."

"Good that makes me feel better." I went and took a set.

"Hold on he said where you think you're going?"

"I'm waiting for them; I said smiling at him.

"You're kidding?" He said.

"No I said I needed them and you said they were coming in. So I wait."

No, No, no, he said you don't wait I call you and tell you there here."

"But I don't have a phone you see I'm leaving back for the north in the morning. I'll just wait I said.

"Look captain maybe you didn't hear me. When I said they were coming in I didn't mean today. I meant six to eight month from now."

"What. I yelled standing up. No way I need them now."

"Sorry he said and went back to some paper's he had on his desk.

I know he just got a shipment in and he had them. So this is the game he plays.

"Who is in charge?" I asked.

He smiled and said. "You're looking at him."

"You; I said who is the officer in charge?"

"Oh him; he said he is over at the main building Officer something."

"You don't know his name?"

"Ha he said I never meet him."

"You are joking?" I said.

"No go see for yourself."

"Then maybe you could tell me who I see to turn over contraband."

"What kind of contraband?" He asked.

"Just some gold and things we captured from the North."

How why did I know his ears would stand up.

"Oh that; he stood up and said. You bring them to me."

"Ha I said. In a pig ass I'll go see the officer in charge." I said walking out the door.

He got up and ran over to stop me from leaving "Sir really; you bring them here. He will tell you the same thing. Look he said taking me by the arm and brings me back to his desk. I'll save you the trouble of walking over there. I'll call him on the phone you can talk to him and you will see; I'm the man. He reached for the phone and called "Major I got this Captain here and he said he's got contraband; tell him I'm the one that he leaves it with. Yes Sir;" He said and handed me the phone

"Hello." I said

"Hello shit Captain don't you know we have a war going on. I don't have time for this shit just leave the shit with the sgt. and go back to the fighting. That is an order;" he said.

I gave him the phone back.

"See; he said smiling. I looked at him and said. I want an inventory of everything I give you." I said.

"I wouldn't have it any other way; he said "By the way what do you really have sir?"

I took out my pad and read off something I had down "One bar of gold weight 30 lbs five diamond rings weight 10 ct Gold chains Weight

14 ct. Then some guns and some pictures. All junk. I said. I was coming back to get resupplied but since you don't have the things I need. I guess I'll just take them back with me till the next time."

"Hold on there; he said. Now just you hold one minute. He took some papers out and said yes, yes, yes, Sir you're in luck. What I got here is the things you need it seems the company they were ordered for isn't coming to pick them up just yet."

"Oh no sgt. I couldn't think of taking someone else order. I'll wait my turn lake everyone else is."

"Lookey here sir; you're not taking his order. He gave a double order in and we didn't catch it. This paper here; he said holding up one is the order; and this one; he said holding up; another one; it's the same. What a fool I was; I was going to ship him two of the same orders. So you see Sir; no one gets hurt. Now where do you have the contraband? I'll help you get it," he said.

"My driver should be coming in a day or two. He was following me but you know them semis they move like shit."

"Look you take your things and when you pass your driver on the road you tell him to bring them right to me."

"Gee's I don't know Sgt. I did need and officers to check them in."

"OK he said I'll throw in a case of Scotch."

"A case of what? I asked; there is no scotch to be had over here."

"Oh he said looking like a rat. "You have your drive here and I'll have a case of scotch ready and waiting."

"Sgt you got yourself a deal." I shock his hand and left.

Shit this was easy I had two days to get it together. I went right to company head quarters and got the man in charge. It was a Major, I gave him a list of things I needed and told him I needed them in two days."

He laughs and said "And where do I get the gold?"

"I just want something that looked like gold. I didn't care if he painted a lead bar; I need it.

"Look I don't know who the fuck you think you are but you just don't come walking into my office and give me orders; you got me." He yelled.

"But sir you read my orders you knew I was investigation the supply department. Plus I was told you would supply me with anything I needed.

"How long have you been with this department Captain? Two month if that and already you're telling me my job. Let me tell you one thing mister; here I run the show and if you don't want to find your self on the first plane out of here you had better back off and let me do the investigation around here. Do I make my self clear mister?"

"But sir I said I was under the impression I was to control it."

"Well your impression is wrong everything has to come to me in writing then I and I alone give you the go ahead. Does that sink in mister?" He said getting up from his desk.

"But "I started to say when he hit the top of his desk with his fist.

"But shit I don't see anything on my desk Mister Do you?" He asked.

"No sir." I said

"Then mister you had better get one here before you do anything else. If not your ass will be the one getting locked up. Do I make my self clear? Mister?"

"Yes sir I said and turned and walked out.

Mother fucker I take it back I don't think I'm going to like this job. I went out to the front and was about to walk out When I heard his voice.

"Mister where the fuck you think you're going?"

"Sir I said turning around.

"Get over there and start your report;" he said pointing at this desk with a typewriter on it.

"Yes sir." I said

I walked over to the desk and took out some paper and started to type. I was told while in training everything was to be written down. Nothing was to be done on less it was in writing on paper first. I guess this is what they meant. So I didn't know. So shot me. I guess being under cover wasn't under cover if I had to hang around here and let everyone know who I was and what I was doing. I guess that was the Marine corps way of doing things; or I should say the Government way.

I made out the report and dropped it on the front desk Again I started walking out the door I needed a drink.

"Mister I heard him yelling again. Did you ever hear of the chain of command?"

"Yes sir I said.

"Well it would be nice if you know it; now wouldn't it."

"Yes sir I said turning around to face him.

"You see that office over there; he said pointing. That is Captain Jones he is over you he is the one you hands your report to. Then if he thinks you got something he brings it to me. Then I in turn approve it and give it back to him. Then it is his job to set you up with what ever you need to complete your investigation. That is our chain of command; do you get that Mister?"

"Yes sir I said controlling myself.

"Well." he said looking at me.

I went back to the desk and took the paper and went over to the captains door and knocked. The man behind it said. "Come in." I did I closed the door not to have privacy but to get away from the Major.

"Sir I said as I stood in front of him."Captain My report for investigation." I said and handed it to him "Good he said Tooking it and put it on top of his files "That will be all he said Check back with me tomorrow he said

That was it They got to be joking

"Sir I said Maybe I over stepped my place here But I arranged a set up for tomorrow I think we could closes this case if I could follow up as soon as I can on it

He looked up and smiled "You do do you "What was the name? he asked

"Goldberg I said

"OK Goldberg You see all of these papers here

"Yes sir I said to make him happy

"They come first Maybe you have something here and maybe you don't. It is up to me to decide if you do. You know it takes money to set something into motion; money is what it's all about. If we are going to spend money on something that isn't going to work; then I have to explain to the Major why it didn't work; not you, me; he said. And if it happens to many time's I am asked why it didn't work?" Before you know it you will be looking into my file. "What did Captain Jones do with the money? I don't want that to happen; do I make myself clear Mister? Just because you came out of the training ready to set the world on fire, going like a bat out of hell. It doesn't work that way mister they didn't teach you to look at what you're doing? Then sit back and go over it again to make sure you didn't miss something. Then you follow it very slowly so no mistakes are made. Does that make sense mister?" He asked

"Yes sir; I said tomorrow;" and turned around and left.

As I was walking out the door this Cpl at the front desk said. "I take it you meet the chain Sir?"

"Oh I said Is that what it was. You know of any good bars?" I asked.

He got up and said he was heading for one himself. He would show me."

I guess he gets it all day long with them two. He to needed something to make him forget. What the hell I needed someone to talk to. "Lead the way." I told him and off we went He had his own jeep he told me to jump in; it was off the base."

What the hell I couldn't do anything till tomorrow and I didn't want to go to the barracks just yet; so off we went. It was a small town; it was just like any other small town a base was set up around. Bars, Bars and more bars. Up and down the main street. You seen one you seen them all. He said his name was Peterson. I told him mine. He knew that already he said he read my file."

"So which is the place?"

He smiled and said Pick one."

I did I just said stop. We got out and walked into the first one. Again it was the same; Dancing girls, smoke and soldiers. No different then any other one in the world. He pointed over to a corner and headed for it. It was a table out of the way; I followed. As soon as we sat this girl came over with her tits hanging out asked.

"You buy me drink Joe?"

"No; he said bring two beers fast; he told her "You do drink beer?" He asked me.

"I was thinking of something a little more stronger." I said.

He yelled to her. "Make that two whiskeys too." She kept going.

"I don't think she heard you." I said

"Ha he said she heard."

"How could she?" I said the noise was so loud."

"Watch this;" he said. He took out a quarter and dropped it on the floor."

"Shit would you look at that?" About five girls turned around and were looking at the floor."

"See; he said When it comes to money they hear." I guess he was right she did come back with the whiskeys.

He just smiled and drank it straight down. "Well he said holding up his beer to me."Welcome." And down the beer the same way. I guess that is the way to do it. I did the same. Oh I needed that. He picked up his hand and snapped his fingers. She was back quicker than a rabbit.

"More Joe; she said you buy me?"

"Yes; he said and no." She knew what he meant; she was gone again.

"You know I said to him that shot didn't do anything."

He laughs; "Of course not it is so watered down it takes three to do the job of one."|

"Oh really I said Then get three." I said."

"So he said looking at me. You're new at this?"

"I guess you could say that."

"How do you like it?" He asked.

"Need you ask?" I said.

He smiled and said. "This is now you end the day." He said holding up his glass again and downed it.

"Every day?" I asked.

"No, I'm OK today; he said smiling This is a good day. Bad day's I get a bottle and stick a straw in it."

"I see I have a lot to learn."

"Ha that is the understatement you never learn. The only thing you learn around here is you become a drunk."

"Something to look forward to." I said and drank mine down.

Just then a chair came flying over our heads and hit the back wall.

"Oh shit." I said getting ready to jump up.

"Hold; he said holding my arm down. Don't let it bother you this happens all night long."

I looked at where it came from; this big guy was jumping on three other guys.

"See; he said it wasn't even meant for you. Just let them go at it."

I looked and before you know it more soldiers were getting into it.

"This is why I pick the back table. One could get hurt out there;" he said picking up his next drink.

"I see what you mean." I said and did the same

"You get a better look back here; he said. Better then TV."

Oh shit a bottle was coming at us. He just lowered his head and let it hit the wall behind him.

"Nice place;" he said smiling.

"I'm glad I didn't pick a bad place." I told him.

"Oh shit he said watch out for this one. It was the big guy that started it. He was hit and he was coming straight for our table on his back.

"Get the drinks." He picked up his two that were left and just stood up. I did the same. The big guy hit the table and broke it into a million pieces. The Cpl just looked at me.

"Got to be quick;" he said.

I had my two drinks in my hand with this big guy at my feet on top of what was once the table.

Mother fucker I know him.

"Louie;" he said looking up at me.

"You big dumb shit. I said what the fuck you doing here?" It was the big guy from my old platoon.

He stood up and yelled. "Gunny."

That mother fucker was here?

"Look who I found;" the big guy said.

Just then this guy came over and was about to hit him. The big guy came up with a chair; I think he left half of it in the guys head when he hit him with it. Then way over at the other end of the bar I could see the Gunny standing on top of it; waving his hands.

Shit it was him I don't know how he got over to me so fast but he did. I mean the floor was full of guys fighting; that didn't stop him. He walked right on top of them without touching the floor.

"Mother fucker; he said coming up to me. Where the fuck did you go"? He said hugging me. I don't think I had tears in my eyes but I felt like crying. It was like old home week. The Snake came over and the rest of the guy's followed.

"Louie," they all yelled. The fighting stopped. I guess they were fighting with each other.

"You crazy mother fuckers; what the hell are you doing here?" I yelled

"Looking for you;" he said.

"You got to be kidding me?" I said.

"You, he said we missed you we were going back to the states to find you."

"Get the fuck out of here; you weren't?"

The big guy looked at me and smiled. "Oh yes we were."

This crazy nut's I bet they would.

The Cpl didn't say a word he just kept drinking. "Gunny you fuck how have you been?"

He took me by the shoulders and kissed me.

"Hey you nut;" that was when I saw he had his strips taking away. He was busted down to a cpl.

"What the fuck happened?" I asked.

Snake said he beat the shit out of the last Louie we had to death."

"You didn't?"

"No; he said a truck ran over him."

"Yea, the big guy said. With the Gunny driving."

"Lets get out of here; he said taking me by the arm. We all left together; the bar was busted up but they didn't care.

I guess the Cpl wanted to stay; he didn't follow. We went out side; the big guy took eight bottles as he left the bar. His hands were so big he held all four in each hand.

"We drink; he said and walked down the street. We followed; we walked to the end of the town. Nothing no lights, no nothing. The Gunny said he parked his truck over there and pointed. I didn't see anything but they did. Shit there it was a truck.

"Come on let's get out of here." Off we went I didn't know where we were going I know I couldn't see anyway; the road was black. They drove with out the head lights on.

We pulled up to a barracks and stopped. "No one will bother us." He pointed to the sign on the building. 'off limits No trespassing Top secret.'

"Shit Gunny we can get into trouble here."

"I put them signs up; He said "Don't worry about it."

I didn't; I got out and we went in side with the rest of them; the whole platoon was here.

"Is this where you're stationed?" I asked

The Snake said "This is home Louie;" he said taking me by the shoulder and picking up a bottle. If you were in the Marines as long as I was you would know how to do it. Thanks to you we did it."

"Did what?" I asked.

The Big guy stepped in and told me "Ever since I did what I did to them gooks; the brass gave us all kind medals. So the Gunny had some signs made up and we put them on the barracks."

Then Snake came in "Now we are top secret and no one knows what we do."

"Oh and you all got promoted."

"No the Gunny said I found out that once you get a metal; everyone sees the brass hanging around you. That is the time to do it. You see with the brass patting us on the back and this signs. No one knows what we do and they don't want to ask because they don't want the brass to get mad. So they just walk by us and don't ask questions."

"How long can you get away with it?" I asked.

"One time in Germany I did it for almost eight month; before someone asked what I was doing and who was I assigned to?"

"Man you can get your ass in trouble doing that."

"No; the big guy said. The Gunny said all we say is that the General that gave us the medals told us to hang out for a while. That is what we did We didn't know how them signs got on the barracks."

"So; the Snake finished "No one wants to fight with a General so they don't say anything; they just put us back in the war."

"And nothing is done about their mistake;" the Gunny said.

"You old fuck." I said.

"A fuck yes but not old; he smiled. Now what brings you back?" he asked.

"It's a long story I said. When I told him he smiled. Shit, give me your job; he said I'll save the government millions I know them all."

"Them who? I asked

"All the fuck's that are skimming off the top."

"You mean you're doing it?"

"Ha he said they don't want to go near me."

"Why is that?" I asked.

"Hey come on Louie I can't tell you. You will have me locked up first. We don't want that to happen, now do we:" he said looking at the men?

"Fuck no;" they say

I didn't blame them he was their god.

We drank and we talked. We laugh and we cried Just like family. When the bottles were finished he told Snake to go get some more. I reached into my pocket and took out some money. "Here I'm buying."

"Ha put your money way. Snake get a move on." He took off.

"Well Louie, how long are you going to be here?"

"I don't know the way they move I'll be here after the war is over."

"Let me tell you one thing; he said there is a right way and then there is a wrong way."

And they all said together "There is the Marine corps way."

"Right; he said That is the way we live; like it or not."

I felt sorry for him he was busted all the way down. "Gunny what the hell did you do to get all them taken away?"

"Nothing he said I just took them off myself. This way no one has rank and no one can get into trouble over it."

"You think of everything don't you?"

"No, he said I just keep one step ahead of them."

The Snake came back.

"Man, that was fast; what do you have a jet waiting for you out side?"

"No sir I got my own store."

The Gunny looked at him. "Easy Snake; he said Remember he's an officer."

"Oh sorry guy's I said taking a bottle."He must have stolen it." I said.

"Something like that; the Gunny said But I'll never tell."

"We drank till we couldn't drink any more. I passed out; when I woke I was in my bunk in my own barracks. The Gunny must have brought me here. Oh shit my head, Man I never drank so much in my life. I went into the shower and just let the cold water hit me. I got dressed and headed for the office. The cpl was sitting at his desk.

"Have a good time?" He asked.

"My old company."

"He smiled and said he know. "Captain wants to see you."

I knocked and he told me to come in

"I read your report; he said. You think it is going to work?"

"I hope so sir;" I said.

"Look I don't want to get your hopes up; but we were after this guy from back with the Germans."

"I know sir I read his report."

"Well he said you got my OK Now what?"

I told him I need a truck and the list of items I had on my report."

"You're going to need some man; he said. Now if this Sgt bits you know it isn't over with; we got to get him and the people that he is connected with. Otherwise it goes on. We got to get it from the top to stop it. This sgt. doesn't have the brains to run it. Someone else is doing it."

"So we get the big one." I said.

"Ha, he said. That isn't going to be easy; here is what I want you to do; he said. I'm going along with you on this but we do it this way. Give him the real stuff and when your man comes back with the order we both know he isn't going to have half the items on it."

That is going to be your in you go back and get him in a corner and tell him your going to blow the whistle on him if he doesn't cut you in on the items he left off the list. That will get him thinking. And to add to it you tell him you have more contraband coming. If that is the way he wants to play you will go some place else with the shit. He won't be able to give you the answer right away. That will give us time to set him up and follow him to see who he goes to."

"Sounds good to me." I said

Just then the Major came in.

"Well Mister I see you're learning? The captain here told me what you did; Thank god we can use a good arrest. Let's hope the sgt. didn't get wind of you and runs."

"I don't think so sir I said With what the captain came up with helped even more."

"See Mister that is why we make out reports. We're a team here; he said not loners."

"Yes sir."

I guess he had a point it was better this way. That is what they wanted to do; drill it into my head. 'Team work'. Maybe this will teach me I always work alone Maybe it was time I forgot about my past and worked on my future. If they didn't find me out by now; I guess they will never. Look at the Gunny he can hide a platoon for month and then not know it, as long as I kept my nose clean and did what the Brass wanted; I would be OK.

Well it was set up and I was given everything I wanted. Truck, Gold and pictures. They were the real thing; the Major said the sgt. was no fool. He could smell the real thing. So he had some flown in. Show time; I went back to the supply house and the sgt.

"You got the stuff?" He asked.

"It's on the way; now remember I want a list I don't want it coming back to me; I get this shit all the time." I told him.

"Well you know where you have to bring it."

"I know I only wish I could keep it for myself." I told him.

"Don't we all; he said. But that would be stealing and you could get locked up for that;" he said.

"I guess you're right."

When truck rolled in I told him I was going to make sure my case of scotch was in the load."

"You got it; he said and I left.

I waited for the truck to head out the gate before I meet it. The captain was with me. The driver pulled over and handed us the list.

"Oh shit something was wrong. He listed everything did he put a case of scotch in?" I asked the driver.

"If he did I didn't see it."

"Shit he caught on;" the captain said.

"God damn it now I have to hear it from the Major. I should have never listened to you;" he said.

"What is the big deal? We get him another way; someone leaked it to him that is all."

"That is all?" he said looking at me you know how much this set the government back? Shipping the gold and setting this up. Maybe a couple of thousand; he said. The Major isn't going to like this."

"So it wasn't our fault someone fucked it up."

"You tell him that; he said. I don't want to hear it."

We drove back and told the Major what had happened. Man did he hit the fan. He was going like a mad man yelling I was the one that fucked it up. They should have never sent me. I was going back and he never wanted to see my face again. All kind of shit."

I guess he was right but I had to get my last word in. "It would of work if someone from this office didn't say anything."

I guess I said the wrong thing. He even yelled louder "Your saying we got a bad CID agent working here Mister; you got any proof?'

"No sir."

"Well mister you had better get your bags packed because you're heading right back where you came from and my report will follow."

"Yes sir; I said and started to back out the door.

"I'm not finished with you yet; he yelled. My report is going to say you spent the night with the base sandbaggers and you wrecked the town bar. You and your so called friends stole a case of scotch to boot. Now get your ass out of here before I change my mind and have you locked up with your friends."

Shit he had them locked up. "Yes sir I said and left. It had to be the Cpl at the front desk. He must have followed me. The major must of put him up to it; that rat fuck he didn't have to get my men into it. As I walked out the door the cpl. just smiled. "Leaving so soon?"

I wanted to kick his ass for him but that would be all I needed. The Major would have a field day on mine. And see to it I was locked up with the Gunny. Just because he didn't want to show the operation fucked up."

I went back to get my thing's packed. The General wasn't going to like this my first assignment and I fucked it up. It seemed so easy. All I had to do was get this mother and I would be a hero again. Oh hell I guess I had it too easy. Now I was getting back to real life. The Major was right I moved to fast. If I would of taking my time this might not have happened. May be the Sgt. Smelt it coming? He did get away with it for a long time what made me think I could walk right in and lock him up? I had to face it; I fucked up now I hope they don't put me on a desk job. I really couldn't see myself working behind a desk. I'll transfer back to combat.

Shit what did I do to the Gunny and the man I bet now he will lose his strips and the rest of them to I had to go see him before I left I didn't know what I could do. I wanted them to know it wasn't all my fault. If the Cpl. didn't follow me they wouldn't have got caught. Shit there I go again trying to get out of it; even with myself. It was my fault I was the one that picked the bar I was the one they took back to their hideaway. It was me the Cpl. was following. So it was me that got them locked up. But what could I do? I didn't know anyone here to help me. The Major seemed to enjoy it. The captain was too worried about fucking up so he was out."

I got my things packed ready to go. The Captain sent someone over to take me to the air port. He wanted me out of his sight. I couldn't blame him. As for the sgt. he was probable going to slow it down for a while till things got back to the way they were. He got off; my friends got jailed and I'm getting kicked out of the country. Nice I wonder what the General will give me next?

The driver was waiting for me when I walked out the door Man they really wanted me out of here bad. I got in and as we drove off I asked where the brig was? The driver told me at the end of the base."

"Could we stop for a minute?" I asked

"No sir; he said The Major said no stops and I was to see to it I got on the plane. Oh hell I guess it was better this way. Knowing I couldn't do anything to help them, knowing the Gunny he'll get himself out of it."

We arrived at the air port the driver pulled up to this plane.

"That is yours."

I walked up the stairs and went in. The pilot told me to have a set he was waiting for clearance from the tower." I sat and buckled up Shit what a mess I couldn't help think of it. The plane started to taxi out on to the run way. It went down to the end and stopped. Now what; I said to myself; It wasn't moving.

The pilot came back and said "Sorry buddy you'll have to find another flight out. Something is wrong with the landing gear. I don't want to change it."

I got up and went to the door. The driver was already down the run way and out of sight. Oh hell I might as well walk. The pilot said they were coming to tow us back if I stayed on He would at least get me back by the brig; and from there I could hitch a ride back to head quarters."

"Why not!"

He told me it was at least two miles back to the hanger. "That far I said. He said they did that just in case the gooks bombed it. The planes were all over the place so they couldn't hit all of them. Made sense to me. He sat back down and waited for the taxi to hook up to take the plane back to the hanger

Shit he did say by the brig." Maybe I'll stop in and see the Boy's."

What the hell it wasn't my fault. The driver should have waited for me. I got off the plane the pilot pointed to the stockade fence.

"Right in front of you;" he said. I saw the main gate "Just tell them to send a jeep for you."

I thanked him and got out; I had my duffel bags. The pilot said I could leave them; he would see to it that they were waiting for me on the next plane."

"Thanks they were a little heavy."

"He smiled and said. Don't rush the next plane out isn't going to be for a while. Maybe four or five hours.

"You're kidding?"

"No he said the rest of the planes are running supplier up north."

"Thanks again." I said and headed for the brig. When I got to the gate I told the guard what happened.

He laughs. "Shit you were lucky I saw that plane coming in They were having trouble with it then It surprised me it landed."

"Look I need a ride back."

"We have a jeep going in about two hours."

"I guess that has got to do."

"Hey what are my chances of seeing someone in the brig?"

He looked at me and said "You got ID?"

I took out my CID card.

"Shit he said the brig is yours. We don't mess with you guys." He got on the phone.

"Who? He asked

"Oh, Gunny Hoff."

He called and told them to let me in; I was CID."

The gates opened and in I went. Another guard met me and showed me where the Gunny was. He opened the gate and told me I had to leave my pistol with him. I took it off and went down the row of cells. I heard the guard yell "Turn key open cell 27." Down the end this cell door opened. As I reached it I saw the rest of the man next to him."

"Hey Louie; they said you come to get us out." Later I told them I have to talk to the Gunny. Knowing I couldn't do anything for them.

The Gunny was sitting on the floor. He smiled and said. "I'd offer you a set but we can't sit on the bunk."

"No thanks; I'll stand Gunny. I'm sorry."

"Sorry for what?" He asked.

"It was me that got you in here."

"No it wasn't;" he said.

I told him about the Cpl. and the Major. He just looked at me when I finished he got up and said "That mother fucker. He did this to me."

"You know him?" I asked.

"Know him! That mother fucker did this to me. He said he would get me if I fucked up."

"I don't get what you mean?"

"Look you got to help me."

"I wish I could but I don't know anyone here." I told him that is why I didn't want to come I can't help him. The Major is shipping me back to Washington I would be on the flight right now But something went wrong with the landing gear."

"Look he said taking me to the back of the cell. Remember I said something last night about me knowing something?"

"Something about the scotch and Germany."

"That was it; he said. I was doing what the sgt. is doing. Me and him ran it; but I was giving the supplies to the Jews. The Major found out what I was doing and he held it over my head. He said if he turned me in I would hang. I was young then and he scared the shit out of me. Saying the firing squad and all that kind of shit. When he found out how easy it was to lose supplies; he started doing it and selling it to the black market. A little at first and then more and more. I didn't want anything to do with it so he had me transferred and his sgt. took over."

"Shit I was glad to just get the hell out of they. He was taking more and more it was getting harder to hide the shit. So I got transferred to boot camp I was a DI for a couple of years. Till the war broke out I wanted to get into it. That is when I meet you. Well you know the rest when I got here and saw the sgt. and the major. I know they were doing the same thing here. Now I really got scared. The Major was just a Louie like you. Now he was a Major in charge of CID. Shit he didn't have nothing to worry about. He headed the investigations on the Sgt. So now you know why he never got caught."

"That mother fucker; that is why he wanted me out of here. And he locked you up so you couldn't tell me."

"Ha he thought I did tell you it all fits into place. I didn't know you were working for him and you were investigating the sgt."

"I couldn't tell you what I was doing here. You know that."

"Top secret shit; I know I had the clearance once myself. I couldn't tell my mother what I was doing."

You said your plane had trouble I bet he was the one the coursed the trouble. Lucky the pilot found it out if he didn't you would be dead meat right now. That is why he locked me up. He was going to pin it all on us. OK we did take a case here and a case there. But that was it I know where and how the sgt. was getting rid of the shit. So it wasn't hard for me to take what I wanted."

"So you and the man would be off to Leavenworth for something they did."

"And you wouldn't have known what had happened you would be dead; he said to me."

"And I would be dead?"

"That is right."

"That mother fucked."

"Shit Hold tight I'll be back." I had to get throw to the General."

I didn't know what to do if the Major had that much pull around here. He could still have me killed and call it an accident." The guard at the gate did say the plane came in with trouble. He must of switched pilots and didn't tell them something was wrong; nice.

"Shit he plays for keeps.

"Wouldn't you; he said When I left he was doing about a million a year. I bet he's up to at least three."

"And with the contraband thing. He must be way out in front."

"Shit that was something new; he said. Just think of what the black market would do with captured good. No one knows what you got or who gave it to you."

"That is what the sgt. was trying to do with the shit I had. I was wondering how the Major got his hands on the gold so fast. Then when we got there the sgt. did everything by the book."

The Major was his boss."

"That is why the Major jumped all over me when he found out I was sent to investigate the Sgt. Shit he didn't want me to find out about him. What about this captain?" I asked.

He didn't know about him he wasn't with them in Germany

"He may be all right."

"Look don't trust anyone; he said. Do it your self or just get back on that plane and get the fuck out of here before he finds out and kills you."

"I got to get to a phone?"

"He told me one was in town. All the rest came throw the base. Use the one in town it was safer." He didn't know who the Major had working for him.

I went back out to the guard

"You guys really got them didn't you?" He was meaning the Gunny. He thought I was the one that locked him up. I had to keep letting him think that. I didn't want him running back to the Major and telling him I had to stay out of sight. I didn't want anyone seeing me; hoping they thought I was on my way and when I landed I would crash. Nice he would have nothing to do with it. He would of caught the bad guys; getting another rank probable out of it.

I went to the main gate and the guard told me the jeep wasn't ready yet. How far is town from here?"

He pointed at the main gate and said I could hitch a ride off one of the gooks. They always picked us up for a price."

"I know I heard anything for money."

"You get it right." He said.

"Oh hell I got time to kill." I walked over to the gate and told the guard to see if he could get me a ride into town. He stopped the next gook coming out of the base and waved to me.

"He's going your way;" he said.

"Hey Joe; the gook said. You fuckey Fuckey my sister Five dollars?"

"Why not; I said. He smiled. Anything to get away from the base. He drove into town; I asked him where the phone was? He pointed and said his sister would meet me over by it. I just gave him five dollars and told him to forget his sister; I didn't need a piece of ass right now."

Shit look at this line it must be about fifty guys waiting for the phone. Shit I had to call; I looked at my watch; it was too late. Everyone left the office. Now what? I can't waste any time. The Major would find out I didn't take off by now He would track me to the brig and he would know I talked to the Gunny. Then he would put a price on my head. He did say he could have me locked up for helping them. Killing me by plane was better; but if he didn't have a course He could shot me and say I was in with them and get away with it. Remember I didn't check right in with him. He could just cover it up by saying he didn't know who I was. Shit I had to get to the phone. I was looking to break in the line when I saw the Cpl. waiting to use it. He didn't see me I ducked quickly and back up behind the building.

"Hey honey" someone said tapped me on the shoulder.

Oh shit I almost shot her. I had my gun out and ready to shot. She wasn't nervous The gun didn't bother her.

"Honey you fucky me?"

"No, go away."

"Honey you fucky me?"

"Look I said get lost. Now her brother came up and said. "My sister you pay Fucky;" he said.

Shit I didn't need this."

"Look man I said it is yours, go."

"No he said fucky sister."

Wait a minute." I said to myself I gave him another five. "You tell sister fucky fucky man over by phone. I showed him the Cpl. He was busy talking to the guys on the line.

"You fucky; he said and pointed to the cpl

"Go I told her; I stayed back and watched." I know he wouldn't want to lose his place in line and he couldn't pass up a piece of ass for free. So what do you do? Have the guys hold your place. Come around the corner and get a quickie. Then go back on line, right? I hope I was right. She went over to him and sure enough that is what he was doing. He told the guys to hold his place He would be right back."

The girl came around the corner and he followed her I waited for him to go into her room she had for fucking and I followed him in. He didn't know it was me at first. He was going to swing then when he saw it was me he started to run.

"Go ass hole I'd love to blow your fucking head off." He stopped and just stood in the middle of the room. The girl started to yell. I took out twenty and she shout up fast. I tired him up to the bed; she started to walk out. I told her in Japanese to watch him hoping she would understand me. She did I took out another twenty and ripped it in half. I gave her one half and told her she would get the other when I got back. She wasn't to let him go. She didn't like the idea; she back away. I knocked him out so he wouldn't give her any trouble. She liked at better; she sat and waited for me to return.

I went back to the line and told them the cpl was getting more then he paid for. He told me to save his place. I was only about two away from using the phone. Now what? My place? Nancy she did say she was going to move in. I hope so. My turn came; I dialed and got my house. Ring, ring, Ring, shit be there; Ring. Nothing I was just about to hang up when I heard someone on the other end pick up. "Hello. I said

"Hello. She said.

"Nancy this is me."

"Oh "she yelled getting excited. I yelled back at her to shout up and listen. I didn't have time they were going to kill me."

That made her stop and listen. I told her everything; I told her I was going after the Major and the Sgt. But I needed help. I wanted her to get a hold of the General and have him back me up on this. I know what I was doing. Have him call the base CO. Anyone not in our department. I didn't know who was with the Major it could be anyone. I need someone the General could trust."

"But where are you?" She asked.

I told her the name of the bar I was in last night and told her to have who ever it was to meet me there."

"Good. "she said and was about to hang up."

"Wait I yelled. Tell who ever you're sending to say "Nancy gives you her love. That way I'll know who he is."

"Oh she said I do;" and hung up.

Now to take care of the cpl. It might take a while for them to get to me. I went back to the room she was still sitting there. The cpl was still out I gave her the other half of the twenty Then took out a hundred and ripped that in half. She would fuck a donkey for that. I told her she would get the other half if she kept him here till I came back. I know she would do it She would kill him for a hundred. That was the way them people were.

I went back to the bar to wait. They cleaned it up and were ready for business already. I took a set at the bar and just waited. The place was jumping already and the girls were all over me. Shit I didn't need this; I should have picked someplace else. It was too late I had no course but to wait. I hope who ever it was came soon. I ordered a drink so I didn't look out of place and kept looking at the door. An Hour passed; where the hell was he?

This gook girl came up to me and asked me to buy her a drink."

No I told her I was waiting for someone." I took the last of my beer and started to drink it when she said.

"Nancy said she loves you to."

I almost choked She couldn't be the one? This was a set up.

"Who the hell are you?" I asked."

She took out her ID and she was a Korean police."

"Your General called and said you were in trouble and no one from the base should know."

"You got that right Can we go some place and talk?"

"Come she said in the back." It was as if she owned the place. She went right to a back door and out into a office

"This is better?" She said

"Much." I said

"Now what can I do for you?"

"First of all have the cpl. picked up." I told her where he was. She opened the door and two more police were waiting outside.

"Bring him here; she said and closed the door; Next?" She asked.

"My man are locked up in the brig I need them. I said. She got on the phone and said something in Korean and hung up.

"They will be here also."

"Now would you mind telling me what this is all about?"

"I don't think I can; I said It is top secret." I said.

"Look I have access to your highest top secret. You can check; she said handing me the phone. That is why your General Greene called me. Now either you fill me in; our I go home. What will it be?"

"If the Generals trust you I guess I have to."

I told her what happened. She back away with her mouth open.

"You know how long we were trying stop the black market?" We could never get close enough; every time we were getting close it would shout down. Nothing it was as if it packed up and left. A week later it would start all over again with someone different running it. You see we can't go on your base and you can't come out here. So the go between was the Major and that is why nothing got done. It was him that controlled it. Your General said he notified the base of what was going on. They are waiting for you."

"I didn't want that. I said I don't know who got their fingers in the cookie jar."

"What does cookies have to do with it?" She asked.

"Nothing. I laugh It's just an expression we say when people are doing things that they aren't suppose to be doing."

"Oh "she said. Well anyway when your ready I'll go in with you to make sure nothing happens to you."

"Thank you."

"No; she smiled. It is I who should be thanking you."

The cpl came in and he just looked at me.

"Your suppose to be on the plane." He said.

"Look ass; I don't have time for your shit Now either you talk; our you do time with the Major;. You decide?"

"Look I know nothing."

"Good I said to her. Lock him up in your prison."

"No wait you can't do that."

"Oh; and why is that?"

"The major runs the show around here."

"He did as of now; I do now do you talk?" I checked your file out and you're too young to know what went on in Germany. That means you're new at it. I'll go easy on you just help with the investigation."

"Hey men go fuck yourself."

"Have it your way; Lock him up."

She opened the door said something the two police took him. "Shit, something was wrong? Why would a guy that doesn't know that much stand up like that?" He knows he is going to do hard time over this. But it doesn't worry him. Something is up with him. Can you have him checked out feather?" I just saw when he entered the service; I stop there I didn't think I had to go back any feather But I see now I have to. Something is wrong here." She called on the phone and read off his ID she took off of him.

"Get right back to me, She said it would take time but she put a rush on it.

The Gunny came in; the rest of the men stayed out side.

"Hey Louie you did it?"

"I said I would take care of it didn't I Gunny?" Now you have your new orders. You're working for me.

"And the rest!"

"Them too." I didn't know what I was getting into Gunny If you know anything else it would help."

He smiled and said "Just about half the base had some thing to do with it one way or another."

"See "I said to her. That is why I didn't want to go through the base for this one."

"Smart he said Mine introducing us; he said looking at the woman."

"Oh sorry Gunny this is Captain Kun of the Korean secret police."

"Don't I know you?" He asked.

"She smiled and said "You're the one that keeps breaking up my bar all the time."

"That is where I know you from; here? Your secret Police?"

She showed him her ID to shout him up.

"Look we have to get the main kingpins; I went this far we can't let them get away."

"All I know is that the Major runs it. The sgt. handles the other end."

"The reason." I asked.

"The whole base is in on it. They know they can get anything they want and no one turned them in."

"Why?

"As long as the sgt. delivered and he takes care of them; what the hell. That is the way it works

"What about the cpl.?"

"The one that ratted us out last night?"

"The same, something doesn't set right with him."

"I know nothing about him but I like you feel something is up with him"

"I'll find out."

"Well captain can you get my men weapons and I'll need someone that speaks your language."

She smile and said "I said I was coming."

"No, it could get a little rough."

"Mister; she said my country is at war and I don't think it could get any tougher out there then it is."

I guess she was right "Well then shell we go?" I want to take the sgt. first. I want to see how he act's once he sees the two of us together. Maybe he will crack and give up who ever else may be connected with them."

"May be; "the gunny said He never did like me I busted his nose once."

"I see you get alone with ever buddy;" she said.

"Sorry mama if I'd of known this was your place we would of went to another one an busted it up."

"No worry; she laugh. How do you think we stay up on what is going on out there? The bar hears all."

She has a point there Gunny; good info center."

"Well how are we going to do this Louie?"The gunny asked.

"I think you owe the sgt. a visit."

"I think he will shit;" she said.

"I'm planning on that I'll be waiting at the office to see what the Major is going to do. Who he calls or what he does. If anyone is in with him he will call them."

"What about me?" She asked.

"You, I said will be waiting outside. No need for you to take a chance I'll need you to do the locking up. You sure the base is informed of what is going on?"

"No "she said you said you were worried about who was in with them. So let's just see I have my men with me. When we find out who is who then I'll do the calling."

"You know you'll be on Military property."

"I know she said. That is why I want to see who backs him."

"You may not get out." I said.

"I got you; she said. I no worry."

The Gunny smiled and said. "See what you do to people?"

"Yea;" was all I could answer?

"Let's go; I said. Gunny, have the man stick by her and don't fuck up."

"Who them?" He said.

"No your fucking grandmother." I told him.

"Is she coming?" The woman Kum. Asked.

"No, we both laugh She isn't here the gunny's grandmother that is."

"Oh You Americans don't make sense."

"We know; I said. That is what keeps us on top."

We got into the car's she had waiting for us and headed for the base. I told the Gunny what I wanted him to do.

"Were ready? He said as we pulled up in the back of the warehouse.

"Ready and willing." I said.

"What the hell happened to able?" He asked.

"We will see about Able after." I said.

"Oh;" he said smiling.

The Gunny went in I head for the office. I told the Gunny to say he had escaped and need money to get out of the country. He didn't want to spend the rest of his life in the brig. If the sgt. didn't go along with him He was going to turn them all in. That should get things moving. Kun came with me. Half the man stayed with the Gunny just in case of any trouble. We didn't know what to expect. The rest came with us.

"How let's see if they bit what I have to say? I'm hoping they didn't know the plane didn't take off."

I walked in the look on the Majors face was enough to make me laugh but I held it back."

"Sorry sir the plane had trouble they told me they would have another one ready in a couple of hours."

"What the hell took you so long to report back to me?" He yelled.

"It stopped at the end of the field I had to walk back."

"He got to the phone quick and dialed some place.

He said "It did;" And hung up.

"Well Mister I guess you were a luck man."

"I think so I said the way it looked we would of never been able to land."

"Well mister make yourself comfortable hey will call when another plane is ready. He went back to his office and closed the door. I got up and went to listen to what he was doing. Just then the phone rang I picked the one up at the desk. I did it so he didn't know I was on it. It was the sgt.: He started yelling over the phone. "The Gunny escaped?" He was going crazy over here. He was going to blow my head off if I didn't get him some money."

"Cool down; he said. I'll take care of it."

Just as I was about to hang up the captain came in.

"What the hell;" "he said The Major heard him over the phone. He dropped his and came running out to see what the hell was going on. He had his gun out.

"OK fucker the game is over." He told the captain that I help the Gunny escape and we wanted money."

The captain was in with it; good thing I didn't trust him. He pulled his gun out on me.

"How what? He said looking at the Major.

"We kill them; he said. Get someone over to the warehouse and get the Gunny."

"What if he gives us a fight?"

"Kill him; he said. He is an escape convict."

"What about the sgt." He asked.

"Kill him if he gets in the way; he said you understand me Captain? I'll called and have his men to meet him at the warehouse."

"Good this way we will get them all."

The Major told me to have a seat. He went to the phone he was talking to someone. I didn't like it. He was speaking in Korean I picked some of it up he was talking to some General of the South Korean army. Then he said. "The Cpl. isn't here I didn't know where he was."

See I know it; the Cpl. had more to do with it. Just then the door broke open she came in with my man.

"Hold it Major I wouldn't do that?" He was pointing his gun at her. Let's say your plane has landed. Who were you talking to?"

"Ha, Don't make me laugh you have nothing on me."

"Oh I thank we do. I said

"With out the sgt. and the Gunny you have nothing."

'Your right there Major we have them. You see the Gunny is working for me. My men are over there with him."

"ha, you got to be joking the Gunny cannot talk."

"Oh but he did; I don't think you can hold it over his head anymore. Oh and Mister I said to him. You will have my full report in written, In your cell, in the morning, on paper."

I just had to say that.

Kun was looking at me funny.

"What is it?" I asked.

"Oh just something I hear when I was at the window. The one he was talking to was General Oh. "He is the one we have been keeping an eye on. He is bad news he isn't a soldier he is the mafia."

"Mafia! You're kidding."

"No, he runs it."

"You mean the Koreans have a mafia?"

"One of the biggest;" she said.

She told me they control most of the Far East. From Japan to China and no one can stop them."

"Something like the Italian mafia?"

"But with slanted eyes;" the Gunny said walking in.

"She didn't like that but it was true she said

"Infect the Italian mob gets a lot of their drugs from him."

"Shit this might be bigger than we thought."

"No she said we know about it for a long time but this the first break threw she had. Oh don't get me wrong we got small people but they wouldn't say a word for fear of getting killed. The General is the one I would like to get but he is with the high brass and no one can touch him."

"But if you know he is doing it why not?"

"That's just it we can't prove it. Just hear say."

"Ok now what?" I asked.

"We get your end taking care of. Now maybe the black market will slow down some. But I doubt it she said they will have someone else running it by tomorrow."

"Maybe we could get this General Oh, for you."

"Ha she said. You know how many people tried to and got killed?" He's get people working in the north. The funny part about it is that every time someone gets killed it always seems to be someone from the north that does the killing."

"Well we can't learn anything standing around here. Lets get them all together and see who wants' to sing?"

"Why do they want to do that?" She asked.

"Do what?" I asked.

"Sing?" She said.

"Oh I smiled. Another expression we use."

"Oh;" she said and went out.

I took the Major with me I didn't want anyone touching him. We waited back to the warehouse getting everyone together.

"Looks as if you got your self a hand full Gunny?"

"Just some ass holes that wanted to make some extra money. He was meaning the small army the captain had with him. Just soldiers from the base that made some extra money selling goods. No one big; Most of them didn't put up a fight. They just dropped their weapons when they saw what was going on. The sgt. and the captain were the only ones that mounted to anything."

"And the Major." I said pointing at him.

Just then a shot rang out. Shit I didn't even have to look I know what it was. The Major took it in the head."

"Shit I saw Snake take off; if anyone could fine the one that did it; he could. Gunny give the rest of them cover. I don't want any more getting hit. They took the sgt. and the captain back inside. They stood around them till we could get them to a safe place. Shit it was the Major I wanted. He was the brains at this end. Oh hell I guess the General was covering up his tracks. I bet the captain didn't even know the general "So much for that I said to her?"

"See she said he always does it. I don't know where he comes from but he knows everything that is going on. He is one step in front of us all the time; you say get him! Ha, she said, how?

Well this was all I could do; my job was finished I got who I was after?" Her job was just starting. She had her hands full. We waited for a truck to come and pick up the rest I didn't think anyone else would get it. The General got the one he wanted. He was in the clear for now. Snake came back with the one that did the shooting. She was right he was from the north. He was a regular from the north. He even wear his uniform.

"See," she said.

"Maybe you could make him talk."

"Ha she said He will kill himself before he talks. We tried that before; she said. She went over to him and rolled up his shirt. "See she said. They all wear it; it was a tattoo of a dragon on his arm."

"This is the sign of death;" she said. the soldier didn't blink; he kept looking over our heads.

We got them back to the brig and started questioning them. She was right nothing but what we know already. "Well I guess I'll leave it up to you." I told her I was calling my General to find out what he wanted me to do next."

"Nice working with you;" she said Come back soon."

For some reason I know she meant it she held my hand and didn't let it go.

"Yea sure thing;" I said pulling it away from her. The Gunny came out behind me.

"Hey Louie she was sweet on you."

"Oh I didn't notice." I said.

"Well she was; take it from me; he said. I know that look them people give. Well Louie where to from here?"

I looked back at him and said. That is what I'm going to check on how."

I got to the phone and called Washington. I got Nancy.

"Hi she said excited. You ok?"

"I'm great is the General in?"

"Hold he was waiting for your call."

"Joel he said I just got the good news you did a good job he said

"Well sir it didn't turn out the way I wanted it to; but we got the ones that were doing it on the base. The Koreans have their hands full over here sir other then the war."

"We know; he said. But that is their problem I want you back here at once."

"Oh sir one other thing Do you think I could bring my own men back?"

"You mean the Gunny?" He asked.

"I was thinking we might be able to use them. I said.

"Bring them back; he said but they are your prisoners they still have to stand trail for what they did."

"What was that?" I asked.

"AWOL; he said and at the time of war they could be shot."

Oh shit now what? "Sir I started to say when he stopped me.

"Mister didn't you hear what I said? Your prisoner's."

"Yes sir."

CHAPTER 6

I was just about to hang the phone up when Nancy cut in "Hold on the line; she said. I think I got something. General she said I ran a check on the cpl the captain said he has."

"Yes;" he said.

"Well he comes up as not being in the Marines."

"Oh I said then what is he?"

She said she was still checking and she would get back with me."

"Shit; the General said who the fuck is he and what was he doing there?"

I guess the only one that could answer that is the Major and he is dead.

"Look; he said. Bring him back with you something doesn't fit;" he said.

"Sir that was my feeling when I meet him. He is hiding something."

"Bring him back; he said. I'll be waiting for you." He hung up and Nancy was still on the phone. She told me she was checking something else to call ever chance I could. She would give me up dates."

I didn't know if she just wanted to talk to me our she meant it?"

"OK I said will do."

Off we went; the Gunny the Cpl. and my men. We got a plane right away. We had to stop over in the Philippines. The flight was long and no one was talking. The Gunny and the men were worried about what was going to happen to them when we got back. It was war time and they were AWOL. Shit they can't hold that against them. When we landed in Subic Bay to refuel I got out and Called Nancy. She said she missed me and she still didn't have nothing on the Cpl. I told her I would call when I hit Hawaii. She told me she loved me. I hung up Maybe she was the one for me I know I was thinking about her too

Well we took off and headed for Hawaii; the same no one talked. We were landing the gunny said he wanted to get out and stretch. I smiled at him and said.

"No you don't I know he was think of taking off."You're going back with me and the two of us will fight it; don't do anything stupid. I told him.

He sat back down and just looked out the window. All his years going down the drain. No way I wasn't I going to let that happen. I got to the Phone; Nancy picked it up. She sounded excited she was about to tell me something when the General got on. He said for me to get the hell out of there as fast as I could. The cpl we had was the son of the mafia big boss and they wanted him back."

"The what?" I asked.

"You heard me you got no protection there; he said. Get back on the plane and get the fuck out of there."

"It was to late I saw these three cars coming down the run way and they didn't look as if they had fuel for our plane with them."

I dropped the phone and started running for the plane. The cars were coming to the side of me. I took out my gun and took a shot at the drive. Shit, want a good shot. I hit him in the head; he fell down on the wheel. Shit he was heading straight for me and no one steering the car. The others were hanging out the windows trying to shot me. Here I was running down the run way with a car out of control chasing me. Plus the guys in the car were shooting at me; not knowing I killed the driver. Lucky thing the car was swaying back and forth. The guys couldn't hit me but the car was going everywhere I was. I couldn't get out of its way. The other two cars let this one to take care of me. They head for the plane. Shit the Gunny didn't know and the others were asleep. They were going to take the Cpl. without a fight.

No one had any guns on the plane either. I was the only one that did. Just as the car almost got me the drive must of hit the gas and full. The car took off and passed me Just as the guy's were getting ready to shot me it passed me and turned over.

Shit was that close; I kept running for the plane I started shooting at the other two cars. They opened fire on me. I hit the ground and kept rolling so they couldn't hit me. That was when I saw the Gunny standing in the door way with something in his hand. Bang I saw this smoke come out from his hand and went right into the car. It was a flare gun. He shot a flare at them. He did the same to the other car and before anyone could get out. The Gunny and the man were out of the plane dragging them from the cars. Shit was that close I got up and ran to the car.

"Good work I said I couldn't warn you."

"He smiled his smile and said. "I saw the whole thing; he said. You ran the mile in ten second."

"Ha, I said you would to if you had a car full of gun man shooting at your ass."

"Mind telling me what this is all about?" He asked.

"The cpl." I said.

"What does he got to do with it?"

"It seems as if he was sent by his father to watch out for his interest."

"And who is his father?" He asked.

I looked at him and said. "They never told me."

"Nice; he said I love it when they don't tell you."

"He did say something about the Mafia."

The Gunny just looked at me.

"Something wrong?" I asked.

He went back to the plane and as he was walking he said something; "That kid bothered me now I know what it was."

He got into the plane and went for the cpl. He took him out of his set and throw him across the aisle.

"Hey; I yelled. What did you do that for?" I said holding him back.

"This piece of shit is the son of Mr.G."

"So, I said. Who is Mr.G?"

"You don't know who Mr.G is?" He asked.

"No, I said who is Mr.G?"

"Mr.G is the big crime boss on the east coast and this piece of shit is his son."

"Hold on how; do you know that?"

He looked at me and said. "Is the plane fueled?"

"I don't know; I said.

"Well check it; he said. We got to get the hell out of here. He's probable got more coming. Go; he yelled.

This was the first time I saw the Gunny scared. I went back out of the plane and saw more cars coming. Then I saw the fire engines coming to. They saw the smoke from the cars and thought the plane was on fire. My men had all the mod guys from the car's holding them together.

"Snake I yelled give me a couple of minute. He knew what I was talking about. He took one of the rifles the mob guys had and got down on the ground. They were still far away and it would take a good shot to stop them from here; but I know he could do it. The guys refueling the plane had stopped. He didn't want the fire from the cars to catch on to the plane.

I yelled for him to get back and finish."

"No way;" he said and started to get in the cab of the truck.

Snake turned his gun on him and shot his heel off his shoe.

"I think you had better do what the man said he told the drive."

He looked at him and got back down. He climbed back and kept refueling. Snake took out the tires of the two cars coming. They both flipped I guess they were moving. You couldn't tell how fast from that distance but you could see them turn over and do crazy flips in the air. They had to be moving to do that.

"OK Snake said. What next?"

I looked at the fire engines coming. Wait till they come and then we are out of here." I said The fire engines pulled up; when they saw what was going on they went back into the truck and started to back up. "Hold on;" I yelled Holding up My ID.

The captain of the fire department came up in a car and pulled next to me. He didn't get out of the car. He to saw what was going on. He got a phone call about us. He said the PD was coming.

"Good I said and handed him a gun. Keep your eye on them for me." I told my men to get back aboard the plane. He didn't have a chance to say no. I was up the stairs and waiting for the refueling to finish. He finished I closed the door. I yelled to the pilot to take off. He did, we were air born with in five minute. Shit that was close. The Gunny was still sitting with the cpl.

"Well what have we here?" I asked the cpl.

He just smiled at me and said; "it is a long way to Washington."

The gunny took a swing at him.

"Hey fool; he said as I blocked him from hitting him. You're going down with me ass hole and who the hell are you anyway?" He asked him.

That I wanted to know myself. What made the Gunny act that way? Something he didn't tell me. I got up and told the Gunny to take a back seat and cool off."

He didn't want to but he did. I looked at the cpl and said "You're some piece of work. How long did you expect to get Away with it?"

He laugh and said "Your dead Jew and spit in my face.

I hit him for the Gunny.

The gunny yelled "Cool off Jew boy."

I guess he was right; something with this kid made me want to take him and throw him out of the plane head first with no shout.

Gunny called for me to come back and have a seat He wanted to talk to me. I had to talk to someone. This was getting out of hand and we still had Calf. to go and then Washington. If was going to be anything like Hawaii we were in for it. I was hoping the General had people waiting for us to protect us when we landed. I guess he would; but you never know.

"OK, You want to level with me?" I said sitting down next to him.

He looked at me and said "We got trouble."

"NO shit Tell me something I don't know."

"You remember what I said about the Major in Germany? I didn't tell you he took on a partner."

"This Mr.G." I said.

"The same. He was in the army at the time. He was doing the same shit as the Major was so they teamed up and made it bigger. Before you know it they controlled the whole operation. Nothing went in or out with out them taking some of it."

"YOU mean contraband taking from the German army!"

"Gold, Diamonds and art work. I'm talking Millions worth. That was when I got scared I told them I wanted out; Mr.G didn't want to hear it so he sent some guys to take me out. I got them first then I went back and got him. I thought I did but I later found out he use it to get back home He went back as a war hero. He said he was wounded in action saving this town single handed." That is what the papers read. He as gone and the Major just let me be. I guess he kind of thanked me for what I did. I know he could have me taking out anytime he wanted to."

"So did he?"

"He just let me be after that I was a no buddy and he knew it. All I wanted was to be left alone." They did; the rest you know."

"You sure! You seem to be coming up with more and more each time something happens."

"No that is it No more but now his father thinks I had something to do with his son getting caught." He is going to come after me

"So you got the US government behind you how."

"Ha he said don't make me laugh."

I know what he meant He was being taking back to stand trail and no one to stand by him

"Look I'm with you I said

He just looked at me and said "It would be easer if he just jumped out of the plane before it landed

"Look I got the General behind me

"You don't know this Mr.G he runs the government He came out a war hero and didn't stop there He is in office now he is a senator

"You're kidding?

"No he said you wait and see."

Again the plane went quite. The kid just closed his eyes and want to sleep. He didn't have a care in the world. We landed at Calf. This time we had a greeting committee waiting for us. It was as if the President was coming. More FBI people then in the movies. They told us over a loud speaker not to leave the plane. They would come board to talk to us. I went to the door and waited. Two guys came up the stairs and looked around.

"You Goldberg?" One said.

"That was me." I said.

"I'm Johnson; one said. And Johnson the other one said.

"Brothers?" I asked.

"No, they said I'm Johnson P and he is Johnson J."

"So P J what can I do for you's?"

They didn't think that was funny.

"We come to take the kid."

"Oh I said. You have that in writing?"

They looked at me and then at each other. "No one said.

"No ticket no shirty. I guess you don't get the kid then."

"You're kidding?" One said.

"No sorry I have my orders. You don't have yours So that means I win."

"I don't think you heard me; one said. We come for the kid."

"Look guy's I don't think you heard me. You're not getting him."

"Hey; one said. You see what we got out they we could came and take him if we have to."

Just then my man stood up. Each one of them had guns pointed at them.

"You can see what I have here." I said I could do the same. Now why don't you two Pj's get the hell off the plane and let us get on with what we were told to do."

"You're not going to hear the end of this. One said. You're disobeying an order."

"A direct order the other;" one said.

"That depends on who is giving the orders. If it is you two stick them up your ass. You two are the only thing I see So now gentleman if you would close the door behind you. We have a date to keep."

One of them was going for his gun. I had mine out first. I held it to his head and said. "Must I?"

"You'll hear about this." He said backing out the door. "I'm sure I will but for now no tickety no shirty." I closed the door and waited for the plane to refuel. They didn't stop it; they just watched us. I could see one was on a radio. The refuel stopped and the truck pulled away. I waved to the PJ and told the pilot to take off. He did; off we went. Next stop Washington. Shit I didn't know if I did the right thing or what. I guess I'd soon find out. Like the Major told me. Paper work, I can't do anything without paper work. So no paper work no Kid it was that easy."

We were starting to land. The kid was looking worried. I guess he thought his father would have him by now. The Gunny walked by him and said "Your father was always a shit head; and so is his son." He said slapping him in the head.

"Good Gunny you feel better now?"

He smiled at me and said. "It helped a little."

"OK now listen up; I said No one goes anywhere." Just keep your set and keep watching out the windows. Don't shot on less I say so."

"Hey Lieutenant. Where in America now. Snake said.

"So I said. Do what I say and everything will be just fine."

"You heard the man. The gunny said. He got us out of shit before. This is no different; he said He will get us out of this. Now hang tight and do what he said."

Again there were a lot of people waiting outside when we landed. But no one I know. The plane stopped and the stairs came to the side.

"Someone was knocking at the door; the Snake said

"See who it is."

Snake went and put his ear up to it. Then came back and said. "More FBI."

"Shit, ask him where CID was?"

He went back and told him. He came back and said "They were on their way."

"Good I said. Close the door and tell them to wait. I could see Snake didn't like doing it.

"Go Man I said they won't bit."

He did He almost took the guys fingers off. He wouldn't take them off the door so he could close it. He got the door closed and ran back to his seat.

"Don't worry; the Gunny said. The man knows what he is doing."

I looked at him and smiled. I wish I did I said to myself.

Just then The snake said "Someone's coming."

I looked out the window. Shit it was about time it was the General. The major was with him. He got out of the car and headed for the stairs."

"Open it Snake;" I said He got up and had it open for the General. The General came in with a big smile on his face."

"You sure know how to make a name for yourself Son." He told Snake to let the others in.

"Let them have him; he told me. We don't want him.

"What ever you say sir. I told the Gunny to bring him He almost chocked him dragging him out of his seat.

"Easy Gunny; the General said. We don't want them complaining we treated him wrong."

I took him off of him then took him out to the landing. "Oh hey kid;" I said as the FBI was coming to get him "I don't like shit like you spitting in my face." I kicked him down the stairs. The agents got him just before he hit the bottom.

The General looked at me.

The Major said "Did you see that sir?"

"Make a note of it." the General said to him. The major took out his pad and started to write.

"How use it to wipe your ass with." The General added.

The Major just put his pad away and didn't say a word.

"Well son you did it again. He took me by the arm and said. "You hungry?"

"Your wife cooking again?" I asked.

"You know it;" he said.

We walked out of the plane together.

"Oh sir my men?"

Oh don't worry; he said I'll take care of them."

I turned and looked at the Gunny and gave him a smile. He smiled back and went back in and closed the door. I got into the Generals car.

"Home "he said the little lady is waiting."

We arrived at the Generals house and to my surprise Nancy was waiting with the Generals wife. Of course the Generals wife had on something different on this time. It was just as see throw as the first one. Nancy had her work clothes on. Day and night; before and after; kind of thing. Nancy and the General's wife.

Nancy came running up to me and so did his wife. That was a good one; who do you take first? I got the both of them together; one in each arm.

They both said "My hero. And started kissing me. It seems they tried to outdo each other. It was like I had twins; one on each side of me. What one was doing the other did; till they got to my ear. Then both of them bit it and sucked.

"Woo I said Getting to hot; I said and pulled away from both of them.

The General just laugh "Come my children lets eat."

I took the both of them by the waist and marched them to the dinner room.

"You know; I said. You two keep that up and I'm going to have to send the General out to feed the dog for a couple of hours."

"Daddy "the Generals wife said; "do we have any dogs?"

"No sweet thing but if you wait we can get one." And we all laugh.

The food was great and the women were out of sight and the General was himself. So all and all we had a good time. He said he had something to tell me tomorrow; Tonight was not the time for it. He always left thing unanswered. Shit what was he going to tell me? Nancy thanked him for the dinner. As we were leaving she turned to his wife and thanked her. Not for the dinner but for making me so hot she would have to take the whole night to put the fire out."

That was one way of looking at it. I did want to fuck the shit out of anyone. It didn't make a difference who; I just wanted to feel a woman under me, on top of me or around me all night long. The Generals wife did that to me. Nancy knew it; she did it to everyone. You just couldn't set at a table with her and not get excited. She moved looked and talked sex. Don't get me wrong Nancy was good looking. She could probable look just as good if she wear what she had on. But she didn't; so I spent most of the night peeking at the Generals wife.

When we left the General said I could take a couple of days off."

"After tomorrow that is." I was welcome to join him and his wife at his pool."

""No thank you; Nancy said. Thanks but no thanks." looking at his wife.

I could see the Generals wife wanted us to say yes."

"Maybe next time;" she said disappointed.

"Maybe." Nancy answered for us.

"We were out the door with her pulling me."

She had her car out front to drive us home. She kept looking at me and saying.

"Don't lose it."

"No; I said I'm holding it. Meaning my feelings.

She said she didn't want to stop on the high way like last time. She was flying we pulled into the drive way almost hitting the house. The both of us ran out and headed for the door. That was as far as we got. She came into me I took her at the door step. She back up against the door and lifted her skirt. I undid my fly. She mounted me with her lags wrapped around my waist. I was in. If it was possible to kiss someone to death? We were trying. Our tongues and lips were working over time. One trying to outdo the other. We didn't care who saw us. We kept it up not caring. All I could hear was her back banging against the door and the both of us making little noises.

Then we came; together of course. The both of us sat on the front step out of breath. She took my hand and said.

"We must try to make it to the bed room next time."

"I know the neighbors are getting a free show. I said pointing to the old lady looking at us.

Nancy waved to her "I hope we taught her something; she said getting up. "Are you ready to try to make it to the bedroom this time?" She opened the door.

"I don't know. I said. That is up to you."

She went in and as she walked in front of me she picked her skirt up over her ass

"Oh shit that isn't fair I got to her just as we reached the steps I think my thing found her before she bent over Well any way she bent over She had her hands on the second step and her butt facing me I was right behind her going at it again

Dog style she called it. She could call it what ever she wanted to all I know is it felt good. I was getting every inch of me into her and more. She kept 'yelling' "Harder, harder.

So I let go of her and took hold of the wall with one hand; and the Rail with the other. I back up as far as I could go without dropping out; then I slapped it in as hard as I could.

"OOOOOh; she said. Yes."

I guess that is what she wanted. I kept it up Slapping my bottom hard against her back side. Just as I felt we were reaching our climax she yelled.""Woooo' and fell to the steps with me on top of her. She turned her head around and asked. "Ready to try again?"

"Here" I asked."

"No she said; in the bedroom."

"I don't know you think we can make it?"

"I don't know; she said but we have to try."

"I know I said. Why don't I just leave it in? This way we can stop on the way."

That was a laugh. Did you ever try to walk with it in someone; backwards and going up the stairs. It was crazy but we finely did it."

I said "We looked like a couple of dogs in heat."

She broke up and fell to her knees on the steps it came out.

"See we can't do it."

"Oh and who said so; she said still laughing. She took one lag and put it over the banister. Then her other lag went on the wall. "This better?" she asked.

I looked down and just reached over her head and rested my hands on the step over her ; then went in.

I was doing bush ups on the steps with her under me. She reaches to the front of her blouse and ripped it off. Her tits were looking right at me. She had no bra on and her tits were as hard as rocks.

"You know; I said I think you get just as hot watching her as I do."

She smiled and said. "What makes you think that?" Squeezed her nipples with her two fingers. She was playing with her self as I was banging it into her.

Well we finely made it to the bed. Just in time to fell asleep. We didn't bother to finish undressing. We didn't have the strength to. The next morning she woke and turned over. I was a wake but wasn't moving. I was thinking of what the General was going to tell me."

"Hey she said; something wrong?"

"No, I said kissing her.

"Then why aren't you jumping me?" She asked.

"Oh I said facing her and playing with her nipples. "It was what the General said as we were leaving."

"What was that?" She asked.

"Something about he will tell me tomorrow."

"Oh that; she said. He always does that. It's a game he plays. He said it always keeps the brain thinking."

"He's right I haven't stopped thinking sense he said it."

"I know what it is;" she said and rolled over to get out of bed.

"Oh shit not you to?" I said.

She stood with her back to me and finished taking her clothes off.

"But he didn't have what I have she said

"No but his wife does

Ooops; the wrong thing again. I could see by the way she was turning around to give me my answer. There was going to be a war. I jumped off the bed and landed on the floor to get out of her way. I know she was getting ready for a fight. When she saw I had moved she just stood looking at me and said.

"No, I'm not going to let you get to me."

"No, she said again and started to walk to the bathroom. She surprised me. She closed the door with out throwing anything at me. I got up and just as I got my one lag out of my pants she came out the door charging like a bull. She landed over the bed and tackled me around the waist. That had me on the floor. She had shaving cream in her hand and started squirting it on me.

"Now she said. Take it back."

This was fun I loved it when she did that.

"No, I said. You'll run out of the cream sooner or later but she will still be there." I said

She just looked at me and smiled. "You're asking for it."

"Oh, I said. You have it in you?"

"Oh honey, do I;" she said.

Again we did it; on the floor of course not the bed. We took the shower together she had more cream on her then I did. When she got out she said.

"Maybe we will take the General up on his offer?"

"Oh, I asked. What did she mean by that?"

"Oh nothing I just think it would be nice to have a dip in the pool don't you?"

She was up to something and I think I know what. "Sounds good to me." I said.

"I'll tell him;" she said.

"Better yet; I said why don't I drop over and tell her." Oh shit wrong words again.

"No "she said again and walked out. "No "she kept staying walking down the stairs. Then she said "yes."

"Oh I said "What was the yes for?"

"Oh nothing I was just thinking to myself." She said.

"Good "Like you said it is always good to be thinking."

"Your right; she said you're so right."

"Well? I asked. What were you thinking?"

"Oh, she said. That wouldn't be fair I do want you do; thinks to her; she said getting dressed.

"Ok play the game." I said and got dressed. Half way throw; I asked again. "What were you thinking?"

"Oh she said you'll find out; and went down stairs.

Oh shit I know I was in for it now. Me and my big mouth. She acted funny I guess I said one thing to many.

"My fault Ok." I said; coming down the stairs "I'm sorry I take it all back.

"Oh No; she said. Too late you started it so now we play;" she said walking out the door.

I followed her. "Come on; I said Peace."

"Oh honey you'll get your piece;" and got into her car. She drove off with me standing there.

"Hey wait for me." I yelled. She didn't stop.

Oh hell I guess I drive my car. I got in and tried to follow her. Shit where was she going? She wasn't going to work. I followed her to this apartment house. She drove into the drive way and got out and went inside. Shit I was to meet the General; I couldn't follow her in. Maybe she had an appointment here?

I backed out and headed for the office. The General was here already I bet he was waiting for me. I was a little late; I ran up the stairs and went right into his office. I knocked before I went in.

He yelled. Come."

I opened the door expecting to just see him. Shit the room was full. Oh my god he had my family here. Seymour was here to. Even the Gunny and the men.

"You're late; he said getting up.

"Sorry sir I said I got lost."

"Oh he said. And where is Nancy? She is late to."

"She said she had to stop some place sir."

"Oh hell I did want her to be here. Well you can see her later. Joel he said Being you are what you are I took it on my self to have your next rank forward. Being you did what you did and all that I arranged for you to receive your next rank ahead of time. You are now a Major. Here son;" he said holding out my Star's.

My uncle and Aunt, Their daughter's. The whole bunch was proud of me. The Gunny and the man just stepped back and got out of the way. Shit this is what I wanted I was on my way.

"General. I said. I wanted to earn them myself."

"Son, you did. It wasn't me that gave them to you It was the President that OK it."

"Really sir!"

"Really, He asked me what I wanted for Christmas I told him Rank. You see son when my report landed on his desk he himself read it. The way it read you saved him and the people a lot of money. Anyone that could do that. Lets say they ask and I they get kind of thing; do I make myself clear?" He said.

"Yes sir; I said and thank you."

Well I guess this is what I was looking for; and no one could say it was giving to me. Even my man said I desired it. I looked at the Gunny and saw he still had his strips on.

"Sir I said. What is the story with my men?"

"Well you see son that was the hard one. The President wanted to have them shot. You know to set an example for others; and all that kind of shit. I had to get down on my knees to beg him; to show he had a heart. I told him they should get a rank boost them self's. Well son he hit the ceiling; I did all I could to talk him into it. But the old man wouldn't budge. He stood his ground. Then I did what I had to do I told him if they get shot he would have to have you shot to."

"Me sir?" I asked.

"You "he said. They are your men; you're responsible for them; are you not?"

"Yes sir." I said

"So to make a long story short He agreed to not giving them the next rank and to assign them to me for punishment; I felt that was fair. So I told him he didn't have to shot you."

"Yea;" I yelled. The Gunny and the man jumped with me.

"See; the Gunny said. I told you he would get us out of it." Meaning me.

Well that was the start of a wild escapade. The General was sorry he ever did it. Oh don't get me wrong we got thing done. It was the way we did it that got us into trouble.

But later for that; Nancy came in behind her was the Major. He had this shit eating smile on.

"Oh good; the General said. You're just in time." "Listen everyone I'm having a little get together at my place. Everyone is invited I feel as if he is my son; he said so why not."

Nancy came up to me and kissed me; Congratulation' she said.

The Major came and shock my hand. I know he didn't like it but what the hell I didn't care about him. Seymour came to me and took me in his arms.

"My brother we both got what we wanted." He was right.

"Well the General said. Let's go before we run out of gas. Nancy came up to me and took my arm

"Hey I said where did you go?"

"Oh; she said I had to finish what you started."

"I started something?" I asked.

"You sure did but don't worry I took care of it."

"And how was that?" I asked.

"Sex what else; she said You didn't for fill me all the way so I had to go see a friend to finish it for you." She said and walked away

Oh this is the game she wants to play. Then I saw her take the Majors arm. That fuck she went to his place. Ok if that is the way she wants to play it. Like my father always told me. Don't get mad get even.' And that was what I was going to do; get even.

The Gunny and the men came over to me and asked who she was

"Oh just someone that works here."

"Oh man the big guy said. What I could do with that."

"I don't think you could ever satisfy her; she loves it morning noon and night."

That should get it started. The men went right out after her. Nothing like a challenge for the young sex starved Marine's. They took her by the arm and as they carried her out the door she looked back at me. I gave her my smile and off they went. The General had cars waiting for us. Off we went to his house. Nancy caught on to what I was doing she played it all the way. She was enjoying it. Look at her the witch. Seymour and My Uncle came with me. The aunt and her daughters went in their car. My uncle wanted to be alone with the two of us. I found out he found out about me and he didn't know what to do. Seymour didn't even know it; was a shock to both of us.

It seemed someone that he knew was in the same camp and know Seymour's mother and father till they died. No son was born they only had Seymour. He still didn't know who I was; but he did know I wasn't his Nephew. He just talked to Seymour as if I wasn't there. He asked him if he knew? When Seymour said. "Yes. He dropped it. He said "I don't want to know you must have had good reason to do what you did." And that was the end of it. He never spoke to me again. Weightier it was us lying to him; or he did know who I really was. I'll never know he just back away from me. He didn't even tell his wife. She and the daughters treated me the same.

What could I say to the man? Seymour said he would talk to him but for now let him be.

It hurt me I grow to love him as a father. He never told me what to do. He said if I lived through what we were through; that was the best teacher in the world. Nothing he could do or say could help us be any smarter. He was a smart man I know he was right but to have him find out this way was wrong. We..I should have told him. At least half of it; no maybe it was better this way. I could never tell him who I really was. No man could forgive that much and if he know it already it was hurting him not to turn me in. So like Seymour said. "Let it be for now."

We got to the General's place. It was hard for me to celebrate with this over my head. Seymour told me to keep the act up or it will hurt his aunt. Give him that much;" he said.

So I did; it was hard all through the day I kept looking at him. He was a lost man; and I did it to him.

What can I say; the party was going crazy. The General's wife was having a ball. Nancy was right along with her. The two sisters were the real Jewish type and everything was shocking to them. My aunt just smiled. They left early; Seymour said something about driving home and the long trip."

He didn't want to have them stay. I was glad they were leaving. The General tried to make them stay but he gave up. He know it wasn't the type party for them. He didn't really care he was having a ball. He just watched the men full all over his wife. His wife didn't like the idea of Nancy cutting in; so it was a battle to see who got the most looks. I guess if I wasn't feeling this way it would have been fun to watch.

Seymour stayed, He didn't want to leave till he talked to me. He said he would stay over a couple of days I was glad of that I wanted to talk to him with out anyone around. For some reason I felt what the general was feeling. It felt good knowing your woman was the center of attraction. As long as it stayed in control. That was hard with the men but the gunny watched them like a mother. All and all it went without any trouble; No fights. The man seemed to understand by the time we called it a night they had played them self's out. The Gunny said he would look after them. Seymour said he was going to a hotel.

"No way. I said. I have an extra bed room." I wanted him to stay with me. Nancy went home to her place or with the Major; I didn't care I didn't own her. The General took his wife up I guess to fuck her. She needed it she ended up with nothing on. The only thing that kept the men from going crazy was the Gunny.

"Look but don't touch;" was what he kept saying.

On the way home Seymour just looked out the window. I could see a lot going on in his mind. When we got home, we went in and I took out a bottle and put it on the table." Well now what;" I asked?

He just looked at me and at the bottle and took himself a glass. I could see it was going to be a long night.

"First I have to find out who my uncle talked to."

"Then," I asked.

"Then it may be up to you. That is if you don't want any more people finding about you."

"I don't get you?" I said.

"You can gain access to whose left from the prison camp; those are still around and where. Then get them to me and I'll check them to see who we know and if they are the ones that would know about you."

"How am I going to do that without being caught?"

"I don't know; he said but it is the only way we could be sure you're not going to be discovered. That is on less you want to be?"

"You crazy; I said you see what I got going here. I would be a fool to give this all up. You know what they are doing to the Germans they are finding."

"I know; he said. I read about it all the time in the paper. The Russians are killing them left and right, and no one is saying anything about it."

"So, we know what we have to do; he said. Look I'll stick by you all the way, he said. You're my brother and you will always be my brother."

"Thanks; I said taking him in my arms. I feel the same way. Man why me?" I said.

"Hey, he said; we knew this might happen. We've been through a lot. What is a little more?"

I know, but some day I would like to put it to rest."

He looked at me and said. "As long as there are people out there that remember what your people did to my people; it will never rest. Not till every one of your people are dead or caught."

"That may take forever." I said.

"We have forever." he said.

"Look, what could they do to me?" I asked.

"Ha, he said, you're not the one to ask that. You know what they could do to you."

"No, I mean what if I come clean with who I am. I didn't do anything; it was my father that did it. What could they do to me?"

"Well from my point of view. If I didn't know you and you came forward with who you were. I think I would go to the end of the world trying to kill you."

"But why?" I asked.

"Come on now, he said picking up the bottle again. Your father killed my father and mother and I'm the only son living. Why shouldn't I seek revenge? You're still alive and my family isn't what gives you the right to live?"

"You mean it would make you feel better killing me?"

"Let's put it this way. I would sleep a lot better, knowing I did something for my family's death and touchier. Your father did a lot of things to my people he didn't have to do."

"He was under orders." I said sticking up for him.

"Ha, he said orders from who?"

"Hitler." I yelled.

"No he yelled back, not at the last days he wasn't. He just did it because he loved doing it. I know I saw the look your father had in his eyes when he shot my people just because they didn't dye fast enough. He looked as if he was killing dirt. You know the way he did it; why should you ask." He yelled.

"He was still my father." I yelled back.

"Will then you should die for him." He yelled.

"Hey if your family would of left when they had the chance they would still be alive." I said.

"Look, he yelled back. Don't get me started on that. My mother and father were good people and you know why they didn't leave."

"They were too busy helping the Germans."

"That is right; he said when he saw the look on my face. Helping the people that killed them."

"You didn't tell me that." I said.

"Come on now who do you think my father was taking care of; Jews? Ha grow up; he said. You should know the whole story before you condemn. My father worked in a German hospital. No Jew had the right to a doctor. Hitler had all the Jew doctors talking care of his man. My father would come home after 19 hours a day taking care of Germans. And instead of going to sleep he would go out and take care of the Jews that were dying. For many of days my father would go without sleep.

The same with my mother, you think she was teaching Jews? Get real; he yelled, she would of been killed long before she was if she got caught teaching Jews. Germans she was teaching."

"That is crazy; I yelled, they saw what was happing. They had the chance to leave. The general even said it."

"Oh look at mister know it all. You weren't there; how do you know they could leave? One thing I remember was one day I asked them why? And you know what they told me?"

"I don't care what they told you;" I yelled, they still could of gotten out."

He jumped up and took his glass and was going to throw it at me.

"Go ahead; I said standing. If it will make you feel any better do it."

"No he said. What would make me feel better is if you were dead."

His words hit me. What the hell was going on? I felt sick from his words. I couldn't move and I couldn't answer him. I just looked at him without saying anything.

"Well; he said you got a gun? Finish what your father couldn't. Go ahead and shot me. I know you could; he said I see it in your eyes. Well he said again, go ahead. Don't tell me you lost your nerve? You're like all the other Fucked up people in the world. You can't do it on less you got an army behind you, or someone telling you what to do. Weak; he said, your kind of people are the weak ones."

I didn't think I could do this to him. He was all I had and if it wasn't for him I would be dead with the rest of my family. I just stood looking at him. Tears started coming down my face. I wanted to hold him. But I didn't think he would want me to; so I just stood there looking at him.

After he finished yelling at me he saw and felt the same way I did; he to just stood looking at me. And then the tears started coming from him. The both of us just stood looking at each other and cried. Neither one wanting to make the move for each other, for fear the other one would reject the other. Rejection none of us needed right then.

I spoke first" Seymour, please forgive me and my family."

He looked at me. "I wish I could say the same to you. But my family and I did nothing to you's."

I couldn't hold myself back any more if he pushed me away he did. I had to hold him. I came into his arms and cried. At first he didn't hold me and then I felt his arms come around me. My brother loved me. I don't know how long we held each other. But however long it was, it wasn't long enough. I didn't want to let him go. He was right; his people didn't do anything. But it was over so now what? Go on hating? That was easy. The whole world hated something or another. If you didn't like what this guy hated, go to the next guy and see what he hates. I'm sure you would find someone you would agree with for hating.

"You could never hate alone in the beginning, someone always had to start you. He pulled me away and finished telling me about his Mother and father.

I guess he wanted to get it all out. And to make me understand what he was feeling.

"You know what the sad part is? He finished. If they run and then the next one runs; then who would be left to help?"

We sat back down again and kept talking.

I answered him with.

"But it was crazy for them to stay."

"I know that and you know that, he said. But they didn't see it that way. All they could see was people needing them and it was in their hearts and soul not to turn and run."

"Did you ever know the reason?" I asked.

"Look, he said,if I have to explain what their reason was; I wouldn't be here. I would have just stayed there and killed you. Then I would have gone back to my people to see if I could help. I was one of the weak ones, he said, I ran."

"No, I told him, you weren't. If you would have stayed you would have been dead or no use to anyone. Now you can help. I said you're a doctor just like your father and you're alive. Your people need you more than ever now. People like you are making your race live on. If you would have stayed you would have nothing."

"It is easy for you to say. He said. I got my people coming to me and wanting me to help find the Germans that did this to my people. How would it look if they know I saved one?"

"But I didn't have anything to do with it." I said.

"You fucking liar," he said getting mad again. Does your memory block all the bad things you do yourself for laughs?" Oh, he said. You don't count them; you and your whip. How many Jews did you whip for fun? Your father standing next to you and you showing him what a good German you were. You're forgetting I was there and saw you."

"Then why the hell did you help me?" I yelled at him.

"Why, he yelled back,I don't know why. I've been asking myself that every time I see what people like you did. Pictures and film over and over again. My people are getting tired of this kind of treatment. More and more bodies are turning up in Mass graves. People that were there and lived are going back and showing where they saw their families killed. It is going on and on, more and more. God what made your people follow that man?"

"I don't really know." I said.

"That is it! You don't know. Come on now; he said, you got to have a better answer then that. What made your father do what he did? He wasn't born that way; or was he?"

"No, he was a good man."

"Well something made him the way he was. Your father was killing for the fun of it." He stopped and just took another drink.

I didn't know what to say to him. He was right. As for me I didn't have to do what I did. But at the time it was fun. I was the guard's enjoyment. Any time I would come down with my father they would hand me a whip and I would beat any Jew I saw. I still remember chasing them and beating them. The guards would point out the ones that were bad and tell me to 'teach them Jews'. I did or at I through I was. They told me the harder I hit them the better they would listen. So I hit them with all I had to make them be good and to show the guards how much I was like my father.

"So how what do we do?" I asked.

"Maybe it would be better if you didn't see each other again."

I know he didn't mean it. He was hurting and it was mostly because of me.

"Please I said I love you." .

"And I love you; he said. But it is hard for me to look at all the pictures and forgive."

"Please." I said.

"No," he yelled and stood up.

He took out a picture from his pocket and throws it on the table." Here he said. Frame it. This is you;" he said looking at me.

Oh shit it was me. I was standing over ten Jews and I had my foot on them and a whip in my hand. Like a hunter killing his game. I remember that day. I was the laugh of the guards. One of them had a camera and was taking pictures of what we did to the Jews.

"Where did you get it?" I asked.

He took another drink and said he had it all this time. He didn't want to show it to me. He felt bad just holding on to it, but he didn't want to throw it away.

"But why?" I said. I didn't know what I was doing. Why couldn't you throw it away?"

"Why? He yelled. See the two on the end; the man and woman? That is my mother and father. You whip them to," he said crying.

Oh god it wasn't; it was. I didn't know it was his mother and father. It was just some Jews to me.

"But why do you keep it?" I asked.

"Why? he said again this is all I have to show me what they looked like. You know how many times I wanted to throw it away. Millions of times; almost as many Jews that you killed. But I couldn't. You know what I would see every time I would tell myself to throw it away? You; he yelled. You and the way you held my head in the car. All I could remember was looking up at you and you crying for me and telling the German I was your friend; not to hurt me. That is why; he yelled. Your face looking at me and your hands wiping the blood away from my face. That is why. You know what is funny?" he said. I look at this picture and I got to look at it half and half. When I want to see my family I look at the bottom and when I want to see you I look at the top."

But when people come to me and show me pictures they have found or stories they tell, about what they went through. I look at the whole picture and get sick. Yes; he said I get sick. How does it make you feel?" He asked me.

"Sick," was all I could say. I didn't even want to look at it.

"You tell me; he said, did I pay you back?"

What did he want me to say? I didn't know, I don't think he knew what the answer was either.

He got up and said." I think I did."

He was going," where are you going?

"Anywhere; he said I got to have time to think. I'll call you;" he said going over to the door.

"You can't go;" I said.

"Oh and what is keeping me? You going to whip me to," he said.

Shit I was hurting and he was even hurting more than me. I guess I should let him go. I didn't want too, but the way he was feeling, it would only hurt the both of us more if he stead. I just watched him go and close the door.

What could I do to say; I'm sorry? Nothing, it was over with and the damage was do. Damage that time would never take away. He left the picture and as I went to pick up the bottle to take another drink I saw it just staring at me. I took the bottle and throw it. I didn't know why. The faces were looking at me and I couldn't stop looking at them. I must of fell asleep looking at them at the table. Did I say sleep? That wasn't the word for it. More like Night mares. I woke up in a sweat. My hands were shaking and my back was drenched for sweat.

All I remember was people I was whipping were doing it to me. And Seymour's face crying. People screaming were the noise I got use to at the prison. To others it was hearing the birds sing. To me it was hearing the people screaming all night long. Trains would come all hours of the night and day; bring Jews to be killed. I remember one officer telling my father Mr. Hitler was proud of the amount of Jews he was getting rid of. He told my father the Furi was going to come himself and give him the medal for his work. Shit I guess I must of blocked this all out of my head. I haven't thought about this in years. To me it was the bad past. I started remembering the day that Mr. Hitler did come. Shit that was the day this picture was taking. My father had me do it. Not the guards. He wanted to show Mr. Hitler how his son was carrying on in his name. Mr. Hitler gave me something that day.

I couldn't remember what it was. I know my mother took it from me and said she didn't want me to have it. My father got mad. But my mother hide it and wouldn't tell him where she hide it. What the hell was it? So many things I didn't want to remember. Now that I think about it I blocked out a lot. Was I telling myself something? Was I so sick I didn't want to remember? Then the bodies burning in the ovens came back in my mine. I just got on the floor and started to throw up. I know what happened that day and I fought it for many of years. Not to remember that day.

But now I did. The people were screaming and climbing over one and other to get away from the flames. The smell still was in my nose. "Kill me', I yelled, and passed out. The pain I was feeling was real so real I couldn't take it anymore.

CHAPTER 8

When I woke up on the floor I went and took another bottle from the shelf and started drinking, and looking at the picture. The only other thing I remember other then the people screaming was getting another bottle. I must have been drunk for days. No one came around and no one cared. I kept drinking and looking at the picture. When I finely came out of it, I got myself into the shower and just let the water run over me for hours. I had my eyes closed just seeing the faces. I open them and almost jumped out of the tub. It was Nancy. She was looking at me.

"What the hell happened here?" she asked.

I didn't know what she was talking about, till she helped me out and I went out into the room.

"Oh shit what did happen." I asked. My whole place was upside down. I mean everything was broken.

"Look, I said go and I'll call you later."

"No I'm not going anywhere; she said taking me to the bedroom. I never made it to the bed room. It wasn't touched. She took me to the bad and throws me on it.

"Stay here, she said I'll make you something to eat."

"No I said I wanted a drink."

"No way she said and pushed me back on the bed.

I guess she was right I had to snap out of it. I couldn't go on like this. I had to call Seymour and talk to him. For what? I didn't know. All I know I wanted to know he was still talking to me. That was all I cared for. I didn't want to lose his love.

She came back with coffee and more coffee. I had so much coffee. It was coming out of my ears. I got up and walked to the bath room and back to bed for a day. She stayed with me; she didn't ask anything she just cleaned up the place while I would pass out. I guess I need it. I know I was feeling better when I woke one time and she had come into bed with me. She had no clothes on and she came up against me. That was all it took I took her and cried as I did it. She didn't know why, she just laid on the side of me; after we finished and we both went to sleep.

The next morning she talked to me. She just asked if I wanted to talk about it?"

"Not really. I said. I couldn't." What was I going to tell her? No way was I about to tell my story.

"Nothing; I told her I just felt like celebrating."

"No she said I don't buy that. No one cries the way you did and has them kind of dreams."

"Dreams?" I said.

"Yes dreams; she said. You talked in your sleep and what you were saying was crazy."

"Look thanks, but I have nothing to talk about."

"Have it your way;" she said and went to take a shower. When she came back in I took my turn. She kept looking at me.

"Look, I said; forget what you heard, it is nothing. O.K.?"

"Have it your way, But I'm here if you want me."

"Thanks again But it is something I don't want to talk about. Just drop it please."

"It's dropped; she said, want to eat?"

"Want to go out and eat?" I asked her.

"YEA I guess you could use the fresh air;" she said why not.

We got dressed and went out. It wasn't as big as the first place we went to.

"It was just a small place with good food;" she said.

Anything, I was so hungry my stomach was growling at me. We ordered and she kept look at me.

"Please you're making me nervous."

"Look, she said. I'm sorry I didn't come sooner."

"For what? I said I didn't finished what I started to do. I would have just kicked you out. You came at the right time."

"You know we all thought you were out seeing the town with your brother. That is why we didn't check up on you."

"We?".

"The general was asking about you."

"He did give me a couple of days off; didn't he?"

"He did, she said so again we didn't worry about you."

"What day is this?"

"Saturday," she said.

"Shit, I was passed out for three days?"

"You tell me she said I don't know when you started."

"What day was the Generals Party?"

"Monday," she said

"Shit that means four days."

"You keeping track?" she asked.

"No, not really. It is something I really want to forget."

"Mined if I ask one thing?" She said before the food came.

"What?"

"Where is your brother?"

I looked at her and didn't know what to answer her.

"He is O.K. isn't he?" She asked.

"Oh,he had to go back."

"When? Before you passed out or after? Did you see him go?" She asked.

"Yes" I said thinking of the way he left." I saw him go."

We eat without saying a word. When it was time to go she took the check and said she had it. I'm glad she did I didn't have any money on me. I forgot my money. She said this was on her for doing what she did."

"Oh and what did you do?"

She said what she did with the Major.

"Hey I said stopping her. You have no obligation to me. You can come and go as you please."

"I know she said but it is the way I did it. Was that what made you go off?"

I was going to laugh at it but I couldn't tell her why I did it so I just use what she said to cover it and said.

"You did hurt." That was all I had to say, he was all over me. I guess she fell for it. Good I didn't want her asking to many questions I didn't have the answers myself. I had to talk to my brother again. That is if he would talk to me?

"Would you mind if we went back home?" I asked. She was glad I said that. She had sex on her mine and I had my brother on mine. We left and drove home; when we got there she ran in. I guess she was excited. I really didn't want to do it. But I didn't want her think why I didn't. She already through she was the reason I did what I did. I had to keep her thinking that. So we did it. My heart wasn't in it and she knew it. When we finished she looked at me and asked.

"You still mad at me?"

"I'll get over it." I said kissing her to show her I was still hers. She rolled over and went to sleep. I waited a while and then went out and tried my brother's line. I let it ring twenty times; either he didn't want to answer or he wasn't home. I know I had to go and see him. I didn't want to do it over the phone.

I left her a note and left. I was going to leave without waking her. She knows too much already. Oh shit the picture. Where did I put it? She cleaned up. Did she see it? Did she know it was me.? Where would she put it? I started looking all over. Then I saw it she had it under some papers. I took it and left. I had to see my brother, I couldn't let it go.

I drove to New York and went to his address. I pulled up and went to his door. He wasn't home. Now what? He did say he worked at this hospital. I didn't want to go there. I didn't want to miss him. I went to the phone on the corner and called. They said he was off and wouldn't be in till tomorrow. Shit that left only one place left. My uncles. Or I should say his uncle's.

Should I go? That was hard. I hurt the man enough. I could talk to Seymour. But with him I could see nothing but hurt. Either it was my lying or him knowing all about me. I just couldn't face him. Not after Seymour made me remember what I did. So I just waited for him at his place, he had to return some time. I went to the store on the corner and got myself something to drink. I had a feeling I was going to be there for a while. I was right; he didn't return. It was getting morning; and still he didn't show. I went back to the phone and called the hospital again. He still wasn't in. So I waited some more.

The sun came up and the people started walking around. I guess it was getting late. I got out and went to the store again. I had to eat something. I got a sandwich and soda and went back to my car. I finished it and was getting ready to go over my uncles when I saw him walking down the street. I got out and waited for him to get to his door. He didn't see me. He was walking slowly and you could see he was thinking. I know what he was thinking about. Me.

"Hey I said as he got up to me. He looked at me and took me into his arms. I was hoping this meant he still loved me. He pulled away and looked at me.

"Man he said. You look like shit."

I guess I did.

"How long have you been here?" he asked.

"A while." I said.

"Come. He opened the door and went in. I followed. "Come he said, you hungry?"

"No I said I just finished a sandwich. Thanks. "You eat." I said. He went to the ice box and took out some food. He put it in the oven and then sat.

"Well"? He asked. I don't have to ask what you're doing here. The thing we got to answer is what do we do about?"

"I was hoping you came up with something." I said.

"No he said I've been thinking. Boy was I thinking. I was thinking so much I had to take a couple of days off."

"You I said. I just woke up from drinking myself to death."

"You mean you kept on going?

I looked at him and said; "about three bottles later and from what Nancy said three to four days of passing out."

"You're kidding?" he said.

"I don't know. I don't remember."

"Man that is some drinking."

"Never again." I said.

"Look he said I don't know what or where we can go from here. I wish I did. The more I think about it the more I don't know what to do.

"Close our eyes and maybe it will go away." I said.

"No he said it is only going to get worse;" he said. I just came from one of them Jewish meetings. The one they started. 'Get the Nazi's campaign.' They had more movies; they got from the German Government. We spent hours looking at them; seeing if we know anyone that might still be alive. The Germans at the camps? he said. Records indicating where they might be. What country they took off to."

"That was the officers. I said. What about the soldiers?"

He looked at me and said. "There were teams out looking for them."

"And then what?" I asked.

"Kill them;" he said.

"So you're telling me what you're doing is the same thing that we did."

"No; he yelled, there is a big difference."

"And what is that?" I asked.

"Numbers;" he said. We're not looking to destroy the German race; were talking about a few hundred; not million's. We just want some satisfaction. So we can go on with our life's knowing we did something for the pain we went thru."

"Is it? I asked.

". Ha he laugh, look who is talking. What side are you on?

"I don't want to pick sides. I said I just want to see where we go from here."

"Look I did all I could, what more do you want me to do? He asked.

"I don't know. I'm looking for help. And you're the only one I can turn to."

"And who do I have to turn to? No one; he said. My uncle doesn't want to talk to me and his wife doesn't know why, so I can't talk to her. So who do I have ?

"Me; I said.

He looked at me and said "I guess we have each other. And that is all.

I know then and there we both loved each other. That was really what I wanted to hear. We hugged and crying like two babies.

"Look he said we just have to keep covering ourselves and hope for the best. We know it was a chance we were taking, but we know this all the time. I had to go on with my life one day at a time and so did he.

I had more to lose. I could end up facing my crimes for beating the Jews and helping kill them. Him, all that would happen to him was the Jewish faith would have nothing to do with him anymore. Something like a man without a country. He would be a man without a race. To him it would be like death. He loved being a Jew and he was proud of it. To take that away from him would hurt him. So I guess we had no chose but to go on and hope no one else finds out. If they did I would have to face it and take what was coming. I stayed over and left the next morning. He told me he would keep in touch and I said I would do the same. I needed him.

I got back at my place and I guess Nancy was at work. It was noon and she wasn't here. I changed and went to the office. Her eyes opened when she saw me walk in.

"Oh thank god she; said coming over to me. I didn't know what happened to you."

"I left a note." I said

"That was a laugh. It said. Have to take care of something see you later. That could have meant two years from now."

"I'm back. I said, she started kissing me.

"Arr the general said as he walking in. "Your both working?"

"Yes sir; we said.,

"Good then get the fuck out of each other's arms if you don't mine."

I guess his wife didn't give him anything last night. He was pissed.

"Well you coming back to work;" he asked?

"Yes sir," I said.

"Good, he said and walked into his office. I guess that meant to follow him. I did.

"Close the door;" he said as he went to his desk. I just stood in front of him and waited for him to talk. He went over some papers on his desk and then looked up at me.

"This might be right up your alley; he said handing me a file. Read it over and let me know," he said.

I took it and asked if he wanted me to read it here?"

"No he said go to your office and read it."

"I asked do I have one?"

"Of course you do, ask Nancy which one is yours?" He said getting back to his work.

I guess he didn't like the way my man acted at his party. I guess they did over act with his wife. But no harm done, at least I didn't see any. The only thing I saw was a punch of guys getting nowhere and his wife eating it up.

I took the file and left. Nancy was waiting for me.

"He is mad, isn't he?"

"He will get over it;" she said. It was the party, he never had low life's attended one before and it shocked him. His guest looked, but don't touch. Your men went overboard."

"Good; I said now maybe he won't invite us again.

She smile and said; "that would be nice." I know what she was getting at. Me and his wife. She didn't want to go through that scene any more. I could see she was trying to keep up with her, but couldn't. She had no practice. The general's wife did it all the time. To her it was a game. To Nancy it was to make me jealous. I think.

"The General said I had an office."

"Oh, she said getting up. Over at the end; yours;" she said and opened it.

"Shit, not very big." I said.

"But comfort, she said going in. It had a desk and a chair and file cabinets and a phone. That is all you need;" she said.

"What about a couch?" I said.

"Oh and what would that be use for?"

"Oh you know when I want to work overtime and get tired."

"Ha; she said I bet.

"No really.

She said; when I was here longer I'd get a bigger office, for how this was it.

"Major, she said.

That is right I did move up a rank.

"I had your uniforms changed;" she said. Looking at the one I had on. I still had the captain's bar on this one. She took out Major's stars and handed them to me.

"Can you do it or do you want me to?" she asked.

"I'll get them." I said and sat down. You have work to do?" I asked her.

"Yes sir," she said and gave me the finger walking out. I didn't want the General to think we played all day. I had work to do. Even thou I would like to try out my new office for sex.

Oh hell what a life. I opened the file and I was looking at a picture of my father. Oh shit what the fuck was this? Did he know about me and was just rubbing it in? My stomach went sour. I just sat and looked. I didn't want to do or say anything. He probable had an army outside my door waiting to lock me up. Then the phone rang. It scared the hell out of me. I jumped and just looked at it. I let it ring I didn't want to answer it. I just stood and looked at it. Then the door opened. Oh shit here it comes.

"You going to pick it up? She asked. Or are you just going to look at it? The General wants to talk to you."

Here it comes. I picked up the phone and he said;"you read it?"

"No sir; I said waiting for him to tell me I was under arrest. He didn't he just said; "well read it and get back to me." He hung up. Nancy just looked at me.

"You O.K.?" She asked.

"I'm all right." I said.

"Well you don't look it; she said. You're as white as a ghost. Oh she said looking down at the picture of my father. "I guess he would make anyone sick. The General said he was the one that killed your parents. Now it's your turn to get back at him;" she said.

What the hell did she mean? "I don't get you?"

"Well read it and you will see." She went back out and closed the door.

What the hell was going on? Something was up and I didn't like it. I turned the picture and looked at the note attached to it. Oh shit they think he is still alive and they want to find him. Why me?

I read on and it had all kind of people's report of seeing him. It ended with he was responsible for the death of 2 hundred and fifty thousand Jews. Plus he was connected to the disappearance of contraband that was taking from museums and Temple's. 'Worth over 20 million dollars'. He and he alone know where he put them. And to this day none of them have turned up. They suspect he took them when he left the country and is hiding some place with millions of dollars to support him with.

I didn't see my father get killed. It was the driver that told me he did. He could have been covering up for his escape; but why me? I got on the phone and called Seymour. I told him what my next assignment was. He didn't say a word. He went quite.

"Seymour you there?"

He came back on and said. "Well what are you going to do?"

"I don't know, that is why I called you."

"Me? You're going to have to make up your own mind;" he said.

"If I don't take the job someone else will, and if I do take it and find him; then what?"

"You and you alone only knew the answer to that."

He was right; he couldn't tell me what to do. If I was him I wouldn't know what to say either.

"My group is looking for him also;" he said.

"Why didn't you tell me this the other day?"

"Because, I didn't have the report on him till this morning; that is why. And still it is only a report. Nothing fact; just here say. You did say you saw him killed?"

"No, I said the driver told me he saw him get killed. I didn't see him."

"So he said it could be true. He could still be alive."

"He could!" I said.

Again he went silent.

"Seymour Please talk to me."

He came back on and said. "I'll give you a 24 hour head start; then I'm taking the file myself and if I find him first I'll kill him." He said.

I guess he change his mine about joining his group. The reason my father was still alive made him change his mind. I couldn't blame him I guess I would of do the same thing. My father did kill his mother and Father and a lot more. I see now what Seymour meant by he didn't have to do it at the end. The war was over and he still kept killing them. Just for the fun of it. I remember the last couple of days he wouldn't come home; he had my mother bring him his food. He wanted to stay and make sure he killed every last one of them. No way were the Americans going to set them free. Hitler wanted them dead and he was going to carry out his orders, even if he died doing it. To the last one; he told me one day when I went to see him. That was the last words I heard from my father. 'To the last one'.

Just thinking about it made me sick. How could he do it? They didn't do anything to him. The door opened and the General came in.

"Sorry; he said. I thought you would rather take it then give it to another agent. I'm sorry son, he said reaching for the file. I'll assign it to someone else."

"No I said stopping him."I'll take it."

"You sure;" he said looking at me.

"I'm sure I said and picked it up. This one is mine."

"Look, you don't have to."

"You're wrong, I told him. I do!"

That was the end of it; he just turned and walked out. I took the file and sat back. I read everything they had in it; four or five times. I wanted to know it inside and out. I don't know the reason I wanted it was to help Seymour find him; or to save him? Or kill him for what he did. I guess the only way to find out was to find him. That is if he was still alive.

CHAPTER 9

It said something about me and my brothers and my mother and sisters. The bodies of my sisters and Mother were found. My brothers from the last report were in the hands of the Russian's. As for me they said my body was so small that it could have burnt up with my mother and sisters. They weren't sure. It said he was in Brazil. So I guess that is where I start looking for him. IT said he goes under the name of Joe Smith.

I got up and closed the file and took it with me. When I walked out Nancy looked at me.

"You're really going to take it?" She said.

"I have to; I said. I'll never get any sleep knowing he is still alive; I said walking out the door. No good bye kiss,Nothing. I had my father on my mind.

I went home and pack my bags and headed for the air port. I guess I had to get started. I didn't want Seymour finding him ahead of me. Who knows my father might get to him first. I didn't want that. I know my father wouldn't hesitate to kill him. Seymour on the other hand wasn't a killer. It was up to me to find him first. All the way on the plane I was thinking of how I would do it. Then it came to me. Why not? It worked once. Maybe it would work again. I had contraband to sell and I had some one that wanted to buy. If he had it he would want to sell it. Ha that would be a laugh. As I was talking to him as a buyer, he would ask me, are you my son? I had to change the way I looked, but how? I know, a beard. That would cover most of my face. Plus he didn't see me for years. I'll have to take a chance and do it that way.

When I landed I checked in my room and did my lag work by phone and the Bell boy. I found out if you want to know anything ask the bell boy. If he didn't know he had a cousin that did, anything for money. I let my beard grow. By the time I got my first lead, it was full enough to walk the streets with. Brazil was a jumping place. People from all over the world flocked here for sun and fun. It was one of the country's that didn't ask questions. They didn't care who you were; as long as you brought money to spend. You didn't have money you were nothing.

I got the word out that I was looking for old artifacts and I would pay top dollar for them. Like I said; Money talks. I had the General set up anything I needed and being I was a new face, it was easy for me to go unnoticed. I wasn't known to the underworld. Nancy said she set a file up on me making me an antique dealer in rear artifacts. So I was ready as far as I know. The bell boy set me up with this guy that dealt in that kind of stolen merchandise. I told him I was interested in per columbine art. Knowing my father if he was here and if he was a live wouldn't have any. I was hoping it would throw them off the track for now.

I had a taxi take me to this bar that I was suppose to meet this guy. What a place, it was dark and dirty. Not a place where terrorist go. The people that were in this place I wouldn't turn my back on. I went over to the bartender and ordered a drink. He looked at me and asked if I look for someone?" Before he gave me my drink. I guess it showed. I told him the name of the man I was to meet. He looked over my shoulder at a table. I followed his eyes and saw this fat man in a white suit with a bottle in front of him. What else; I said to myself. He fit the pictures I saw in the movies once. I took my drink and walked over to him.

"Mr. Bull?" I said.

"That is me; was his answer. "Sit;" he said, kicking out a chair for me.

"I hear you have something I might be interested in?" I said sitting.

"Maybe I do and maybe I don't," he said.

"Well if you do, I'll drink. And if you don't I said I'll see you." I started to get up.

"Where you from?" He asked.

"Does it matter?"

"No, he said as long as you got the green. You could be from out of this world. It wouldn't matter," he said.

So do you or don't you?"

He looked over his bottle and said 'drink'. The sun is getting hot."

"I know I feel it, so do you have anything for me?"

He looked again and said" I have anything you want."

"Good, where?"

"Ha he laughs. Slow down it is getting hot outside."

"You said that before."

"Look you want to do business with me; you do it my way." Taking a drink straight from the bottle.

"And what is your way?" I asked.

"First you got to tell me how much you got to spend."

"You have what I want; the price is no object. I said. But don't think you can fool me."

"No my friend I don't fool people."

"No I said. Either did Hitler."

Ha, the man of men. He just smiled. What; you don't like him?" He asked. .

"Let's just say he got what he deserved."

"Oh my friend, there are more people out there just like him."

"I know that;" I said and lifted my shirt sleeve. He saw the number tattoo on my arm.

He laughs again and asked; "how did you escape?

"You're a funny man; I said, the same way you did." I acted as if I was getting mad. He backed down and changed the subject.

"You go back to you Hotel. My friend and I will get back to you."

"When?" I asked.

"My friend I said it was getting hot outside and the sun makes me hurt. I told you my way." He said again.

"I know; I said, but what is your way? Today, tomorrow or when?"

"That is right; he said, anyone of them will do.

You want, you wait; he said. I don't rush for no one my friend."

I could see why he was so fat he couldn't rush if he wanted to. I had to take my time I wasn't going to blow it. I got up and looked at him.

"My friend; I said. I well be here no longer then Fri. I hope we can meet again;" I said.

"We will see;" he said and took another drink from the bottle.

I left and when out to get my cab. It was gone,. Shit I told him to wait. Now what? I didn't know where I was. Find another cab; I said and started walking. What the hell I had all day knowing the way he moved.

I walked to what seemed to be the busy place in town. Shops and food markets, people were running around buying anything in sight. Then I saw this shop that said Pre-Columbian. I went in and looked around. The place was filled with statues of all kind. What the hell I might as well get to know what I was looking for.

"May I help?" This old man asked. He was sitting between the shelves.

"Ohhh I said, you scared me."

"No mean to; he said. Just sitting, you got money?" he asked.

"Did everyone ask that question?" I asked.

He smiled and said." Most people just look. You got money I get up. You just look I stay down. I guess he told me where it was at.

"Maybe both; I said. Now what do you do?" I asked him.

"Me stay till you call;" he said.

I could see no one moved around here.

'Good; I said you do that." I kept looking. The place had all kinds. What were real and what was fake? That is what I wanted to know. I picked one I liked and showed it to him. "How much?" I asked.

"Oh he said you pick good one."

"How much?" I asked again.

"You know it is very old;" he said. For some reason I didn't believe him.

"Get out of here; I told him. You just made it."

"Ohhhh; he said, you know?"

"Look I can see all of them are just made. Where are the real ones?" I asked.

"You pick out one;" he said.

Was he kidding? I couldn't tell.

"You so smart; he said you tell me."

This must be his way of finding out if you know, and if you didn't they were all old. He would charge you an arm and a lag for one.

"No, I said you can't fool me. How much?" I asked again.

"Oh you talk big; he said. You just look; he said and don't bother me." He laid his head down as if he was going to sleep.

Crafty old man I said to myself. I just looked at all of them, just to know what they looked like. Then over in the corner I saw one. It didn't look any different from the others on the shelves. But one thing stuck out. It had a cloth under it. It was places in such a way you wouldn't notice it. If you had something priceless that is what I would do. Place it on something that would protect it.

"How much?" I said getting ready to pick it up. His head came up and his eyes opened and he smiled.

"No touch and not for sale," in the same breath.

"Oh I said then why you have it out?"

He got up and came over to me." For ass holes;" he said.

"Oh. That is a good reason. This ass hole wants to buy it." I said.

"Who are you?" He asked.

"Oh no body; I said. I just came down for some sun and fun. I'll give you ten American dollars for it;"and went to pick it up.

"No; he yelled you no touch."

I stopped and looked at him. "This the only one you have?"

"You smart man;" he said. You find only old one. Now go; he said. I don't sell."

"But you got it on the shelf for sale."

"No; he said, for ass holes;" he said again.

"Let's stop the shit. I said. I know the real from the fake. You want to sell it?"

"No;" he said.

"O.K. I said then I'll go. I'll buy mine off of Mr. Bull."

"Ha he laughs and said; that fat pig."

"Oh, you know Mr. Bull?"

"I know; he said and went back to his chair.

"Why you laugh?" I asked.

"You will find out;" he said and put his head back down as if he was going back to sleep. I know I wouldn't get anything out of him so I started to walk out.

Just then two men came in. They went right over to the man and pushed him. They said something In French. I know what they were talking about. They were Mr. Bull's man.

The old man looked over at me and smiled. I didn't want the two guys to see me so I left. I waited out of the shop on till the two men left. They were carrying something. They got into their car and took off.

Ten to one this Mr. Bull was setting me up with new statues. I had to see the old man again. I went back in. He wasn't sitting in his chair. I looked around for him, he was gone.

"Hello; I said walking around looking. The place was small and he couldn't hide that good. He must have a back door. I was about to walk out when I tripped on something. It was dark I didn't see what it was. The mown came from whatever I hit. It was the old man. The guys beat the hell out of him. I got him up and sat him back on his chair.

"What happened?" I asked.

He looked at me and said; "water please." He pointed to this bowl. I went and got him some and took a rag he had next to it. I dipped it in and wiped his face off. He wasn't that bad. Just his nose.

"Thank you;" he said as he drank.

"You want me to get the police?" I asked.

"No; he said laughing. They do no good."

"What the hell happened?" I asked.

"You're Mr. Bull;" he said.

"Come, you got a place to lie down, you don't look to good."

"Oh, no worry they do it all the time." He said.

"Do what? I asked. Beat you?"

"No, he said. I did that;" he said.

"Oh you beat yourself"? I asked.

"No, he said. I made them mad."

"Oh I see."

"Would you help me;" he said getting up. I took his arm and helped him to where he wanted to go.. He walked over to this shelf and went behind it. Then he went into this room. I know he had to have some place else. He walked over to a bed. I helped him sit down.

"Thank you, he said; now go."

"I guess it is none of my business. But I got to ask you one thing. He just looked at me.

"Were they the statues Mr. Bull is going to try to sell me?"

He smiled and laid down on the bed.

I guess he didn't want to talk. If they did this to him, they could come back and finish the job. I didn't want the old man getting hurt so I left. I found a cab and went back to my hotel. At least I know the pre columbines weren't real. That might work out for the better, me knowing about them.

I got to my room and hit the shower. They were right the sun did take it out of you. I was feeling tired. I got on the bed and closed my eyes. Now for him to make the first move. I went to sleep.

When I opened my eyes again the sun was gone and the stars were out. I called down to the desk and asked if anyone called for me.

"No sir; the guy at the desk said and hung up. Oh hell I couldn't wait in here. I had to get out and breathe. With just a fan it took some getting used to. I took another shower and got dressed. I went to the hotel dinner room and sat down. A waiter came over and took my order. I eat and when I finished I went to sign the check. What was this? There was a note on the plate with the bill.

"Your room." Seymour.

Shit he was here to. I looked around but he was nowhere to be seen.

I got up and headed for my room. He was sitting in it already.

"How did you get in?" I asked.

"The bell boy will do anything for money."

"I found that out." I told him. Well Brother how are we going to do this? I asked him. Work together or separately?"

"I would like to work together. He said. But I don't know if we can."

"I don't get what you mean." I said.

"Your father; he said what happens if it is him?"

"I don't know; I said, take him in and have him stand trial. Kill him, what?" I asked, what do you want me to say?"

He looked at me and sat down." I don't know, but we got to do something about him." He kept looking at me.

"What?" I asked.

"Your beard.

"Oh I said. I didn't want to take any chances. You like?" I asked him. He laughs and said, it didn't fool him.

"You seen me only last week. I said. My father hasn't seen me for years."

"True, he said, it looks good, kept it."

"Thanks I will."

"So now what?"

"Look I didn't like what my father did any more then you did."

"That was after you saw what he was doing. When you were with him you enjoyed it."

"Let's not start that again." I said. The way I feel now I'll take him back and lock him up."

"Would you?" He asked.

"I think so;" I said.

"Then he will tell the world who you are."

'That is the chance I'll have to take; I said.

"You're willing to take that chance?" He asked.

"I'm willing;" I said. He didn't believe me, but what else could he do.

"Just remember I'll be right behind you;" he said.

"I hope so;" I said and took his hand. "Brothers" I said holding it.

"Brothers" he said and taking mine into his.

"So what have you got so far;" he asked?"

I told him about Bull and the old man in the shop.

"Good he said. It is smart of you not to ask directly for the German. This way it will throw them off.

"Maybe I was hoping it would and how about you?" I asked.

He took out a file from his pocket and opened it.

"You know him? He asked. He showed me another man's face.

"No, I don't think so;" I said.

"Look close;" he said.

"No, he don't look formulae to me."

"You sure?" he asked.

"I'm sure I don't know him."

"He is your father's brother.

"Hold;" I said remembering the time he came to the farm to tell my father about Hitler. "Yes I said. He does look formulae. He is him. I only saw him once and I was very small. But something about him I remember. That is him."

"You sure?" he asked.

"Almost;" I said. It did something to me when you said that. I saw his face again. Younger but his face, yes that is him."

"He is with your father here;" he said and the two of them work together."

"Shit; I said, how come we didn't pick it up."

He said. We dig deeper. You just want to find all the money. We intern want our scrolls back."

"You're what?" I asked.

"Temple Scrolls worth millions; dating back to the beginning of our time. Your father took them from temples along with all the gold he could find. The gold we don't care about, it is the scrolls we want back. Hitler may have destroyed my people; we don't want him to destroy our history. If we don't get them back he will have done that also."

"Do people know how importune they are?"

"Any Jew knows."

"What about my father?" I asked.

"Maybe not; he said. Oh don't get me wrong he knows they are worth money. He just doesn't know how importune they are to us. If he did he would have destroyed them by now."

"You think so;" I asked.

"Yes that would have been like killing all of us at once. He doesn't know what they mean to us."

I know he didn't want to get into it about how my father was. I know he was telling the truth. My father would have destroyed them just for the hell of it, if he knew what the Jewish people felt for them; and enjoyed every minute of it.

"What else do you have?" I asked

"Nothing; he said he just got here."

"Good, I think it would be best if we weren't seen together. He agrees, but we have to stay in touch."

"How?" He asked.

"Where are you staying?" I asked him.

He told me a hotel on the other side of town.

"Good, I'll call and ask for a doctor anything." The key word will be doctor. Once you know it is me, I'll just give you numbers, First will be the time and the next will be the place we will meet.

"Good, he said, but how will I know what you're talking about?"

I took out a piece of paper and wrote down a simple code I learned in class.

"Easy, I said remember it and throw it away."

"Good," he said and got up. I just took him and hugged him. That was all we said. He left and I lay down to rested.

I didn't need it but what else was I going to do? Mr. Bull should be contacting me soon. I hope. I was right. He sent someone to my room. It was one of the guy's from the shop. He told me Bull wanted to see me.

"About time to damn hot here." I said and went with him.

He had a car waiting out front. The same car they drove this morning. I got in and off we went. We didn't go back to the bar we went the other direction. He pulled in front of this house. We got out and he opened the door for me, he didn't say a word he just showed me in. There he was Mr. Bull, as fat as ever. This time he was eating.

"Come; he said sit and join me."

"No I said. I just finished eating thank you. You have something for me?"

"In due time; he said. First I eat."

"Look why don't you just show me what you have and while you eating I could be looking at them.

"You going someplace?" He asked.

"Yes I said to other sellers if you don't have what I want."

"Not here;" he said.

"Oh, I know that;" I say. You control it all here."

"Smart man;" he said picking up some kind of lag to eat.

"So I said can we start."

He looked at the guy that was standing at the other end of the room.

"Bring" was all he said. The guy left and came back with four Pre Columbine.

"Nice; I said as he brought them to the table. He put them down in front of me." Nice very nice." I said picking one up.

"Be careful they are a lot of money."

"Oh I said. And how much is a lot of money?"

"Oh, he said eating again; for you; if you buy them all I guess I could give you a good price."

"You still haven't told me anything;" I said.

"Look and make me an offer."

"Come now you must have a price in mind?"

"Oh he said I do, but you may not want to pay it."

If they are the real thing I'll pay. You can bet on that."

"The real thing; he said laughing. I deal with nothing but the best. I got my name on the line." He said.

"May I," I asked picking one up.

"What is it they say in your country? You brake you pay? It goes in this country also."

I laugh and said priceless pieces like this have to be touched by only people that know;" I said.

"Ha, he said I don't touch them; he said. One time I dropped one. The grease was on my hands and I dropped it;"

I smiled and say. "You always have grease on your hands."

He didn't think that was funny. I did. I put the first one down and picked up the next one.

"Good" he said with his mouth full.

I didn't answer him. I went from one to the other. On the last one I just held it.

"How much;" he asked.

"Do you know how to tell the real from the fake?" I asked him?

"No he said I just sell them."

"Will; I said holding the one I had in my hands up high. "You drop it."

He choked on whatever he was eating.

"No; he tried to say.

But I said first. "I don't know what you take me for. I said, but your game isn't funny."

"Oh he said after he finished what he had in his mouth.

"They are good; I said but anyone could buy good statues. I'm not anyone and if you think you're going to sell me these, you're crazy".

"You doubt me;" he said getting up.

"Let's say I do. I throw the statue in the air to see if he would try to go for it; to save it. He didn't. "See I said, you know they are fake."

"You are a smart man; he said. How did you know?"

"Look let's stop the shit, now do you or don't you?"

"I don't;" he said.

"What the fuck you doing to me?" I asked.

He looked over at the other guy and said, checking you out."

"For what; you have nothing."

He laughs and said. "If you would have bought them I would have had more for you."

"Well I didn't, so stop playing games. Get me back to the hotel." I said turning around to walk out the door.

"Wait; he said not getting away from the table. I didn't think he would leave his food." I got something else;" he said.

"What, more shit?"

"No gold; he said. Old gold.

"Sorry, I don't buy gold."

"But he said, you will buy this gold."

"No I said I don't think so. Take me back;" I said. Just them someone came in from behind the curtain.

"You a Jew?" He asked.

"Who the hell is he, I asked Bull. Look I said I didn't bring any money with me if that is what you're thinking."

"Oh no; Bull said; we don't do business that way."

"Good I said taking out my gun and pointing it at his head." Take me back; I said. For a minute I thought he was going to lose whatever food he eaten. He took a deep breath and before he could say anything the guy that came out from behind the curtain took his gun out and held it on me.

"You see; he said you're not the only one that has one."

Oh shit it was my uncle. I tried not to show it. So I just kept my gun on the pig.

"So it comes to this. O.K. I said when I count to three we firer. You get me, but I get him I said and maybe I get you to." Pointing my other finger at him.

"Go; he said, he is a pig anyway." My uncle said to me.

"What the fuck is going on here?" I said. I come to buy now I got a shootout. This is crazy." I said.

"You must forgive my fat friend; he likes to play games.

Bull was sweating as we talked. He didn't say a word; he just watched us with the guns..

"You mean he doesn't run this show?"

"No my good man this pig can't run nothing. If it means anything to you sir; he said to me. I'll let you shot him."

"Hey, the Bull said. Let's call it a bad day and forget it."

"You my fat friend have do this to many times. This Man here has a right to shot you. He saw what you were doing. Be my guest;" he said to me putting his gun back.

"Oh hell why not." I took a shot at him. I aimed at his food plate. I blow it off the table.

"That would hurt him more." I said. As the food went all over the place.

My uncle laughs at it.

"Come he said. He walked out the door and I followed. The bull must have been thinking of getting sick. His stomach was moving like a volcano as I passed him.

I got into this big car with my uncle. We sat in the back. "Now you wish to go back to your hotel?" He asked.

"I think so; I said. I have other business to do."

"Maybe I could interest you in some other rare treasures."

"Oh; you have some Pre columbine?"

"No, he said I much better."

"And what might that be?"

"Artifact from Germany."

"No; I said I don't think so."

He looked at me and asked if I was Jewish again?"

"What does that have to do with it?" I asked.

"Oh nothing he said it is just that we have these scrolls."

"Hold on; you're doing what the fat man did." I said.

"No, my good man;" he said these are real."

"Where did one obtain such scrolls?" I asked?

"Germany of course." He said.

"If it is true what you say, I would have to have them looked at by my people. Too many of them are fake."

"So, he said. You are interested?"

"Let's put it this way, if they are what you say they are I might be."

"Oh my good man; believe me they are."

"You said "WE" before, you're not meaning the fat man again?"

"Oh no; he laugh he is only our front man. He finds out the real buyers for us."

"This "US" if I might ask."

"Oh just me and my brother are the only ones you will deal with."

"You have to admit you're not giving me too much to go on. Let's say I have a bad taste in my mouth over this."

"My good man; he said. I don't blame you. I would also have one if it happened to me. The fat man will pay for this;" he said.

"It isn't the fat man I'm talking about. He knew what I meant. German's and Jew's don't mix.

"How do I know you're not bringing the war here with you?"

"Money my good man."

"YOU being Jewish know the meaning of the word Money. You see us German's learned from you Jew's."

"Yea I bet you did."

"Well my good man, what shell it be?"

"How many scrolls are we talking about?"

"Say one hundred of them."

"Sorry my good man; I said to him. You're lying. I know for a fact there isn't a hundreds left from Germany. We have traced them and most of them were destroyed. If you said you find two or three we would be happy. You say a hundred. You Lye; I said. Take me back to my hotel." I said taking out my gun.

"What if I show you them?" He said.

"Look my good man you see this? I said showing him my numbers. I know I was there and I saw a lot of them destroyed."

"You think you saw them destroyed. What you saw was copies of them going up in smoke. The real ones were hiding before they were set on fire.

"The only man that could have done that is dead." I said.

"I see you do know what took place."

"Like I said I was there. He went to reach for something.

"Hold it," I said putting my gun up.

"No my good man; he said. Allow me; he took out a pen. "Now you see it. Then it was gone. Now you don't. That is how the scrolls did it." He said

"If you say you have is real. Then you would have no trouble letting me look at them. All of them?"

"Of course not; my good man; he said. You see one thing about this country here. We pay for protection and no one can leave if we don't want them to. So you can look all you want; he said. I'll drop you off at your Hotel and I'll have my driver bring you one to have it checked out. Now does that sound as if I want to fuck you?"

"That is only one." I said.

"If you like the one and we come to some kind of price you may check them all. As I said you cannot leave the country so we have nothing to lose." He said.

He was right the Government works that way. You could come and live here and bring money all the money you want. But you can't leave without them saying so.

"You got yourself a deal." I said

He told the driver to head back for my Hotel. When I got out he smiled and said" Luckhime.

I didn't want to answer him. I got out and walked into the hotel without looking back. What he said was an insult to the Jewish people. Here was a German talking Jewish and getting rich over their dead bodies.

For a moment I forgot he was my Uncle. Now I knew my father was still alive. I didn't want to rush it. I still had to see him for myself. I still didn't know what I was going to do with him once I came face to face with him.

I went back to my room and called Seymour. I gave him the place for us to meet. He hung up without saying a word. I left my room. I went out and sat at the bar. I had time to kill. I didn't want to run right out. I had to make sure no one was following me. What the hell was I doing? I must be crazy. Me and my brother can't handle this by ourselves. I needed help, like they said, team work. I got to the phone and called Nancy; she was to be my contact. We had it set up so she would know what I was talking about when I called.

"Hi I said when she got on the phone.

"Well? She said. You have anything for us?"

"I think I have better; I said, but I'm going to need some help with it."

"Oh she said, sounds good. She was acting as my buyer. Just in case someone was listening in on my call. They know I was here to buy, so it sounded as if I bought.

"What is the price? She asked.

"Have them bring the bank." I said. That meant I need men and back up.

"Would tomorrow be O.k.?" she said. That meant the day after. I had to stall them till then.

"That would be great; I said. I see no trouble in getting them out of the country. That meant I might have trouble with the Government here, so be ready for it. "Love you;" I said. That meant I wasn't in any danger.

"I love you to. That meant she loved me. Ha that was a laugh. No code for her saying it.

I walked out into the garden and looked around. No one was watching me that I could see. So I went out over the wall and on to the street. If anyone was I guess I lost them. I waited to see if anyone went over the wall to follow me. Good No one. I walked to the place I told my brother. All the way I was looking behind me. Nothing. I saw him coming, he was on time.

We went down this alley and to this little cafe. We sat and I told him I meet my uncle.

"He asked;" was my father was with him? What did you do?" He asked.

"Nothing. I said. I set it up to meet them together."

"You did?" He said. Just like that?"

"Just like that." I said

"No trouble?" He asked.

"None so far." I said.

"They brought your story?" He asked.

"Hook line and sinker." I said

"It is going to easy;" he said.

"No; I said, this made it go." I said showing him my number.

"You're kidding?" he said. He knows you're a Jew?"

"Am I?" I asked him.

"You're my brother." he said.

"Good then you wouldn't mind coming along with me the next time we go."

"What?" he said. You told them about me?"

"No I just said I needed someone to verify the scrolls."

"What scrolls?" He asked.

"Oh, he said him and my father had over a hundred of them."

I could see it took his breath away. I guess you had to be Jewish to appreciate what they meant.

"You joke with me." he said

"No brother they said they didn't burn them. They said they had them."

"Do you know what this means to my people?" He said almost crying.

"What ever it does. I said. You're going to tell me."

"Yes, he said. We have our life back again."

"But there only paper." I said.

"Paper no; he said. Our great Rabbi's wrote them many years ago and they tell of what our people are. I can't wait to tell my people what you have done."

"Hold on; I said. We're not out of the woods yet. First we have to make sure they are what they say they are, and second how are we go to get them, my father and Uncle out of the country without the government stopping us? Don't get too excited just yet. The hard part is yet to come."

"We can do it; he said. I'll have my people come and help us."

"Hold on I said. I have my people coming and that is enough. We don't need to start a war."

"Your right he said I'll let you handle it."

"The only part that has me worried; that is when I meet my father I don't blow it or he recognizes me, and blows the whole thing."

"I will be by your side." he said. So how what"? He asked.

"They said they would drop one off at my hotel for me to check out. The one thing going for us is they think the Government is going to protect them at all cost. This is why they feel free dealing with us."

"That is good," he said

"But it is also bad. As I said before we may not be able to get the scrolls out of the country without starting a war. What I'm saying is that we might have to forget about; my father and uncle for now that is. Just on till we get the scrolls out of the country. To take both of them out may not be a good idea." I said. He just looked at me and said.

"That is a tough one."

"I know, so what will it be?"

He looked at me and said "Let's play it as it comes."

"No I said, we have to make up our mind now. We can't go in blind. We have to know what we are going to do. One or both or which one do we do?"

That is going to be up to us. He said and no one else."

"Just you and me." I said. Oh my uncle said Lock hem when he left".

"That pig. You sure it was him?" He asked.

"As sure as I'll ever be."

"O.K the scrolls are more importune than them, he said you could come back later for them."

"Oh one another thing. It is going to cost a lot of money. They know what they have and they plan on getting every penny they can from the Jews for them."

"For them the war is still on, he said. Kill the Jews any way you can." He said.

I didn't know what to say. It was my father and Uncle he was talking about. Was I getting feeling for my father? I kept thinking back to when he was the man I looked up to. He was the man that took me over my brothers; he was the man that made me feel like a king when I was with him. He was the man that thought me how to hate.

"Maybe it would be better if we came back for him." I said. If the scrolls meant that much."

He looked at me and said. Thank you, they do. Maybe this will show the world you're not the Generals son." He said. Wouldn't that be nice if you didn't have to worry about them finding out about you anymore? You could come right out and said it." I was the general's son but look what I did. No one would hate you."

He had a point they. Maybe, it would turn out for the better this way.

"So what about the money? I asked.

"We will get it; he said. Just find out how much?"

"Then we will meet with them."

"You'll have to give me a couple of days." he said.

"I would expect that and so will they. They knew I didn't expect to buy them.

"That was a good plan he said that gives us time that way.

"So my brother go and do what you have to do. I will call you when they bring the first one to me. Remember you are my expert on it and only that. No getting into a fight whatever they do.

"Lock hem;" he said and left.

I got up and went my way. It was getting late and I was feeling tired. I got back to the hotel and went to my room. For some reason I felt some one was in it. I guess they were checking to see what they could find out about me. Lucky thing I didn't have anything to give me away. Then I remembered the picture. The one of me standing on Seymour's mother and father. Oh shit it was gone. They got it. How what? They would find out about me.

I had to think fast. I had to go see Seymour before they came with the scroll. I know they would come and get me. But for what? Having the picture? Who was I to carry this picture? What did I want? I know that is the questions they would ask me. Just then the door came opened. My uncle was standing there with three other men.

"I wouldn't; he said pointing his gun at me. One of the other men came and took my gun from me.

"How would you mind coming with me?"

Shit I know it was going to easy. How was I going to warn Seymour?

"What is this all about? I asked. You are doing a Mr. Bull?"

"We don't work that way;" he said.

"Then what is it?

"My brother and I want to talk to you."

"So I have a phone."

"You're a funny man; he said. Now please don't make me shoot you."

"I'll try not to; I said. But it would be nice to know what is going on."

"You will find out; he said now move."

They took me down the back stairs and out to the waiting car. We got in and off we went. He didn't say anything he just looked at me. Shit I hope he didn't recognize me. I tried to talk to him. He just told me I would find out when we got there". I could see he wasn't going to talk.

We drove out of town and into the hills. We pulled up to what looked like a fort. The main gate had guards. It opened and they let us pass. Then we came to this big house. More like a castle. We stopped and he got out.

"Would you mind if I went back to my Hotel? I forgot something."

"Funny; funny man." he said. I didn't know Jews were so funny? Get out;" he said and held the door open for me.

Two more guards at the door. Shit he didn't have anything to worry about. He had an army protecting them. We went into this big room. That was when I saw my father for the first time since the day the Americans came. He was standing looking at us. He got old but he was still a handsome man. He kept his weight down and he grow a mustache. His hair was all white and he looked like a king standing there.

"Well what have we here? Another Jew I see." He said. At lease he didn't know who I was. I didn't know if that was good or bad. I would soon find out I bet. I take it you two know each other;" he said looking over at the other end of the room. Oh shit it was Seymour. I started to go for him but my uncle held me back.

"How touching; he said. You Jews always had that about you's, even when you were dying. Nice; my father said but you will have time for that later. Sit he said to me, pointing at a chair next to Seymour. We have some questions we would like to know."

"Look whatever your name is? I don't know what the hell is going on, but this here man is the man I have to check the scroll out. What are you doing?

"Look sir Jew; my father said. Something doesn't smell so good to me."

"I didn't know it was supposed to smell good I said all we want is our scrolls back. And we are willing to pay for them. I don't see a problem with that; I said. We can get the money." I said. We just want to make sure they are what you say they are."

"Where did you Jews get that kind of money first or all?" My uncle asked.

"The same way you krauts did. I said. We steal it."

"See I told you he was funny." My uncle said to my Father.

"That is good; he said. He is going to need it."

My father took out the picture and held it up to our faces. Seymour didn't know they had it. He looked surprised to see it. I had to do all the talking before he said anything to make it worse.

"Oh that? I said; that is my friends he left it at my place when he came to see me. It was the last picture he had of his mother and father."

"Of course you two didn't know I was the general at this camp?" My father said.

"Oh we did." I said quickly.

"So he said you're not here to kill me?"

"That thought entered our mind." I said fast. But you see us Jews think before we do anything."

"Oh my uncle laughs, listen to him. The funny Jew thinks."

"Yes, I said; if your kind of people did that you might still be in Germany."

My father came over and hit me with the back of his hand. "You're not being so funny now;" he said.

"Go ahead you ass hole; I said to him. Kill two more if it makes you feel any better."

"Oh yes; he said; it will; and walked over to Seymour. So my little Jew this is your mother and father?"

I looked at Seymour and hope I said enough for him to catch on to what I was doing.

"Yes;" he said.

"So the two of you are going to kill me and become heroes to your people?"

"Now look who is a funny man; I said. Killing you would mean nothing to my people. Your dead anyway."

He came at me again and hit me.

"Arr you do that good; I said I can see you didn't lose your touch."

"He is not only funny; my uncle said but a little crazy to boot."

My father looked at me and asked; "how I was intending to get away with it?"

"Look if you're that stupid what is the sense of me talking. Kill us and get it over with."

My uncle said to my father; do it and get it over with."

"Ha, I said laughing.

"You find it funny?" my father asked.

"Oh yes I said that goes to show you's haven't change, your still as dumb as ever."

He hit me again.

"We are not dumb;" he said.

"Oh and what would you call it?" I asked.

"Killing you is not dumb;" he said.

"Look ass hole, I told him. You have a chance to make some money and the two of you are going to blow it. Just, Like your Mr. Hitler. He blow it too."

I got hit again.

"He did not blow it;" my father said swinging at me.

"Then what would you call it? I asked. Here you got the means to sell something that no one else will buy, and all you can think about is killing Jews. You tried that once and didn't do such a good job. Now the two of you are going to try again. I should have guessed it would come to this." I said.

"What are you talking about?" My Uncle asked.

"The scrolls; I said. No one will buy them off of you except the Jews, and we are the only Jews that can. So you kill us and what do you have? Nothing; like your Mr. Hitler had."

"You know we can kill you and get away with it."

"This country protected you and we would be shot on the street. Plus with your army you have outside. We are not as stupid as you Germany were." I had to keep talking. I couldn't stop. "Besides the scrolls are more importuning then the likes of you's. We the Jewish people for give."

"See; my uncle said. I told you he was crazy."

"No; Seymour came in with, my mother and Father live on the inside of me. The same thing with the scrolls, they live on inside of us. You can burn us and burn them, but you can't burn our souls."

"See, My father said to my uncle this is why Hitler had to get rid of them. They all are sick with this Jew thing."

"Oh what do you call a Jew thing? Money."

They both looked at each other.

"You heard me, I said. Money. If you do anything to us. No Jew will want the scrolls after that. So again you will have nothing. No brains and no Money. I said. Your Mr. Hitler was mad; we Jew's had all the money and brains. Isn't that why it all started?"

"Some Jew will buy;" my uncle said.

"No, Seymour said. This is it; if we don't bring them back my people will never buy them."

They looked at each other and then told a guard to take us away. I know it would get to them. They needed money. He took us to this room and locked us in. Seymour was going to talk when I held his mouth. I pointed to my ears. Meaning they were listening to us. He knew what I meant so we did our talking with our hands and eyes. I know how to do this from watching the Jews at the camp. They couldn't talk so they had this way of talking. I told him I was sorry but the greed of money will help us. They didn't know who we were. And if that failed; I'll tell them who I am."

"No, he said you can't do that."

"I have to, I said I'll tell them to let you go and give you the scrolls. They won't hurt you;" I said.

I didn't want to do it. For some reason I didn't want to have anything to do with them. But if it meant saving Seymour life I had to.

About an hour later they came for us. They took us to another room. It was like a big safe.

"Come, my father said and see what your people gave to me."

Seymour went in first, I could tell by the way he stopped and looked, it was something. Tears were coming to his eyes.

"See my father said. We have everything from your people.

There were painting, statues, gold cups, and a wall of rolled scrolls, plus Books, hundreds of them.

"This is my Jewish temple." My father said, laughing.

"May god strike you dead?" Seymour said?

"Oh, my uncle said, he tried that already. But he didn't make it."
They both laugh at that.

"You're a funny man now." I said.

My father looked at me and said. "What would a Jew give for all this?"

I looked at Seymour. I know by the way he looked it was all real.

"You're the one that has to give the price." Seymour said.

"Oh how let me see Brother, what would you say?"

"Oh my uncle said. How much do you have?

"I could see they were going to play games."
Seymour said to them.

It almost chocked me when he said it. "We have ten million dollars set aside for recovery and investigation. That is all the money we have. Take it or leave it;" he said.

My uncle said, "ten million? We were figuring at least twice that."

Seymour looked at him and said. "That is all we have; so either you take it or you don't," he said firm.;

"Oh I don't know, my father said, we have to think about it. Come he said you seen enough." He pulled Seymour out the door and closed it. "You see we have what we say we have. I think you had better come up with a lot more money than that."

"You fucking theists." I said going at my father. The guard held me back.

"Now, Now Jew;" he said.

"Look you could never spent all that money. You couldn't destroy us before you will never destroy us now. Take what we have left and forget about us."

"Oh how touching. Take them away;" he told the guard.

They put us back in the same room.

"They aren't going to go for it" Seymour said. They want more. We don't have it. We don't even have the ten million. I know once I tell my people what they have my people will come up with it."

"Ten million?? I said. Where will they get that kind of money?"

"Do you know what they have there?" He said.

"Our whole life, we can't just let them destroy it. And that is what they would do if they can't sell it. Just for the hell of it. I can see it."

"Look, what if you tell them you just want the scrolls. And they can keep the gold."

He looked at me with the tears coming.

"I guess I couldn't expect you to understand what it means to us. You're not Jewish;" he said.

"I guess I can't;" I said. But what are you going to do?"

"I don't know; he said. It was different before I know what they had. Now that I saw, God help them," he screamed. I took him and just held him. He was losing it. I couldn't let him do that. He had to have it together. We had to have control, we had to outsmart them.

"Look I have to tell them who I am. That is the only way we will get out of here. Knowing them they will take the money and destroy the scrolls any way. I know what they are thinking. Man like my father will never let a Jew win."

"Maybe your right; he said, but what will you do?"

"I don't know I said whatever I'll do it once you're away from here."

"You're my true brother," he said, holding me.

Well the time has come. I had to face it. It was me or Seymour and his whole Jewish Race. I felt I had to do it.

"Guard, I yelled. Get me my father." I said.

"You're what? He said laughing. You have gone crazy. Get back and keep quite. He went to push me. I took the gun off of him and had him on the ground. I stuck his own gun in his mouth.

"Now do I shot you or you tell my father I want to see him? I didn't have to waste;"

Another guard had his gun at my head. I didn't care if you shot me I just wanted to see him."

My uncle came running down the hall.

"Stop; he yelled. What is going on?" He asked the guard.

"He is going crazy;" he said as I got up.

"No, I said, Uncle Hans. It is me Joseph." I stood up and waited for him to say something.

"My brother will kill you; he said looking at me. No one says that about his Joseph. Joseph is dead."

"No Uncle; I said the day you came to my farm to tell my father Hitler wanted him. That was the day we left home and the German soldiers took the farm over." I said to remind him I was who I said I was.

He didn't say a word he just looked at me. I added "You came back in the first car we ever saw. My mother and sister's feed you. The picture you have is me holding my foot on the Jews. Remember Mr. Hitler gave me his gun?"

He came to me and hugged me

"Joseph it is you;" he said hugging me. By this time my father came down the hall.

"You gone crazy; he yelled to my uncle. He saw him hugging me.

He yelled to him. "It is Joseph."

MY father stopped in his tracks and just looked at us.

"You? He said. My son is no Jew;" and took out his gun.

"No father I said it is I; your son Joseph. Remember the day Hitler gave me his gun?"

My father stopped and looked close at me. Remember the day I ran away from the ovens?"

"But you're a Jew;" he said.

"No father. Thanks to this man I was saved."

This throws him off all together.

"You lye; he said not wanting to believe me. He pointed his gun at me again.

"My brother the time I hit him over the head for taking my gun. The whip; I said; you gave me. That did it; the Whip. "I never went out in the prison yard without it. He knows that.

"Joseph; he said dropping his gun and coming to me. God it is you."

"Yes father it is me."

"My son; he said holding me back; what happened to you?"

"It is a long story." I said.

"Come; he said crying with joy. Come and tell me."

I guess I would act the same way knowing I just found out my son was still alive. He wasn't a Nazis then. He was a father. I myself had tears in my eyes. I didn't want to but for some reason I did. My uncle came behind us holding his hand on my shoulder.

"Joseph it is you;" he kept saying.

I guess he was glad himself knowing someone else from the family was still alive.

My father didn't let go of me, he kept his arm around me all the time, just crying as we walked.

"Joseph My Joseph." he kept saying.

We got to this room and he let me go. "Joseph, talk to me. Tell me it is really you?"

I did and by the time I finished he was still crying. This was the father I once knew. He just sat across from me holding on to my hand. He wouldn't let it go.

"Joseph, He said when I finished. What are you doing here?" he asked.

I had it all figured out to what I was going to say to him. And hoping he would let Seymour go. I reminded him of Seymour and the time I ran away. And what Seymour did the day the bombs dropped, plus, all the rest.

"Look Father you have to let him go."

"No," My uncle said.

"But father I said I owe it to him,"

"You owe a Jew nothing;" he said.

I stood up and said "Father if you want me to love you the way I did, you have to let him go."

"No;" again my uncle said.

My father told him to shout up and he looked at me. "Why?" He asked.

I told him that I owe him and I didn't want to owe a Jew anything. I wanted us to be even. It was hard for him to understand but I did something I haven't done in a long time. I remembered what use to make him go my way.

"Please," I said, and gave him the same look I did when I was a boy

"You are my son; he said holding me. Only you know my weakness. He held me and said. You will stay?"

"You let him go; I said and I will stay."

"Go; he told my uncle. Bring this Jew to me."

He did not liking it. When Seymour came in he knew I did what I had to do.

"Jew" My father said to him. My son here said you saved him. For that you will live. You have my son to thank for that. Now go; he said before I change my mind."

"Father what about the scrolls?" I asked.

He smiled and said since you won't let me kill him. I'll burn them instead." He said smiling.

"No father;" I said.

"No, he said looking at me.

"What, living as a Jew, made you think Like a Jew?"

"Yes, father I said. The money is all they think about. I myself was looking for a way to get the Ten million off of them. Don't you see they mean it; no other Jew will buy them. It's either the ten million or nothing; I know this for sure."

"My father laughs at that." Oh you are my son he said. "So My son what do you want to do with this Jew who you owe?"

I hope Seymour didn't take it to heart what I was saying.

The Jew will live for another day and we will have his money. I said; they will not send anyone else to deal with you. So we take the Ten million and let him go. This way I owe him nothing and I could rest. Knowing the ten Million was in my hands would make my rest a lot easier."

"You, he said" I always said you were the smart one."

My uncle said. "Then they will know who we are and where we or."

"So I said with ten million I'm sure the government here will protect us. Who cares if they know where we are. Let them try something." I said.

"He is right my brother. My father said to my uncle; with the Ten Million who cares. And my son is with us now. Give the Jew his garbage and let us go on with our life; with my son by my side."

My uncle didn't like the idea, but my father was the boss. Oh I didn't tell them about me in the C.I.D. I was hoping Seymour wouldn't let it out I was. I couldn't let him know what I had planned. My men were on their way down here, and hopefully they will get me out. I needed Seymour out of here to do this. With him on his way with the Scrolls; nothing would stop me from getting to my father. I had to make him pay for the crime he committed. Even thou I felt for him. And that I did. I was feeling his warmth inside me all over again. I couldn't let that happen. He did what he did and he must pay for it.

CHAPTER 10

Well Seymour got the money sent." They raised all Ten Million together. My father used his soldiers to load the scrolls ; but nothing else; pictures and gold stayed. Then they took him to the air port where a plane was waiting for him to take him back to the U.S. Out of arms way.

My father kept saying was how he was going to start his own army here and finish what, Mr. Hitler started. He was a sick man. It was hard trying to act the loving son roll. I had to make sure Seymour was out of the country. And hoping Seymour could reach my man in time to stop them without telling them why. I didn't want to tell the world who I was. And I couldn't just walk away from my father. I didn't what to. I had to bring him in, and stop him before he could do what he said he wanted to do. He was getting his army ready. He didn't think of nothing else but finishing what Hitler started.

Seymour saw this and knew how importune it was. We had to find out all my father had. Meaning his money, supply, people and how he was going to do it. It wasn't funny, he had it started and almost in full swing whatever it was. I went to his training camp and got sick. My father was acting just like Hitler.(Like The Bull said there is always another Hitler out there.) God was this scary; seeing a dictator being born. The hate these kinds of people have. And the hate the people that wish to follow them have. Make you think twice about yourself. Could I follow in his foot step's? Seeing how they worshiped my father and did anything he ordered them to do, scared the hell out of me. Most of them were young Germans that grow up as the war ended, and didn't like the way the outcome turned out. My father kept their dreams alive with his money and his dream of taking over the world.

Days went by. I played the part of a son; excited with what was happening. My father was in his own world and being I was at his side again, he was more so. He felt his power and it was getting bigger. Just over the two days I was there, he recruited ten more man. That is the way it would go. More and more man were coming. He had people all over the world looking for what he called soldiers of fortune. The Brazilian Government didn't care; they just looked the other way. Little did they know their country was the first one my father was going to take? He said he had to have land to own and soil to stand his feet on to call his own. Every one of the soldiers felt the same way. It was as if they were drugged.

Scary wasn't the word for it. Fighting was more like it. He even had dogs trained to kill. He raised them from puppies and had them attaching dummies dressed up like Jews. I guess it brought back memories of my dog. I guess you could say I fell in love at first sight. He was just like my dog Mike. When I saw him for the first time his tail didn't stop wagging. My father told me to take him and train him. He didn't have to twist my arm. I felt love for him. I picked him up and from that day on he was mine. I named him Mike also. Don't ask me why. I didn't know why, he just looked like a Mike.

My third day here and nothing. I was hoping Seymour got through. Maybe my father had him killed. Shit what if he did? Now what? I had no way of getting to the outside. My father only had certain man leave his camp, the rest stayed behind. He said he didn't want anyone knowing what he was doing. On the fourth day some new men came. He was talking to them in the yard. I just walked around trying to find out as much as I could and where he kept the files. I had to get to them without letting him know what I wanted them for. Any time I'd ask questions. He would tell me I didn't need to know. He just wanted me to train. To him I was to be the best and no man should be better than me. My training and my will to live made me good. He liked that and used me as a example for the other man to learn. Once again in my father's eyes I was his son.

As I was walking with my dog looking at the new man. Something stopped me. My dog spotted it first. It was a flower. Where did that come from? No flowers grow here. I bent down to pick it up and when

I looked up I saw Snake looking at me. He was one of the new men. I didn't want to give him away so I just put it in my packet and kept on walking. My men were here. Seymour made it. Now to get to talk to them.

My father finished with them and was taking them to their barracks. I went along with them. I had to find out what they had planned. My father left me and went back out to get some gear for them. He treated them all like his sons.

Snake came over to me and started to play with Mike. He was saying thing to him, that was meant for me. I didn't look at him, knowing we were being watched. He kept talking and playing with Mike. I found out the Gunny was coming in tomorrow and most of the other man to. It was easy to fit in. My father was looking for all military man that wanted to fight. He didn't care who they were. He know once you got here you couldn't leave on less he said so.

I did get all the Government officials names. A lot of good that will do, this was their country and they ran it the way they wanted to. The U.S. had no control over it and if we got caught here there would mean a lot of trouble for The U.S.

That meant we had to take my father out without them knowing anything about it. Knowing the money my father was paying them. They wouldn't want to see him go and would almost go to war to keep him. So we had our job cut out for us. I didn't want to give Snake away so I just kept away from him. I had to wait for the Gunny to come. Snake said he had it so the Gunny knows me. When he came he would be a long lost friend. That way I could see what they had planned. That meant I couldn't do anything till tomorrow. I didn't want to start another war right now. We were still fighting the one in Korea.

Talk about walking on eggs. That is what I was doing. Me and my father eat all meals together. And we talked all night long. It was hard not to tell him what I really through of him, but I couldn't. Every time he would bring up something about the past I would remember it, and now I could see how wrong it was.

Was it really me; he was talking about. He even said I liked getting blood on my hands.

"I still do; I said" And I meant it. I still did like the feel of blood on me. Maybe he was right. I was his son and my mother kept saying,, your fathers son. I wonder if she knew something I didn't. Well I had my day set for me tomorrow. I couldn't wait to get out of here. He was getting to me. I wanted to smack him the way he smacked me the first time we meet, but I couldn't. His men would shoot me on the spot. That is how much they would follow him. To them he was god and no man could touch him.

I didn't get much sleep that night. I was waiting for the morning to come. It came and went and so did the afternoon. I saw Snake and he just gave me the look as if he didn't know what was going on. It was getting sun down when the phone rang. The guard gave it to my father.

"Yes" was my father was saying and he had a smile on.

They found them out. I had to make my move now. It may be my only time to do so. My father hung up the phone and turned to me.

"You know a Gunny sgt. named Huff?"

I started to go for my gun. I had to do it now. He broke out in laughter.

"He wrecked the whole town;" he said laughing. I stopped my hand from going for my gun. I felt the sweat coming down my face. Shit I couldn't do it. I couldn't shot my father.

"Did you hear me? He said. That friend of yours and his man got locked up.

"You're kidding?" I said trying to smile. The Gunny is here.

"You know he fuck up the town real bad. That was the chief of Police and he said it took all of his man to take them."

"So how what?" I said.

"Don't worry my son; he just called to see if they were my man. They are on their way here now. If there anything like you, he said. We could use them."

"Oh believe me they are father."

"Good he said maybe this could push my plans up."

We keep getting good man like them and before you know it we will be ready my son," he said. How would you like to be King of the country?" He came and put his arm around me and hugged me.

"It isn't that easy. Other countries won't stand for it," I said.

"Ha he said. Hitler did it this way one at a time and before you know it he had half the world at his feet."

"One country at a time?" I said.

"That is right, and this time we don't make the mistake he did."

"What was that? I asked.

"Greed; he said. Adolf got to greedy. He didn't know when to stop."

"Oh" I said not thinking. You do?"

"Yes he said. Once we take the rest of these countries down here we stop and rebuild."

"What makes you thing you can take them?" I said.

"My son like Hitler I to know the weak. All these countries are weak," he said with that look I saw on Hitler.

"What about it the U.S.?" I asked.

Then his look changed. "You getting soft for them?"

"No" I said quickly.

"They are so worried about the war they started, they will look the other way."

"Japan thought that, I said, and looked what happened to them."

"Stop he yelled you're not thinking clearly. This isn't going to be like that. We can pay the government of these countries off and before you know it we control them. See; he said, we don't rush. We take our time and everything comes to you. You will see my son; tomorrow I give a party and you see how the heads of state come to kiss my feet, hoping they can get more money out of me. You'll see, he said. I could run for President right now and win," he yelled.

He really believed it. He really through he could. I had to stop getting him mad.

"Any nice woman coming? I said to throw him off. He stopped and looked at me. He broke into a loud laugh. You are my son;" he said. I have plenty coming. Drink;" he said getting the wine out. Tomorrow I show you how easy it is."

Well the Gunny came. Oh shit did he look mean. The whole bunch of them were covered in blood. The police drove them up in two trucks and just dropped them off at the gate. The Gunny was drunk. Or at least he made my father believe he was.

"Men; my father said when they reached the front steps. You make me proud."

The Gunny came running up to me. Taking me in his arms and picked me in the air.

"Fucking Louie" he yelled. Men look who the fuck is here? See I told you he was coming." He said to my man. They all came around me as if they haven't seen me for years. My father just looked at me proud and said," My son".

The Gunny looked at me and didn't know what he meant by that. So he just kept up the act. Shit I guess Seymour didn't tell them everything. Now what? I didn't want them to know just yet. I didn't want anyone to know who I was. I was still afraid for being found out.

"Come" I told them. I'll show you where you sleep. I had to get them away from my father. I looked at him and told him I would take care of them. I had a lot to talk about. He smiled and went back in the house.

"Go My son, they are your man."

Just like my toys. That is how he sounded. Look what daddy brought you to play with.

The Gunny looked at him and then at me.

"Come; I said before he could talk. I took them to the barracks. Marched them in and closed the door. When we were inside he pushed me away.

"Seymour told me he thought you were his son. Shit I didn't believe him. I guess he was telling the truth. Did he see your Jew number? He asked.

"No, you crazy he would kill me on the spot.

"Man you got yourself in some deep shit. He said to me.

"I know and we are going to have to get out of it. That fucking nut is going to take over this country if we don't stop him now."

"We know; the Gunny said, and we can't do anything to stop him. The shit heads down here think he is the greatest and don't want to hear it."

"They will find out soon enough what he is. He is getting ready to make the move on them. He is giving a party tomorrow and that is when he is going to talk them into making him President.

"You're kidding? He said.

"No you wait and see. He knows money buy's anything down here and he is going to pay them off so the people will elect him.

"What the hell is he going to do with this country?"

Use it to take the others," I said

"You mean he is going after Chile and the rest?"

You got it; he is starting just like Hitler. One at a time. On till he owns all of South America. Then he plans to sit back and make his army the biggest in the world. Then march up to Mexico. And then the U.S."

"He can't be serious." He said.

"Oh no, to hear him he owns the U.S. already."

"With what? He asked. He doesn't have the man power."

"Oh that he does. You see all the man he has here."

"A hand full;" he said.

"That may be I said but each man here is backed up with at least hundreds. See the guy over there?" I said looking at a guy in the corner.

"That young kid?" he asked.

"Him I said, he is the son of a state trooper captain, from some southern state. His father has two hundred men that will follow him. He sent his son down to make him a leader. Each man here are from different parts of the world with man waiting to follow. My father planed it this way. This way no one would know till it was too late. He could have his army ready to go within a week and believe me he had the weapons to do it. They may not be too many men here, but he has the weapons to arm almost a half a million soldiers. Planes and tanks and anything you could want to start a war.

And. See that kid on the other side. His father is a general In Pure. He is just waiting for the orders and his air wing will join him. He has mostly military men that didn't like the way things were going in their country. He has them convinced he will make a change.

"Just like Hitler said .

"Don't people see what is going on?

"No I said the money blinds them.

"So he said your father is going to finish the job with the Jews."

"No; I said. He wasn't the niggers first. He said more people hate the niggers now. If he started with the Jews he wouldn't get that many people to back him. People hate the niggers now. Money is coming in from all over the U.S. to support him. The K.K.K. has men here, I said. A lot of German solders that served under him with Hitler are his main guards. It seemed as if they all fled here.

"Shit this is bigger than we thought. The General said to just take him out and give him to the Jews when we do it. He didn't know all this was going on."

"No one did. That is why the Police just drop you off at the gate."

They don't care. They could give a shit what he is doing, as long as he keeps their pockets full. This party tomorrow might be a good time to make our move." I said.

The Gunny didn't say a word he just looked at me. "Anything wrong?" I asked.

"You can't mean you still want to go throw with it?"

We have to; I said, someone has got to stop him."

"You kidding we would never get him out of the country if what you say is true."

"We have to try." I said.

"No, he said it would be suicide."

"What if we kill him?" I said.

Ha and have all the man come down on us for killing him. No, I don't think so; he said. We would never get out of the country. The government would have us locked up and throw away the key."

"So, I said, the general will came and get us.

"Ha, he said again. That is out to. The general told me to tell you that if you don't do what you were sent down here to do, don't come back."

"He said what?"

"Well, he said not in them words. But he did said he didn't know anything if you got caught. In other words he said the U.S. isn't backing you and as far as they no. You're on your own, seeking revenge for your people. Case closed he said. So How what?"

"Shit," I said.

He looked at me and said "that is what I say. I wish Seymour would have told me about this;" he said.

"He didn't know; I said. I'm the only one from the outside that knows. The government doesn't even know what he is doing here. They think he is just protecting himself from the Jews. Most of the man came here a terrorist and never leave. They don't keep track of who leaves. They just care who comes and how much money they bring with them."

"What about weapons?" He asked.

"They think he is running a plantation here. Coffee and it takes years for the trees to give coffee beans. See the boxes over there?" I said

"The ones marked Machines." He asked.

"That is right, you know what he had sent in them?""

"Guns;" he said

"No, I laugh. Airplanes."

"You're kidding;" he said

"Oh no I'm not he has two hundred jets ready and waiting."

"But how?" he asked.

"He said something about directing them from one war to another."

"I don't get you;" he said.

"Look, they are all parts to a jet. You get enough parts together you have a whole. That is how he did it. He said he had men at a supply base that would switch the place of destination, from Korea to Brazil."

"Just like that." he said

"Just like that?" the proof is in the hanger. I saw them. And he has the pilots to fly them.

"Shit you telling me he has our own people shipping him supplies?"

"One big deal he is working on is from the Columbians. He said something about drugs. He is meeting with them all the time. He promised them they could ship all the cocaine to the niggers in the states they want. And in turn they pay him to get his idea going."

"Nice, he said, what else you have to tell me?"

"Oh I almost forgot. The atomic Bomb."

"The what?" He said almost chocking.

"He did say something about some scientist from Germany are coming to finish the work they were doing for Hitler. And the bomb was mentioned."

"You kidding? He said. Man this is getting to fucking crazy for me. I was sent here to bring back a Jew Killer and that was all. Not it's the whole fucking world."

"Quite" I said to him. This place got ears."

"Ears; he said this place get everything, from soup to nuts. And Nuts is what it got the most of. Fucking nuts;" he said. You mean fucking world war four is going to start right here?" He asked.

"What happened to world war three?" I asked.

"Oh that one?" he said is still being forte remember. They don't want to call it a war just yet."

"Oh, when do they call it a war?"

"Maybe never;" he said, if this one breaks out they don't have to worry about world war three, four, or five. I won't be around to see it.

I started to laugh.

"No, it isn't funny;" he said.

"I didn't say it was".

"Then what the hell are you laughing at?"

"You, you're so fucking nasty you'll never die."

"Get the fuck out of here," he said pushing me.

The rest of the other man saw that and started to get up to stop him."

"Hey cool it. They don't like anyone touching the Bosses son."

"Go fuck yourself;" he said getting up to kick some ass.

"Hold on now Gunny;" I said taking hold of him; we are all in this together."

My man started to get up with him. Oh shit I didn't need this.

"Look guys, I said to the other men standing between them. Sit the fuck down. We are one. No fighting. This is my brother in combat and if you are as half as good as he is, we will take over the world. That was what got them started. That was what my father used to get them going. This here man won't let no Nigger or Jew fuck your woman. Tell them Sgt." I said pinching his neck.

"Your right there;" he said. No Nigger or Jew is going to walk on the same side of the street I walk on. No, he said I take that back. No nigger or Jew is going to walk on my earth."

Oh shit he got them going. They all stood up and started yelling "get the Niggers and skin them white. Take a Jew and make him light."

My father came in and when he saw how fired up we got the man, he smiled. I know what he was thinking. That's my boy. But he was wrong I could have shot him right then and there. I know if I did, we all would be dead. If not his troops the Government soldiers would do it. So I just had to go alone with him for now. I know one thing I wasn't going to let this happen. Not as long as I lived. The Gunny knows it to so we just went along till we could figure out something.

I left them and went back to the house with my father. I asked Where is Uncle Hans?" He said he had to go out of the country for a couple of days. He will be back tomorrow and I hope with good news."

"Oh? I asked. And what will that be?"

"Remember when you said Hitler didn't do something with the Japes when he had the chance to? Well my son. I listen to what you said and realized what you meant. So my son my brother is in North Korea right how inviting some generals to come visit us. And hopefully they will accept my invitation for the dinner party tomorrow."

I don't know if I showed it, but I almost throw up. He was going all the way. This fucking man was going to do it. He was going to take the world.

"Come, he said. I have something to show you."

What now? I said to myself." Hitler". He is still alive and he had him locked up in the basement all this time? Oh shit he was heading for the basement. This I got to see. He went down the stairs and when he came to the bottom he took a key out. The key opened this big steel door. Mother fucker what the hell was this? I couldn't believe what I saw. It was like a hospital of some kind. I mean an up to date lab with people working in it. What else didn't he show me? I just stood looking, what a place.

"I can see your impressed my son."

That wasn't the word to describe it. Breathless was more like it.

"This, my son; he said, was Mr. Hitler's dream. I had it shipped over piece by piece, from Germany.

"But how?" I asked.

"Easy my son. I saw what was happing to us month's before and started shipping the lab over here without anyone knowing. Mr. Hitler and I only; of course".

"But why did he die if you both knew this?" I asked.

"Please my son, we still don't know if Mr. Hitler is dead. The man has so many different ways of escaping. He still could be alive. That is what I'm doing this all for. Maybe someday he will hear of me and come out of hiding to stand by my side once again."

God that was a scare feeling. What if he was alive?

"Come, he said walking around the place. He stopped at each person and said what they were doing. By the time we walked around the large room, my knees and stomach were trembling.

This man was really out of his mind. The people that were working here were also out of their mind. Each and everyone thought what he or she was doing were going to work. I don't mean inventions to help the house wife either. I mean sick thing from making strong and larger babies; to having a 7 ft giant with a brain to match no other. Then there was a super bug that carries a deadly bit. The bug also came with a brain. It was mixed between a black widow spider and a roach. This was my father's pet. He said this was the pride of Germany. He took me to a window and told me to watch. He told me it was a one way glass the person on the other side couldn't see us. I saw a man sitting at a table, reading. This man that my father called a doctor came over to join us. He was the one that was working on the spider.

He had a spider in his hand. Or whatever it was. It was big, almost the size of your hand. It had 8 lags more than the spider. Its body was long like a roach but hairy like a spider. It just sat in his hand, not moving.

"Watch this;" my father said getting excited.

The doctor went over to this slot in the wall and put the spider into it. Then the doctor held up a little bottle of something and said" watch". He went into the room and started talking to the man at the table. He had his hand on his shoulder as he talked.

"Watch;" my father said. He is going to look at his neck and as he is looking he will put a drop of the drug on him without him knowing it."

I watched and saw the doctor do what my father said he would do. It was nothing the man didn't notice the drug. Then the doctor came back out.

"Now my son, watch."

I was watching I couldn't take my eyes off of the man. He kept reading as if nothing was wrong. The doctor presses a button. I saw the spider fall to the floor. It didn't move.

"Watch;" the doctor said.

Both of them were getting excited.

"I'm watching; I said but what am I to watch?"

"The man;" he said. In two minute he will rub the drug I put on his neck. It will give him a little burning feeling, just enough to make him rub it. They, he is going to do it. Now watch the spider."

The man just wiped his neck as if he had a itch, then went back to reading. The spider was a different story, it was as if he just found out something good to eat had come into his web. And he hadn't eaten for days. The spider moved so fast it was as if he had wings. Before you know it he was across the room and up the lag of the table and on to the man's pants. IT was heading for the drug spot that was on his neck. The man didn't even know the spider was there.

The spider got to his shirt collar. He was only there a second and started coming back down his lag.

"See;" my father said.

"He doesn't even know he was bi**tten**." The doctor said.

They told me why. The spider and roach cross breed mixed gave them speed. The drug was a food like sent that had some other commercials mixed into it. That was what spider's enemies would give off. So the roach part wanted the food smell, and the spider part wanted to kill its enemy.

"He said it was as if it had two brains working together."

Then my father said;"watch." The man that just fell on the table. See, he is dead and he didn't even know what happened."

"How come he died so fast?" I asked.

"Ohhhh very good; he said. You tell him."

The doctor took me by the arm and went to the slot to get the spider. It was there waiting for him.

He came right back with it in his hand.

"Trained." I said.

"Ha the doctor said he loves me."

I could see why. The doctor looked like a big spider himself. He took it and went back to his table. He had a lot of them in cages. He also had snakes.

"You see this pretty snake?" he said pointing at the little red and black snake. This is a coral snake; it has the deadliest vein going."

"What the doctor did, my father said, was have the spider part reproduce the snakes poison into the spiders young through the roach's part of reproduction. You see a roach has something in it that make its self hymned to anything. So with that and the spider's natural poison; it has to kill other insects with. Together;" My father said. They kill anything they bit"."

Oh shit this was more than the Atomic bomb

"As you can see;" the doctor said my friend isn't hurt at all. And he can go and do it again in a couple of hours. His body has to reproduce more poison."

"He is on empty" my father said.

That was a big laugh with them. It wasn't funny to me, this thing was sick.

"Show him" my father said to the doctor. It was as if the doctor couldn't wait for him to say it. He took out his bottle and put a drop on the end of this glass rod.

"May I?" He said looking at me.

"Get the fuck out of here." I said backing away. Another joke for them. They laugh.

"No" my father said you show him. The doctor put the glass on his arm. I didn't even see anything go on his skin, but he did press it there. Then he took the spider out again and placed it on the table.

"How watch, he said what my little beauty does."

He rubbed the place he put the drug. The spider was on his arm in nothing flat. He did something and was back on the table like lighting.

"Fast little bugger, the doctor said picking up his arm for me to see what he had do."See the little blood here;" he pointed at a little drop of blood.

I guess that was where the spider bit him and put the poison in.

"As you see he doesn't have any left. If he did my father said the good doctor would be dead looking at his watch;" right now, when the small hand hit 12. As you see he is still alive.

"That is what I have to improve;" the doctor said. I want him to carry enough poison to kill at least ten people before he runs on empty."

Another joke.

My father picked up the spider and talked to it as if it understood him. He will; my little baby won't you? You see with this little baby we could go around and wipe out whole armies with none of our man getting hurt."

"But how would you get it on the person?" I asked.

"Ohhhh he said happy. The doctor was more excited with showing me, he took up an after shave bottle and said. With this?"

"You got to be kidding, I said. You know how many snakes you would have to have to make that much to supply a whole army?"

"See, My father said. I told you his was smart."

I guess meaning me.

"Oh but that is what we are working on now, he said. You see what I am almost about to discover."

My father picked up a bottle of shaving lotion and held it to my eyes. "Go" he said to the doctor. The doctor took his little bottle and his glass rod and put it into the shaving bottle.

"See; he said the little red dot on the top.

"Yes;" I said.

"That is the poison. It will always stay at the top. So that way you put it on you with the first splash of the lotion."

"But what if you don't put it on your neck?" I asked.

"See;" my father got excited; he is smart," meaning me again.

"Oh, he smiled and said. You dye a little later. The neck is the quickest, but any where you have it will kill you. Even if you but it on your dick."

Another joke they were laughing like crazy man.

"So what is the problem?" I asked.

"The doctor said; "watch." He held up the bottle again and said; "see the red dot is going away." "That is what we have to improve. My father said we have to make it last till they use it. Who knows how long one will take to wash him and shave himself?"

"When you're in the field it may be weeks before one splashes something on himself."

"See my father said again. He is a genius. That is what we have to do. But we can't make it work. The mixer in the shaving lotion breaks the poison up."

"Well my good doctor; get back to your work and find me the answer. With this we can start my war." I said feeling better they didn't have it perfected yet. I couldn't believe what they had.

With this super bug we didn't have to shoot a single shot to win. All we had to do was send everyone a bottle lotion for Christmas. And take over their country by New Years."

My father like that one.

"See he said again, he has got a brain. My son has giving me a good idea. 'Christmas gifts'. That would be nice. And what a way to celebrate the New Year."

He couldn't stop laughing. The doctor agreed with him.

"You would have to have an army of spiders." I said hoping I would take the fun out of it, but that didn't work.

"Come," my father said. He took me to another window and put on this light.

Oh god would you look at this. The whole room was filled with the spiders. I mean ever where.

"There must be a million of them." I said.

"That was a bonus;" the doctor said. You see when we mixed the roach with the spider the roach reproduces twice as fast as the spider did; so we can have all we want of them little buggers. All they want to do is reproduce."

"Beautiful; my father said. Look at all of them and they are hard to kill like a roach," he said laughing again. And they reproduce with the poison already in them. Isn't he wonderful?" My father said holding on to the doctor. And he is a Jew;" he said.

"You're kidding?" I said backing away.

"No, he said. Aren't you my good doctor?"

"Yes; he said. You see all Jews aren't bad." My father said.

I had to get out of there I was getting sick.

"Can I go? I asked him.

"No, he said, we have more to see."

"Now what?" I asked.

"Ohhhh he said you will like this part. I was saving it for you till last. This is my pet; he said I love coming here. It makes me feel young again."

"The fountain of youth I bet."

"No; he laughs, but almost right. He opened another door and it looked like a clean stable. Two rows of half walls all white and clean. It had a glass wall for a door.

"Come, he said. He pressed a button. This big tall good looking blond woman came out of what looked like an office.

"Oh sir; she said; this is your son?"

"Yes furline;" he said proud of me.

"My" she said, he will do nicely."

She looked at me as if I was on display at some fashion show.

"Yes" she kept saying, as she walked around me touching me all over.

"My son, my father said starting to take off his clothes. "Come; he said to me. Take off your clothes."

"Do what?" I asked.

"He smiled at me and said. We don't want any germs getting in. We must clean our self's first."

"Come" the woman said. I'll help you."

She came at me and started to take my pants down. I pulled away as she did it. That started my father laughing again.

"Oh look at the baby; he said. You did ask me for woman! He said. Didn't you?"

"Yes"

"So I'm giving you the woman for the future. My super woman;" he said pointing at her. Show him;" he said.

She back away and took off her uniform, it came off with a snap. Oh shit was she built. Not a wrinkle on her body and she was soft as snow.

"See; my father said taking hold of her breast and kissing them. This is a perfect machine. She is the answer to what Mr. Hitler wanted to do."

I must admit she did have it all. I was getting hard just looking at her.

"Tell my son about yourself," he said holding her all over and kissing every part of her body. He was making me embarrassed. I tried to look away but found I couldn't. She was a goddess. She let my father do whatever he wanted to do to her, as she looked at me.

"Tell him" he said taking his mouth off of her breast."

She smiled and said" I Judy have giving birth to twenty seven babies and I'm 49 years old."

"You got to be kidding!" I said with my mouth open.

"No, and I can't wait to have your baby;" she said looking at me.

Oh shit so did I. I wanted her in the worse way. Man could I fuck the shit out of her.

"I see you feel the same way" she said taking hold of my pants. You have a big one, good."

I didn't pull away this time. My father stopped doing what he was doing and looked at me.

"She will take care of you; he said. Judy show my son what we are doing here." he said and walked away. Naked.

"Come she said, take this things off your only smothering your body with clothes.

"Gladly" I said taking my clothes off. I stood naked in front of her. She smiled and took my dick in her hand and just looked at it.

"Oh yes she said looking at it. This will do very good."

I hope so, I said to myself.

"Come; she said still holding on to me, as if it was a leash on a dog. I followed her. I guess you would say I had no chose. Either have her pulling it off, or follow. She had strong hands for a 49 year old. I wasn't about to find out just how strong she was.

She took me into this room that was a shower. She turned it on and started washing me down. She washed me all over. She didn't miss a spot. She did it twice. Then she took hold of my dick again and led me out to another room, where she dried me. Then she took hold of it again and we went into another room. This was the room I first saw, but we were on the other side of the glass now. Soft music was playing and you could hear people making noises. Oh shit they were making love. You could tell by the way they sounded. I was right, the first booth we came to I saw to people doing it. Their heads were up at the end so I couldn't see what they looked like, but I could see them doing it. This guy was going to town.

"See, Judy said we have to still do it the old fashion way."

"I'm glad to hear that;" I said reaching for her tits.

"Oh, she said, don't rush it you will get to me soon enough. She didn't pull away thou. She let me touch her.

She walked to the second booth and the same. Two people going at it. This was making me hotter then I was before, if that could be possible. By the time we got to the end I couldn't hold it in any more. I took her in my arms and went to town on her. She was bigger than me and I was 6'2". So you could imagine the feeling I was getting. She was all women, from her head to her toes. She moved us into one of the booth. She sat me down on the bed like table and started to go to work on me. With her body and her age and how many children she said she had, she knows everything you would want to know about sex. She even knows when I was coming. She would stop and let me relax so I didn't come.

She told me why she did it. She said the stronger my sperm was. The stronger the baby would be. Oh it would take weeks for her to build me up to have her baby." She said.

"Oh? I asked. I'm not ready for it yet?"

"No, she smiled and said. First I have to take your sperm and have it checked out. Then when I see you're as strong as you sperm can be I let it enter my womb and see if I take it. My body is built to only take the strongest of sperm. Any weak sperm will not take."

"Ohhhh, and how do you do that?" I asked.

"I'll show you." She took it out of her hand and started sucking on it. She knows again when I was coming. She took her mouth off and finished it by hand. Then she took a cup from a shelf and shot it into it. She closed it up and got up.

"Come;" she said walking out the booth with the cup. She held it up and was looking at it in the light. "You are very strong; she said, but you don't do it that much."

"Oh, I asked, you can tell?"

"Oh yes; she said. Just by the color, the whiter the better."

"I didn't know that." I said.

Who the fuck looked at their come? I said to myself.

She entered a room that looked like another lab. Inside it was three other women with nothing on. The only difference between them was their color of hair. They all looked the same. Well close to it anyway. What I mean is they were all goddess looking. Big, strong and beautiful. It was like I died and went to heaven.

"Come, she said showing the other woman my sperm.

"Let's see what this hunk of a man has." One said.

She took the cup and places it on the table. Each one of the woman took some out of the jar and placed it on a glass slid; the kind that you put under a microscope. They all had a microscope to look at. They all did it as a team, and by the numbers. Judy just held on to me and was waiting for what the other woman would find. They made some remarks and kept looking. At the same time they picked up their heads and said together, he is good. Then one said he is a little week. The other one said about three weeks. The other one said; more like a month."

"See; Judy said. I told you so. You don't get laid enough. You have to use it to improve it. The more you come the stronger you get."

"You know, I said your right, but with my kind of business you just can't find the time to be doing it all day long."

"Oh she said taking my dick in her hand, did you ever think of just jerking yourself off? That sometimes helps."

"No, I said. I didn't think of that."

"Maybe you should start;" another one said coming down and sucking it out of Judy's hand.

"You see; she said you have to keep your body working. It makes it for you whenever you want it. So you have to use it up, so it can make more. The more it makes, the stronger it gets."

"You mean if I do it 24 hours a day, I'll make giants."

"No" they all laugh. You can over do it. Look at the niggers they do it all day long and look what kind of babies they have? Too much makes it weak also."

"Twice a day is the right mix;" one said.

"Ohhh, I see; I said. Does it make any difference when in the day you do it?"

"Ohhh yes; one said, in the morning and then when you go to sleep."

"You see; another one said, when you wake up it is better to get it out of your balls, so you have room for the new supply to start building.

"That is good to know." I said.

"Then at night; another one said, is better so you can relax after you do it. Relaxing makes the stronger of the two."

"Oh I see; I said, so if you want to make a boy you want to make sure the morning one is the one that gets into making the babies?"

"That is right;" they all said. They all came at me.

"He is a smart one," they said attaching me.

What they did then only a man dreams about. Having four women that know what to do, working on you at the same time. The only thing I could do was lay back and let them go to work. And I do mean work. Not one of them had anything to do. They all found a part of me to work on without getting into each other's way. The fun part about it, they all know when I was getting ready to come. They all back off and let me go back down. Then they started all over again. I don't know how long we kept it up, but I do know it was hours. I enjoyed every minute of it.

Then when they finely let me come they all got a cup and filled it; back to the Microscope again they went. I just sat and waited for them to talk. They did and what they said made me very happy. They all said within two weeks I should be ready to give Judy a baby."

"Oh that was nice; I said. So that means I got to have you work on me twice a day for two weeks and then you say I'll be ready to give a baby?"

"US" Judy said kissing me, aren't you happy?"

I don't know how they felt about it. I do know I was out of my mind with it. Having all four of them working on me when I wake up in the morning.. Then having them return for the night class; was out of this world. Dream land for any man.

"Come, Judy said. We go."

"More?" I said.

"Oh you can do it again?" She asked surprised.

"I don't know I said, but I'm willing to try."

That got a laugh out of them.

"Bring him back when he is ready," the other three said.

"You bet; Judy said, let's see what he is made of."

They all giggled as we left.

She took me into this other room. Shit it was a nursery with babies in it. There were at least ten babies in cribs.

"See" she said looking throw a glass window. No one can go in. The room is germ free."

"What are they doing in there? I asked. Three more women just like the other three were sitting in chairs reading.

"They feed the babies."

"Oh I said that must be an easy job."

"Watch, she said as one of the babies started to wake up. One of the women got up and took the baby and let it suck on her tit for the milk. They didn't have any clothes on either, so all they had to do it stick their tit in the kid's mouth.

"Boy; I said now old are the babies?" I remember seeing a friend's baby and it was half the size of these babies. She said most of them are three week old in this room."

"Three weeks? I said almost chocking. You're kidding?"

"No; she said the one that she is holding is the youngest, he is only two weeks."

"My god I said, they look almost a year old. Look at the size of them."

She smiled and said. "See what good sperm can do and the right food." She pointed at a table that was filled with nothing but food. The women eat all the right food and the babies drink the milk from them and grow to be big and strong."

"I see." I said.

She then started turning on a voice box. It was tuned into the room. I could hear a radio on and it was saying things I didn't understand. "What was that?" I asked.

"It is an advance form on math. We play all kind of thing to let the baby hear it. And when he grows up he knows everything. We develop the brain at an early stage."

"You said he?"

"Oh yes, this room only has Boys in it. The girls are in another room, we keep them apart. Boys learn different things then the girls do. Listen she said to the woman."

She was talking about the one that was feeding the baby. She was talking to it in Japanese. We talk to it in all kind of languages. This way he knows all of them when he reaches the age of two.

"You mean by talking to them when there this age; they know what you're saying?"

"Oh she said they do. See the other woman reading? They read all the time to them. And what they read, they tell the babies when they hold them what the meaning of what they read. See, asked one of the women to hold up a book."

"Shit I didn't even understand that one in college.

"Oh you didn't? The baby will be able to tell you all about when he is five."

"You're kidding?"

"No; she said. You will see."

She walked to another window. In it were kids about six. I would guess by their size. "Six?" I said?

"No, two.

My God they were walking and talking like old people. If you know what I mean? And the same radio was playing but saying different things. Also three more women were with them. All nude of course.

"I guess the clothes didn't matter?" I asked.

"Oh it does; she said. When you cover your body it stops it from breathing. That meant less oxygen to the brain. We need all the oxygen we can get to make our brain work the way it should."

"No wonder I have trouble thinking when I have clothes on." I said.

"See; she said. You do feel the difference with your clothes off. Just imagine if you had them off all your life. You would be a wiz." She said.

The next room was girls, they were about ten I guess, but I know I was wrong. She told me 5. Boy they were big. Some of them had breast already coming out. They learn how to please a man, she said; besides being smart."

"At this age?" I asked.

"Oh yes;" she said Look.

This room had man taking care of the girls. These guys looked like mister universe and gods all in one.

Look at the size of them guys," I said.

She smiled. "They all think they are gods; she said.

"Look at them I said, they are!"

"No she said, they are the small ones. The big ones make the babies. They are the ones with the most brains so they teach."

"Oh I said that is nice. How stupid of me."

The next room got me sick. She said it was the babies that didn't live up to their standing."

"What do you do with them?" I asked.

"We experiment on them to see what went wrong and then we get rid of them."

She didn't have to tell me anymore. I saw what she meant. It was a door to an over. I saw that door before. I still see that door in my dreams. It was the same oven they killed the Jews in, but smaller. I turned away and she knew it.

"Oh she said. You have a weak stomach? You don't even think about it:" she said without any feeling. You just think of them as bad product and get rid of them. They have no use to us or the world. Once we open them up to see where we went wrong."

"Stop, I said. I heard enough."

"Oh this is nothing; she said. The best is for last. Come; she said walking me to the last window. This one always gets you."

Inside were boys and girls. I would say about 15 or 18. I was wrong again. She said 10 and 12. They were doing it to each other with other man and woman in there. They would watch them do it. They were teaching them. Then I saw my father, he was the man doing in right in front of the kids.

She laughs and said. Your father likes this part. He said it shows them how he wants it done."

I couldn't believe my eyes; my father had three young girls on him. He was doing it to them." Oh God;" I said and went away from the window. He didn't see me; he was enjoying it too much. Judy came to my side and held me.

"That is normal; she said, if it wasn't your father you would be hard as a rock watching them do it. But being it is your father we expected you would act like that."

"Oh, I said looking at her. You knew it already?"

"Oh yes; she said pointing at this glass. Inside was a doctor. He smiled at Judy and said. "I won the bet."

"Bet". What bet?" I asked.

He bet you would do what you did. And I bet you wouldn't. I bet you would get hard and ask to join in with your father."

I couldn't believe her, she was just as sick as the rest, even more so. She acted like a robot, no feelings at all.

"Shit. I have to go." I said feeling myself getting sick again.

"Come; she said this way. She opened a door and we were back in the room with the first three woman.

"Is he ready?"

"No; I said and walked out the door.

Judy followed me and took my arm.

"Don't worry; she said. They said you would feel this way. You see we monitor everything that goes on here. We like to know how the human brain works and what makes it do things."

"So you would say I was an experiment for you?" I said.

"Oh yes she said. A very good one. You see your feelings have made us see what we could change in our self's to not have them."

"Like you?" I said

"Yes, she said. I have no feelings. I just use my brain for other things. Feelings are for the weak."

"You're saying I'm weak?" I asked.

"Oh yes, you're so weak we may have to work on your sperm along with your brain for three week instead of two."

That did it I walked away from her and left the room. I found my clothes and put them on. I walked back to the main room, to the doctor that was working on the spiders. He asked did I enjoy myself."

"No", I said, and went out the other door. I found myself in another room. Not the one we came through. This room was more like a jail. They must be a way out of here. I said to myself and kept walking. The first cell I passed no one was in it. The place looked empty. I was wrong. One of the cells had someone inside it. I could hear them crying. I walked up to the window and looked in. There was this woman with no clothes on. She was sitting on her bed.

"Hello, do you know the way out?"

She looked up at me and said. "Call the guard." "Thank you is anything wrong?" I asked her.

She got up and came to the window so I could see her.

"Oh shit what the hell happened to you?"

Her nose was twice as big as her face.

Just then someone touched me on the shoulder.

"Oh shit you scared the hell out of me." I said jumping almost out of my pants. It was my father, he was dressed this time.

"Will my son I see you didn't like what we did to the bad ones. I told them you wouldn't. You still remember the ovens." He said walking away with me.

"Yes, they will never leave me." I said to him.

"Maybe someday;" he said.

"No, I said never." I was forgetting myself and that was no good. I had to stop and think. I couldn't let him know what I really thought about him. I change the subject.

"What did she do?" I asked meaning the woman in the cell.

"Her? She was too ugly to be one of us."

"That was all?"

"Look" he said walking back to her cell." She is beautiful and has a good brain, but look at that face. Would you fuck it?" No, he said laughing. No man would."

The woman had tears in her eyes, but didn't say a word.

"So let her go. She doesn't desire to be put in a cell just because something went wrong with her face."

"Ho; he said. Can't you see if she was to be let go she would tell the whole world about us. And that we can't have. So she is kept here for good use."

"Oh and what is that?" I asked.

"Ohhhh he said laughing. She fucks the men that I send down that have been bad."

"Oh for punishment, fuck the ugly one for being bad."

"Something like that; he said. Come let's go eat."

"Now many of them do you have down here?" I asked.

"Oh now let me see. I think five of them. Don't worry; he said, when they get to ugly we burn them."

I knew he was going to say that.

"Show me the way out." I said to him and walked away from him.

"Still don't like the burning part?" he said again.

"No, I yelled and kept walking. I didn't care where I went. I just had to get away from him.

He followed and told me the way to go, but he stayed behind me. I guess he know he over did it once again. I'm glad he did. I was going to kill him right there if he kept it up. I guess he knew it also. Besides I would put the rest of my man to death if I did. No way were we getting out of here without him. I got up into the open and just ran. I didn't know where I was going. I didn't care. I was doing what I did many years ago.

Running, running as fast as my lags would carry me. I just took off. I found myself on a beach. The water was clean the air was fresh. I didn't stop to see if anyone one was following me. I kept walking till it was up to my head. Then I started to swim. And when I couldn't swim any more I stopped.

Oh shit I was far out, now to get back? That was if I could make it. I was out pretty far. Oh shit I know I couldn't make it. I was too tired. I felt so much hate for my father I forgot about myself. Oh well this is how I was going to die. I might as well accept it. "Get it over with." I said out loud and went under. I was going down so deep I knew I couldn't make it back up. No sense prolonging it. What the hell was this; something came from under me and started moving me back to shore. When I was back to where I could stand. The thing came out of the water. It was a frog man. My father was standing at the shore waiting for me.

"You ran away again;" he said. Just like when you were a boy. But this time I know what you would do." he said.

"Leave me alone." I said and walked pass him. I went back to the house and went to my room. I got out of my clothes and took a shower. Not to get the salt off of me. I was trying to make myself clean from the inside. I know I couldn't do it. God knows I tried many of time through my life. It just didn't work. I got out and took a drink. I needed it. Before you know it I was drunk. I didn't want to but I couldn't stop myself. I passed out.

CHAPTER 11

The next think I remember was something playing with me. I opened my eyes and sew it was Judy.

She smiled at me and said. "You have to keep it up. We have to get you strong for my baby."

"Oh what the hell, I knew I couldn't stop her. I let her go. She made me feel good. I almost forgot what was going on around me. But like always when you come, you come back to real life once the high is gone.

She got up and said. "Your father told me to dress you. The party was to be in about two hours."

Oh shit I had forgetting all about it. I jumped up and said I would dress myself. I told her to leave. She didn't want to, so I made her. I had to see the Gunny before this party started.

I dressed and headed for the barracks. When I went inside the Gunny was sitting with my man in their own group. "Hey, he said jumping up, where the hell was you?"

"Don't ask; I said. Look there is going to be a big party tonight and if we are going to do anything tonight is the night to do it."

"What do you want us to do?" he asked.

"Just be ready for anything. I'll let you know.

"How? He asked.

"I don't know yet. I'll just do it."

"Oh he said that is good, and if I don't know? He asked. Then what?"

I looked at him and said. "Were all dead."

"Oh just like that?"

Little did I know my dog was following me? He followed me all over the place. Snake was playing with him, he like snake.

"This dog was smart;" Snake said.

"Ha. I bet my father is breeding them to."

"What?" The Gunny asked.

"Nothing I told him. I would tell him when we were away from this place."

"Come on Mike." He did seem real smart. My father was probable breeding him with the woman to. As I walked with him I was giving him commands. He knew everything I was telling him. It was almost as if he understood me. Shit it was scary; he looked at me and gave me a wink. I know he knew what he was doing. He did understand me. What else was my father doing? Shit I didn't want to know. He had to be stopped. I went back to my room. Judy was still there, she had some different clothes for me to wear.

"What the hell is this?" I asked.

"Your father wants you to look like a King." she said holding up this uniform. He said you would do him honor if you would wear it for him."

I held it up and looked at it." Mike you want to wear it?" I asked the dog. Shit he shook his head, yes.

"Did you see that?" I asked her. He said yes.

"He can do more than that;" she said.

"Don't tell me. I said. My father is breeding them with humans."

"No, she laugh, you can't do that."

"Oh I bet he tried."

She didn't answer that. I know that meant he did.

"No, she said, he is taking the smartest ones and helping them along. You see; she said some dogs are smarter than others. And with a little extra something they can almost be like a human."

"Don't tell me. I said. I don't want to know what that little extra something is. Mike did he hurt you?" I asked. Mike ran under the bed. I guess that meant yes. What else is this man doing? I asked myself.

Judy got me ready. When I looked at myself in the mirror; I almost laugh at myself. Oh shit a KING.

I had more gold hanging from me. And the medals on me were all for different things;" she said. She went over to a box and took out her dress. She said she was to be my escort for the night.

"Now nice I said. Do we do it after?" I asked.

Oh how stupid of me. I forgot only twice a day. Right?" I asked her.

"No; she said. You could do it three times without hurting yourself. But it should be after midnight when the party is over. That will start the next day; she said smiling, if you're worried about over doing it."

"Oh good. I did want to have the super baby for my father."

"Oh how nice of you. She said looking at me half dressed. You will. I'll see to that."

"I bet you will." I said.

We finished getting dressed. Then she did something to Mike.

"Your father wants use to bring the dog, she said.

"What the hell he might be the only one I'll be talking to tonight." She put something around his neck.

"What is that?" I asked.

"You will see."

It looked like a collar of some kind. What the hell he's got to look good to.

Well it was time. She took my arm and out the door we went the super couple and dog.

For some reason I felt that way. It was something about the clothes I was wearing; power all over me. I felt this way one time before. That was when Mr. Hitler gave me his gun and everyone saw it. The Power of feeling good I guess you would call it. Oh well down the stairs; down to the main room. I had to stop before we reached the bottom step. The place was filled with people.

"Where the hell did they come from?"

"Your father flow them in;" she said.

"I bet he did."

My father was the first to meet us. "Very nice he said looking at me. Very nice you will do;" he said.

"Oh thanks. I said not trying to get into convocations with him.

"Judy and you will make any man or woman eyes turn."

"Thanks you sir," she said to him.

"How, he said, let's get started."

What he meant was to show me off.

The first one we went to was with my uncle. He was with the Korea. He was in uniform and smiling. When I was told his name I almost shit. This was the general that I almost arrested for selling the drugs and contraband. This snake was ever where. He had my father, Mafia and Hitler. and him. My uncle said he was here only to tell us he couldn't join us."

"Oh, my father said. And why is that?"

"He said something about the Russians helping him with the war. And the Russians didn't want anything to do with the Germans."

"I could see why, the man has a point. But uncle wouldn't it be wise for him to see who has the better offer first? That is before he leaves."

My uncle looked at me and my father stepped in.

"You see general my son is a leader of man and he talks with wisdom."

"Thank you, he said. You took the words right out of my mouth." Giving me a look.

"My father's son; I said.

My uncle didn't like me taking over the way I did. I could see he was going to give me trouble.

"You are so right; he said holding on to me.

My father took the other side of me and said. "General we will talk;" and walked away with me at his side. The next person was just as big. He was from some other country, but had just as much to add to my father's army. This went on and on. If everyone that we meet joined my father no one could beat him. He would have the world in his pocket by year's end. The thing that got to me was no one cared about things till it was too late. Someone had to know this meeting was going on. But yet they allowed it to take place.

Well we meet everyone that was worth meeting. My father took me to the center table. There we sat at the middle of it. My father in the center, my uncle on one side and me at the other. Mike was at my feet. Judy was to my left. My father didn't say anything about Mike so I kept him by my side.

Then the band stopped playing and my father stood up and thank everyone for coming."

"Now we must get down to the real reason for my little get together."

I know why he didn't say anything about Mike. He called him. Mike got up and went to his side.

"How gentleman I would like to start with the simple achievements. This is one of our research developments.

"The dog." Everyone laugh.

"But "my father said, he is not an ordinary dog. He understands the human language. As we all know a dog understands tone not voice. What we have done was developed his brain to understand the human voice.

"Does he talk?" one asked.

"In his own way. My father said. Sir he said if you would like to ask him some questions. Limited to a yes and no answer. You will find him must intelligent."

The gentleman asked a question. Are we going to make money? Mike shock his head yes.

"Am I going to make money?" Another one asked.

Mike got down and went over to him and smelled him. Then he came back on the table he shook his head, No. The people didn't know what to say to that. The man that asked the question just looked at my father.

My father said." Enough. I'll show you what he really can do." Show me a Korea? And while you're at it piss on a nigger." Mike left and went right to the general. He took his hand to bring him over to my father. As he was doing it he stopped and lifted his lag on one of the waiters that was black. The crowd clapped. The general came up and sat next to my father and uncle.

"Now my father said, this is all well and good, but this isn't the reason. Mike he said to the dog; go get Doctor Frew." The dog jumped and left the room. He came back with the doctor; the doctor that had the spider. "Come, my good doctor. My father said for him. Join us." He did. When the Doctor sat at the table the dog came back to my side." How my good people my father said this is what we all came for. I'm sure you will not go home dissatisfied. Doctor if you will please."

"Dog," he said. Mike went back over and stood by his side. The doctor took two bottles and told Mike to bring them to two different people. One was a German and the other was an American." How gentleman if you would please. Open the bottle and smell the after shave.

They did.

"Does it not smell good?" He said.

"Yes; they both said. It is good."

"Would you wear it?" My father asked.

"Yes" they said.

"Then put it on;" he said.

They did.

"Good, he said. Now sit."

Then the doctor took out this cage." Now gentleman I guess you all know what we are here for and that it to reunite the White world from blacks and any one that agrees with them."

"Here, here;" they all said.

"So what better way could we do this without firing a single round?" No one had the answer.

"Animals;" he said.

That got everyone in the room talking.

"Yes, my father said. Animals instead of humans. Sound good?" He asked.

"Good, but not sensible;" a man said.

"What is sensible? My father asked. To die; or to live with riches."

"Live with riches;" they all said.

"Good, then we agree. You sir; he pointed to one of the man that put the shaving lotion on. "And what do you think?"

The man looked at him and stood up." I think he said; that it is all bull."

"Oh and why is that?" My father asked.

"Because sir; he said. I got word that you're on your way down and you're only making noises."

"And where did you hear that?" My father asked.

"Oh I got my ways."

"Good;" my father said. And you sir." He said pointing to the other gentleman that had the lotion on. What do you have to say?"

The man stood up and said. "I hear the opposite. From what my people tell me we could be ready to go with in the next four month."

"Wrong." My father said.

"Oh? Why is that?"

My father looked at everyone and said. "What if I tell you we start today?"

Everyone stood up and yelled "Yes."

Then my father said. "Let me show you how we can. Doctor;" he said. The doctor stood up and put the cage on the table.

"Now gentleman please don't be alarmed just keep your sets and don't get nervous. I can ashore you nothing is going to happen. Now please sit. The doctor took the spider out of its cage and held it in his hand over his head. "What you see my good men is the latest in armies."

"Ha; one laugh and said. We have bigger ones in my country."

"Another one stood up and said. I could crush it with one foot."

"And then the man that had the lotion on stood and said. "See this is what I mean you're taking our money and doing nothing with it. I say we all back out now," he said to the other man at the table.

"Gentleman the man has a good reason for talking like that. You see I just found out that this man is going over to the Russians. Something about the wheat he is growing. And the Government is giving him a lot of money to employ the niggers from the south to work in his fields. I don't blame him. My father said. But what I do blame him for is talking to the Government about what we are doing here."

"No" the man yelled. I haven't told anyone about us and yes it is true, I did get the contract to ship Wheat to Russia. So? He said. I won't be sending money from this date forwarded."

"Thank you. My father said. It was nice of you to tell us this. How back to my friend the good doctor. What you see here is his answer to the war. Doctor;" my father said.

"Now gentleman once again please don't panic, stay seated at all times. No one will get hurt."

I was watching the two men with the lotion on. One of them went for his neck. The spider took off and went under the table and out of sight.

"Now please don't move;" my father said again.

It only took three seconds for the spider to reach the man and bit him. He was so fast I was the only one to see him do it. He came right back to the doctor. When he got on the table and everyone sew him. They laugh. "He did a good job they said. Now what?"

My father still standing turned to the man that said he could step on it.

"Did you see it sir?" my father asked.

"No, he said, but he didn't go anywhere." The man said.

"Oh but he did, my father said. What would you say if I told you he went to the end of the table and did something to our friend that isn't going to be with us much longer?"

"No way; someone said. No spider could run that fast."

"Well then gentleman I see you will want proof. Watch the Wheat man," my father said. All eyes turned to him.

He stood up and said. "You're going to be sorry for this."

"No; my father said. You're the one that is sorry."

He looked at his watch and said. You're going to die in twenty seconds."

"What are you going to do; shot me?" He yelled.

"No my father said. My new army is going to do it." Just then the man fell to the table right into his plate. Would someone check him out and tell us what you find!"

One man checked him and said. "He is dead."

That got them all moving.

"Now gentleman. Please be seated. I have to finish what I was doing in order for you to understand my reason for doing what I did. Please."

They were looking on the floor and all over for the spiders.

"No; my father said. The only spiders that are in this room are right here with me. Now please."

"I stood up and yelled." Sit the fuck down." Everyone looked at me.

"Now if you babies have finished yelling. My father will continue."

They all looked at me and sat.

"Thank you son; he said "Now as I was saying. My army can be in the millions. And I could give each and every one of you your own army to command."

"How could you do that? Someone asked. Without the Government knowing what is going on."

"Easy, he said. Then he pointed to the band. It played music. Behind us the curtain came up. "This gentleman will answer any questions you have." When the curtain was raised the light came on. I mean real bright lights. In the center were a white and a black man standing with nothing on. Both were big and strong looking.

"Now that is and army," one yelled.

"Please;" my father said again. Doctor pleases." The doctor called Mike again and gave him two more bottles and said something to him.

Mike ran on the stage going from the table to the stage in one jump. He walked up to the white man and gave him a bottle, then went to the black man and did the same.

"Now gentleman if you would please apply the lotion." They did and then just stood back at attention. My father pointed to someone behind the curtain and out came six guards with guns. They walked out and went around the two men on stage.

"Just to make sure they don't run. My father said. Now Doctor if you would."

The doctor came to the microphone and started telling them about what his spiders could do. When he finished my father stood up and looked at his watch.

"As you can see;" he said, both man put the lotion on, but one of them has the right one. I've had them set up on the stage so you all can see the swift movement of my soldier. And for the gentleman that said he could step on it before. I'll give him the chance to do so once my demonstration is over, if he wishes." Doctor." He said as the black man went for his face. It was the burning drug working. The doctor took out another spider. Before he could let it go. It flow out of his hand and headed for the nigger. They saw it coming and tried to run; both the nigger and the white. The spider was too fast, but with the white back ground you could see everything it was doing. Once it bit him the spider ran back to the doctor.

"Give me a soldier that can stick that fast. My father said. And get away without being caught." The both man stood back. "See; my father said. It didn't even bother the Nigger. Now did it boy?" He asked.

"No; the nigger said. I didn't feel it."

"Good. Now tell the gentleman about yourself."

He started talking and when he got to his place of birth he dropped to the floor dead.

"See, my father said. No pain, you just dye. And when and if someone checks to see how you died. It just comes up as an insect bit. Case closed."

"That is great; one said. Now do we get them?"

My father said. We are breeding them now and by the months ends we will be able to ship them out. But; he add, one thing is standing in our way."

"Want is that?" One asked.

"Doctor;" My father said again. This time the doctor came on stage.

He took out a lotion and put it on himself and then took the same bottle and gave it to the white guy that was still standing. He put it on himself.

"Now; my father said. The same two spiders he took out. They waited for the doctor to feel the burn. Now we will see the both of them feel the burn. That means the spiders will bit both of them. Before he saw them get the burn the spiders took off up on the stage and up to the neck of the both of them. It bit and came back to my father.

"The good doctor will dye;" one yelled.

"No; the doctor said. That is what I have to work on. That is why we need your money. The spider can only kill one person every five hours. I'm getting so close to having him reproduce enough poison to kill four men an hour."

"How long can he keep killing?" Someone else asked.

"Well sir so far the ones I tested will keep going for years."

One man stood up and said. "You mean one of them spiders could kill four men an hour for years.

"That is what I said;" the doctor said.

My father stepped in and said. Could you imagine what hundreds of them could do to a country?

People started to ask all kind of questions now.

"Wait; my father said. One other thing, the drug that we have it only last four hours in the lotion. We also want to further that two months. This way all you had to do it give a bottle to a friend and let him decide when he wanted to die."

They all laugh.

"But, one asked. What can kill the spiders?"

"Nothing," my father said.

"Oh I find that hard to believe;" the man said.

"No, the doctor said. With the cross breeding of the roach it builds an amenity up to anything and any poison invented on the market today."

"What if like this man said? You step on it."

"Oh the doctor said. Come here; he said. The man looked at him and didn't come up.

"Come, he said. I'll let you try to step on one."

"No thank you;" he said and sat back down.

"I guess the man is chicken," my father said. So I'll do it to the dog. You all know a dog is fast and if he can't stop it; no human can. Agreed."

"Agreed, they all said not wanting to have it tried on them. My father called Mike to him.

"No, I said wait. His is my dog." I said looking at my father.

"Oh, he said. You come attached to him?"

"Yes," I said

"Good then, he said you take his place."

So this is what was up his sleeve.

"Everyone said. Your own son you would test it on?"

My father said. This will show you all how it will work. My own son will demonstrate to us."

If this is his game, I'll play it. If the spider has poison in it then he wins. If it doesn't then I'll win. I got up on the stage to show them who I was.

"Now my father said; to show you he is no push over."

The six guards put down their guns and took off their uniforms. Shit they were like giants. And they know the martial arts good.

"Now son;" he said pointing at me.

What the hell it was now or never. I took off my uniform. The only thing I had on was the pants Judy made me wear. This is why, she know it all the time I'd would be doing this.

I stood ready for them. They came at me holding nothing back. I must say they were good, but I was better. I beat all six of them. I killed two of them. I didn't want to. At first six was too much. I had to get some of them out of the way.

"Now, My father said. Is he not fast? And don't you think he would make some country a good king."

One guy stood up and said. He can marry my daughter and become KING tomorrow."

"Good My father said. I'll talk to you later."

They all laugh.

"Now, he said to me. Son, take this lotion and put it on."

I did without waiting to ask if the spider had poison. I didn't care. I knew I had to stop the spider to make my father look like a fool. I felt the burn and then the doctor let the spider go. Man was he fast. I did everything in my power to keep away from it or to step on it. Nothing I did. No matter how fast I move he came at me. It was almost as if he knew where my feet were going to land. He was there and then he wasn't. Mike even came on stag to stop him. The dog couldn't. The spider was flying and jumping all over the place. Then he got me.

"Now my father said. Anyone else think they could stop him. Please come up and try?"

No one moved.

"Now, he said. You're all guessing if the spider had any poison left in him. He didn't, one bit is all he has, till he builds it up again. Now it is up to uses; you want to have a spider that can kill one every four hours. Or one that can kill four and hour none stop."

"How much money?" One yelled.

That is what I want to hear. "Now my son get dressed and come down to your place at my table. He was proud of me once again. I could see that. Judy came on the stage to help me. The man liked her. She had a dress that you could see right throw.

"Oh and gentleman, if you like Miss Judy? We have more of them. Thanks to the doctor's I have working day and night to better the human body." The band started playing and the woman started coming on the stage. They all had something on, but it wasn't much. The man started going crazy.

"Hold on gentleman. Money first."

Boy did he know how to get money. My father was the best. Only he could think of this. I got dressed and went back to the table. By that time the man were lining up. Like a wedding, when you give the money to the bride. But this time they were giving millions and I do mean Millions. Mike and Judy came back down with me. The rest of the night was shaking hands and meeting people. If I was going to take my father out, the time was now. Most of the man were taking their woman to their rooms and were in for the night. My father and my uncle were taking the money they collected and were counting it. To make sure everyone gave.

Now how was I to get the Gunny here?

Judy came up to me and said; "it was after 12."

I guess she wanted to go have sex. I took hold of her hair getting ready to kiss her, and to tell her later. That was when I pulled a flower out of her head.

Shit that was it. The flower.

I told her I would be right back and took the flower to the hall with me. I know Mike would follow.

"Now My good dog, let's see if my father was right, can you understand me."

He shook his head yes.

"Take this flower to Snake, the Indian you meet before, then bring them back to me. I'll be with my father. You understand me?" I asked.

He shook his head again yes.

I hope so. Now go."

He didn't wait for me to turn around, he took off.

I went back out Judy was waiting for me.

"Ready?" She asked.

I told her to go to my room and I would meet her there. I had to talk to my father first."

She left and I went over to my father.

"My I watch." I said.

"Come; he said. We count it in the other room. My uncle pick up what he could. I helped them. We went in to this study like room.

"Now, my father said. This is going to be the start of it."

"Mind if I ask you something Father?"

"You can ask me anything; he said. You're my son aren't you?"

"How will you get the countries away from the people?" I asked.

"The same way they are letting them take it."

"With the spiders." My uncle said.

"You see my son I control the amount they received and when they come in power. I make myself known to its people so they know I'm second in charge; or you. My father said. And when we have the people on our side, then we get rid of them."

"Just like that?" I asked.

"Just like that," my uncle said for him.

"Would you look at this?" My father said holding up a diamond necklace. "What would you say this was worth?"

"Ohhhhh my uncle said, at least a Million."

"That is if it is real;" I said.

"My son you get to know what is real and what isn't just by the feel of it. See," he said handing it over to me.

"Heavy." I said.

"The heaver the better; look at all this gold;" my father said. He had it on a cart it was so heavy. And more to come;" he said holding up pieces of paper. "This is money being transferred to my account from their banks."

"Is it enough?" I asked.

"Oh yes my son it is for now."

I heard Mike scorched at the door. Mike I said, would you mind if he came in?"

"Let him in." He said. He has the right to see what he did for us."

I went to the door and saw Mike alone." Hey Mike didn't you give them the flower?"

He shook his head yes. Maybe they didn't know what I meant by it. Shit now what? I had to take them now. Just then I saw something hit the door. It was the flower. I look at where it came from and saw the Gunny peaking around the corner. Good. I waved for them to come. I opened the door wide so they could come in. They piled in before my father and uncle could see them. My father looked up and saw them standing there.

He smiled at me and said. "That won't be necessary. We don't need extra guards."

"I'm sorry father, but you're going to have to come with me."

"What; MY uncle said, you crazy? What has come over you?"

My father didn't say a word. My uncle was doing the talking. I told him to shout up. That was when I told him I was with the American C.I.D.; he stopped talking.

My father just smiled and said. You didn't think you could get away with it do you?"

"I have, I told him. Now you're coming with me."

"My son he said, I love you."

"No father you love power and you have to be stopped."

"Ha, he said laugh. You can't do it."

"No, I said. We will see."

May I remind you about the government down here and not to say about my own guards? You will never make it, and all for want?" He asked. The U.S.?

"Yes father I said the U.S. and all its people. For the world. I said. After I saw what you are going to do. You're just like Hitler. Didn't know when to quit?"

"Oh but I do son; he said. I just haven't decided when."

"Well I'll do it for you;" I said. You're giving up now."

"No I don't think so my son. He called to Mike to take the gun away from me. Mike didn't move. He just looked at me and then at my father.

"See, even he knows what you're doing is wrong."

My uncle started to go for his gun. The Gunny stopped him.

"No sir; he said. We don't want to carry dead bodies with us."

"So my son. My father said. You think you and your little army is going to take me?"

"Snake go and get a helicopter ready for takeoff."

My father had four of them taking the man back and forth. "Tell them my father wanted it to go to the bank; he had to bring his money."

"They won't believe you," he said.

"Then kill them; I said to him.

"Yes sir;" he said.

"Snake take Mike with you."

"Will do;" he said.

Mike liked him and he would be the key to the guards believing him.

"No, my father said coming at me. You can't do this."

I don't know why, but I did the only thing I could do. I didn't aim to wing him I aimed to kill. I shot my father right in the head. He didn't even close his eyes; he just fell with the look of shock on his face. The Gunny looked at me he didn't know what the hell was going on.

"Now Uncle you next?"

"No," he bagged on the floor.

"Good I'll let you live. But one more wrong move you're dead to. Do I make myself clear?"

"Yes, he said crying. He was weaker then my father. I know he wouldn't give us any trouble.

"Now Gunny how would you like to take back over forty million to the General?"

He just looked at all the gold and money and Diamonds. "Well get a move on and get it loaded. We don't have much time."

"What about your father?" He asked.

"Leave him, they will find out that their dreams aren't going to come true."

"But what if someone else wants to pick up where he left off?"

"I think this should stop that. Banger, do your thing."

He smiled and asked. Where?"

"Have fun; I told him "Gunny I'll meet you at the chopper. Take my uncle with you and if he makes any wrong move kill him. You see uncle even if we don't make it. The whole place is going to blow, so you decide."

I took the keys off of my father. Me and the Banger went down stairs. I opened the steel door to the lab. The whole place was empty. I was counting on that. My father gave everyone off for the party. "Well can you do it?" I asked him.

"I think so;" he said opening up his jacket. I know he never went anywhere without his shit. This will be easy; he said. See all the shit they got down here. Good stuff." He said. It will add to the firer works."

"Good."

"How long?" He asked me.

"Give us about an hour."

"One Hour? He asked. That is to long; he said. Someone could find them."

"Hide them; I said. I need at least an hour. I don't want anyone getting killed. I got to give them time to get out of here."

"You're the boss;" he said and started to go to work.

"Oh sorry sir; someone said behind me. It is you."

"Man you scared the shit out of me doc." It was the doctor. Good I was just looking for you. I can't leave you here;" I said.

"Oh and why not?" He asked.

I told him I killed my father and I was going to blow the whole place to bites. I didn't want him around to go to the highest bidder. He didn't seem to care. I guess deep down inside he know he was doing wrong. I hope so because a man with his brain would be a shame to kill. He could do some good for the world, if he wanted to.

"Come I have to let the people out that my father is holding in his cells."

"No, he said. You can't do that."

"Oh and why not?"

He said they will kill him if they saw him. He was the one that did it to them."

"Come on now Doc I saw some of them. They aren't that bad."

"Ha he said backing away from me. You said you only saw some of them. The ones you didn't see was the ones your father kept to remind others what could happen to them if they fucked up. They are the ones that I'm worried about."

"How bad could they be?" I asked.

"Bad; he said. They aren't human."

"We have to let them out."

"No; he said. They would be better off dead, believe me. Dead is better."

"No, I can't do that."

"OK he said. Come and I'll show you the ones your father didn't show you."

I yelled to Banger. "I'll be right back and if I wasn't back, do it anyway; and headed back for the chopper with or without me. That was an order. "Let's go doc; I said talking him by the arm.

He went down the same hallway I did and into the same room. He walked down to the cells. The girl was still crying." Open it a told him."

"Her? He said. She is crazy."

"I know, open it."

Then I went to the others one by one. Oh god what did my father do. I couldn't believe what they looked like.

"See; he said. You can't let them go. They would kill anyone they meet."

I couldn't stop looking at them. "What the hell did he do? I yelled. These were people."

"No more; the doc said. They are no good to anyone now. Please he said. I can't let you take them."

"Isn't there something you could do for them?" I asked him.

"No. I tried but this is what happened. Nothing could help them believe me."

When they heard his voice they all came to the window. They made sounds that weren't human. The hands that were reaching out to get him weren't human. Maybe he was right. What would I do with them? Fly them back to be stared at for the rest of their lives?

"Doc how could you?"

"Your father made me do it. I was only testing animals, your father made me do it to them."

I know he was telling me the truth. No one but my father could let this happen.

"One other person would. Mr. Hitler. The doctor said he was the one that started it. My father picked up after he left off."

"No, he said. He was coming with your father. The two of them had sent me here a year before to set it up and they said they would follow."

"Is Hitler dead?" I asked him. .

He looked at me and said. He didn't know. "My father would talk as if he was coming, but he never showed up.

"My father's dream. I guess. Well I hope he is dead along with my father."

"Please let them stay. They would want to dye;" he said.

"What about the girl?" I asked.

"Her to. He said. You don't know her. She could kill you with her bare hands. She is a woman but with the strength of Ten man and her brain isn't all there. Please," he said again.

"Let's go." I said. I know I was doing the right thing. I felt it as I left them trying to break their doors down to get out.

"This way; he said. It goes out the back way. I don't know why but I followed him. Just as we got to the door this guard came out from nowhere.

"Halt; he yelled and had his gun out."Oh it is you Doc; he said putting it back. Look Doc you know you can't keep coming out this way."

"I know; the doc said, but we have to catch a plane."

"Doc I don't know. I'm going to have to call and find out. You got me in trouble the last time I did it for you."

"Oh don't worry I won't tell anyone;" he said.

"It's not that doc the alarm goes off in his office. He knows I opened it."

"Soldier do you know who I am?" I asked.

"Yes sir he said, but I still have to call. Father or no father.

"Good soldier. I said and turned to talk to the doc. I back kicked him under the chin." That should take care of him." Now lead the way doc."

"He was right; he said it did set off an alarm. "So, I said. We will be long gone when they come down."

"I hope so;" he said.

He opened the door. I could see we were almost by the beach.

"The choppers were just over the hill;" he said.

I hope the banger did what I told him to do. Set them and leave. We got to the choppers and the Gunny said; let's go." I got the doc on and was about to get on myself.

"Banger; where is he?"

"He was with you." He said. He didn't come back yet."

Shit I got back off and told them to wait five minute and if I wasn't back take off, you got what you needed, the doc will tell all. Won't you Doc!" I asked looking at him.

"You can bet on that;" he said. Just get me out of here"

"Five; I said to the Gunny.

"Ten, he said. Now go."

I took off back to the doorway. The one we came out of, so far so good. We did it without anyone knowing about it. The sun was starting to come up so I had to move fast. I got to the door. No one was here the guard was still out. I jumped over him and headed back the way we came. As I got close to the cells I could still hear them yelling. Oh shit; when I turned the corner I saw the woman. She was holding something in her arms. It was Snake. The doc must have forgotten to lock her door back up. The Snake was just lying in her arms not moving.

"Put him down;" I yelled. That was when I saw him move, good he was still alive.

"No, she said. I love him."

"Look please put him down and I'll get you a new lover."

"No;" she said putting him over her shoulders.

God was she big.

"Snake, can you talk?" I yelled.

"Yes;" he said.

".Where is Banger?"

"Over here;" he said.

It was coming from the woman's cell.

"She won't let me out;" he said.

"You have anything left?" I asked.

"Shit no, if I did I'd of used it on her. I got nothing."

"Look Banger I have a gun, if I throw it to you do you think you could hit her?" I can't from here. I told him without hitting Snake."

Just then I felt something behind me.

"Hold on Louie let me at her;" he said. It was the big guy.

"I'll get him."

"Don't." I stopped him. Who sent you?" I asked

"No one, but where you go I go; he said. Look I could take her."

The Banger yelled, "no way is she strong. She will kill you;" he yelled.

"No woman can beat me;" he said trying to pass me.

"No wait let's see if this works." Banger here it comes. I took the guards gun and throw it at the door. "Good shot;" the big guy said.

"Now Banger;" I yelled. He ran out picked it up and ran back in the cell.

"How what?" He asked.

"Shot her;" I said.

"Do what? He yelled.

"Shot her in the lags; I said. Make her drop him.

"I can't do that;" he said.

"Snake yelled shit the mother. She is squeezing me to death and her breath is killing me. She kept kissing him on the lips.

"Do it;" I yelled.

"I can't;" he yelled back. She is a woman. Can't you see the tits on her?"

She did look good from the shoulders down.

"How could I shot something that looks like that?" The big guy said, lets rush her.. All four of us can take her. Come on she is a woman.

"Banger please shot her."

"No;" he said I can't."

Snake started yelling. Her fucking breath is killing me. Please Banger I'll give you anything you want. Shot her."

"O.K. Big guy; I said. You lead. I'll follow and if you can't take her let me know I'll shot her." "That will be the day a woman comes by I can't take."

"On three;" I yelled, we are coming. Banger get ready to help just in case."

"I'm not going to shot her; he said. You see her body?"

"Fuck her body;" Snake said, let her kiss you and you'll change your mind real fast."

"One, Two Three. He jumped over me and headed right for her. She didn't know he was coming she was too busy kissing Snake. The big guy hit her with all he had.

Shit she didn't even move. The big guy landed on the ground.

"More" was all she said dropping Snake and picking up the big guy. Man she didn't even strain. She held him off the floor and started kissing him. Snake moved away fast. I got Banger out to help him up. I went up to her and looked straight up at her.

"Sorry lady he has a girlfriend."

She stopped kissing him and looked over his shoulder at me.

"Oh honey;" she said. You came back for me! She let the big guy drop and started to come for me.

She remembered me from the other day.

"I know you would come back for me. You love me." The Banger was right, you couldn't shot her. God did she look good. That was without her face. I pointed my gun at her and told her to back away. She didn't even know what a gun was.

"For me;" she said and took it out of my hand. She was not only strong she was fast to. She took the gun and looked at it.

"This is nice; she said. You do love me?"

The big guy got up and the split second I turned to look at him; she had me. Oh god was she strong, she was breaking my ribs. And she wasn't squeezing me. Then I know what Snake was talking about. She put her mouth over mine and kissed me. Her breath was like nothing I had ever smelt before. No I take it back. I did smell it before. It smelt like dead bodies rutting in the sun and more. I couldn't breathe it in, it was making me sick. Short of breath and with her holding me I could feel myself going out.

"Shot her." I yelled.

I couldn't see what the fuck them ass holes were doing behind me so I kept yelling till I couldn't yell any more. Then I felt her dropping me. What the fuck was going on? She was looking over my shoulder at something. When I hit the ground I almost went out. The big guy grabbed me and dragged me away from her feet. I saw Snake standing in front of her with something in his hand. The big guy stood me up. I saw what it was. The flower. Snake was holding it so she could see it.

"Give it to her;" I yelled, and let's get the hell out of here. How much time?" I asked Banger.

"We got plenty of time;" he said half an hour.

"That isn't that much time. We have to get everyone out of here before it blows. Let's go;" I yelled at Snake. I turned around at started running back. I saw Snake turn to so I know he was following.

The big guy led the way. Banger followed and then me and Snake. Good we all got away. I went out and headed straight for the chopper. The Gunny was watching for us. I yelled for him to take off and to get on the loud speaker. The chopper had one on it.

"Tell everyone that the place is going to blow. They had better get their ass out of bed and leave. They got ten minute to get out; I was going to say when I saw the Gunny looking over my shoulder." Banger how long?" I asked. He too was looking.

"Now what? I asked, and turned around. I couldn't believe what I saw. The Snake was running with the woman hand and hand, like two lovers.

"What the fuck is that?" The Gunny asked.

Banger said. He is in love."

"The doc said he can't take her. She will kill us all."

"Oh shit now what? Gunny shot her."

"You crazy?" he said. Would you look at her body?"

"Fuck her body;" I yelled. Look at her face. Shot her."

"No" he said giving me the rifle. You shot her."

I took the gun and pointed it at her.

Snake yell, don't she isn't going to hurt anyone. .Let me keep her."

This is crazy the fucking Indian is sick. No one could love anything like that. Before I could get my rifle back up they were to close.

"Please Luoy, she love me."

"Gunny if she makes any wrong moves shot her. Get in." I yelled

"This is crazy; he said. You shot her."

"Take off. If she goes crazy she will kill us all. Now shot her or take off."

He took off. I got to the loud speaker and started yelling. "Get up and out of the house. It is going to blow." I didn't care about the man in the barracks; they didn't hold any threat to anyone but them self's. They would find another war to fight. The house was what I wanted clear. The lab was right under it, and from what the Banger said it was going to go.

It didn't take long for the windows to open and heads to stick out. I said it again, this time I gave the time." In 15 minute the house is going to blow with everyone in it. Now get your asses out now." I didn't have to say it again the door opened and they all started running out. Some with clothes and some without. Then the shit started to hit. The soldiers and the guards started shooting at us.

"Get it up Gunny; there is too many of them down there." He did before I finished. We were climbing.

"Oh Shit; the Gunny said. We have company." He pointed at the ground. The other chopper was coming.

"Oh shit Gunny, you didn't take them out?"

"You didn't tell me to."

"Gunny when I get you down on the ground me and you have got to have a long talk."

"Yes sir captain;" he said smiling.

He was a nut. As I watched the chopper take off the whole house went up.

"Shit Banger what the hell did you do?"

He just smile and said. "My job sir."

The house just lifted up into the air and came back down to earth. The people were running all over the place. It took out two choppers doing so. That left only one more." Snake let that woman alone and get your ass up here."

"Yes sir, he said taking off his jacket and covering her with it.

"Here" I said handing him the rifle. Take it out." I pointed to the chopper. I know if anyone could, he could. He did. I looked at my uncle to see what he was doing. He didn't want to look at me.

"Home James." I said.

"I hope we make it;" the Gunny said.

"What do you mean, make it?"

He looked at the gold and said we are overweight. And we are burning a lot of fuel.

"Where is the ship?" I asked. He did said we had a ship in the waters waiting for us."

"It's about 25 miles and we have gas for about 20."

"So take a short cut."

"We can't;" he said.

"Why not? I asked.

"It will be over the air field and the Brazilian won't like it. They must have the word by how and are coming up after us. He was looking out the window. He was right here they come.

"Oh shit now what?" I asked.

"You're the captain," he yelled.

"Fuck you. Brake radio silence and get our ship on the line. Tell them we need help."

"Will do;" he said taking the radio and yelling. May day, May day, we need help."

We all went silent waiting for the answer. It came. "That is a Roger;" the radio said."

"Yes;" we all yelled as the first Brazilian Jet flow over our heads.

"Oh shit here they come."

The other jet was getting ready to shot.

"Out run them;" I said.

"Ha you got to be kidding;" the Gunny said. Throw the gold out and we might be able to. With that load in here, no way."

Everyone looked at me. They acted as if it was theirs.

"Start throwing;" I said.

The first box was just about to go out the door when this loud noise came right over our head.

"Mother fucker what the hell was that?"

"Yea;" the Gunny yelled. It's our fly boys coming. The mother almost hit us going right over us and into the Brazilians Jets.

He almost hit them head on. The Brazilians didn't even put up a fight they saw the other jets coming and turned around and took off back to their base.

The Gunny yelled back. "The gold has got to go, were not going to make it."

Again the box was going out the door.

"Wait" is that our ship?"

"It sure is;" the Gunny yelled, hold the gold."

The ship was coming for us. I guess it heard us.

"Can we make it Gunny?"

"It's going to be close."

"Give it your best." I said. Everyone get ready to crash. Heads down and pray."

"Hey Louie how do you pray In Jewish?"

The only thing I could think of. "God save my ass."

"Lock hum. And hope he hears you." The Gunny was making it. We were close to the ship. We were about ten feet from landing when the engine stopped.

"Hold on;" he yelled. Down we went.

Ten feet didn't seem like much but with the load we had on. We came down with a bang. The landing gear gave out. We got two feet shorter. The choppers belly was flat on the deck. We made it.

We all started piled out. The deck craw came over with the hoses to spray. The Medic team was on its way. They all were running for us.

It was like the movies, time stands still when the woman came out. Everyone stopped in their tracks and just looked. The coat blow off and all you saw was this 7 ft naked woman standing on the deck. I heard the guy in the tower said over the loud speaker "WHAT THE FUCK IS THAT?" And clicked off.

The captain came running over and he stopped. He couldn't believe his eyes.

"Good god man where the hell did she came from?"

"You got any more of them aboard?"

"No sir I said laughing getting way from the chopper. "Captain I want General Greene on the horn right away."

"His is. Follow me; he said still looking at her. "Good god is she real?" He tripped over his own man who also weren't watching what they were doing.

"Watch where you're going Sir. I said trying to hold it in. He got back up and turned and yelling. "Get something to cover her with."

I followed behind him to the tower.

"General Green he said handing me the head set.

"You fucking nut what did you go and do now?

"Stopped a war sir I said.

"I don't think so he said, the Brazilian are pretty pissed off.

"Tell them for me to piss off General.

"It may not be that easy. He said. I'll get back to you. Tell the captain to get the hell out of their waters and don't stop..

"Will do sir I said and sign off.

CHAPTER 12

We headed back to the states. Wouldn't you know it? We were heroes once again. Seymour came forward and told the General everything that he knew. And when the doctor told the rest, along with my uncle as proof. The general was sitting on top of the world. Of course he received another star for it. Little did they know how close it really was? My father would have controlled the world in a few short months.

So it was rest time for us. Boy did I need it.

Nancy was glad I was back. The general gave us a week off. Nancy and I headed for the beach. We rented a place and made love in the sun. I kept trying to remember what Judy said about sex. Two times a day. Oh hell there goes my wonder man. I didn't care; we did it at least four times a day. To hell with her.

Well it all went off without them finding out who I really was. Seymour did a good job on that. He told them my father was out of his mind and when he remembered seeing us he thought I was his son. Seymour said we did work in my father's house as servant. He did know me, but he thought as his son. Not as a prisoner. It worked out for the better, everyone was happy. Mike came with me. He was mine forever. Nancy loved him. She couldn't get over how smart he was. She played with him all the time. That is when she wasn't playing with me.

When we got back we checked in. I had another assignment waiting for me. It had something to do with the General that got away and the Russians. Things weren't going to good over there. It seemed as if the Chinese were getting into it to. So back to Korea; I couldn't wait. I really didn't want to go, but I had my orders. I was to land somewhere in the north and try to get the general out of the picture. Easy wasn't it? Kill the gook and leave just like that. I didn't know if they thought I was superman or what. This isn't going to be that easy.

I rounded my man up and off we went. Oh in case you're wondering what happened with Snake? He married her. He said it was love at first sight. They spent their honeymoon in the lab. The government wanted to check her out first. He didn't mind. He was with her all the time. God I could just see the babies they are going to have. He was short and she; well you know how big she was! Time will tell I guess. So he stayed back with her. The rest came with me. The Gunny was glad to get out of there. All of them did. They love war. I guess I did to.

We landed in Soul and were greeted by the Korean police. I asked where my friend Kum was. They told me she was already up trying to get to the general. That's crazy she can't do it by herself. They said she wanted to and she was the only one that could. Knowing her she would. So what did they need me for? They told me they lost contact with her and didn't know where she was. Nice I said and left without saying another word.

We got air lifted as far as they dared. Then we were on our own the rest of the way. We had check points mapped out to where and when they would come back for us. If we weren't waiting at one they would go and come back the next day. This was to go on and on till they retrieved us. One small catch. They would only do it four times. Then we were crossed off as missing in action. Nice of them. So off we went. He was somewhere up north. My guess is he was with the main troops. He always wanted man around him. He felt safer that way.

We went from village to village looking. He was nowhere to be found. Time was running out and no word of him or her. It was as if he never came back from Brazil. Intelligence said he did; so we had to find him. He was doing all the talking with other countries. Making them join forces with them. The only thing that stopped the countries from doing it was the atomic bomb. They know we wouldn't hesitate to uses it again. Thank god for that, if we didn't drop it on Japan the whole world we be after us. That was the only thing that kept Russia and China from really joining them.

Well we were out for a week. We had three days left to get picked up and still nothing. It was hard going; we traveled mostly by night;

resting in the day. Troops were all heading south. The more we saw of them the less I liked it. One day we came to this big troop camp. I mean two or three battalions of man. The Gunny pointed out a lot of Chinese soldiers mixing with the north.

"This may be the place." I said.

"Let's hope so. He said, we are running out of time. And I'd hate to walk back."

"We will camp here and go down and see what is going on."

Me and the Gunny went. I had the rest of the man watch. If anything happened they were to head back for the check point.

Here goes nothing. We had Russian uniforms, and I did speak Russian. So we were to walk right into the camp and tell them we got shot down. We wanted to get back to mother Russia. It was the only way we could get close and find out what was going on.

"I hope it works;" the Gunny said looking kind of nervous.

"So do I."

Off we went. Knowing if it didn't work we would be right in the middle of them with no way out. What the hell. We got to the main road and just walked up it. No one stopped us. The troops just waved at us and yelled. I guess they thought we were joining them. That was on till we got to the main gate. The guards didn't speak any Russian so I tried Japanese. That didn't go over either. Finely this officer came over and took over. He understood me and told me to follow him. We did, the more we walked the more I was sure the Chinese were joining the Korea's.

The place was filled with them. Trucks were coming in with Chinese weapons. Oh shit I think we hit pay dirt. This was a massive movement to the south.

He took us to a tent and left. I guess he wants' us to wait. The Gunny didn't like it.

"What if the general is here?"

"We kill him." I said.

"What if he sees' you?"

Oh shit that was right. He knew me.

"No, I said he didn't know it was me that took my father over. It was you and the General that took the credit for it. Seymour saw to that.

The Gunny looked at me and asked." He was your father wasn't he?"

I guess he know all along but didn't want to ask. "Does it make any difference?" I asked him. He didn't answer me. I guess really knowing took it out of him.

Just then this officer came in.

"You he said. You come with me."

We followed and went into this other tent. This one was bigger.

"Come, he said taking me back to this place they had curtained off.

Oh shit it was like old home week. Captain Kum was with two other man. She almost died when she saw me.

"Yes, one of the men said. What can we do for you?" He spoke in English.

I didn't speak at first then I said in Russian. "I need his help."

"Oh he said In Russian. He spoke all languages I guess. I told him we were shot down and we had to get back to see general Oh."

He smiled and said the general was coming here so I didn't have to go anywhere." You bring good news?" he asked.

I told him it was for the Generals ears only.

He didn't like it, but he respected it and back down from asking any more questions. I asked about the woman and something to eat. He laughs and said, she was ours and food will be brought to our tent. The General wasn't do for a day. He was coming tomorrow.

"Big meeting with the Chinese." He said. They will join if you do?" He said.

"This is what we are here for." I said.

That got him so excited he almost jumped in the air, he was so happy. "Good he said. We will take the Americans.

The Gunny looked at me and didn't know what we were talking about. All he did was smile. If I pulled this off. It would be a miracle. What the fuck was I doing anyway? I was right in the heart of the Korea army with nothing but a hand gun and ten men. Our uniforms were like that of a Russian pilot. They even looked as if we crashed. But how dumb could they be? Kim was looking at me and didn't want to say anything. She was still dumb founded. She couldn't believe her eyes. When she heard what I was doing she just sat back and looked, along with the Gunny. Poor Gunny, he didn't know what I was up to either.

The officer went over to her and told her to go with us, and show us a good time. He said she was a woman from the village, and she knows how to treat a man. I could see Kum was glad to go. She got up to leave; the office told her she had better be good." We needed our friends the Russians. He told me if she didn't treat me good to kill her.

"Ha, I laugh; right in the head." I said pointing my finger at her.

They showed us the way out. As we walked throw the tent Kum was looking at a desk, trying to show me something. It was the layout of their troops.

"Arrrr I said and stopped. "This is very good."

"He smiled and said. It was the latest troop placement. And as you could see we had the Americans surrounded.

All they needed was the Chinese to come from the south and Russia from the north.

The Gunny just wanted to get the hell out of there. Not I. I wanted to look at it more. If I could remember what was here. What the hell am I talking about? If we ever got out of this; we'd be lucky.

We went back to our tent. When we were along the Kum came up to me and put her arms around my neck. Just in case someone comes in.

The Gunny just went to his bunk and sat. "What the hell he said, you're in charge."

"Look fellows I don't know how or why your here, but if I was you I'd get out of here as fast as I can."

I told her I was worried about her.

Ha, tell me another one."

"Look I'm here now what?"

She started to talk when someone came in with some food. She came right into me with her tongue and body. Oh hell we had to make it look good.

The soldier that brought the food just laugh. He was talking to the Gunny. The Gunny didn't know what the hell he was talking about so he just laughs. I think she was a little over doing it, but I didn't stop her. She only had on this silk dress. I could feel even her public hair against me. She was like a wild cat.

The Gunny waited till the soldier left and said. "Food guy's, food is here. He just sat and watched us going at it and ate." Man this is better the T.V." he said and kept watching and eating. When she knew the soldier was gone she pulled away from me and said. "These soldiers are stupid. When the General come he will know what you are. I don't know if she felt anything but I sure did. She was something else.

"Are you listening to me?" She asked.

"You said something about the General."

"Stop being a fool, she said I had to make it look real. Now listen to what I have to say."

"O.K. I said taking her back in my arms and kissing the hell out of her, she started to fight me, then stopped and joined me. If the Gunny wasn't here I'd of had her on the floor by now.

"Stop" she said pulling away from me. "You crazy we may never get out of here alive."

"So, I said, what a way to go."

"Here, Here;" the Gunny said. My turn."

I just looked at him with my look.

"Just kidding;" he said and went back to eating. "Look she said this isn't the time or the place for this."

"Oh I said. My doctor said twice day."

"You're what?" She asked.

"Nothing. Now what do you have for me?"

The Gunny said again. We can see what she has, don't ask."

"Shout up the both of us said to him. He went back eating.

"First of all the General just came back from this meeting in Brazil and he seems to think the war is over. The way he talked is as if Mr. Hitler was coming himself.

Oh shit could it be. No I couldn't be so lucky I said. "What"? The Gunny asked.

"Did anyone see when the general left? Maybe he didn't stay around. Maybe he left before the shit went down. "So what if he did the Gunny said. He still knows you. "He does but in a different way. If he did leave and didn't know what had happened to my father. Then I think I can convince him I was here to see what he was doing On behalf of my father.

"You crazy he said. Everyone knows what happened there. Maybe the outside world does, but not on the front line they don't.

"So now what," he asked?

"We play it by ear."

"Ear? he said. Our last pick up is in 15 hours and if we aren't there we walk. She asked what he was talking about. I told her.

"Good she said. You had better go. You can't do anything here. Take back the information you have. It will help win this war.

"What about you?.

She smiled and said. You know where to find me if you win. I'll be here .

"Funny girl I said. You know what they will do to you. Your coming with us.

"No, I could do more staying.

"Just then someone else came in. She came to me again. This time they had another girl for the Gunny. I guess they wanted to take real good care of us. The Gunny jumped up and ran over to her.

"Hey he said now this is what I call eating. The soldier asked if we need any more. I was about to say no, when the Gunny said about five more.

"What the fuck you doing I yelled. No I told the soldier this was enough. He looked at me and smiled." Go I said and let us have fun thank you." Gunny you take the lady and have fun;\" I told him. I didn't know if she was a plant or what.

"O.K. honey I said to bed. Take your clothes off and do the right thing. She knew what I meant. We couldn't talk with her in the same tent. But if we were in bed together we could talk under the blanket and the Gunny could keep her busy. I got under the covers and took off my clothes. She did the same. The Gunny had his off and was doing it to the girl already. I guess he would keep her busy for a while.

"Look I got to stick this out. If everything goes the way I plan we all should be gone by tomorrow.

"How are you going to do that? She said.

"The General himself will fly us out."

"Ha she said laughing. You are crazy."

She put her hand down and it touched me." Oh she said what this is.

"My gun; I said. What the hell do you think it is?

"Oh that's nice she said putting both of her hands around it. You have a big gun mister, and it feels hot.

"Now look who don't want to talk I said.

"We talk later she said and went down and started sucking.

"What the hell go for it I said to her., she did oh boy did she. We would do it. Then as we rested we talked. Then we found ourselves doing it again. I could hear the Gunny going at it. I didn't think he stopped once. I told her all about what happened in Brazil and what I had planned with the general.

"Look Kim if it doesn't work. It doesn't work. We got nothing right now.

"You're the poppa son she said, and came at me again. She was so small she felt like the wind over me. Her nipples were like little pebbles on a hard ball. She didn't have much, put whatever she had she know how to use it.

"War? What war?. I said and went to sleep.

We were wakened by soldiers yelling.

"The general was coming. He was on his way." We jumped up and started to get dress.

The Gunny looked at me and said. Give me another ten minutes."

"Get the fuck up I said to him. You're going to fuck yourself to death."

He looked at me and said. "So what the fuck is wrong with that?"

"Get up I told him.

"No he said. You go and let me know what the hell is going on. If we are going to die he said, what the hell good I would do. Just tell them to shot me in bed. I always wanted to die in bed with a woman. He took the covers and covered him and the woman.

"Maybe he would just get in the way she said. Better leave him here.

"Thank you he said from under the covers without coming out.

She was right he would only foul it up if he opened his mouth. We got dress and followed the soldier to the main tent. Everyone was running around like crazy. The general didn't land yet, but I could see him coming. "Well I told her it is now or never.

We sat and waited. Of course you know where we sat. Right in front of the map. Looking at it and trying to remember everything on it. Then it happened. The General came in with his armed guard and yelled something. "Oh shit I heard her say. He wants us killed.

The guards came over and stuck their guns in our face. Oh shit he knew. They had the Gunny outside and when they took us out he smiled and said. "I didn't get the chance to die in bed.

They took us to this make shift prison. She was thrown in with us. She said they are going to shot us. Where is the general? I kept asking. They kept hitting. Mother fucker. Then little fucking gooks. Before we got to the prison I was bleeding all over the place. She kept yelling for them to leave me along, but they would hit her to. By the time we got put in the cage we all were beat up pretty badly. The Gunny was out, they had to drag him in. What the fuck happened. I didn't even see the general. We were on the cold ground. I could see something was going on over at the main tent. The general must be inside. Shit he know who I was and it was over for us.

About two hours later the officer that spoke Russian came over and stood looking at me.

"You dye American he said poking at me. How he spoke English.

She looked at him and said something to him. He started to go after her. I pulled her away from his reach. Then he left. She told me what he said. No shit they had it all wrong. Them stupid mother fucker's. They thought I was a here to kill the general. He said he was getting into trouble for taking us in. He said the general checked and found out no Russian Plane went down and the only other thing was we were sent here to kill the him. They found out who she was and that was it.

The General didn't even know it was me. He also said that we were to be shot for being spy's. He said he would be back to do it him self. Shit I would never get to see the General. They were going to shot us. The Gunny was coming to. He was in bad shape. His teeth were out of his mouth and his ear was hanging off.

"Hey guys looks like we don't get to party for this one, he said and went back out.

"Look she yelled, there he is.

It was the general coming out of the Tent. He was going over to the chopper. Shit he was leaving.

"No I yelled trying to make him look at me. To him I was just another American spy caught. He didn't even look to see who I was.

"You mother fucker I yelled. He stopped and turned to look at me. Shit that was the wrong thing to say. Shit why did I said that.

What the hell else was I going to say. I know I said to my self.

"Spider. "Spider I yelled. He was walking away by then. Shit I don't think he could hear me. The choppers was making a lot of noise." Spider" I yelled again. This time I think I blow out my voice I yelled so hard. The next one was just a squeak. I didn't have anything left in me to yell. I fell to the ground and just looked at her.

"Well it was nice knowing you I tried to say. She came down to me and held my head in her hands and cried. I just looked at the Gunny and then at the ground. What a way to go. Beat up, muddy and dead. I wiped the blood from my eyes and saw a pair of boots standing out side the bob wirer. I looked up. The mother fucker was coming to kill us. I could just see the shadow of him, the sun was right behind him.

"Go ahead you fucking gook I said. You don't have any brains anyway.

Then I hear him say "Spider.

Oh shit he did hear me. I tried to get up to see who the fuck I was talking to. But I was to weak. I just p73 pulled my self over to the wirer and shaded the sun with my hand. Oh god it was the general.

"General Oh I said. What the fuck you doing to me? I passed out. When I woke I was in a bed. The General was standing over me.

"Mr. Kaufmann what brings you here .

I sat up and said "You.

He had someone help me up .

"Now would you minute telling me what brings you here. I looked at him and said .

"If I had a spider with me you would be dead I said to him.

He didn't laugh. He helped me up and took me over to a table.

"Come he said. Drink it will make you feel better.

He gave me something hot. I drank it and almost chocked. "What the fuck was that. I asked.

"Make you strong he said. Now please tell me .

I looked at him and said "My father sent me here to see what kind of army you had and to talk to you. I was hoping he did leave before I killed my father .

"I told your father I would get back to him when I left.

"I know I said, but My father is moving fast and he said it would be better if you joined him now. With the spider you will save many of your man.

He smiled at me and asked, did I have any with me.

"No I said. You know it will cost you money to get them.

"Arrrr so he said. This has been on my minute. My Russian friends Don't want anything to do with your father .

"But what can they offer you? I asked.

"Men.

"Ha I said. Man won't stand a chance with our spiders and you know it.

"Arrr so but one thing I forgot to ask your good doctor.

"What is that?

"The spiders will only live in warm climate. You see he said it is very cold here.

He had a point. Now what.

Shit why not. "Mr Oh do you have roaches here? In your country.

He smiled and said. That is what my soldiers eat most of the time out in the field. Good protein he said.

"Mr Oh what did the good doctor breed the spider with? Roaches I said. They can live anywhere. Weather is nothing to them. If you want you can have some send here to show you. My father will be glad to. I said.

"No he said. You made your point. The Russians don't want to come in with me all they want to do is sell me weapons. p73

"What would you rather have. Spiders our guns.

"Look he said I know what I would do. But I don't control my country.he said. Not today I said but tomorrow like my father said it could be yours. But what is the price must I pay,he asked. I'm sure my father will work some kind of payment plan for you I said.he finely laugh The American way he said. No I said my fathers way. He looked at me and said your father has a wise son.

No I said not to wise. If I was wise I would of not got my self almost killed. Then why he asked. oh I said I wanted to see if your army was as good as you said they were. Well he said. waiting for me to answer him. I looked at around the tent and smiled. They stink I said I would shot them all. I found out everything you are going to do and they even gave me a whore to make me happy. he called over his shoulder and the officer that spoke English came front and center. This is the officer that you talked to he asked. That is the one I said he didn't even ask to see my papers. he took me in and gave me the whole thing. That was very stupid of him to do so He said. he is one of many I got like this. So I said you know how to get reed of them I said. Oh he said but you didn't bring any with you he said smiling.

They he did it. I didn't even see him take out his gun he had it to the officers head and pulled the trigger before I saw what he was doing. Oh shit he blow the top of his head off. the blood went flying all over the place. You see he said. a bullet still work. the officer didn't even know what had happened. he was still standing. I guess he was dead but didn't know enough to lay down. he just pushed him to the side and handed me a rag to wipe his blood off of me. Pig he said Your way is much better he said smiling. We told you so I said,So now what he asked. your father isn't going to back out because of what my man did to you. No I said he will only say it was good for me for doing what I did. he didn't want me to come but I had to see for my self. Well he said you see now what.

I looked at him and smiled. You got any real food I asked. that fish and rice isn't hitting on shit I said. I know he said,once you eat it your hungry an hour later. I know the joke he said and laugh. You got it. What about my man I asked. Oh he said he is being 03 looked after by my doctors. he will be O.K. And the girl I asked. Oh he said he was sorry for her. he called another man over. and said something to him. I trough he was telling him to go get her. I was wrong. he shot him to. Right in the head. Oh man I said I just cleaned my self. Come he said I got new cloth for you. He just stepped over the other body as if it was nothing. What was that for I asked as we walked. he gave you that spy he said. Spy what spy I asked. the Woman he said she is Police for south. Shit I said how the hell did she get here. Oh he said my man like woman and they bring woman from the village to make them happy. so she joined them. See what I mean I said.

You are so right he said. If I ran this country I would do like your father does. and what is that I asked him. Kill the weak he said. I trough to my self and said if he did that he would have none to order around. they all were stupid. Good idea I said to him you should start now I said. he went into this part of the tent and it was like a dinning room. hey I said look at this. Food. He had a turkey on the table with all the trimminutegs. and wine. You like he asked. Just like home I said and sat down. I eat till I couldn't eat any more. Well he said I must go. You tell me what you want he asked and He will do it. he was getting tired of this war. he wanted to live like my father was. Good Life I told him. he agreed with me. I told him I wanted a plane and all the money he had/. If I took that back to my father he would be happy. Money he asked. I just laugh and said see what your man did to me. I don't think my father would have anything to do with you after seeing what had happened here.

Please he said,you must make him understand it was not my fault. If you would of came with an invitation,This wouldn't of happened.I know that I said but you know my father. He didn't like giving up his money I could see that. I had to make him less powerful,and taking away his money would do just that. With out money he was nothing. With out money,anyone was nothing. That was the way the world went around. Either you have the ability to have people give you money, or you have it to start with. either way you had to have it. Hitler had nothing but he had the ability to have people to hand him money. Caesar had money. two of the worlds leaders from different back grounds. General Oh was one of them man like my father the only difference was General Oh lacked something. I didn't know what it was,but I know he wasn't going to last.

The General asked if I could give him some time to collect it.I told him I had to get back My father would be worried about me. I wanted to get out of there as fast as I could. I didn't want him to find out what p73 really happened to my father, I didn't want to be laying on the floor like the other two. I'll give you till tonight and then I have to go I said if you don't want to I told him he would just have to take a back seat.

My father didn't want to wait. he had plans and it didn't need any set back. he was ready to make his move with in a couple of days. This got the General excited. he didn't know it was that close. Your father said a couple of months. Ha I said that was before the good doctor found what we were looking for.,Right after you left. Good man the general said,you will have it here tonight. he said now I got to go and arrange it,he said. Oh general The girl I asked him. Oh he said he will take care of her. No I said leave her to me.

He didn't even ask why. He told the guard to bring her to me and to give me anything I needed. He will return he said and left. How all I needed was to not have him find out about my father. I had to make sure my man left. I was hoping they obeyed my orders and went back,but I had to check to make sure. I went in to see the Gunny. Man did they do a number on him. He was still out of it. Then I looked at my self in a mirror. shit they did one on me too. I had two black eyes and cuts all over. That was o.k. it didn't bother me. I know it was all worth it. just to bring the general down. I went out and told the guard I needed a jeep to get the rest of my man. he know the general was my friend and what he did to the other two that fucked up. I didn't have any trouble getting what I wanted. I went out and when I got free of the camp stuck my white shirt on the window of the jeep. Hoping they would see it if they didn't go.

I got to the spot I told them to wait and no one was around. Good I was glad they obeyed my orders. I started going back when something hit me in the head. a rock Shit where did that come from. I stopped at looked all around Nothing I started off again and another one hit me. What the fuck I got out and walked around. Captain I heard someone calling. It was banger. Shit they didn't leave What the fuck are you still doing here I yelled. waiting for you he said. Where are the rest I asked. He said he sent them back He was the only one that stayed. Get in I said. he looked at me and said your kidding. No I said it is o.k. we got the run of the camp. Now get your ass in here. Man he said getting closer. what the fuck happened to you.

Oh I said you think I look bad you should see the Gunny. Your crazy he said and you want me to go back with you. No way he said backing up. Get the fuck in I said and started to drive off. he jumped

in. I told him what had happened and what we were up to. I also told
p73 him that if the General finds out were dead. Nice he said If it is all
the same to you he said I'll wait out side and when our ready to leave
pick me up.No I told him I wanted him with me. If I had to leave in
a hurry. I didn't want to stop for nothing. When we got back she was
waiting in my tent. she was beating pretty bad her self. The Gunny was
coming around and they jumped when I came in. They didn't know
what happened to me. When the Gunny saw Banger he smiled The
troops have landed. No I said but we don't have to worry about them
they took off. Banger was the only one that stayed.

I always know he didn't have any brains. he said to him.. I should
of left he said. But no I trough you would be glad to see me he said. Yea
ass the Gunny said you can watch them shot me first and then you. The
Gunny didn't know. What had happened; when I told him he smiled
and said you mean he is going to get all his money and have it on a plane
waiting for us to fly out of here with and he is going to wave as we take
off? You got it I said. No I can't believe it he said it sounds to good to be
true. Then I told him. That is if he don't find out I'm lying. Then what
he asked. I said kiss your ass good buy. Oh he said looking at her. Man
do I look as bad as the two of you. Worse she said. Thanks he told her.
so Now we just wait. Banger came over and said sir one thing."

"What is that?" I asked. When I let the man go I told them to
report that there was a big build up going on and to have some jets do
their thing.

You're kidding?" I said. No sir he said I don't know how long it will
take them to get here but you can bet they are on their way. "Oh shit I
said now we have time against us. Gunny now long would it take them
to get back and send out the fly boys?"

"Oh he said by morning they should be here."

"At the crack of dawn;" he said.

Shit that changes our plan. What about the General she asked. we
had to wait for him. Let's but it this way I said if he isn't back here by 2
we had better get our ass the hell away from here. Other wise we aren't
going to have any ass to worry about. How are we going to do that The
Gunny asked. Just get in Jeep and drive the hell out of here. I said. just
like that He said. Just like that I said the solders don't want any part of

us. after the general shot two of there officers in the head. What ever I want I get I said.

No she said we got to wait for the General. We got to take the money off of him. he is making the war go out with all he has. He is buying the Chinese with it. Well I said if it comes down to that I would say we will have another day to try. No she said by that time he will know about you and trust no one.We have to wait she said. Good the Gunny said then you wait. I say we get out of here right now. No I said we still got Time. That is if they didn't radio the information ahead. If they did they could be right outside our door right now. I don't think so I said,"something this big they wouldn't put it over the radio. They had to conform it first with headquarters first and you know how long that will take. I hope you're right; he said but I wouldn't bet on it".

What time did they get picked up I asked Banger. This morning He said around 8. So that gives them 4 hours to fly back to our lines and another four to get the story straight. and then another 4 to have them check it out. then another 4 to map out the air plan. So that is into the night. I know they wouldn't want to drop at night. They want to see what they are hitting. so Your guess was right at the crack of dawn. That is if they didn't know about it before and they were just waiting for us to get out of here The Banger said. So we are still here I said. No he said I told the man you probable got you self's killed. I was just handing around to make sure. Oh that was nice of you. How was you going to get back. he took out his radio and said I was going to act as the point and direct them. and Hope they would send a chopper for me after. The radio I said that is it. No sir he said they can pick us up. as soon as we turn it on. I found out they have a tracking station here and we had to hide two times from them coming to check us out.

Once you turn it on they pick it up. I would only stay on half a minute. That was all. And hope someone heard me. So we only use it if we have to I said.

"And when do we have to?" The Gunny asked.

"When we see the first bomb drop. Something like that;" I said. Oh that is nice The banger said. By then it will be to late. Look the both of you knock it off. we leave By 2 if the General isn't back. I told him I had to get back to rush it. So we wait I said now just relax and eat I said pointing at the table. The banger was sitting down picking already. The Gunny didn't fell like eating; he couldn't with no teeth. Man was he a mess.

She came over to me and just sat next to me a cuddled up to me. I know I said you want his money out of the way but we got to think of our self's I said, No she said my people come first. What do you want me to do I asked her. Get on the radio and have them call it off she said. and wait for the General to return. I can't do that I said you heard what the banger said. Once they know what we are doing they will call the General. If he had any brains he wouldn't bring the money here. No we got to do it this way. Even if he comes with it we got to get right out. I don't want my own jets shooting at us as we take off. It is going to be close either way you look at it.

What if the Generals hears about them coming and changes his minute?" She asked. What if he finds out about me I said and what if I said, Nothing; the if's are driving me crazy. Let's just wait and see what happens. We play one card at a time. I guess that is all we could do. She tried to get some sleep. I couldn't, The Gunny was out and the Banger walking around. I told him to stay close I didn't want any gook shooting them. They know of him so they knew he was with me. But you never know what they will do. He said he just needs some fresh air. So we waited. I kept looking at my watch. Shit it was getting close. 12, then 1, then1:30. O.K. I said let's start getting ready to get the hell out of here. I asked Banger if the jeep was still in the front. he said it was. Good then let's get the old man ready for a ride.

"Wait; the Banger said I hear something." He was right it sounded like planes. Two or more. Shit that wasn't the General. He was only coming with one. Oh shit it was our boys. They were doing a night drop. No jets just bombers. Let's get the fuck out of here;" I yelled. I ran over to the Gunny and started to get him Up. Oh shit two guards came in. Mother fucker kill them;" I yelled to the Banger.

"No she yelled they said the general is on his way.

"Hold it Banger." I yelled as he was taking out his gun. you sure I asked he That is what they said It was the general coming in. Let's go I said we don't have any time to waste. Banger got the Gunny and I took her. Tell them we want to go meet the General. She did and they helped us in the jeep. I drove to where the planes were coming in. Shit two of them.

Let's hope he had the money on one. I didn't know what the other plain was for. Maybe he found out about me and had his own guard come along to shot me. Whatever it was I didn't have time to play. I told Banger to keep the jeep running just in case they found me out and make a run for it. You got to be kidding he said and how far do you think we would get. I say let's turn around and get the hell out of here while we still have the chance." Maybe he was right. The plans were just landing and no one was watching us; we could just drive off and they wouldn't know which way we went and wait for our plane to came. That is if they were coming. I wasn't even sure about them. Maybe my man didn't make it back. Maybe the top Brass didn't want to send any plane. Maybe and if." Two words that could drive you crazy.

No I said let's go see the general." We drove up to the side of the planes and I got out; the door opened and the general came out of one.

"Well he said I'm giving you it all he said. This mother had both plans filled with money of some kind. My father will be pleased. I said now I must go." I don't want my father worrying about me. Oh he smiled don't worry about that I have a call into him right now. I'm just waiting for his answer.

"You have?" I asked.

"Oh yes he said I had him call the base here. I'm sure you would like to talk to him and tell him how much money I'm giving him." You bet." I said. He will be so happy I bet he has a load of spiders ready for you already."

"Good he said you can send them back in my plane. "That was a good idea." I said

Come he said and we eat. No I said I wanted to get the hell out of here. I didn't want the money to fall in the wrong hands. Oh he laugh we are to far north for that to happen. The Americans won't dear come this far north. Just to be on the safe side I said I still like the cover of darkness. If you don't minute I said I do want to get back. I have other Countries to go see. My father is going to make his move and I would like to be there when he does. You love your father he asked. I love him to death I said laughing. Go he said my man will fly you. Oh shit I didn't think about that. Oh hell why not I didn't know how to fly. and the Gunny was in no shape to. So I guess I needed his man to do the flying.

Good I said and they will bring you back your spiders. just use them wisely. I said to him. You know how it works I asked. Oh yes he said, How many do you thing he will send me he asked. Oh maybe a hundred. I said. what is that all he said. You are taking all my money and all you are going to give me is a hundred. Cool down General. I said remember what the good doctor said. they double every three weeks. Roaches remember. By the end of the month you'll have thousands of them. That is the best part I said good things come in small packages. Ar so he said your father is very wise man. and remember we got other countries that gave money first we got to send them to. he was getting so excited he was shacking. The world will be ours In months he said clapping his hands together. Come I said why don't you come with us. I said.

No. he said he was to start planing who he was going to start with. His own people or the Americans. I told him to start with his own. We would take care of the Americans. Oh he said laughing. I guess your father hates them more then me. I guess you would say that. Go He said and hurry back. I went over to the Gunny and told him I wanted him and the banger on one plane and My and the lady would go on the other. he asked where was we going. Brazil I said. You crazy they will shot you out of the air you go anywhere near it. Just till we get out over our own air space. then you take the plane over and make them land on our air field. What if they don't let us he said you know we are in Korean Plans. Get on the radio I said what else.

Well the General watched us get aboard his plans with his money with a smile. I had to get out of they before he got the phone call and before the sun came up. Just in case our jets were coming. and far away not to have Our jets taking shots at us. We were to head up and over China and down to Russia and the along way around but the general made plans for us so we could refuel. we had to stop at least three time he said. The nearest place I could see was Alaska Once we got in the air I was going to get on the radio and tell them who we were and hope they believed us. No one know what we were up to so I had to make them believe us. I didn't want to p73 come all this way to be shot down by our own man. Just as we started to taxi down the run way I saw this jeep flying out of the main camp. Oh shit it was the phone call.

Get a move on I said to the pilot. He had two man in the cockpit and two more in the back with us. I guess it was the same in the Gunny's plane. I saw the general waiting for us to take off. the Gunny went first. It was a small air field and only one at a time could take off. I kept watching them and the general at the same time. the jeep got to the general just as the Gunny took off. Now us. I told the pilot to go. Oh shit here it comes. I saw the general jump into his jeep and head straight for us.I told her to get ready to take the two in the back I think we were in trouble. Now I yelled She took out her gun and told the two to drop theirs. Good I said now tell them to come up front. Then you tell the pilot to keep going. he was going to have the general on the radio soon and we couldn't stop. he know about me. She took the two to me and I just hit the Pilot in the head lightly with my gun to show him I had tone. I was right the general was yelling over the radio for them to stop. I hope the Gunny is seeing what is going on and is doing the same. I will never know.

The pilot didn't want to do it he started to slow down. Oh shit he can't do that. I put the gun to the co pilot and said do it. He still kept slowing down. I turned my gun on the two that was in the back and shot both of them. Now I yell get this thing up in the air. she started yelling something to him also. he looked at the two and changed his minute. he started to take off. Good I said now get the fuck out of here.. The General was gaining on us. Move it I yelled. he was shooting at us. The plane turned around and started picking up speed for take off. the General was right in front of us and he wasn't about to move. I told her to tell him to run him over if he had to. then I saw the Gunny's plane coming back Oh shit they heard the general and took Banger and the Gunny. Now what?

Shit I guess it was over I couldn't let them take the fall. I was just about to tell her to tell them to slow down when The base started to blow up. What the fuck. Did our plans get there already. Then I heard the Banger on the radio. Get the fuck out of there he said. I got the whole place ready to go. That mother,he must of did it when he took his walk. Yea I yelled tell them to get this fucking thing in the air our I'll blow his fucking head off. She told him that. He know we meant it. The general stopped to see what the hell was going on back at the base. I guess he trough his life was more importune then money. he stopped and turned his jeep around and was heading over to the choppers. I p73 guess he wanted to get the hell out of there to.

O.K. I yelled when the wheels lifted off the ground. I was just about to go to the back when Bang,shit she shot the fucking Pilot. what the hell did you do that. She turned to me and said he was going to land. Now what I asked her. I don't know how to fly this. You nut I said to her.She didn't look worried. she just pulled him out of the seat and took the wheel. Where to she asked smiling. You know how to fly I asked her. No she said but someone has got to. Your kidding I said sweating. She just smiled a winked at me and went to flying the plane. Can you see the Gunny I asked her. he is right on the side of us she said looking out the window. I climbed over the bodies and sat next to her.

She gave me the head set to talk to him. Hey Gunny what the fuck happened. he smiled and waved at us. I guess the same thing that happened with you, This gook wanted to turn around and head back. The banger got on and said How did it look. I know what he was talking about. Oh shit she said we are in trouble. I looked a head to where she was looking. Gunny we got trouble 12 o'clock high. No he laugh, They are our's. Gunny who's plane did we steal. Oh shit he said,get on the radio and tell them it is us. Oh shit she said it is to later they spotted us already. One was coming right at us then the other's were going for the base.

May day,Mayday I started yelling. It is us don't shoot. I didn't know what to say my tongue was dry and the words wouldn't come out. Don't shot I yelled again.

She yelled at me to turn the radio on first. How the hell did I know I yelled back at her. Well do something he is getting ready to make a pass at us.I turned the radio on the way she told me to. and yelled get the fuck out of here. I guess the pilot heard me he didn't shot he just fly over us. and I do mean just flow over us. he rocked our plane with he power. Say something else she yelled at me. What I yelled back at her. Any fucking thing she said just keep talking. I got back on and said,If

I get you on the ground I'll kick your ass I said. She looked at me and said is that all you can say. Tell him we are friendly, Americans tell him anything .But don't get him mad. she yelled at me.Oh shit here he comes again. Well say something fool, she yelled.

They the pilot came on our radio. Identify your self's he said. Tell him she said hitting me or he will shot us down. Stop yelling I said to her and don't hit me. Will you answer him she said hitting me again. Keep your hands on the wheel I told her. Oh shit she said he is going to shot at us. Mother fucker he did. He shot rounds over our heads. Identify your self's he said p73 again. It is us I yelled into the radio. Big fucking deal he said who is us. he said back. Tell him she said hitting me again. Us you know Captain Kaufmann. Captain who he said back. Oh shit I slipped. Captain Goldburg I said. How who is it he asked Goldburg or Kaufmann. Kaufmann I yelled. And how do I know that he said coming around for another pass. I couldn't think. She was hitting me and the jet was coming and the Gunny was yelling and I didn't know what to say. Well the pilot said you got three seconds to answer.

As he flow over us I saw the way he turned around, he did a roll over. That was the same pilot from the other time. Roll the plane over I told her. Do what she asked,You know do a roll over. You can't do that with this type of plane she said. Do it I yelled at her. Your crazy she said. you can't. I took the wheel and turned it all the way. Oh shit what did I do. The fucking plane went to one side and before you know it we were up side down. Oh shit I heard her say. we had it now. I felt the gold bouncing around in the back and all of a sudden the plane started to drop. You did it now she said. I told you this plane couldn't do it. Do something I yelled. The only thing we can do she said was kiss our ass's good bye. The plane went straight down. Oh god do something I yelled.

I couldn't even look at her. The plane was dropping fast. I heard her say she couldn't control it. and them I took the wheel again and turned it the other way. Oh shit she yelled take your hands off the wheel. But before she could finish it we were right side up again.Still falling but this time we were looking at the sky,not the ground. Well I said make us stop falling I yelled. How can I do that with out any engines running. She was looking out the window. Oh shit the props weren't turning. Start them I said.Don't make me laugh she said you start them.

How I asked her. Go out and turn them she said. you crazy I said looking at her. Just as crazy as you are. she said You do it I said. Then something happened I looked out the window and one of the props started to turn. Look I yelled it is turning. Shout the fuck up she said to me. I could see she was doing something. I just sat back and watched her. we were still falling. I kept watching the prop and praying it would start. It did and she did something else. oh shit it worked we were stopping falling and she was going forward. See I said I told you we could do it. Shout the fuck up she said not taking her eyes off the gages. Then we started to go faster. How close were we to the ground I asked. Look out the fucking window she yelled. Oh shit that was a tree. we just missed it. That close I said and kept my mouth closed.

When we got back in to the air,she looked at me and put her gun to my head. You touch that stick again and I'll shot you. You got me. I throw up my hands and didn't go near it. Now get on the radio and tell them who you are. How she yelled. I think she was mad at me. May day, I said. Not that shit,she said .Tell the man who you are. This is Captain I know who you are the pilot came back with. What the fuck he said. Oh I said smiling. you do,do you. She just looked at me and didn't say nothing. Your the only one I know that would try something like that and live to tell about it,the pilot said. You do it I said. ha he laugh it is you. Where the fuck you going he asked. She got on and said down she said and the sooner the better. this man is crazy she said looking at me. That is a Roger he said just hang on my tail and I'll bring you home. he came over us again and she followed him.

The Gunny came on the radio. is that you he asked. no I said man he said we saw you going down and. Look she said stopping him. you know what we did. Now don't bring it up again she said and shout it off. hey I said I wanted to talk to him. Your getting to me she said it is a big joke with you. Do you know we were close to crashing. Oh I said I know you could fly. She gave me the back of her hand and right across my face. I guess she meant it. she didn't say a word till we came to what looked like a air field under us. The pilot came back on and said rest the land down. She did and when we came to a stop she got up and went to the back and throw up all over the place. Glad you didn't do that when we were up side down I said. she turned around and shot at me three times. I jumped and hide behind the chair. Hey you crazy I yelled. Put that gun away I told her. I didn't want to stick my head up she may shot me. What has came over her. hey I yelled cool down. I was only joking. hey you hear me I yelled. Oh shit you scared me. It was the Gunny. You can come out now he said looking down at me behind the set.

Where did she go I asked. Who he said. You know who I said peaking over the set. Oh her he said she left already. Oh I said standing up. what was all the shooting about he asked. I looked at the three holes she put in the wall and said she shot at me for no reason. No reason He said. You got her pretty mad he said she didn't even stop to talk to me. she just pointed her gun at me and kept walking. what did you do to her he asked. Nothing I said. Man look at this shit he said Looking at the cargo that turned up side down. Some mess he said Man how did you do that he asked. I didn't know you could fly. he asked. I can't I said walking out the door. Hey he said wait for me.I told him to stay with the plane and let no one in.I will be back. I had to find her. Witch way did she go I asked him. He p73 pointed and I ran. I had to catch up with her.

Shit there was nothing out there. the field only had two tents and a run way. She was walking out into the boonies. I started yelling for her. Shit I had to find her she must of flipped,went crazy. something. No one just walks out into the woods,not knowing where they were. You she said jumping out from behind a bush at he. you she yelled with her gun in her hand pointing at me. I tackled her to the ground and make love to her. It was the only thing I could think of I mean real hard love almost as if we wanted to hurt each other with it. hard banging skin slapping mad love.

When we finished she came into my arms and started crying. I guess we both need it. I picked her up in my arms and carried her back to the plane. The Gunny was on the radio and he yelled out the window. Where the hell did you go. For a walk I said. Well he said You had better got your ass on the line. We got more trouble.. I got into the plane and put her down. The Gunny came to meet us. he said the North was sending everything they had in the air looking for us. The base as telling us to take off. This air field isn't ours. Oh shit now what I asked. We got to get back in the air. the command post said they were sending everything they had to help us but we had to get back in the air and head south. She picked her head up and asked the Gunny how much fuel he had left. He said quarter. She got up and said how far do we have to go. He said they just want us back in the air. they didn't say where.

Man she said getting up. she went to the cock pit and on the radio. They told her where and she was starting the engines. Will she said to the Gunny you going to fly you's or you want me to do the both of them. The Gunny left and went back to his. I looked at her and she didn't want to look at me. I started to get in the co pilot set. when she stopped me No way she said get the fuck out of here.I guess she meant it. I didn't want to get her any madder then she was. so I went to the back. Man look at all this gold. I heard her yelling for me. I went up to see what she was yelling at. Oh shit I saw what she was yelling at it was ground troops coming and they weren't ours. We got to make us lighter. she yelled. How I yelled. she said throw something out. Like what I asked. Anything she said. I went to the back and opened the doors. the only thing I could see to throw out was the bodies of the solders.

So I did one my one. Move she yelled faster. she was At the end of the run way and was turning around More she yelled. I went and got the Pilot and co pilot and throw them out. How's that I yelled. we will see she said racing down the run way. The troops were shooting at us p73 put with rifle firer only. She was getting to the end of the run way and she kept yelling more. More what I yelled back Weight she yelled. There was a box of gold at the door I opened it and started throwing out the gold bars. More she kept yelling. the more I throw out the door. One my one. I didn't want to throw any more then I had to. One by one. she kept yelling more. Then I felt the plane lift off the ground. I stopped throwing. I didn't want to throw any more then I had to. That good I yelled back to her. You fucking cheep Jew she yelled back .You almost got us killed.

Me not being Jewish. I didn't know what she meant by that remark. then. But later |i know what she was talking about. Jews didn't like to throw away money. I guess that is what she was talking about. My throwing one bar at a time. I guess it would of been better to throw the whole box out. Oh well we were air born. The Gunny was waiting for us in the air. Hey I said walking up to the front. we made it. I was going to sit next to her. but changed my minute when she pointed the gun at me. I want back and sat. I guess she didn't need my help.

I sat right in the middle of the gold bars and started to stack them. like building blocks. Get the fuck up here I hear he yelling. No I said not looking at her. Bang the fucking nut shot at me again. The bullet hit the gold and made a spark. hey I jumped and hide behind them. Get up here she said again. Oh you need me now,I said peaking over the gold. No she said I just want you to see how your going to dye she said. I jumped up and ran to the front. Oh shit what the hell is that. I asked. Birds. No she said the enemies. the sky was black with them. and they were heading right for us. get on the radio and find out where our planes are she said. I jumped in the seat and started yelling where the fuck are you. She yelled at me to turn it on again. shit I always forgot to turn it on.

I did and said again where are you. Just then the plane rocked. I wish he wouldn't do that. It was the same Pilot he came right over our heads. and so close it made our plane shack. that is a Roger he said we see the bogies and have it in hand he said. Then as he passed over our heads I saw the whole fucking air force behind him. My look at all those jets. The General must have sent the whole Korean air force up. I know he didn't tell them what we had of his; he would be crazy. He still didn't run the country and the ones in power would find him out and shot him. So it was like fourth of July for a while and then the Korean's turned and ran. The pilot did his roll over as he passed us and called on the radio. He said he would guide us back. That was nice of him I had to meet this guy.

Well we landed and before you know it the air field was filled with M.P. and a truck convoy was coming to take the gold off. I guess I'll never see that again. Who know where it would end up? That in itself was top secret. I couldn't even find out where. So much for that; I did my job and make other people look good. The war went on and Me and my man got different assignments, from one part of the world to the other. Most were just little thefts under a million. But you add them up and by the end of the year; we stopped over twenty million in contraband stealing. Everyone wanted to get rich quick. My job was to stop them.

CHAPTER 13

One case made me stop and thing. It was so small it almost didn't seem the trouble to check on. ; but we did. Someone was taking little locks from the jets and before you know it they didn't have any more locks to lock. I got so bad that we had over a hundred jets waiting for them locks. They couldn't be ready for combat without them locks. It was only a small box but it had over two hundred of them in it. The cost was about twenty, lock's and the box got lost. We had to find it. The factory that made them didn't have their line set up to make more and for them to do so it would have to wait. No other company could make them as cheaply as this one could. Something about setting up and having this machine do the shaping.

No big deal I trough. That was on till I got into it. This one little box cost the government say four thousand dollars. Witch wasn't that bad. being you needed it to make the jet fly. But if they reordered it the price jumped up to three hundred a piece. That made the little box worth sixty thousand. Something about setting up cost. I guess sixty thousand wasn't that higher price to pay for having a hundred, three million dollars worth of jets sitting doing nothing. So off we went to find the little box and how do you find a little box?" You start from the end and work your way back. That was when it got interesting. The man that signed for it didn't remember seeing it. So we had to set him up to see what his roll was in it. It didn't take too long to find him out. He would do anything for a buck. I had a hunch about him. After you handle cases like this you could almost guess what made them tick.

With this one he was a nickel and dime guy; anything for a beer. I had one of my man deliver something and had one case shout. Nothing big; just a small case. The sgt. caught it. That was good but what he did wasn't. My man offered him twenty to sign the voucher anyway. He convinced him it was nothing and he would make up for it the next time. All well and good no harm done; who would miss a case of paper clips? What the hell they only cost ten dollars and he was making twenty for turning his back. That is how it started. This guy probably didn't even receive it. So the next step who delivered it. It came right from the factory; along with a lot of other things that day. It was a big order; who would miss this little box anyway?

So the next thing was to find out who the drive was and start on him. How we did that was to follow him for a couple of days and watched and see what he did after work. He was the ordinary guy and lived on his income no extra; just the stop at the local bar before going home. So I had one of my man hang out in the bar and become friends with the driver. You know buy him a beer once in a while shot the shit with him .Then ask if he could get you something the factory made as a favor. You were willing to pay him for it. What the hell why not he would bring the thing the next day. Then you had him. Before the end of the week you had him bring home the kitchen sink for you.

So the next thing you had to do is to have a man working inside to see how the driver was doing it. That was the hard part. Getting someone in when no one was hiring. Even the lowest man; or boy I should said kept his job. So we had to find away to get someone inside without letting anyone know what we were up to. I got a file on all the people that were working at the place and went right to the bottom. Here we go; I said this kid right here; I said to Nancy. Draft him. She did and the day he got his draft notice we had a man at the door looking for a job. He got hired right on the spot. If that didn't work we would have kept going. I remember one time we couldn't find anyone to draft so we broke his lags to make him be out of work for six months. That was all we needed.

Well any way we got our man in side. He found out it was the dock foreman that you had to see if you wanted anything on the side. He was the man that took from stock and made sure it got on the truck. When I went to check him out he didn't seem to rich. But, when I had him followed that was a different story. He didn't live where he said he lived and his car wasn't the car he drove to work. My man came back and told me he followed him to a garage and lost him. He went to his home and he didn't show up when he went to the door the people inside didn't even know him. When he ran the license plate it came back to him with the same address but he didn't live there.

This was getting interesting. I did most of my work from the office. Why not; I had Nancy to sit on my lap and I was doing my job. This one was getting to me. I had Nancy bring me all the records from this company. At first looking it didn't look to bad. They under bided most companies for the goods and kept their profits low. Then when I turned to the back of the page I almost shit. This was reorders. Would you look at this? They made one hundred times the amount for the goods on reorders. Letters were all copied to make it official. And it seemed as if they had the rights to over charge according to the contract. Something about setting up again and stopping work for the reorder; all well and good. You do what you have to do.

But they seemed to be reordering every other week, it was costing us plenty. Something was wrong here. I guess I had to go and check it for myself. Just this month alone they got over three hundred thousand dollars in reorders. So I headed for this garage the kid said he lost the Foreman and waited. He did it every day so I know he would be here. I was right I ducked down when I saw him coming in and he went up to the floor above him, I got out and ran up the ramp to see where he was going. I no sooner got to the top when this Caddy came racing down. It almost hit me I jumped out of its way. "Fucking nut." I yelled; he blow his horn at me to say "go fuck yourself."

Oh shit that was him. I ran back down and got in my car. But by the time I did it he was gone. Shit another day I had to wait. I went back up and looked for his other car. There it was. Nice; he didn't want anyone to see he had a new caddy. I guess I wouldn't if I was making all that money. What people didn't know didn't hurt them. You know the old saying. When someone got better then you; you get jealous of him and want what he has. So you don't let that happen. You keep a low profile and no one knows about you to fuck it up. Well I guess I have to wait for tomorrow.

Wait, what is this; a match book with a club on it. He had three of the same match book in the car. He kept it like a shit box; he just throw the garbage in the back seat. now Nice of him. What the hell I wasn't doing anything tonight and maybe Nancy would want to go out.

I took the book and left. I went back to the office and ran a check on the club. A night spot and it was owned by this guy that was clean. Nothing wrong with that; maybe he picked up some girls at this place and maybe he never been to it. That was the chance I had to take. I had nothing to do till tomorrow and I just remembered tomorrow was the week end. So I would have to wait for Monday to follow him again. Nancy was ready to go out for the night and what the hell I needed some relaxation myself. So we went home and dress.

We got to the club and it was swing. It look like little Italy; all the Italians with their Caddy's and girls. I pulled up and we went in. I didn't want to act like an ass so we just sat and looked around. Nancy had a picture of the guy; real Italian looking. Greasy hair, mustache and smoked a cigar.

We ordered drinks and watched the people on the dance floor. Nancy wanted to get up and join them but I didn't know how to dance. I never learned. I was too busy getting a head and worrying about being found out. So I didn't go out to much. I didn't have to know how to.

She smiled and said she would teach me.

"No, I said not here; some other time." She know I didn't want to so she didn't push it.

Well it didn't look as if he was here." I said; so we just drank and watched the crowed. We were out for the night. About two hours later Nancy said she had to go powder her nose. I had to go to so we both walked to the bathroom. I left my jacket on the chair so no one would take our table the place was starting to get crowed by this time. I guess it started getting hot after midnight.

Nancy said that is when most clubs started to jump; after midnight. Again I didn't know; I wasn't in to this type of life. We went in and when I came out, I waited for Nancy to come out. That was one thing I did know; what a woman did when they went inside no one know but they would take forever doing what they did. I went over to watch the girls dancing. I must say they enjoyed them self's. The drunker they got the more they moved. I guess you could say it was getting me hot just watching them. Nancy finely came out and took my arm. You like watching young girls shack their asses."

"I did." I told her and it was making me hot."

"Oh she said then maybe we should go. I don't want you coming before I get you home."

"Sounds good to me." I said.

As we were heading for our table Nancy stopped me; "there he is;" she said.

"Where?" I asked.

She was pointing at our table.

Look at that mother; I said he was talking my jacket and putting it on the floor. That got to me. Nancy held me back.

"Don't;" she said you don't want to blow it. Let me;" she said. You back off and let a pro do the work."

"Oh I said and who is that?"

She turned around and slapped me across the face. I mean real hard. "Hey." I started to say. But she walked away from me and went over and picked up my jacket and throws it at me before I know what she was up to.

"Now don't bother me;" she yelled so everyone heard her.

What the fuck was she doing? "Hey." I started to say again. But she stopped me by saying. "Don't you get it ass hole you're not my type." And got her drink from the table.

Oh now I see what she is doing, she is counting herself in on the investigation. I was about to go over and take her out when two guys came from the table and stood on both sides of me and took my arm.

"You heard the lady; one said. Now beat it before you get hurt." These two guys were big, but not that big. I was going to smack them both till they showed me what they had under their jackets; Guns now nice. I didn't want to blow it so I just back off and walked away. That nut I said to myself and went over to the bar to get another drink. I watched her doing her thing and before I know it she was sitting next to him; Like they were old friends.

What the hell is she up to? I turned to order a drink. I know I was going to be here for a while. I wasn't going to leave her with him. "Hey bartender a drink over here." He was moving like crazy keeping up with all the people. That is what I trough at first then went he slowed down I called him again. He looked at me and came over. "Hey buddy didn't you get the massage you're not wanted here, now go before you get carried out." He walked away again without getting me a drink. I was about to pick up a glass and throw it at him but the glass I was going to throw was this young ladies. She held my hand as I grabbed for the glass and said "It isn't worth it;" she said looking at me.

"Oh I think it will be." I said.

"No it won't; she said still holding on to my hand. Johnny D owns this place and what he says's goes. He wants your girl he takes her and you don't do anything about it. That is on less you want to live;" she said. I don't know any, Johnny D. I told her and whoever he is I don't give a fuck."

"You really don't know who he is; do you?"

"No I said I'm from out of town."

"Oh honey she said Johnny D is the mafia. His father is Mr.D the big gangster." Oh shit how stupid could I be that was the solder that I locked up in Korea. The one with the Sgt. I know he acted like a big shot. How what? I had to get out of there before he found out who I was. But I couldn't leave Nancy with him.

"Hey little lady; how would you like to make yourself a couple of bucks?" Slap I got it again across the face. "Hey I said I didn't mean it that way." I told her; it was to later. The bartender was coming over and the bouncers were on their way for me. I looked over at Nancy; she was looking at me and winked at me. I was hoping that meant she was coming, because I was about to get my ass thrown out of the place. I could have stayed but I would have been found out. So I had to leave. The bouncers took my by the arm and walked me out the door. They know what they were doing. They didn't want any trouble inside and they were pro's at it. Once I got out side they also showed me what they had under their jackets. I guess it would stop most people from making trouble.

If it was any other situation I would take the guns off of them and make them eat it barrel first. But I just had to back off and walk away. How what? I guess I just had to wait for her outside the door. I went to the car and waited. What the fuck was taking her so long. Did you ever wait for someone? The time goes by slower. Shit ten minute's went by and it felt like two hours. That did it a half hour went by and No Nancy. I had to go back and get her. Fuck the case. I had all I needed to bust him. The mob was into the Government supplier. I got out and started to head for the door.

Just then I saw something coming from around the back of the building. It was Nancy. "Let's get out of here;" she said going for the car. I didn't agree with her more at the time. She got in and told me to hurry; she didn't want him coming looking for her. I got in and drove off. As we pulled out of the parking lot I saw someone opening the same door Nancy must have came out. It was a back exit. It was him; he just stood and watched us go. He went back in and closed the door. "What the hell were you doing?" I asked her.

"Your job;" she said.

"Oh now you're doing my job?' I said.

She looked at me and was breathing heavy.

"You know who that guy was?" Before she could answer me I told her Johnny D. the one I locked up in Korea."

"You knew?' she said looking at me. "You fuck;" she said slapping me on top of my head. I hit the brakes and stopped.

"Look." I said holding up my hands to protect myself from her. She hurt.

"Look I just found out myself. I didn't ask you to fuck him."

"Oh she said looking madder. I trough I was helping you;" she said.

"You were; I said but I didn't ask you to."

"That is the thanks I get for almost getting rapped and..."

I stopped her with a kiss. She came at me with all of herself.

Here we go again. "In the back seat;" she said. Right on the high way. People were beeping their horns at us by this time.

"Let me pull over I said pulling away from her. Fuck them, she said; let them get their own lay." I pulled over with her still on me. Boy was she hot. We did it and then we drove home she didn't say a word till we pulled up in front of my place.

"That fuck;" she said wanted me to do Coke with him. Right there at the table. Could you believe that?"

"Knowing him, He could, He owned the club." I said.

"You know it? She said and everyone around him. His men were selling it right over the table." "What made you want to leave?" I guess I said the wrong thing, she slapped me again and got out of the car and went in the house. Shit, she hurt. I got out and followed her. I guess I was lucky we did it in the car; because I wasn't going to get any more tonight. She had my pillow out on the couch and the bedroom door closed when I got in.

Oh hell Mike would keep me company. He was looking back and forth at her door and at me.

"You got it. I said she is mad." He came up and gave me his paw to shack; meaning he was still my friend. He was something else. He did understand every word you said. Sometimes I used him to help me out in a case. He loved that, he didn't like lying around the house doing nothing. Me and him got along great. "Man's best friend and more." We both got to the couch and went to sleep.

The next morning Nancy was up and had breakfast ready for us. Mike ate what we eat; why not he was part human and he didn't like dog food. He told you so by dumping it on your plate. I guess he was trying to tell us something. Would you eat that shit, was the look he would give you.

Nancy came to me and said she was sorry for hitting me. She just didn't expect what had happened. She told me the Johnny D was all over her and got mad when she wouldn't go under the table and give him a blow job. "That did it she said he was acting as if I had to do it to him and if I didn't he would fuck me up."

"Oh I said he would off. How did you get out of it?"

She said "I told him I had to take my underwear off first; this way he could fuck me right in front of everyone and they wouldn't see what we were doing. That got him excited; excited enough to let me go." She said and then I went out the back door hoping you were still waiting outside for me."

"You know I wouldn't leave you." I said taking her in my arms. Mike barked at us and wagged his tail showing he was happy we weren't fighting any more.

We got dress and headed for the office. She couldn't wait to tell the General about her night.

"Maybe he will let me go out in the field with you next time;" she said as we drove to work.

"No I said you're doing a good job right where you are."

"Oh she said you don't think I could do it?"

I didn't want her to get started so I just kissed her.

"Oh now see; she said you don't want to answer me. I hate that; she said.

"Ok. I said I won't kiss you anymore." "No she said not the kissing; it is the way you try to shout me up that bothers me."

"Oh I said; would you rather have me slap you the way you beat on me last night?" "No; she said looking like a little kitten. "I'm sorry;" she said coming into me as I parked in my spot. I took hold of her and then someone was knocking on my window.

It was the General. "You two working?"

I just looked at him.

"Good he said let's get to it." and walked away.

I hate when he does that;" she said getting out; "he knows we are. Why does he ask that?

"Maybe he is Jealous." I said.

"Ha for what. He had his this morning."

"How do you know that?" I asked. "He tells me;" she said.

"Oh. I see." We went in and I got all the papers on this Johnny D guy. I wanted to have it all in order before I showed it to the General. He liked it that way; he didn't like to see things half done. He had his hands full with more importune things he would say, "take care of it;" that is what I was getting paid to do. Just hand it in when I wrapped it up. He like it that way he was looking good and he got all the glory for doing it. I didn't mind I liked working with him. I didn't forget what he did for me either and I was still waiting for the day they would find out who I really was. That was still hanging over me.

CHAPTER 14

I saw Seymour once in a while and it would always end up with him telling me to tell the world who I was; no one would condemn me for what I did. Not even the Jews. No thanks I like it just the way it was. "Maybe someday." I told him; but not right now." and he would leave being mad at me. But he still loved me and I him. He worked hard at what he was doing and was getting a name for himself. He was seeing this girl and was thinking about getting married. He needs it he had no sex life at all. The way I found out about it made me sick but now I know.

He told me what my father had done to him for running away. He didn't kill him because of me; but he did make sure he could never have any children. He cut his balls off and made him eat them. It took a long time for me to face him again. He would call and I would tell him I was busy. I felt sorry for him knowing he could never have children because of my father and I know he loved to have some. But I got over feeling guilty after a while; what I found out I missed seeing him. We cried and it was all forgotten with. I guess that is all you could do. I couldn't give him has balls back.

Nancy came in and I came back to really life; she had more on this Johnny D guy. More wasn't the word He was into everything and the Government was paying him; to boot. Well it ended up with his father owning the company that was making the parts for the Jets. Not out right, but the bottom line was he owned it. He had some other name on it and it took a lot of checking to get to the bottom. And at the bottom was Mr. D pulling the strings. To anyone looking at the records would think a Joe blow owned it. Not Mr. D. but somewhere down the line his name came up. It was small but if you know what you were looking for it was there.

How what? I had him but I didn't. Not to take him to court. I found out later why he didn't do any time for the time I got him In Korea. Something about him having amnesia. Some doctor sign him off and he walked free as a bird. Nice if you got the right people backing you.

So this time I was smarter and I know I didn't like him so that made me do a good job digging up everything I could on him. I didn't want him to walk this time. I went back to the garage and waited outside for him; I know the kind of car he was driving so it wasn't too hard to follow him. Just as I expected; he live in a big house with guards around it. Nice; the government was treating him o.k. I was glad to see that. I did pay taxes; you know. And this house was my tax money being used. Nice place I wouldn't mind moving in myself. I drove back to the office and got the guy that I had in the factory. We went over everything and when he finished I know what, where and how he did it.

To update it I had Nancy type out it in a report. What they would do, if they don't ship a certain part. One that would hold up the completion of whatever it went for. Jets or jeep. Something small but needed. So the first price wasn't that much. That is what made it look legal. The when it came time for reorder; that is when they stuck it to them. The government didn't want to think it was their fault it got lost so they just ordered it again. Something small could always get lose. So no one could blame anyone for it. So it just went through as "miss placed". Then when the reorder came in Johnny D would write this letter explaining how it set back the factory to set up the machines to remake this order. And all the time he didn't touch anything he had the part waiting for redelivery all the time. But his contract made it clear he had to get compensated for any extra. Work, hours and labor; all within the contract.

That is if no one followed up on it. Like the General said the first time he handed it to me .Small; but he had nothing for me to do; look into it." That I did and look what we got. So far in the last two years they got the government for 30 million; of the tax's payers money. It made you think of how many small jobs were out there? Well I was ready to hand it in. The general was up to his neck with the war; it seemed as if it was about to end and everyone was excited about it. The Gunny was getting out and most of my man when back to civilian life's. The only one that stuck with me was Snake. He married the woman and they live on the base. He had nothing to go back to. We took all his land. I mean the Government took it. Most Indians didn't have anything and the ones that did didn't sure it or lost it by fast talking White man.

It was sad to see what the U.S. did to them. It was almost like my father and Hitler tried to do, but they did it; and got away with it. I guess life goes on. You sometime thing of how it would be like, if this happened instead of that, what would the world be like. I guess everything had a reason for turning out the way it does. But what got to me is who was holding the cards. Who was running the show? Who was the director? All that kind of shit, I guess we will never know. Each religion has his idea but nothing to sink your teeth in. They all can say what they want to and have people believe in what they said; but it all boilers down to no one not knowing; just guessing.

Well the war was over and we won. What did we win? Now that was a good question. All I know that from my stand point being a solder I felt good. For others it was stopping people like Hitler from taking over the world; you had to start from some point. All the big powers didn't want another Hitler in their time anyway. So stop it before it got out of hand was the thing. One man wants someone else's land stop him because he will never stop at just one; he will want more and more and before you know it he was at your back door knocking to come in. So I guess Hitler did something; he made people look and listen to some big mouth that meant nothing to start with; but look at him now. The man would have kept going till he owned the world along with my father and then the two of them would of had to have it out sooner or later. They weren't room for the two of them to rule.

Well I was sent to Germany for a while; Nancy went with me and we got married. She quit her job and we were thinking about a family. Seymour got married; his wife was something else. He did pretty good for a guy not having any balls. We made a joke out of it; that was all we could do. Just between our self's that is; no one else; not even our wife's.

The big treat was Russia. They called it a "cold war". I don't know who thinks up these names but they should go back and rewrite them. The Korean War was called only a "Police action". Could you believe that? The many of man that died over they couldn't even said they died in a war. All they could say is here lays John Doe he died in a Police action." What the hell was a Police action? To me it was when a gang for kids shot it out and the police came in and broke it up. That was a Police action to me. Not all the man we lost. Come on, let's call it world war three and be over with it.

I mean if they were worried about running out of numbers to call the wars; they had a long way to go. Shit we could have a war every ten years and never run out of numbers. Shit I could just see it. Big headlines "World war 69." Shit I don't think anyone will be around to fight it. So what did they care what you called a war. All I know is it was world war three to me; and I was looking for,world war four to start. I was ready for it. What would they call the next one? I know it would be called a dispirit. That was it; a dispute. Imagine dying and spending billions of dollars over a "dispute". Don't make me laugh.

Well things look quite to the rest of the world. The press was down playing anything that was happening. As far as fighting was going. But it was out there and getting bigger as the day was long. Russia was getting ready to take over where Hitler and my father left off. They seemed to want land for some reason. Any one that didn't like the way things were run would go to the Russians and get help from them to over throw the guy that was sitting in the driver's seat at the time. They didn't care who or where they came from and all the time we and Russia were making bigger and better bombs; to out show the other.

Hey it worked in Japan. Two bombs and they throw up their hands and ran. Why the hell not. If that is all it took go for it. So now the race was on. How many and how much damage could one do before the other one got wind of it? Destroy him first.

I was beginning not to like being a solder. I was the old type; Give me a rifle and mud and I'll take the hill for you. Not sitting back in a chair and pressing buttons to see how many buttons the other one had and hope you had more than he did. Otherwise it was back to the drawing board. Then Russia did something we didn't like. He came close to us. He had this Cuban named Castro. He was the Hitler type but small potatoes. He didn't have the brains. At first he was the good guy' on till he got a taste of what power could do. Then it went to his head. Before you know it he was thinking about getting in his row boat and taking Florida. The Russians played him along; just to see how far we would let him go. Why not; it was only a game. If they lost; the only one that would get hurt was this ass hole named Castro. Not them and if he won it was just another step to taking the world over. So what did they have to lose?

Well that was my next Job. I sent Nancy back to the states and Found out she was having a baby. I guess I should of got out then, But I didn't I still was a solder. I guess I love it when I got saluted and man called me sir and jumped up when I went by. I had my own power trip I guess. Most people do and again there are some that don't. The world is made up of givers and takers. I guess it is born in you. Ok. You're a giver and then the other one you're a taker for this life. You can change in your next life if you want.

Life goes on. Well back to this ass Castro. What the hell was he trying to do anyway? The place was a paradise and we even had a base on it. What the hell was he trying to do? Or I should say what Russia was trying to do. At first we helped him but when we saw what he was up to we back off. He got what he wanted; but he seemed to want more. So we backed away from him. We had our base on the island so we could watch him. I guess the only reason we helped him was because the Mob was moving in and taking it over more and more; gambling casinos were going up and the poor people were getting pushed out. Just like the Indians. That would have been the end of it; if Russia didn't stick it's nose into it.

So I got my orders to go down and find out what the hell was going on; and what we could do to stop it. So I did. Nancy went back to D.C. to set up house for her and the baby to be and I went to Cuba. What a place. It went from a paradise to a hell hole over night. Then I got word that Russia was planning something. I wasn't sure what it was but we know something was in the wind. You see they couldn't do anything without us knowing. All we had to do is look out our back door and see. They called the base Gitmo bay. Never know why and I didn't care why, the real name was Guantanamo Bay. Must be named after someone with that name.

Well the fun started. The Russians started coming by the boat load. They said they were just helping Castro got back on his feet. I found out we got most of our sugar from Cuba so that stopped. Big deal we got it from someplace else. It didn't hurt us and Russia needed it; they didn't have any country that grows it; so why not. That was the only really lost we had over this Island. Other Caribbean country picked up where Cuba left off. It was still the place to go on vacation. Cuba. No one missed it except the Mafia. Who cared about them they would work there were in somewhere else. So I stayed down in Gitmo and waited to see what the hell was going on.

One day we got a surprise. Castro had a foot solder around the whole base. I mean for miles. Now what; he may of had us out numbered for the moment but all it would take was a phone call and we would have half the Marines here in nothing flat. I know; we had drills all the time for this and we always had a fleet of ships waiting for something like this. The called at a "med cruise to make it sound good to the man that pulled it for duty. I guess it wasn't that bad. Hey they got to see the other islands; fun and sun was the name of the game. But all the time they were showing Castro what we could do to him if we wanted to. I guess the man was sick in the head. He believed Russia was bigger and could stop us any time they wanted to. So he went ahead and had his own money printed up; his face on everything; Bills and coins. Shit we even had Cubans working on the base. They would come to work every day and go back and tell Castro what we did. I couldn't see that we were paying them to do what any solder could do and a lot more than the solder was getting.

So that was he was here for; he was to make sure no one came off the base on till he made his money. So who the fuck gave a shit? The only thing I didn't like was right outside the main gate was his main gate and it was guarded by Russians. How the hell we stood by and let this happen was beyond me. But I wasn't in charge I was just a officer with people over me. I took orders just like the next man; that was what being a soldier was all about. It uses to make me laugh.

The workers get paid in American Money and would walk out the gate and the Russians would take the American Money off of them and give them Castro's money. That wasn't bad; they couldn't spend the American money anyway. The thing that I liked about it; Castro used the money we paid the workers to feed his people with. You see the worker would make; lets said a hundred dollars. Castor would give him back what was the amount of maybe five dollars in his own money. So the workers worked all week for five dollars and Castor kept 95 American dollars to spend.

Good man I think every country should have a deal like that. This went on right under our noses and we did nothing about it. What the hell he had to eat to. One day all hell broke loose. President Kennedy got some pictures back and he found out the Russians were setting Missiles up and they were aimed at us; and the U.S.: Boy did they have balls. That was almost asking for us to sell them land in the U.S. so they could put Missiles on them. Sure why not; with the range they were getting out of them. It didn't make since. The only thing we could figure was that they were getting ready to strike.

Well Kennedy had to do something. He couldn't let them build missiles right in our back yard. More and more Russians shops were coming in. Boy did they move fast. If we didn't stop them when we did; they would have been ready to fire them next week.

Kennedy calling in the Marines; and I mean he called them in; we had more ships off the coast of Cuba then all of Pearl Harbor. The Russians didn't know what to do; we had them out numbered ten to one with ships and double that with man in less the 24 hours. Man did that practice work. It went like clockwork; No fuck ups the marines have landed. No, I shouldn't say that we kept them on the ship for the time being. Kennedy got on the T.V. and said straight out. "Get you're fucking shit the hell out of Cuba or we will do it for you." And he gave them till sun down Like in the old western movies. And he meant it. He didn't need all these man; he had six nuclei sub's park right outside Castro's door waiting for the orders to press the buttons. And Cuba would be no more. I mean right down to the water line. The only think we had to worry about was getting off the island before it took place. And that was practice also. We could be gone within the hour. Not packing anything; but who the hell gave a shit as long as we were clear when the missiles went off.

Time was ticking and we were getting worried; maybe world war three would start over this bearded nut. Everyone was waiting. It was like waiting for the ball to drop on New Year's Eve. The whole world waiting to see what we would do. I know what we were going to do. But it was top secret and only a few know; so I'll leave it at that and get on with the story. The Russians back out, they know it was a no win deal. So what the hell they tried and lost; no harm done; except to Castro. He was really on our shit list now. The Russians kept him happy by sending him food medical supplies and he gave the Russians all the sugar they wanted. It still wasn't enough to feed his people so he kept them skinny. No one got fat in Cuba; except Castro. All kind of word was getting out from the workers that worked on the base. Castro was a fag and did it to young boys and all kind of shit.

I was about to pack up and go. Nancy was about to have our baby and I wanted to be home for it when it came. But Castro didn't see it that way. I was just about to board my plane when; Bang what the hell was that. One of our planes crashed over his side of the fence. I get off the plane and took the jeep to the fence line to see what the hell was going on. There it was; one of our jets over ran the run way and landed on Castro's side. The pilot was getting out and the Cuba army was running to get him. "We can't have this;" I said taking a Marines rifle. The pilot was out of the plane and was running for the fence. The Cubans were right behind him. I pick out one of the head man. The one with the biggest mouth and shot him right in the head. Oh shit I heard everyone say. "Now you did it." I didn't know what he was talking about on till I saw what I shot. Oh shit it was a cow. I hit a cow not the man.

By this time the Marines were lined up with their rifle's pointing at the Cubans. If push came to shove they would have lost. We had them out numbered with rifles. And with the dead cow at their feet I found out later it was a no, no to kill a cow. The cow was the only means they had for milk to feed his babies. I could of shot all the Cubans I wanted to and that would have mattered as much. But to shot a cow that was the wrong thing to do. Hey I missed what could I said shot me. The pilot made it over the fence and was laughing.

"Thanks he said what a shot. You got that cow right in the head."

I told him I wasn't aiming for the cow;" he laughs again. "Just like the way you fly a plane;" he said laughing.

No shit I finely meet the Pilot that saved my ass all the time in Korea. "Hey I said hugging him; how the hell have you been?" I don't know how many times I missed him. We just never got together.

At last I meet him and what a way. I told him we are even;" I took him back with me in my jeep. He was the same rank I was. Oh I made Major. After the war and I was made colonial just before I got here. Rank meant nothing to me. I guess I was losing it. What I need was another war. I felt better with one going on.

Well that stopped me from going home; the base commander was all shock up and didn't want to take the blame for what I did. So I hung around till things got back to normal. What the hell I had to spend some time with my friend; didn't I? His name was Paul Woods he was Black. That surprised the hell out of me. One would never guess it by the way he talked. Over the radio that is. You could tell he was black when he talked off the radio. So what the hell I liked him anyway.

We headed for the officers club and had some drinks. I mean we would have drunk all night, if it wasn't for Castro acting up again. Some M.P. came in and got us. They told us the base commander wanted us. "On the double."

Oh shit now what. Woods came with me; he wanted to see what the hell was going on himself. The M.P. drove us right to the fence line. It looks like day light there were so many lights on. How what? Will look who we have here? It was Castro himself; and his army.

The commander came up to us and said; "see what you started?"

"No, I said; what?"

"My men;" he pointed to.

I saw about ten of our man standing right up against the fence and one of Castro's solder's standing right next to them. "Anything wrong?" "Anything wrong?' he said can't you see."

I really couldn't see what the hell he was talking about.

"Castro wants to cut their dicks off."

I didn't think what I heard was what he was saying. "He wants to do what?" I asked.

"You heard me; cut my man's dicks off." As he was saying it he was walking up to the fence.

Oh shit now I see what he was talking about. Castro's solders had my solders dicks in their hands holding them to the fence.

"How the hell did that happen?" I asked.

"Well the Cuban women come here every night to make extra money."

"You mean the fuck throw the fence." Woods said. That is how it is done, through the fence."

"So I said what is his beef?"

"That is just it; he said the beef the cow you shot. He wants us to pay for it."

"Tell him to go fuck himself." I said and started to walk back to the jeep.

"American." I heard someone call. He was on a loud speaker. It was shit head himself.

"You the one getting in the jeep; you don't think I do it?"

I stopped and turned around, "No I yelled not while you're standing there you won't."

"Ha; he said and what will you do?" he asked. "Kill you." I said and picked up a rifle and pointed it at him. Well shit head make you move." The commander was having a shit fit by now. "Well I yelled what will it be fag." I guess that got to him; he came right up to the fence and started yelling.

"My man will cut them off just for saying that". "Look ass hole I said take your other ass holes and go before you get me mad."

He didn't know what to say. He just stood looking at me. "You think you are funny? he said I'll show you." He reached over and took one of the women that was getting fuck for money and held her to him. His arm around her neck and he was behind her. "You think I joke;" he said and before I could answer he cut her throat. Oh shit did she bleed. He almost cut her head off.

"You see; he said I don't joke."

I tried to not look but something made me enjoy it. "Hey I said can you do another one for me. I like the way she screams."

This again stopped him. He let her fall and then just looked at me again. "You pay he said or your man will be next." His man showed me they had big knifes ready to cut.

"I wouldn't do that. I said. On the ready." I yelled. The whole marine guard locked and loaded and aimed. "Let's see who can dye first." I yelled.

The commander was by my side now. He said for me to stop this shit he was in enough trouble already. "How; I said by letting him have his way?"

"No he said offer him a new cow."

"Fuck no I said maybe a pig, but not a cow."

Just then a jeep pulled up in a hurry. The driver stood up at attention and was holding the phone in one hand and saluting with the other.

"The President sir is on the phone and wants to take to you."

"Shit good news travels fast." I said.

The commander went to take the phone.

"No sir the driver said. The President wants to talk to Colonial Goldberg sir."

I smiled at the commander and took the Phone. "Colonel Goldberg here sir." He was short and brief. "Don't fuck up he said give the ass hole whatever he wants." And hung up.

"O.K. I yelled that was my boss. He said he will send you two cows and that is it"

"You crazy; he yelled I want more than that". "Look ass hole I do what I'm told. Two cow and that is it. You take it or we shot. That is the bottom line." I said.

"No he yelled two cows and ten thousand dollars." "You got to be out of your mine; I said no cow is worth that."

"Give it to him;" the Commander said to me.

"Not so fast I told him. Two cows and Ten thousand in medical supplies; that is it; no more Now let my man go or I'll shot you right in the fucking head. Now." I yelled.

He yelled something and his man back away from the fence. Our man dropped. I guess there dicks were hurting. I know mine would if I had someone pulling it throw the fence as hard as they could.

"How I said you will have you supplies by tomorrow."

"You lie to me;" he said and this. His man took the rest of the woman and did what he did. They cut their throats. Man this man was sick.

"How he said your man will never get pussy."

"Good. I said; how you can send your boys to take their place."

"Pig he yelled; you will see. He got back in his jeep and took off; his man started backing away. "See I said that wasn't so hard."

The commander was sweating. "Hot out tonight?" I said. Me and Woods went back to the jeep.

We went back to the club and finished what we were doing Drinking. Paul Looked at me and said he was glad to meet me and we drank. It was getting dawn when we stopped. He looked at me and said

"I looked like shit."

"Good I said I feel like shit;" and we laugh. He didn't look to good himself. We walked out and just in time to see an ambulance come flying past us. A solder was running behind it. He stopped to tell us what happened. It seemed one of the solders went back to the fence line to get some ass, when he got there the girls were waiting, When he stuck his dick in her he came out with nothing but raw meat. Castro had put razors inside the woman and where you entered you couldn't feel them but try to take it out, OH boy were you in trouble.

I guess he got the last word." Woods said to me. Good that will teach your man to keep their dicks in their pants. I guess so he said but it was pretty bad here nothing to do and no place to go. The man had two years to be here and no woman. the only time they got off here was once every six month the fly them to Portico for the week end and back here for another six months. You get tired playing with you self you know. I guess you would. Let me see if I can change that I said.

"Well my friend. I got to go now; my wife is having a baby and I did want to be there when she had it.

"Hey man; he said congratulation you're a daddy." "Not yet, I said. I don't think she had it .But soon. I said. Look I said, thanks .I hope to see you again some time."

"You bet:" he said and walked away.

"Well I did my job here whatever it was I was supposed to do. So now back home to my family. The commander made sure I got on the plane. I guess he had enough excitement for awhile.

I flow back and had a car waiting for me at the air field. Nancy was at the hospital, she was in labor. We made it in record time. By the time I got to her room she had my little girl. That is right I had a little girl. Seymour and his wife were there.

"Hey daddy how does it feel?" I don't know, I said I don't feel any pain."

Nancy looked at me and said; "you would say that."

"Well I don't." She took something off her table and throw it at me;"now you do."

"Hey can I see my daughter. I asked.

"Come Seymour said I'll take you. Let the two ladies talk."

I guess he wanted to talk to me. I hope it wasn't bad news. I hated having this feeling. We went to the window and he pointed her out to me.

"Hey I said where is her hair; she is a girl?" I asked.

"She will grow it;'" he said.

"O.K. what is up?"? I asked him looking at my daughter.

"Nothing he said I proud of you;" he said.

"Yea I said and you believe in Santa Claus. I know you remember."

"I was just wondering If you picked out grad parents yet?"

"We did. I said Next question. I asked.

"How are you going to raise her? I mean what religion?

"That is up to Nancy; I said, third; I asked. "Would you be the father of my child?"

"Woo;" I said come again.

He looked at me and asked. My wife and I have talked it over and we want you to be the father of our child."

"You know what you're asking?" I said.

"Yes he said and now that we saw your daughter. we want to go through with it."

"Hey; I said let's talk about it."

"Yes or no?" he said.

I looked at him and saw the tears coming.

"Hey; I said holding on to him. If you want me to I'll do it. But I don't want your wife falling in love with me."

He pulled back and smiled. "That is the chance I got to take. He said. You will;" he said.

"Look I said I will. Now we have to ask Nancy."

"I was hoping we didn't have to let anyone know." That maybe a hard one; can we talk?"

"What do you mean?" He asked.

"I mean you don't want me to do it right now do you?"

"Get out of here;" he said. Look I know it is a hard thing to ask, but you're the only one I would ask."

"Look, say no more I'll do whatever you want."

"Thanks he said coming to me. I hope I was doing the right thing. I did owe him and what better way could I repay him then to give him a baby. That is what he was living for. His whole life was around babies. He was a good baby doctor and he helped a lot of people out. He was a good man and if it made him happy; then why the hell not.

He seemed a little more relaxed now. I hated seeing him up tight. "Well he said lets go back and see the ladies."

"Wait; I said I got to say good bye to my little lady." I just looked at her in that little crib and waited for her to move.

"She is sleeping; he said. And she is beautiful."

"If she was ugly would you still want me to do it?"

"It would be from you that is all that counts." "You're the boss." I said. I didn't realize how it would affect me on till I went back to the room. His wife just smiled at me; she knows he asked me. Shit I was turning red I could feel myself. I was embarrassed. Nancy went to sleep and we left together; Seymour his wife and me.

"Look I said come home with me."

"No he said they took a hotel and they wanted to take me out to dinner."

Why not; we had things to talk about. I kept looking at her as we drove. Was I doing right with this? I guess I was. I would be the guard parent anyway so what the hell. We got to the hotel and we went up stairs. She said she had to freshen up some. She looked good enough to me; but woman always said that. When we got to the room Seymour walked behind us. As she opened the door and walked in Seymour turned around and left. Oh shit I guess he really meant it.

It was just the two of us; her and me.

"Hi she said.

"Look I really don't know what to say." I said. She turned and started to take off her dress. Oh shit she didn't want to waste any time. Man what she had on made me hard. She had black lace everything and with her red hair she looked beautiful.

"You like; she said.

"Look I said I'd be crazy if I said no. But let's not get into that. I started to take off my clothes; might as well get it over with. There we were, the two of us standing in the middle of the room naked.

I was feeling like a school kid. "What if I don't get you pregnant?" I said.

"Then we try again."

"Oh," I said.

She walked over to me and got on her knees. "Please she said let me warm up to it. I'm nervous." She said.

"You I said look my knees are shacking."

"Oh you poor man; she said taking my dick into her mouth. That was the end of my knees shacking and the start of a hot fuck and I mean real hot.

She was wild and with mirrors all over the room I was dancing with her around my hips all over the room. My dick was in her and she move up and down as if she was born that way. I started to head for the bed.

"No she said let's keep going." I walked her over to the wall and rested her back against it and went to town on her. Her tongue tasted sweet and she took mine in and almost sucked it out of my mouth.

Well we finished and she said. "Seymour was down in the bar waiting for me." I guess she wasn't coming. "Oh she said and thanks it meant a lot to us."

I didn't know what to say. I just turned and left. In a way I felt guilty, but then I didn't.

I went down to the bar Seymour was sitting at the end having a drink. "Want one?" he said.

"I could use it." I said sitting next to him. He had one already for me.

"Wasn't she nice?" he asked.

"Seymour I really don't want to talk about it". "Sorry he said I won't speak of it again."

"Good I said.

"You have a pretty woman." I said.

"Hey he said now you don't talk either."

"Sorry I said.

"Was she good; he asked?"

"Look; I said stop talking." I said and ordered another round.

"Yes she was;" I said.

"Hey he said let's cut it out."

"Sorry;" I said and drank my drink. She is a real red head;" he said.

"I know; I said. She was red all over. Look; I said we have to put it out of our mines; you were the one up there not me; you got me." I said to him.

He took my hand and held it. "Thanks he said. we had another drink and then I asked. What if it didn't take?"

He looked at me and said; "you'll have to do it again."

I finished my drink straight down and ordered another one. "You really mean that don't you!"

"I do; he said and he drink his down. "What makes you thing it didn't take?" he asked.

"I don't know I said you're the doctor; you tell me."

"Would you like to do it again?" He asked.

"Look I said; stop the shit you're getting drunk and I don't talk to drunken man."

"Oh he said and you're not."

"I have a right to get drunk. I said my wife just gave me a baby."

"And so do I; he said you just gave my wife a baby."

"Good I said. I'll drink to that". And we finished another round.

"Now what?" He asked.

"You go up stairs to your wife and I go home."

"No; he said I want to go home with you."

"You can't you got your wife waiting for you." I said.

He looked at me and started to cry. "Oh shit cut that out she loves you." I said. Why else would the two of you go through this to have a baby?" Love I said, now get up there and finish what I started."

"You mean you didn't come in side of her?" That did it."

I got up and took him by the arm and said; "go ask her. I got to go."

I took him to the elevator and left him. "Go I said she is waiting for you." I waited till he got in and the door close. Now that wasn't so bad now was it?

I went home good old Mike was waiting for me. One good thing about him, he understanding what you tell him, he gets his own food and water; you can leave him home alone and he even goes to the bathroom on the bowl. Believe me he does. Well home at last. I got myself something to eat and sat down in front of the T,V. The news was coming on. Oh shit here we go again.

I was hearing talk about this, I guess it was true. It was about the French in Vietnam. They were pulling out. I guess they couldn't fight the war. Shit let us get over there and we will show them a thing or two. Little did I know but in a couple of years we were on our way. We did we picked up where the French left off.

CHAPTER 15

The general was retiring and my daughter was growing. Seymour had a boy. I just did it that once and we forgot about it. I was glad no more was said. Nancy was having another baby and I was second in charge. The general goes I move up to leader of the c.i.d; why not I was running it anyway. Thing's were moving in Vietnam I mean really moving. We weren't in yet but we were if you know what I mean. I almost forgot who I really was. Once in a while I'd have some dreams, but other than that my daughter kept me busy and my mind off of it. Seymour came around a lot and we went to see them. Our kids played good together. Nancy never knew about me giving Seymour's wife the son. And we didn't tell her. It was better that way.

Well life was one big ball of fun with my daughter. Things were pretty quite around the office. All I had to do was over look paper work. At first it boarded the hell out of me; but as time went by I got use to it. Being home with Nancy and my daughter; Kim was her name.

That didn't last to long the war was on its way and before you know it we were into it full swing. Things started jumping around Washington and everyone was going crazy. I wanted to go over to Vietnam but Nancy didn't want me to, so I didn't put in for a transferred. I just stayed in D.C. It was like a nine to five job and home with the family. One-day Nancy called and asked me to pick up something from the store before I left. She did it once in a while. But most of the time she had the house in order, she was a good wife. I couldn't ask for any better. We still had our fights but always made up before going to bed. I guess you could say we were happy.

Seymour his wife and son were coming for the weekend and she wanted to make some special Jewish food for them. She was good like that; she always knew what to do to make people feel at home when they came to visit us. Seymour was the only family I had. And friends well you didn't make too many in the job I had. So we welcomed them with open arms whenever they came to town. Nancy had her own little group of woman; she would go to the park with. But that was for Kim. She needed some kids her age to play with. So when she asked me to do little thing for her I didn't mind. I left the office and headed for home. On the way I stopped at this corner store to get what she wanted.

I parked and got out. They should have what I had to get. It was a big store. When I went in I felt something wrong. The girl behind the cash register was looking at me then to the side of me as if she was scared.

"Hi I said. And walked to the back, as I walked I looked at the mirror. The ones they had overhead. I saw what she was scared about. Two guys had guns on people in the other isle. Oh shit the store was being held up. I still carried my gun and I still was in shape. I took it out and kept walking to the back. How many more were there? When I got to the back I stop before I got to the end and looked in the mirror at the back, two more with people. One was waiting for me. I took a loaf of bread off the shelf and stuck my gun through the side of it so the guy wouldn't see it and kept walking. The guy waiting for me jumped out and said. "Don't do anything stupid," he said holding a shotgun at me.

"You got it." I said. He took me and put me with the other people he had with him. He yelled to the two in the front; he got me and to hurry up and get the money." "How," the other one said. "I know you all have money on you. Let's do some shopping," he said holding out his hat. Every thing, he said, rings and all."

"I don't what to get him mad, he said so don't fuck with him." The one on the side of me poked me in the head with his shotgun and said. "You heard the man; start digging."

It was now or never, the both of them were watching the other people taking their money out. I pointed my loaf of bread at the other one and shot throw it, as I fired I gave the one standing next to me a chop across the neck with my other hand. That was that.

"Hey what the hell is going on back there?" I heard the other's yelling. They couldn't see us so they didn't know what happened. I told the black guy that was back with us to tell them. "Nothing, it was under control." I couldn't say it. They were black and I was white. Like they wouldn't know I wasn't one of them that said it. "Ha." He looked at me and then said it as if he was one of the hold up men.

They bought it. They yelled back "How we doing back there?"

The black guy just looked at me waiting for me to tell him what to say.

"Just say Money." He did.

"Good, the other one said.

"Move it we don't have all day."

"Tell them were coming." He did.

"Hey Leroy, you got a woman back there with you?" The one in the front asked. "You sure sound sweet." The other one said.

"No" I told him to say.

"No man." He said.

I guess that was the wrong thing to say. The ones from the front didn't buy it any more.

"Hey man who the fuck are you?"

I could see them from the mirror in the meat case. They both had people in front of them as they talked. Shit now what?

"Hey mother fuck you hear me? What did you do with Leroy and Freddie?"

"Your momma." I said and jumped to the floor of the isle they were down. I took out the one that was walking down to see what the hell was going on. The guy he had with him dropped to the floor when he saw me with the gun. Good thing he did. I hit him right in the chest, he dropped. Now that left the other one. He had four people around him. No way was I going to shot him. I got up and walked straight at him.

"Look son; I said your friends are dead. Why don't you drop your gun and be the smart one."

By this time the cops were starting to come. I could hear the sirens. "The cops will be here. You still got a chance to run." I told him.

"You crazy you mother fucker. I'll shot him," he said; holding the guy next to him. He had his shotgun to his head.

"Get up here, he said. I'll shot him."

The guy was Korean I guess he owned the place. They all owned a grocery store nower days.

"I'll do it he said. Drop your gun."

I could see he would. He had the look in his eyes and I saw that look before. Shit I didn't want to; but I had no chose. I was half way down the isle and no place to hide.

"O.K. I said but don't shot."

"Get your ass up here." He yelled.

I walked up to him; just as the cops came in the front door.

"Hold it mother fuckers," he yelled I'll shot his fucking head off. Now back out." He was looking at the cops.

I got close enough to give him a flying kick. I took hold of the corner of the rack and held on as my feet went in the air and came across the top of his head. I landed on the ground and waited for his gun he dropped.

"That was easy," I said standing up. The people he had with him didn't move. You." I told one of them; go tell the cops it was O.K."

She started to walk for the door and then realized what had happened and started to run.

"No," I yelled don't run." She did and I know what was going to happen. Bang; she got shot. The fucking cops shot her. "Everyone down," I yelled. Just keep you heads down and don't move. Don't give them any reason to shot." I got down and started yelling. "Don't shot we give up."

The others started saying the same thing, "don't shoot". Before you know it everyone in the store was yelling. "Don't shot."

It worked. I guess when they saw who they shot that made then think twice about shooting anyone else. They came in with body armor on and stood by the door.

"Everyone O.K. in here?" One yelled.

"We would be if you put down that gun." I yelled.

"Who are you?" One yelled.

"Colonial Goldberg I yelled; U.S. Marines." I said.

"Stand up and show your self" One yelled.

"Not till you put down them guns, I said, you already shot one innocent person. I don't want to be the second."

"Don't get smart," he said.

"No son I said. I'm just careful. Now you lower you guns and I'll stand up. They are all dead, I said. So you have nothing to worry about."

"Just stand," another one said. And show us your face." Shit I hated this. I got to my knees and looked at them. "See," I said, I'm in uniform."

"Stand up, he said, with your hands over your head.

"You got to be joking." I said.

The other one said just stand up please. He was a Sgt. I guess he had more time in. I hated when some rookie was acting the tough guy.

"You got it Sgt. I said and stood. You got two in the back," I said looking to the back; and other people back with them."

The Sgt. yelled for them to come forward. They did. "Now would everyone please line up out side so we can see what the hell went on? And no one else gets shot. Please," he said.

They went out the front one by one. "You the Sgt. Said to me, wait there." I stopped that was the first time I looked at the Korean the guy had the gun to.

Mother fucker it was he. General Oh. I'll be dipped in shit. He knew it was me; he tried to hide his face from me.

"You mother fucker what the hell is you doing here?" I took him by his jacket and throw him to the ground. "Hold it, The Sgt. Said pointing his gun at me.

"Hold your ass, I told him. You know who this motherfucker is?" I said looking at Oh.

"Yes, he said, he owns this place now let him go."

"You're wrong, I said, this man is wanted for war crimes. He is General Oh. Look Sgt. I'm from C.I.D. here is my I.D. I want this man locked up. No; I said I want to use the phone." He isn't getting out of my sight.

The Sgt. Said, I can't let you do that Colonial.

"You what?" I yelled. You know I out rank you ass hole; now don't give me any shit. I'll have you busted and watching cars go by if you open your mouth again."

I was mad and he knew it.

"Yes sir he said. The phone is over here." He pointed to it.

"Thank you," I said pulling Oh with me. How go get the rest of them from the back and while you there I would like my gun back. It is in the isle. It is the 45 on the floor. If you wouldn't mind," I said.

"Yes sir," he said and told one of his men to get it for me.

The others get the two in the front and cuffed them. Three went to the back, one got my gun and came and gave it to me as I was dialing the phone. I guess they all respected me now. "Here sir," he said as he handed it to me.

"Frank, Goldberg here, guess who I got? Oh," Frank was one of my men. He had night duty.

"You shitting?" He said; when I told him.

"Look I said I want some one over here right away and make it snappy. I don't want the locals getting into this."

"Right away," he said.

I told him where I was and hung up.

"Well how General Oh; we meet again."

"Ha," were the first words out of his mouth. You get in trouble Mister big shot."

"Oh; I said and what makes you say that?"

"You see," he said smiling.

I don't know what came over me but I hit him. I bunched him right in the face.

"Hey," the Sgt. said what the hell was that all about?" "That, I said, just taking care of some old business." Oh went down with the first shot. The Sgt. said. You're the one that did it. I don't want anyone saying we hit him. We got enough trouble with the woman we shot."

"As I said you got nothing to do with him."

"Good, he said and walked away.

"O.K. Oh you're not hurt." I bent down and picked him up. Nice shot I said to my self. I got some teeth the lip and the nose in one shot. The blood started coming. "Hey would you look at this; he does bleed. You got some balls, I said to him as I pulled him back to the front. You kill our man and now you come here to live. I don't know how you got here, I said. But you're going back. No, I change my mind, your staying here and I'll see to it you get the firing squad for the shit you did."

He looked at me and smiled. "You got no room to talk, he said. Mr. Kaufmann."

Oh shit was I forgetting my self? He did know who I was and he never knew any difference. "Ha, I said, you didn't hear I wasn't his son. You fool I was a plant."

He kept smiling at me. "You'll see," he said.

What did he know? He had something up his sleeve. "You did pretty good, I said looking around. America is taking good care of you."

"You too," He spit on the floor next to my feet. It was nothing but blood. I gave him a sidekick before his spit hit the floor. He went flying into a rack of cakes. The Sgt. came around again and yelled. "You crazy you're going to kill him."

"So; I said picking him up. That is my business. You take care of yours."

Frank came in with two other agents. He was holding up his I.D. as he walked. "What the hell happened;" he asked?"

"Oh nothing really." I said.

"You had better cool this man down, The Sgt. Said, or we all are going to jail." Franks looked at Oh and then at me. "You do that?" He asked.

"Yea, I said smiling. Franks took me by the arm and told the other two to keep an eye on Oh. He wanted to talk to me alone.

"What's up?" I asked. I knew him by now, something was wrong. He said he did some phone calling on his way here and guess what?

"I don't know, I said. I get money for getting him?"

"Ha, he said you're in trouble."

"I'm what?" I said not believing what I was hearing. "You heard me. I was told to get over here and lock you up."

"You got to be kidding?"

"No, he said that came right from the top."

"The general said that?" I asked.

"No, over him, the C.I.A director him self."

"What the fuck does he have to do with it?" I asked? Did you call the General?"

"I did and he said to bring you in, he would meet us at the office."

"What about that Gook?" I asked.

"I got to let him go. Something about him making a deal with the CIA."

"No fucking way, I said. I'll go with you but he is coming. No way am I going to let him go. I saw this man kill right in front of God and me. God only knows how many others he killed. No, he isn't getting away with it."

I walked out front again and picked Oh up. I walked him out to my car. I throw him in and drove off. "You fucking move you gook motherfucker and I'll blow your fucking head off like you did to your own men. You got me gook." I yelled.

He just smiled at me.

Bang I smacked him across the mouth with my gun.

"You're a big shot now", he said. But tomorrow your will be shit."

Oh shit I did it. I shot him in the head. His smiled turned to a surprised looked and he died. What the hell made me do that? Oh shit now what? I needed a drink. I did a U-turn and headed back. I had to think this out. Why didn't they tell me? How could they let shit like this go?

I pulled up to this bar and went in and ordered a drink. The bartender just looked at me. "Man what the hell happened to you. You O.K.?"

I looked up and holy shit it was the Gunny. I lose contact with him. I know he was around but being I was on the go all the time I never got around to seeing him. "Louie is that you?"

"Oh man am I glad to see you." I said; getting up.

"Hey, you all right?"

"No." I said.

And told him what I did.

"You're kidding, he said.

"No, I said. He is right out in the car."

"This I got to see, jumping over the bar and going out the door. He came back in and looked white. You sure did he said. Now what?" He asked.

"I don't know."

"Look I still got some friends that work in the office." He went to the phone and called.

I just looked at him and saw the way he was looking. It wasn't good. He hung the phone up and came back and sat on my side of the bar. "Well he said, I got good and I got bad."

"Ha, I said so what else is new?"

"The good is you aren't going to lose any rank."

"The bad?" I said.

"Well that depends on what you call bad."

"Well god damns it, give it to me." He took a drink out of my glass and said. "You pissed a lot of people off." "Big fucking deal, I said, give me it straight."

"Well so far the General isn't backing you up. He was ready to retire and he couldn't."

"I don't blame him for that," I said. I don't need any backing up."

He looked at me. "Oh yes you do. It seems you stepped on the CIA and they are all over us."

"I know that shit, I said let's not drag it out." I said.

"Well the way I see it you got two maybe three ways to go."

"Man I said, you're a dick."

He smiled at me and went on. "One, Get out with full retirement and nothing is done. You go on your way. I need a partner," he said.

"Man; I said. He knows he was getting to me.

"Two, he said. You get transferred out of the C.I.D. and go where ever they but you."

"You got to be kidding," I said.

"No, they don't want you around. You made them look bad. So for that they want to hide you somewhere out of sight."

"What is three?" I asked.

He smiled and said, "Shoot your self."

"Get fucked," I told him.

"Will I did say there might be a third way out."

"No fucking Gook is going to make me kill my self."

"So; he said what one will it be?"

"What if I fight it?" I said.

"Ha, he said this is what they told me. I didn't even tell them you killed the motherfucker. It may all change when they find out he is dead."

"Then?" I said.

"Hey, he said. You know what can happen. They may shoot you them self's."

"What the fuck did this Gook do?" I asked.

"Oh, he said something about him turning on his country and turning anyone and everyone in he knew about."

"That is crazy he was the main man doing all the shit." "You know it and I know it, but the boy's on top don't know it. They agreed to give him asylum here for what he knew."

"He knows everything he was the one doing it. That was with the Korean War," he said.

"But this mother had them in Vietnam. And being we were getting into it we wanted to know everything about it so we paid for information from him?"

"That is crazy." Again we both know it.

"That is the way it is. And they feel you fucked it up. Now no one will trust them. They said you set them back years."

"I did dick." I said getting up.

"Where are you going?" He asked.

"I got to call Nancy." I went to the phone and called.

"Hello, she said; she was crying.

"Hi it's me."

"Where are you?" She screamed.

"I'm with the Gunny." I said.

"Get home here," she said. We got people all over the place."

"Look I don't want them in the house, tell them I'll meet them at the office."

"Hello," it was Seymour.

"Hey, I said I'm sorry."

"Don't be sorry, he said, get the hell out of here. Run," he said.

Someone took the phone off of him. Oh shit, what did he know that we didn't? He would never say that to me on less something was wrong.

"Hello," someone said. "This is General Peterson."

Oh shit he was the Major that Nancy was going out with. He got him self transferred to CIA when I made him look like a fool. "Hey guy how it is going; long times no see."

"Cut the shit out, he said you got to turn your self in."

"In a pig's ass I do."

"Look, he said it is only going to go worse for you if you don't."

"Look, I need time to think this out."

"Where is general Oh?" He asked?

I told him in my car.

"Good, bring him here and maybe we can get this straighten out."

"And if we don't?"

Then; Gunny said, "You got to go old buddy."

"I bet you're the one controlling it, aren't you?" I said to him.

"Hey, he said, what goes around comes around."

"I know, I said; just remember that for further reference."

"Look, he said, you can hide but we got your family. So do your self-a favor and turn your self in."

"Like I said I'll meet you at the office. I don't want my wife and daughter to see what an ass hole you really are."

"We will see who is the ass hole; he said when we get you. Now either you come in or we come get you."

"I'll be at my office." I said and hung up.

"Oh well so much for the marines," I said looking at the Gunny. He was getting his coat on and shouting off the lights.

"Where you going?" I asked.

"With you," he said.

"No," I told him I didn't want to get him into this.

"Try and stop me," he said walking out the door.

He waited at the car. He was just looking at Oh. "I guess he got back at us." He said.

"No." I said, at me."

"Look, he said. I don't want to ride with him in the front set."

I opened the trunk and said, "He will look better here."

We both took him out and put him in the trunk. "Now I said; what?"

He looked at me and said. "You were the one with the brains. I go where you go."

"I guess I got no chose. I have to face it."

"Good, he said. I was hoping you would say that."

So we drove to my office. I park down the street and just sat. "Well, I said, here goes." Just them something came jumping right at me from the out side. It scared the hell out of the both of us.

"What the fuck was that?" The Gunny yelled.

"I don't know, I said, it is gone."

Then whatever it was jumped on the hood of the car came around to the side door. Oh shit it was mike; my dog. "Hey Mike," I got out of the car. He had something around his neck. He kept trying to get it for me. "Good dog," I said and took it off of him. He went to the Gunny to let me read it. It was from Seymour. It said they know all about me and this General wanted my ass. He said for me to go see Greene. He was the only one I could trust."

Shit maybe he was right. He was the only one I could trust. "Gunny; who told you about Greene?"

"My friend." He said.

"Did he hear it from him, him self?"

"No, he said he was just passing what he had heard."

I got back in the car. "Let's get out of here."

"How where?" He asked.

"To the general's house; I have to see him."

"Well what ever you're going to do, do it how. I don't like the looks of that car coming down the street."

"Hold on." I said waiting for it to pull up to us. He was right it had CIA man in it.

I hit the gas and took off. It took them by surprise. They thought I was coming in.

"Here they come," the Gunny said looking at them from the back.

"I can see that." I said. Tell me something I don't know."

He yelled. "You got two more in front of you blocking the street off."

"Thanks; I didn't know that."

"You going to stop?" he asked.

"Does a bare shit in the woods?" And I floored it. "You're not going to make it," he said bracing him self. I can't stop how and went up on the sidewalk and hit the back of one of the cars. I bounced off and scraped along the building.

"Oh shit." The Gunny yelled. They were Brown stones and lucky they had stairs on both sides. I started up one side and down the other, like a left side ramp. The car almost tipped over but I landed back on all fours when I hit this statue. It stopped me in my tracks. But set me up right. I backed up and then want around it. I chopped it in half.

The three cars started after me. One didn't see the statue and went right into it. He ended in to the front of the building. That left the other two following me. Off we went with them right behind me. The streets were empty. It was early in the morning by this time. I took the corner on two and oh shit a garbage truck was blocking the street. I tried to keep the car up on two wheels for as long as I could. I had to make it pass the garbage truck. Once I did that I was home free. The Gunny was screaming and I was holding the car on two wheels. I was almost passed the truck. Bang I heard something hit. I didn't know what it was till I passed it. When I got back on all fours I looked up and saw the roof. I mean the sky.

"Shit, the Gunny said. "I always want a convertible."

Off it went I must have hit something on the truck. Whatever it was; it did the job. No roof. The two cars behind me crashed into the truck one at a time. Going around the corner you didn't see the truck and no way to stop.

"Yea, the Gunny said. "Just like the plane." I guess he was meaning the Generals Plane the time I did a roll with it. "Yea," I said with him. "Now, to the generals House."

We park far away from it. I know he would have men around it waiting for me. I was right he did.

"Now what, the Gunny asked?"

"Night raid." I said and got out. "Mike you stay." I said to the dog.

"Hey man, the Gunny said, take him with us. He may come in handy."

Mike liked that; his tail was going like crazy.

"O.K. I said let's go."

We went around the back way into the back yard by the pool. The Gunny stopped and pointed at the patio. It was the general he was standing out side with three other men. "Now what?" He asked.

"Mike; I said, go get the general and tell him I need him."

Mike took off and when he got to where they could see him; he stopped.

"Hey general, I heard one of the say. Is that your dog?"

The general looked and saw it was Mike. "No; he said. It was his neighbors." He walked over to Mike and told the three he would be right back. "This dumb dog didn't know how to find his way home. Good dog," he said taking him by the neck and walking with him. Mike was walking him instead. He was bringing him right to us. When the general came he just looked at me. "You lied to me." He said.

Oh shit he knows who I was. "Sorry sir I said but I didn't have any other chose."

"No, he said you did."

"How's that?" I said.

He looked at me and said. "You could have told me the truth."

"Maybe yes and maybe no; I said. But you can believe me or not I would have told you some day."

"You have Seymour to thank for that;" he said.

"I got Seymour to thank for a lot;" I said.

"And he has a lot to thank you for to;" he told me what you did for him. And anyone that would risk his life for a son whose father killed his parents. Have more the thanks to give."

"I know; I said But that isn't going to help me now."

"No, he said he did all he could do and I think I did all I can do. You're on the shit list:" he said. And with General Oh out there Gods knows what they will do to you. He was the one that told them about you. He didn't finish telling them. But he was holding it till he made sure we lived up to our part of the bargain. He said something about your father and him meeting some place. That is all I know."

"You mean setting him up for the rest of his life."

"Something like that;" he said.

"So now what?" I asked.

"Well when Generals Oh gets throw you won't stand a chance. The way he put it you took the money from him to help your father. They still don't know if it is you or some other German doing the same thing. That he made sure he didn't let out. But anyway He said you took the money for you self."

"But you know we turned it all in."

"I know that but they don't. They don't even know who you are yet. General Oh saw to that. He left them hanging with you. He gave them a lot more people but you he was saving for last."

"Good, then you are in the clear." The Gunny said.

"How's that?" The general asked.

"General Oh isn't going to talk a lot about you now."

"From what I heard you beat him pretty bad."

"He killed him," the Gunny said.

He looked at him as if not to hear him.

"General; he said again, the General is in the trunk Dead. You want to see? he asked. Dead never going to talk again; that kind of dead." He said. Then the general knew he was telling the truth.

"Oh shit; he said now what?"

The Gunny said if he can't talk then the Colonial won't be found out. Yes? he said; but they still had to get more out of him. The CIA will be mad."

"So. I said let them be mad. The only thing I did was act on my training. They can't hold me for that. Look the way I see it we can yell at them for not informing us what they were doing with him. And it was there fault I ran into him the way I did."

"That is it," the general said. It might work. You sure he is dead?" he asked.

"Want to see him?" the Gunny said

"No, I take your word for it. Well you ready?"

"I don't know. I said. What do you think?" I asked the Gunny?

"Don't ask me I don't want anything to go wrong. Ask the dog," he said.

"Why not, he can understand. Mike do I go with the general?"

He shook his head "yes." Well I said; lead the way." I don't know if I did right. But I did it.

Well he was wrong. The other ass had something up his sleeve. He knew all alone who I was. He knew when he left the department. How he found out was by the number tattoo on my arm. Some how he had the records from the prison camp and it had names with the numbers. And my number didn't match the name. He checked it out and had proof. I guess he was waiting to get back at me. Well he got his wish. There was nothing the General could do about it and with the Korean General dead it just looked as if I did him in for this reason. So I was the bad guy now.

CHAPTER 16

The weeks that followed were hell. I got court Marshal and had to stand trail. That was a laugh. Seymour stood by me and so did Nancy at the beginning that is. I had a good lawyer. Seymour got him for me and said he was the best. Then it started, Jews from all over the world started coming in. To hear them tell it I was the one that did the killings; not my father.

I don't know what they tried to prove by it. We didn't tell my side of the story till they finished. I had to sit through the whole thing. The judges were four officers and no jury like civilian court. It was up to them, the four officers. My lawyer didn't cross examining any one of them, he just let them talk. None of them had proof; just hear say. Even the ones that were at the camp; and were still alive; didn't have much to add to what was already known. I was my father's son and no more. Then it came time for us to show or case. First he had an officer that was at the camp testified. He said he knew of me but what could a child do? I was just for fun. He told of how my father would bring me along to make the soldiers laugh. I didn't really hurt anyone.

Then he called Seymour.

This is what took the longest. At first he asked him how he felt about me. Seymour looked at the officers and then at me and said. "I would trade places with him right now. This man isn't a killer. He was lead by his father. In watch he as you can see by his record couldn't rest till he him self killed his father. Not for the crimes he had done. But for the crimes he was going to do."

"Here stands before you, the Lawyer said taking out a report. This is what this man did to save the world. And I do mean world. Not some million Jews. And mind you sir I am very Jewish," he said to the officers. To what Hitler did to my people. This mans father was going to do more, a lot more. My people came here to seek justice. And what is justice? He asked. My family was killed by this mans father or Hitler witch ever you wish to call it. I'm here defending him as if he was my own. Not a German that killed my family. I'm sure once all the records are turned over for the world to see. No Jew alive today will cast a stone in order to harm this man," he said.

The lawyer asked Seymour about the scrolls. Seymour said we kept this mans name from our people because of his pass. I told him to let me tell my people he was the one that recovered them for us. And if this would have been known I don't think this here trail would be going on. This man and only this man risked his life for them. And at the time he didn't even know they existed. I didn't even know of them. I was sent to find this man's father so we the Jewish people could hang him for his sins. Little did he our I knew, his father had our history in his hands. We had giving up on them. We had trought the Germans destroyed them all.

Today we have pictures to remind our children what their pass was all about. But years ago we had nothing but our scrolls; to remind Jewish children of their past. The feeling I got when this man came to me and told me he could get them back. Was nothing I could ever describe? No one could. And believe me I saw the same look on others when I told them about it and they too would say. Nothing in words could describe their feelings of joy. The lawyer stood up and said I bring Rabbi Hina to the stand. This was the rabbi that was in charge of the scrolls. Seymour looked at me and smiled. "Rabbi if you would please with out me putting words into your mouthtell the judges what your feelings are; please."

The Rabbi stood up and started. "I didn't know Seymour my lawyer had him and I didn't know if he was going to help me or hurt me. I listened to him as the judges would for the first time I didn't want to miss a word. It was my life on the line. This Jew could do more damage to me by just saying what he did was wrong, this man must be punished for his crime." But he didn't. He stood there and didn't move. He looked at everyone and said. "I don't think there is one Jew in this courtroom that will disagree with me. The others will have to judge for them self's.

This man; he said is not a killer. He is a saver. For what he did it took not only a Jew to do; but a man. I stand before you and say I being a Rabbi will bless this man and allow this man to become a Jew if he so wishes."

I guess he said it all, then the people that were in the store at the time of the shooting. The girl that was at the front when I walked in comes up first. The way she told it. As if I didn't know what was going on when I entered the store. And the people that were being held in the back said the same thing. Now the big question was why did I shot him? That took some time. First I had to make them believe I wasn't going out of my mind and end up in a nut ward. I did the best I could the rest was up to them.

My lawyer called the Gunny to the stand and had him tell about the beating that we received from General Oh when they found out about us. And the way the General killed the two man right in front of us. Also other soldiers were called in; ones that know the General. They told of the way he was planing to over throw the Government and take power him self with the help of my father.

Then my lawyer called the Korean woman to the stand, she was living here now and she followed the General after we left. And had records of all the crime this man did. She her self said she would of shot him if she would of know he was let off the hook and allowed to live a good life. No, she said the only place for a man like that was dead. He would have never changed."

The lawyer came in with a little surprise. He had a record of things that were found up in Generals Oh store when inventory was taking cocaine and guns. "My lawyer said "I guess the CIA was supplying him with these? I rest my case;" he said. Seymour came over and said something to him.

"One more thing your honor's," he said; I have one more witness to take the stand."

Who the hell was that? It was Seymour's uncle. He looked at me and went to the bench and sat.

"Sir would you mind telling the judges who you are." He told them and held up the same picture Seymour gave me. "This; he said is my brother and his wife and this is my Nephew; when he said that tears came to his eyes. I know he had forgiven me. I got up and ran to him. I hugged him till they took us apart. Tears were coming out of the both of us.

"Gentleman," my lawyer said that is it. I have no more to say. The C.i.A general stood up and said "Touching," and looked At the Judges. I wish to point out an on going investigation we had with General Oh and it did point the finger to Colonel Goldberg or Kaufmann what ever he is called."

"Hold it right there." General Green stood up and said. You can stick that reports up your ass. They means nothing. This man has never done anything but good for the United States. And the Marine Corps and if you say he didn't. You're going to have to say I didn't either. Because I knew every step this man took. And if you're saying he took then your saying I took to. You see these here stars;" he said reaching on his shoulders. You can take them from me first. I gave him the orders to do what he did. Do I make my self-clear?" he said looking at the judges and then at the CIA shit head.

"General" one of the judges said; you made your point he said. Now let us do our job please sir."

Well that was that. Now we had to wait for the answer. As we went out in the hall to wait the CIA ass stopped Nancy. He said something to her. She did go with him so I didn't think too much about it. Nancy pulled away from him and followed us out. Seymour's wife was outside when we came out she ran up to me.

"I'm so glad for you;" she said hugging me.

Nancy just watched. I could see something was on her mind.

"Hey hon. I said don't look so down."

She looked at me and then at Seymour and asked. Did I give his wife their son?"

Oh shit not this. How the hell did she find out? I didn't know what to say. Seymour just looked at her and was thinking the same thing. How the hell did she find out?

"Well she asked again. Is someone going to tell me?" Seymour's wife went up to her and tried to hold on to her. "Can we talk some place," she asked her?"

Nancy went crazy.

"The three of you are sick," she said.

"Nancy please let her talk."

"No; she said your life has been one lye after another." You know I have been faithful to you and I loved you. Now I find out you're not the man I married and you're going around fucking other people to have babies. How many others have you done it to?"

"She was the only one," I said.

"Oh; she said you expect me to believe that, she said then she said something and the only way she would of known that was the CIA general told her. That mother fucker. He just didn't quite.

"You father had a lot of Jews balls cut off. So I guess you had to go and fuck all of the Jewish woman to make up for what your father did?"

We didn't know what to say to her. We just stood with our mouths open. She looked at me and then turned around and left. Seymour came to me and just held my arm. What could you say? Nothing. Like always I should have told her about it and asked her what I should do. I guess I was so use to lying I didn't think the truth was the right way to go. Now I see it was the only way to go. Maybe it would have turned out different. I guess I'll never know. I lied to my uncle, to the general and to my wife. Now what? I didn't lye to the court lets see what they do.

Seymour's wife went after Nancy. I couldn't go. I was still under arrest. The General and Seymour stayed with me.

"Woman, the Gunny said. That is why I don't want to ever get married."

I know he meant well; but I didn't need that right now. I loved her and my daughter and the baby on its way. Shit that motherfucker did a number on me. If he didn't get me one way he found another way. The judges were back and we were called back in. I really wanted to run after Nancy but I had to see what the truth meant.

The judges told me I would have to resign from the C.I.D but that would be it. I was free to stay in the service and hold my rank. As far as my name goes it was up to me to keep whatever name I chose. The Marines would honor it. And as for the death of the general that had to be looked into a little more. He said looking at the general From the CIA; meaning; they wanted to know how they could let this guy in the country knowing what he had done and not watch him more closely.

Case over." he said.

I walked up to the C.I.A. general and just looked at him. I was hoping he would say something first. He did.

"Well he smiled and said there will be another time." "Your right about that." I said.

The Gunny came to my side, he knows me. He was there to make sure I wasn't going to do what I did. You see I still was fast. I hit the ass hole with all I had. He went down. The four judges stopped and turned around to see what had happened. Gen.

Green yelled. "Oh my god I think he had a heart attach. He just fills right to the floor. No one touched him." The Gunny took my arm and walked out the door with me. I looked at my hand and it had the Generals blood all over it. I said, "Now I feel better." Wiping it on to the other hand, I may never wash again." I told him.

"You're a sick fuck," he said to me. And we went out the door.

"Hey the Korean woman said, "Can I get a lift from someone."

We both looked at her and took her by the arms and carried her down the stairs. It was good seeing her again. I wondered about her.

"Come I said you know we wouldn't leave you behind. That brought back memories. "No roll oven's, she said? That got us all laughing. Seymour called. He was coming out behind us.

"I'm going over your house. Give me some time with Nancy."

"I'll be at the Gunny's bar," I said looking at him.

"That he will," the Gunny said. And off we went.

Well I guess I didn't win after all. Nancy didn't want to see me any more and she was going for a divorce. I just couldn't talk to her. I know that she was strong that is why I loved her. But this strong I didn't plan on. She was hurt and there was nothing I could do to stop her. Seymour and his wife didn't get anywhere either. They both felt bad. But what was done was done. I couldn't change it. I wouldn't change it. They loved their son and I was glad I could do it for them. The only thing I would have changed was to tell Nancy. Maybe not if she acted this way, who knows how it would of turned out. I had the easy life this far. Now it was my turn to gave back what I had taking. And with Seymour's son I felt I did just that.

CHAPTER 17

So life goes on. I still had my rank and I move to the base housing. It was a small place and I missed seeing my daughter. Nancy was about to have my second child so I didn't ship out till I know what she had and it was all right. That was the both of them. I did care I did love them. At the divorce she didn't say much and her lawyer got her everything she wanted. I didn't go with a lawyer. I didn't want to fight with her. All I wanted was to see my children when I could. That she didn't fight, she knows how much I loved them. The only thing she wanted was for me to give her notice when I was coming. For some reason she didn't want to be there when I came. She said she would arrange to have someone sit with the kids and me. I guess I really hurt her.

Well I had a son and he was doing great. Nancy was doing well to, so I guess it was time for me to leave. I couldn't stay around knowing a war was going on. I got transferred to the Far East. We were called advisers for the time being. That was O.K. by me. I was glad I was here and not behind the bars, or behind the bar with the Gunny. This was my life and I accepted it. How let's see what we have here. The French had all but pulled out, and the Vietcong were over running the place. The regular army was holding; but not by much. We were sent here to hold them together till the top brass decided what we were going to do. Mean time I was in charge of the advisers; as we were called.

We were sending in supplies by the ton and getting ready to set up shop for our next war. I could smell it. No way were we going to just stand around and be advisers. That wasn't the American way. The fighting was getting heavier on the front line and the North was making its move. Well it was now or never. We had to make up our mind before there was nothing to make our minds up about. The Russians were supplying the north and I guess that was reason enough for us to come in. That is what the President use to get us in. He was hoping the American people would see it that way. He found out later that he was wrong. He was faced with a new generation of Americans. I didn't have much contact with the civilian people. But from what I was reading, it seemed as if the whole younger generation was on pot. The kind you smoke and it didn't take much to start them up.

Word was going around that the Russians had something to do with it, but I guess we will never know. Kids were running from the draft and heading for Canada. And the ones that stayed around made a lot of noise about the war. The kids that did go were confused. Seeing the news about their friends back home not wanting to go and hearing it from letters they received from home. Saying how wrong the war was. And they should come home. Families split down the middle; one son in the service and the other running. The father an All American and the mother not wanting to go throw what her parents went throw with Korea. War, what was war nothing for the fat and lazy. That is the way it has always been until it was at your front door, than and only then did you say "Hey, why didn't we see it coming?' By then it is too later. What we were doing here was stopping it before it got out of hand.

Some may disagree with me but just look back a little and see if I was right; meaning my friend Herr Hitler. He started with just wanting a little more land. That was all and the Jews bothered him. He figured since the beginning of the Jewish race. People couldn't stand them. For what reason to this day no one knows but it was fact. People hated them from the time the first guy stood up and said. "I'm a Jew." The guy next to him looked at him and said; "sit down your rocking the boat". The Jew just kept standing and saying what he was. Not paying any attention to the other man. As if he wasn't there. He was a Jew and that was all he cared about.

So on and on the Jews got more and more people to stand and be counted. I guess you could call them a union of their time. So how he picked the Jews; they were the most likely to have people go on his side. Next would of been the blacks and on and on. Like the saying goes 'where it stops nobody knows'. We were here and we weren't ready to back down. Not yet that is. The war went on and the people back home hated it more and more. For me I just loved it. I had what I wanted; 'A war'. At first it was like playing a game. Don't shot until you were shot at first and only give advice; nothing else. Ha, that was a laugh. Try telling that to someone that killed for a living. The only thing I didn't like about this war was the same thing I didn't like about the Korean War. You couldn't tell the good from the bad. The guy next to you could be a bad guy. So I did what any good soldier would do. Shot first and ask questions later.

They finely said we were in it to stay. By that time we had over two hundred thousand man over. And more equipment then we knew what to do with. I guess being the French did such a bad job with the first try, we didn't want to look like fools. So we went all out. The north did a good job fighting. They know what to do to us was what we called gorilla action. Small groups of man attaching and running. By the time you got your man into position they were gone. This went on for most of the time I was here. You just couldn't get your hands on them and they were doing a lot of damage. Then for some reason they got wind of drugs. Ha I know what the reason was to win the war and nothing else. You see our boys were so out of it. They needed anything to help them live with the fact their mothers and brothers didn't want them over here; helped. Drugs were found all over the place. If they didn't find it in some village they brought it on the street. Why not; it was easy to get.

Then one day I got a surprise. Guess who was waiting for me at headquarters. Miss Korea Sue. She had joined up and was assigned to work with me. That was nice of whoever did that. I could use someone friendly right about now. The fighting was getting to me and there was nothing I could do about it. Most of my man was drug addicts and I didn't blame anyone for not wanting to go on patrol with them high. I guess this will never get out. But that is no way to fight a war. Even the officers were doing it. Oh hell it can't hurt. It is just like having a beer. That is what they all accepted. Just like having a beer. Some fucking deadly kind of beer. I remember one time I had to go check on this out post. We didn't hear from then for a couple of hours.

They still had the joint in their lips. They all got their throats cut. The gooks came up on them with out them even knowing it and did what they were trained to do. Take us out. It wasn't like that all over but you could see it coming; more and more each week. Maybe the people back home were right; this was no war for us to be in. I guess I really can't say what the truth was here. Stand up and fight for our country Americans. Maybe they were war'ed out if there is such a thing. Well I wasn't the one to judge. I was here to do my job and that is what I did. I tried to stay out of arms way as much as I could and just did my thing. It made it a lot easier when she came.

The first night I went to bed with her. I guess she wanted it just as much as I did. Who knows? All I know is the next day I got my orders to go and find this drug dealer. And he was the one supplying the base with the shit. They said he was Vietcong but he was living in a south village. She came along with me. I guess she knew her job and besides she was good to have along.

We arrived in this Village around sun down and before you know it. We were surrounded. Oh shit it looked like a set up. They know we were coming and the whole village was in on it. My four guards were killed right off the bat. They didn't even have a chance. How stupid could I be? I let my guard down just this once and bang I got my ass in trouble. I can't blame her for that even thou I was thinking about her and what I was going to do to her that night. Sex was on my mind; not the war. So now I pay. She paid to. They took the both of us out of the Village fast.

For what reason I didn't know then; but I was about to find out. It seems they had a price on hers and mine head. Little did we know? The Vietnam people put it there but we were wrong, the Mafia put it there. Could you believe this? I guess this war was making a lot of drug families rich. The way we found out was when we arrived to our destination some officer that was collecting the reward for us greeted us. How nice of them. He said it was the Korean and Italian Mafia that put it up. Two hundred thousand in gold. Where in hell was my government when this came about? I'm sure they know about it. Why didn't they warn me about it? And why did they send her here with me. Something smelt and I didn't like it. It was almost as if we were set up by our own.

They treated us good and didn't even ask us anything about the war. Who the hell cared about the war? The money he was going to get would take him right out of it. So he didn't give a shit who was winning. We were kept there for days, her in one cell and me in another. We could see each other but we couldn't touch. May be it was for the better. They didn't want anything to happen to us so we had guards around the clock watching us. Then it came. Oh shit I couldn't believe it. They were Russians. They didn't say much they just came and took the both of us away. They took us further north to a city. I didn't know what one but it was one of the main ones. And we were taking to this building, a real cement and brick kind of building.

She said it was the capital. "I guess we made big time." I said to her. She looked worried. She knows what was in store for us. I didn't. That night two Russians officers came in.

"You are the famous Colonel Kaufmann. Yes." I looked at him and smiled.

"Now what can I do for you. I asked?"

"Dos good; he said you like to make jokes. Good I make jokes to;" he said. Did you hear the one about big foot?"

"About what?" I asked.

"You know the big foot; you people believe in."

"No," I said I didn't know what he was talking about. "Well never you mind; we got big dick and pointed to this big fat sumo wrestler looking guy.

"Him big dick," he said smiling.

I couldn't believe what it was. He was so fat I didn't see he had no clothes on. I did see this thing hanging from the middle of his lag. At first I trough it was a rope of some kind holding up his pants. But as I looked closer I saw it was his dick.

It was dragging on the ground it was so long. "He can't be for real" I said.

"Oh isn't he wonderful?" he smiled.

"That all depends on what you call wonderful?" I said. Me I said he does nothing for me. Maybe he does something to you. Everyone has his own thing."

"No, No he said for your lady friend. Look at her; she can't take her eyes off of him."

"Oh no you wouldn't." I said.

"Oh but I wouldn't; he said he will".

And stood back to let me watch.

Two guards took her and held her down First. They held her on her back and then when he finished they turned her over on her stomach. I know she was going throw a lot of pain. She was a small woman and to have someone that size forcing there were into her had to hurt.

"You see, he said she likes it. She didn't yell one word."

She just looked at me with tears in her eyes. The pain was too much for even me. I jumped at the Russian. Hoping to get his gun from him.

I forgot about the two guards that were watching me. I got reminded real fast. I felt the rifle hit the back of my neck. I didn't go out but I was almost did. The Russian said; "don't leave us just yet. The show isn't over yet." He picked me up and put me back in the chair. "How you watch; he said maybe do you some good."

"What do you want?" I asked.

"Oh he said we what nothing. We just hold you for someone."

"Who" I yelled,"

"Oh he said. You will see. This is just entertainment for us. You see we don't get very much of that around here."

I looked at the big guy and he was still going on her. He was like a horse in heat. I had to do something .I couldn't just let him stand there laughing at her. I came off the floor with my feet and caught him in his nuts. This time I was waiting for the guards. I took a rifle off of one and shot him with it. I hit the other one with the butt and in the same swing I shot the big guy. O.K. now I said get away from her;" I told the other guards that were holding her.

One guard turned her over and smiled; she dye;" he said. He was holding a knife to her throat. I could see the blood coming. He wasn't fooling he was going to cut her head off. The big guy I shot was just looking at me. I guess he didn't feel it; he went right back to doing it to her. By this time the Russian got back up. He took the gun off of me and said; "now I play" he said. Taking out a whip he had outside the cell. I hear you are pretty good with one of these." He said cracking it. I to am pretty good with one to." His next swing came at me. I grabbed it with my hands and tried to pull it away from him. Little did I know the other guard came around and was behind me? He hit me again with the butt of the rifle. I dropped the whip and went to my knees. That was all the Russian needed. He went to town on me.

"Now My German; let's see how you like it." He started whipping. I lost count. At first I felt where they landed. But after a while I couldn't care where they landed. I didn't feel them. My whole body was numb. All the time he was talking. He said something that made me sick. He said something about it was my own people that wanted me. I didn't know if he meant the Mafia or what. I looked over at her and the big guy was still going to town on her. I guess that was the last I remembered I most of went out.

When I came to I didn't feel a thing. I didn't know if I was dead or a live. All I know is I was awake. My eyes weren't open but I could think. And the first thing I remembered was that the Russian said.

Now who did he mean?" The Germans Jews who. He left me in the dark. Who were my own people he was talking about? I guess you could say I didn't know which one he was talking about. I just laid there waiting to hear some sign of life, nothing. I couldn't hear anything. I couldn't move anything. I just had my brain working and that was it. Maybe I was dreaming all this. Come on I said to my self-wake up; nothing. I don't know how long I stayed like this but I know it was for hours. But again they say your dreams are only seconds. Who the hell knew? All I knew is I couldn't move or feel anything.

I must have kept going in and out. I remember something and then I would go out and then come back. Who knows how long I was like this? Maybe I was dead and this is how you stayed forever. I tried to think of my son and daughter but every time I did someone would come and whip them so I didn't think of them any more. I couldn't stand seeing them cry. It was a dream. When was I going to wake up? Or was I ever going to wake. It didn't seem like I was. Then one time I hear voices. Oh shit I was alive who was out their .I tried to talk but nothing. The voices went away. Oh shit another dream. This was driving me crazy. Let me go who ever are doing this to me. I can't spend the rest of my life this way. Let me go I yelled. Ha no one heard me. At least I didn't think anyone did. How would I know? I guess I wouldn't. Back out again. This was for the birds.

Well if this is the way my life was to be I guess I had better get use to it. Who knows how long I got to stay this way? Forever and how long is that? Then I felt something cold on me. What the hell was that? It felt as if I was outside somewhere and being moved.

"Hey I tried to say. But like the last time nothing. Oh shit I was moving I felt something I was rocking side to side. As if I was being carried by someone. Still I heard no one. Then I felt as if I was flying. I went out again and then back to nothing all over again. No movement or cold; another dream.

Then I felt something going in my arm. Someone was holding my arm and playing with it. Almost as if they were sticking a needled in it. Then I heard the words. He will make it and that was it. Were they talking about me or was I dreaming again. Shit this was driving me crazy. What was real and what wasn't? Or was any of it real. I went out again. His time I was sure I wasn't dead I had my eyes open and I was looking around. I was in some kind of room; it looks like a hospital. But something was different then the ones I was us to. It was painted a dark color and didn't have all the machines you would see in one. Then it hit me I was in Russia. The Russian had me ship to Russia. Them mother fuckers what the hell were they up to? I started getting movement in my body. I lifted my arm and shit I had whip marks all over it. That mother fuck tried to whip me to death. That was why I couldn't feel anything. My body was whip all over. I could feel them now.

It was like long burning lines and when I moved they would burn more. He got almost every part of my body even my lags. I had a tube in my arm I guess to feed me. Someone wanted me alive; if not the tubes wouldn't be in me. Now to wait to see who come to see me and what they want with me. I know the woman wasn't going to be anywhere around. Not the way the pig was going at her. No one could live after what I saw him doing to her. The next two-day's the only one that I saw was this nurse if that is what you want to call her. She didn't talk she just checked me and left; no words spoken; just wiping something all over me and changing the bottles over my head. I tried to talk but she acted as if I wasn't even there. I saw she locked the door when she left. I was a prisoner but what the hell did they think they could get out of me?

On the third day I got my answer. Two officers came in. They were officers of the Russian army. They said they were K.G.B. and had some questions to ask me.

"And if I don't want to talk?" I said. Then what?"

One did all the talking the other just looked. Your name is Kaufmann. Your father was a German officer for Hitler at Docktow. Well he said; is this not you?"

And if it was? I asked so what?"

"So; he said. You tell me you are?"

"No" I said. I just what to know if you are who they say you are."

"If I am; then what?"

"Look he said you are close to death and you may not make it. Just for our records; he said.

"Look just let me dye and get the fuck out of here."

"I'm sorry we can't do that. You must answer us."

"Or what?" I said. I closed my eyes and waited for them to beat me or leave. I didn't care what they did. They left.

What the hell was going on here? What did the Russians want with me? I just couldn't figure it out. Koreans Germans Jews Italian; even the Vietnamese. But the Russians what did they think I know? Something was wrong and I didn't like it. I was in no shape to get up and walk around so I guess they will wait till they could beat me some more. What ever it was they wanted. It must be very importune for them not to kill me. Then I remembered the Vietnam solder saying I had a price on my head. Maybe it was alive not dead. That is why they were taking care of me. I still didn't know who put the price on my head and for what. If I know what for if I'd know who did it. The only thing I couldn't figure out was what the Russians had to do with it? Maybe Castro had them get me. That was it Castro was the one behind this. Now it made sense. The Russians were doing it for Castro. Son of a bitch that was it.

Boy this Castro guy was a nut and the Russians were just as sick for taking the chance in taking me. The U.S. won't stand for this. They will come for me. The door opened again and the same two came in. You ass holes know what this means?" I said.

"One said you want to talk to us?"

"No I said. I want to talk to the American ambassador". "Ha he said you're no good to the Americans; he said they don't want you."

I said; "how do you know that?" I asked.

"You see comrade it is like this; he said taking a chair and pulling it to my bed. I tell you; he said. You know what a price on de head means?"

"Look I said if you're going to talk like an asshole get the fuck out of here."

"So I take it you know. He said smiling. Well your CIA but it on your head."

"Your shiting me? I said.

"This shitting you; it means what?" he asked.

"Joking," the other one said.

"Oh look he talks. I said to the other one. He smiled at me and said "Yes I talk and what of it?"

"Look would someone mind explaining what the hell I'm doing here?"

"That is what we are trying to do Comrade but you what to do this joke with us."

"Look; the other one said. He spoke better English. We saved you and now we would like to know why your government put a price on your head. We know who you are and what you have done. But what we don't know is why the price. Did you do something we didn't know about?" "You tell me." I said.

"From what we know he said you're a hero and no reason for this here price on your head. But you see when our comrades in Vietnam said they had you and they were waiting for the reward. We took you from them with the understanding we would return you when we finished with you. Now how would you like that;" he asked.

"So far what you two are telling me doesn't mean shit to me.

Oh he said and what can we do to prove it was your own people that did it to you?"

"Give me a phone." I said.

"Ha this comrade is full of jokes; he said; give him a phone. What, maybe you call room service or something.

"Or something would be the right thing." I said.

"No comrade he said I don't think so; we don't have any phones that do that".

"So I guess I go back to sleep." I said and rolled over. You sleep Comrade he said .we will be by tomorrow. You see we got lots of time. You're the one who don't". They got up and left.

This was sounding crazy. I know they were lying to me; but for what? Any case I worked on was over with and the files were open for public review. I had nothing to hide. The General made sure of that before I left the department.

Other agents that had open files could help them out. But me I closed all my cases. And as far as this war went I know nothing about it except drugs and even that I didn't know that much about. I didn't even get started on my case. I know nothing. Maybe I shouldn't get to mad at them and try to find out everything they knew. That is if they were telling me the truth. One could never know about the K.G.B.. I got it; they want me to come over to there side. They said they heard what happened to me maybe they figured I was feed up with the U.S. and would go over to their side. That was it. By them telling me the U.S. put a price on my head would make me think twice about returning. Like he said they have all the time in the world. Seeing all I did they figured I was worth the wait.

The next day they came in and smiled. Well comrade how you feel this day?"

"Pretty good I said. But can you see about getting me some real food; this shit going up my arm isn't hitting on it; you know what I mean?" I asked.

The one looked at me as if I was crazy. But the other one know what I was talking about.

"Maybe tomorrow he said .Our comrade did a good job on you. You mean the ass hole with the whip. What was up with him?" I asked.

"Oh he said you don't have to worry about him; he is far away."

"I see; good for him. So how it is your turn to do whipping?" I said.

"No comrade he said the other officer was one of the men whose father was whipped by your father. He just wanted to pay back for his father. You see he didn't know we wanted you so he said the Vietnam didn't care what he did to you; the price was the same dead or alive. He paid the Vietnam solder that got you a lot's of rubles to do what he did to you. To him he was just getting back for his father.

You should thank him for doing it to you."

"Oh yea I said .I should kiss him for it".

No the one said laughing. If he didn't pay to whip you the Vietnam would have shot you and waited for his money. Being my officer did what he did; it kept you alive that extra day. That is when we found out about you. One of our officers was passing the tent and looked in. He found out what was going on and called us. That is when we knew about you. My officer wanted to see you for him self. He didn't believe it was you. So we took you back with us. And how if you don't talk you go back. You see we don't have anything to lose. We just want to know why your country wants you dead."

"Maybe I said. I'll think of joining your side. Yes Comrade." I asked.

"Maybe we could talk about that;" he said.

I know it that is what they wanted.

"But what good will I do? I said .I could never go back to my country if what you say is true."

"Yes you are right comrade but from what you have done we feel you would make a good leader".

"Leader of what?" I asked.

"The east Germans division; you know they are ours now. And most of the young solders would jump at the chance to follow a German such as you."

"Being who my father was." I said?

"See one said. He is him."

"Thank you comrade for that piece of information; them sneaky mother fuckers. They did get it out of me. "Ha I said you are good; now what?"

He smiled at me and said; "you will see." They both got up and said good bye. So that was all they were after. Just to see if I was my father's son.

I guess they would put me on trail for what my father did to the Russians at the end of the war. He did kill Russians along with the Jews at the end. He said Hitler ordered it. Well I guess I can sleep now knowing what they wanted me for. I guess they didn't want to pay out that money if I wasn't the one. And the only way they could find out was by me telling them. I had no fingerprints saying who I was but Joel Goldberg and people's here say. Maybe the U.S. set it all up to have me join the Russians. I know how they think. They don't even trust them self's. Let alone what the American papers said. Now they knew. So now a firing squad; I guess. American was, but you sure as hell couldn't call what we had over there.

CHAPTER 18

The next morning two officers came in, one was one of the ones that had been here before and I didn't know the other one. He was much older then the others and he look wiser for some reason. The one that was talking to me; stood and the older one sat. "Well how are we doing?" the older one asked?"

"What; you don't know?" I said.

"No; he said I would like to hear it from you," he said.

"Look I don't want to play your game any more you found out what you wanted. So let's stop the shit and get on with what ever you are going to do with me."

"Oh he said what makes you think we are going to do something with you?"

"Look it may surprise you but I'm no idiot."

"Good I'm glad to hear that," he said. Let me introduce my self he said. My name is Hans Kaufmann."

My whole in sides went turning around. I didn't know what to say. This was some kind of joke he was pulling on me. This man was saying he was my brother. No he couldn't be.

"Well, does the name mean anything to you?" He asked.

"Look I know you know who I am so big deal. You know my brother's names. But to say you're my brother you got to be joking."

"And why is that Joseph?" he said just by the way he said it I got cold all of a sudden. His eyes just look at me. It was him he was looking like my father. Shit that is why I know something was different in him. He looked like my father. I didn't know what to do. I sat up and just studied his face. "Hans is it you." I asked.

"Yes Joseph it is I your brother." His hand reached to touch mine and then I know it was him. "Hans." I got the word out and reached to hug him. He came to meet me with his hug.

"Joseph," he said almost crying. You are my brother." "Hans" was all I could say. My brother wasn't dead. I had my real brother alive. He pulled away from me and told the other solder to leave. He out ranked him so he left with out saying a word. Hens turned back to me. "Joseph what have you done? And how have you been?" all in one breath.

"My brother I don't know what to tell you. I don't know what you mean by what have I do and to how I feel you can tell me that. I don't know what happened to me. It was your man that did it to me."

"Come he said you getting out of here." He got up and went to the door. He yelled something In Russian and came back to my bed.

You're going home with me," he said taking my hand.

"Hans is it really you." I asked. Not believing it.

He let go of my hand and moved it to his far head," "see." He lifted his hair and there was a scar. "That was the last day I saw you my brother.

"I said; you were mad at me for getting Hitler's gun. "Yes my brother; he said it was the day me and our other brother shipped out. This here cut you gave me saved my life."

"I don't get you." I said. What was he talking about? "Well he said our other brother got on a ship and I had to stay behind. You see you hit me harder then our father thought. When I got to the ship I passed out. You cracked my skull and they had to put me in the hospital. So I missed my ship with our brother. Two days out it got torpedo and went down."

"But mother didn't hear anything about it."

"I know, he said father did but he didn't let her know."

"When I got better I got my ship and was captured by the Russians; the first week out. Again Father didn't tell mother. But he knew. Being I was so young the Russian army took me in after the fall of Germany. Like you I loved war and made it my career. Now I am one of the top men in the K.G.B. like you in the C.I.D. but I never know about you till your trail. I thought my family was gone."

"Me also." I said.

He rolled up my arm and said. "So it is true you were saved by a Jew."

"Yes, I said a good Jew."

"Oh he said you need not worry I'm a solder I don't hate anyone anymore. I just kill because I'm ordered to. Just like a job to me."

"Like our father." I said.

"No he said. You know better then that. You know our father killed because he loved to kill."

"Yes I said and you must know I killed him my self."

He looked at me and said. "I know someone had killed him, we got the report over my desk and believe me if you didn't do it I was going to have to do it. Once they found out what he was doing. The Russians got very worried about him. Hitler tried it once. He had to be stopped."

"That is what I said when I found out what he was up to."

"Did you know Him and Hitler had this all plan years before the Americans came?"

"Yes, he said we do now. But back then we didn't know. At first we were too worried about making it over the winter. And then when the war was over we worried about the Americans coming and taking everything we had left. So we had to build our self back up and be ready to fight if need be."

"You talk like you're a Russian." I said to him.

"You talk like you're an American." He said. Smiling.

"No I said like you, I'm a soldier. I have no country." "Good my brother; he said helping me up. You come home with me I will take care of you."

"But what will the Russians say?" I asked.

"Nothing I said you're my prisoner. I do what I want with you. Come; he said we go eat. My men said you asked for good food then that is what you will get; good food my brother."

The other soldier was waiting outside the room for us. He had a wheel chair. "Come my brother I drive you."

You could see he was as happy as I was finding him out. Boy was it a good feeling to know I still had a brother living.

"Hans I asked as he helped me into the chair. Was it you that put a price on my head?"

"No; he said but we will talk about it when we eat. No more talking, he said. I got to sneak you out of here first."

He was really doing it; he didn't have orders to take me home. But he was and the other solder was helping him. We got out of the hospital and in to his car.

"Now; he said we go."

He drove to this little house and pulled into the driveway. Nothing like a general would live in back in the states but this wasn't the states. He got out and the other soldier got out and the both of them carried me into the house. They sat me on the couch and the other solder left. My brother told him something and he left. He came back to me and smiled. "I told them to tell the office I wouldn't be in. I was sick for a couple of days. So my brother you hungry?"

"You don't know how hungry." I said.

"Good we eat," he said he yelled something and this pretty little woman came out from I guess was the kitchen. 'Food,' he said to her.

"You married?" I asked.

"No; he said I just play around Like an American Playboy." he said and laughing.

"Now how do you know about American Playboys?" I asked? Oh he said for five years I lived in America for the U. N. I was in charge of security for personal. That is why I speak good English. I got the feel of the better life. But I got some girl in trouble and they shipped me back. They don't like that, he said so I got my hand slapped and that was the end of it. But you my brother you fought the war all by your self. You are a good soldier".

He said getting up to help with the food.

"I tried I said but like you I did something wrong."

"No he said you did what you thought was right. You did no wrong. Come we eat. Knackwurst and sauerkraut Boy I haven't eating this in a long time."

"Eat my brother," he said and the woman brought a bottle of vodka. Then we drink; he said. Come my pretty woman he said you sit and hear all about the brave Kaufmanns By my brother Joseph."

We eat and talk mostly of our mother and sisters. He didn't know how they died. He was hoping some day he would find them alive; just like he found me. He drank heavily but it didn't seem to get him drunk. I only drank half of what he did and I was out. He must of put me to bed. Because the next day I woke and I was in bed underdressed. He was up already and came in.

"Come; he said my woman will look at your cuts".

She came in with some thing to clean me with. He said he would be back later for me to rest. He left she came up to me and started to take my underwear off.

"Oh she said bad." She saw what I looked like. There was a mirror on the wall. I went over to look at my self. Oh shit he did a good job on me. I even had them across my face. I felt them but I didn't see them. Man did he do a number on me. I don't think he missed one spot on my body.

"Come;" she said and pointed to the bed. Oh shit I said. Looking at the sheet it was filled with blood. I guess some cuts opened up.

"You got to get well;" she said. She laid me down and started putting something over the cuts. It burnt but in a way it felt good. I could feel it working; she did one side and then I turned over on my back was facing her. She started with my face and worked her way down. When she got to my dick she kept looking at it. It was hard by now. She just took it in her hand and jerked it off till I came.

"You feel much better;" she said and kept working on the cuts down my lags. She was right it did make me feel better. I didn't know what she was to my brother so I didn't move. I didn't want to get him mad at me. After she wiped what ever she had on me she took another sheet and covered me. "How get some rest; she said. Putting a bottle next to the bed.

"God no Not for me."

"What you don't drink?"

"No I said not this early."

"Oh she said taking the bottle and taking a long drink from it. Das good she said and left with the bottle. I guess she was going to finish it. She was pretty in her own way. I guess with some make up and a new dress she would turn some heads. But for some reason Russian woman didn't dress up. They always looked like washerwoman if you know what I mean. Oh hell who was I to judge? I went back to sleep, she gave me something to make me sleep. Boy did it make me sleep.

My brother came home and woke me up. He sounded excited. He had a file with him.

"Hey he said you want to know who put the price on your head?" He opened the file and pointed at it.

"That is good but I don't read Russian."

"Oh he said smiling; sorry." He read it for me.

Shit it was the Mafia that Mr.D had it put on me. That mother fucker. "What else does it say?" I asked?

"He said we got a full file on you my brother. You see you were getting into our business and we had to know where you were at all times."

"What is this?" I asked.

"Oh he said this is someone that we pay for information from time to time."

"What is his name?" I asked?

"It looked like the CIA General. It was him you mean to tell me he works for you?"

"No he said he just gives us a little information when he comes around. And we pay him. Nothing big he said just little things. He in turn gives us some little things."

"A spy a fucking spy." I said. That is the motherfucker that started all the shit about me."

"He is? He said. How did he do that?"

I told him how him and I meet and about Nancy and my two children and Seymour and his son. We talk most of the night away. He said he got some days off so he was going to hang around with me.

"But what did they say when they found out I was missing from the hospital."

"Don't worry I told them you are under house arrest with me. They know I'm your brother. Oh yes they knew that once you hit the papers. They know everything that goes on in the U.s. The papers tell it all and what the papers don't tell we got people that talk, we know when the president has to take a shit."

"I bet you do, we know the same what goes on over here I said.

"I bet you do," he said.

"This is crazy, we all try to hide what we are doing but we know. Like Cuba."

"I was there, he said.

"I must have seen you. I remember when Castro had that trouble at the fence. We were sitting back watching and waiting for something to happen."

"We got the jet that was all we wanted. Castro got out of hand with the cow. He thought since we were there we would back him up; but not since Kennedy put his foot down. We were just testing him to see how far we could go with the Missiles."

"That was kind of crazy you knew we wouldn't let you do that."

"Hey we tried."

"Yea you sure did."

"To bad I didn't know it was you I would have come over to your side then. You mean your willing to come over to the American's." he smiled I did live in New York for a while boy do you Americans got it made; woman all over the place. This is just between the two of us. He said they would kill me if they heard me talk like this."

"Hans your welcome to come over any time you want." "Really, he said. You know you can; we don't kill your kind when you come to our side."

"No; he said but we do."

"You're right The K.G.B. is bad."

"No; he said we just are afraid. Men from the K.G.B. get in trouble all the time and get shot for doing so. That is why we are the way we are. We live in fear of doing something wrong. We have teams that are all over the world just for that purpose."

"To kill your own man?"

"Yes he said to kill anyone that tries to go over to the other side. And they always get their man."

You see your general." Holding up the picture; he once killed someone for us."

"You're kidding How, why?"

"No my brother he said it is better you don't know this. Let's just say he got paid a lot of money for this and let it go at that. Your people don't know it was us and if they did nothing would happen anyway. It would mean a real war so we just let it drop."

"Some day you will tell me." I asked.

"Maybe he said but for now we drink."

He got another bottle and put it on the table. "To the President." he said. I didn't know what that meant but I had an idea. Kennedy!

"Can't we eat?" I asked.

"Yes we do that. He yelled to her she came out with food. We don't eat like you do in the states but we fill our stomach. This time we had cabbage soup. And bread. It was good. I guess if you didn't have to eat it all the time once in a while it tasted good.

We talked and eat. "He said; tomorrow I go and get you a woman. You like a woman?" he asked.

"I was going to ask you about your woman."

"Oh her she lives with me. Her father can't feed her so he gives her to me. Pretty isn't she; taking hold of her. She is a young lady; he said she just turned 16. Isn't she filling out good; he said picking up her skirt. Good pussy, he said taking hold of it. Strong hands."

It was as if he was trying to sell a horse.

"Pretty;" I said and got up. Hey is that your room I'm sleeping in."

"For you I sleep here. But when you get better you sleep here. For now you need good bed to rest."

"But; I started to say.

"No; he stopped me; remember I still owe you. You want to finish fight now?' he said holding his head where I hit him when we were younger.

"No I said I'll use it and thanks." I said hugging him. Good to have you back even thou we are in Russia."

"Go get some sleep. Tomorrow we go find you a girl." That sounds good and while we are out maybe we buy a stake for supper."

"Ha, he said a woman would be easier to find." He laughs and went back to the girl on his lap.

I can see he was going to have some fun tonight. So I went in and went to sleep. While I was trying to go to sleep I started thinking how I was going to get the hell out of here. It wasn't going to be easy. I couldn't leave without my brother. He would be killed if I did. I don't think he would come with me. I knew it. So I had to find out a way for the both of us to go. I know once I got him out I could protect him forever. I got my real brother. It put part of my life back together for me. The part I was missing. Even thou it was only one part; he still made a difference to me. Then I fell asleep remembering the fun we use to have when we were kids.

That night I fell asleep and for the first time I woke up with out sweat all over me. He came and got me up the next morning he had something to show me. When I got dressed he was waiting for me in the living room he pointed at the table.

"Eggs," he said.

"No shit I said so."

"So; I had to steal them this morning.

"You did what?" I asked.

"Oh you know it isn't like The U.S. where you go to the market to buy your eggs. Here you got to take. I took them from a farmer he will not know."

"But what if you get caught?" I asked.

"They shot me," he said laughing.

"You're kidding!"

"Yes I kid; he said Come we eat then we go shopping for woman." He said. He was serious about the woman.

We eat and we talked some more. I wanted to see if he really wanted to come with me. If he didn't I guess I would have to stay here with him. I wasn't going with out him. I didn't want to leave him ever again. For some reason I felt good, better then I felt in years. Almost the way I felt when my daughter was born. I guess I would have felt the same way when my son was born But Nancy change that. For some reason I didn't blame her for what she did. I guess it was all my fault and I had to live with it. Maybe some day we will get back together again. That is what I was hoping for. But now it is going to be hard.

That Mr.D. wait till I get my hands on him. I'll show him who the fuck I am. I should have killed his son when I had the chance to. First I had to get out of here.

We went out and he took some bikes out from the side of the house.

"Come he said you know how to ride?" You kidding I had one I rode to school all the time? Me and Seymour got them when the bus stopped picking us up. My uncle gave them to us for Honaker one year. I took it out and jumped on it. "I'll race you; I said and started to go. Oh shit I guess I forgot about my cuts.

"Hey he yelled stop you're bleeding. I stopped and got off; he came up to me and said your back is covered with blood. Come; he said tomorrow we will go. He took my bike and walked it back to where he got them from. You should let me take you back to the hospital," he said.

"No I'm o.k. I just got to let them heal." He yelled for the girl to come and help me, she came and helped me into bed and took off my clothes.

He watched her do it and then said. The man that did this to me he will kill him. No my brother he did it for the same reason you will want to kill him for. It was what our father did. He hates us. Let him be he got what he wanted. So just forget about it. We got each other now he can't take that way."

"Father always said you were the smart one. I use to get mad at that but now I know what he was talking about. I go he said and she will take care of you." He left she did the same thing as she did the other day. But this time she gave me a little extra. She sucked on it. I even had a whip mark across my dick. "That guy wanted to kill me didn't he." I said to her.

"Almost," she said and gave me more of the shit to knock me out. I guess I was kind of rushing it. It would be better for me to heal before I think of getting out of here.

The next day my brother came up. He was looking like he eat all the cookies in the cookie jar he was so happy. "Come he said you're going to sleep all the day, we eat."

"Sounds good to me." Then it hit me. Hey I said what is that I smell?"

"Come he said and got me out of bed. I got dressed and followed him in. There he said pointing to the table.

"Oh shit who did you steal that from?" It looked like a whole side of a cow.

"My brother wants stake; he gets."

"You got to be kidding where the hell did you get it?" I asked sitting down.

"The farmer owes me big favor."

"Boy it must have been a real big favor. Look at the size of this."

"You eat he said and happy birthday," he said kissing me.

"What day is this?"

He told me. He was right it was my birthday.

Now the hell did he know it after all these years. I guess I had tears in my eyes he handed me a rag and said "You still a baby. To my little baby brother," he said. Picking up his bottle and drinking.

"Hey I said to my Big brother." And I took it from him and took a drink.

"Now he said for your other present. Come he yelled. And out came his girl and someone else. "For you; he said.

"Oh I said and what do I do with her?"

"Ha he said you want me to show you."

"No I said I'll take it from here. I got up to have her sit next to me. Why not, there wasn't anything else to do. And I really need it. Like my fathers woman said twice a day and you will have strong children. I took their word on that when I did it with Nancy. I made sure I was strong. "Well," I said looking at the big stake.

"Wait," my brother said. He got a candle and lit it. He put it on the stake and said, "make a wish and cut the first piece."

I did it was just like when we were at home. My mother always baked a cake for our birthdays. "You wish?" He said.

"Yes brother I hope it comes true." I cut a piece for her and one for me I let my brother cut for him and his girl. I didn't want to ask how old she was. All I know she was looking good. And with a stake in front of me; and a good looking woman next to me what more could one want.

We eat till we couldn't eat any more and then we drank. Then she got up and took my arm and took me to bed. She was soft and warm and her body was like she just started getting tits. I felt bad at first but I know I couldn't tell her to go. That would insult her. So I let her stay. She was not a virgin she had had it before. I was glad of that I think I would have stopped if she was. But she wasn't so I had a good night.

Even when we woke the next morning she still wanted to do it. "Oh hell; go to it." I said to her. She didn't understand a word I said. But boy was she good. She was in no rush like most women. Hurry up and get it over with. I got things to do. Nancy was like that once in a while. Not all the time. I guess you got that way once you got married. Who knew? All I know is she felt good to me. And I didn't care if I never got up. She also knew about first aid and she took care of me from then on. My brother got her from the village; he said the father was glad to see her go. He had too many mouths to feed. It was about time she moved out. It was sad but I guess that was the way they did it here. I found out where we were. He had a map. So I looked it over. We weren't to far from the boarder.

If we had to go this was the way to go. It was only a hundred miles this way and the closes. He said it was guarded with dogs and towers. "You don't like it here?" He asked.

"Hans I got no reason to stay here if you go back with me. But if you don't want to come I well stay."

"He looked at me and said. "You will do this for me?" Hans I'm never going to leave you again and if you chose to stay here then here we will stay, no more said."

Well I got better and with the four of us living in the same house we started getting on each other's nervous. Little things like pick up your socks or don't leave your draws out. "Look I said one day I got to do something. Staying around here is driving me nuts."

"Good my comrades would like to have a talk with you." I was waiting for that. I know it was only a matter of time before they wanted to hear what I could tell them about the U.S.

After all we were at war with them. Russia was sending more and more adviser over Vietnam then we did at first. Again they were testing us to see how far we would go. You don't know how the other country was thinking. Were they trying to take over the world them self's or were they worried we were trying to. And like us they wanted to stop it before it got too late. They to had a taste of Hitler and saw what he could do when left to do what he wanted to. But again you don't know.

Well my big day came. Hans had set up a meeting for me to meet the big shots. I know what Hans wanted. He wanted me to come over to his side. They had him so scared of what could happen to him if he would get up and leave. They had everyone scared, even the ones that were scaring were scared. No one trusted each other for fear his friend would turn him in for the hell of it. No this was no way to live. Give me the good U.S.A. This stealing food is not for me and one meal a day wasn't hitting on it. This place was good if you liked to drink Vodka you could get all that you wanted. But I missed a cold beer once in a while. You know the little things like hot running water and a good book to sit down and read. Or maybe just walk to the corner store and buy a cake or two to munch on. That was UN heard of. I guess you could say I was home sick.

CHAPTER 19

Well off we went. I didn't worry about what they would do to me. I guess being who I was made me importune to them. And I was in charge for the time being. That was if I was going to go over to their side. If I didn't then I guess it would be a different story, but for now I had center court. Hans had a car come pick us up and off we went; to the big city. The country was beautiful and peaceful. One would never guess it was at war. Not with other countries but with it self. When we got to Moscow it was different. People all over the place; but still as you drove by you could see Stores empty Lines waiting for small handouts of food and no one smiling; no this wasn't for me. We got to the headquarters and got out. Hans was proud of having me with him. You could see it in the way he walked.

"Come my brother," he said heading right for the main office.

When we went in side the place was filled with all fat people sitting around one big table. I wonder if they had to steal food, it didn't look like it. That is what bothered me. How come so many were fat and no food to eat. Something was wrong. It couldn't be all Vodka. I said to my self. And laughed out loud.

"Comrade you find this funny?"

"No sir I said. I just remembered what some one told me about Russians. And I don't see it."

"Oh and what was that?" He asked.

"They said your people were staving and were skinny. They lye I said no one is skinny."

"Ha he said. You see they lye good." He said that was a good sign he laughs.

"Now comrade you sit besides me and we talk."

Here it comes I know I was in for a long day. Well we talked and we talked .It was mostly one sided. He was trying to find out what I know and if I would be of any use to his side. I didn't have anything to hide. All my cases were closed and anyone could look at them. I had nothing to hide. It was my work record that they were interested in and what I did. We eat all the time we were there. If that is what you would call it. Caviar and bread and of course Vodka was on the table. The one that was asking me all the questions stood up and said.

"This is good. You go now and enjoy our country."

Hans came over to me and smiled. "Come my brother he said, we go now."

I guess they had all they needed to know for now. I got up and smiled at the rest of the fat man and followed Hans out the door. He was happy; for what I didn't know. But when we got out side I found out.

"What makes you so happy?" I asked.

He said, "They didn't kill you."

"Oh I said, "I guess I should be happy."

"Yes he said they like you and maybe they give you good job."

"That was nice of them; when do I hear?'

"Oh he said don't rush them they take there time to decide. They will let us know. So for now we go and enjoy."

Ha I said to my self, enjoy what? We got back home and Hans had got some fish when we were in Moscow. He said a friend owe him. I guess that was the only way to eat around here was a friend. Potato soup and cabbage soup was just not my idea of eating. Oh you got filled up on it but that was about it. Once a week you would get a chicken or duck to eat and the rest of the week potatoes and cabbage. Oh did I forget the bread. Yes you got lots of bread to eat. The bread was used to soak up the juice of the cabbage. No butter.

Well we waited for three more weeks and then someone came and told us they wanted to see us again. Hans was more excited then me. He was hoping I would get to stay here with him that was all well and good. But I needed my own place if I was going to be staved here I wanted to do in by my self not on someone else's couch. Everything was getting to me. The couch the cabbage; even Hans and that I didn't want. That night I was walking around the village when I heard a shot. I hit the ground and was looking for someone shooting at me. No one was so I got up slow and look at where I heard it come from. It was in this house I just passed. The door was open I walked up and called.

"Hello anyone hurt?" I looked and saw what the gun shot was. This old guy shot him self. Oh shit what the hell did he go and do that for? I ran back out and got my brother. I told him what had happened. He got up and came with me. It didn't bother him much he walked behind me as if he didn't believe me. When we got to the house and went in. I heard my brother laugh.

"Ha he said, he was going to do it and he did."

"He told you he was going to shot him self and you did nothing to stop him."

"Yes he said people do it all the time around here. This is nothing we get two or three a month. This month was only him."

"But why?" I asked.

"Oh he said something about the K.G.B. wanting to talk to him, he was worried they found out he took chickens and sold them. Something like that."

"But did he?"

"No Hans said he took them because he was hungry. He eat them," he said and laughs.

No this isn't the life for me. "Hans we got to talk." "Come he said we talk."

"What about him?" I asked.

"Oh someone will come and get him."

"Doesn't he have any family?"

"Four sons but they are in the Army and no one knows where. They will bury him don't worry. Come we talk," he said and walked me out.

We walked back to the house but I didn't want to go in, not just yet.

"Hans lets walk." As we walked I asked him about the time he was stationed in the U.S.

He smiled and said he loved it and he wishes he could get stationed back there." I told him I think I know of a way we both could go back if he wanted to."

"No he said. We can't run away. They will kill us."

"No your comrades will send us. I have a plain to make them see it would be better if I go back. I can get a lot of information by doing so."

"How?" he asked. This General with the CIA I could black mail him into giving what ever we need. But he gives us it anyway," he said.

"No your wrong; he give you only what he wants to give you. I can make him give top secret files. Not small shit."

"What if he doesn't?"

"Oh I said, with what you got on him he has no chose. You know he was the one that made my wife brake up with me. I owe him and believe me I want him in the worse way. And the both of us could go together .I will ask for you to come with me."

"No he said they will never let the two of us go. They don't do that. One has to stay behind so they could us him if the other one don't come back."

You mean they would kill you if I didn't come back?"

"Yes he said. No I said I will make them see it my way. You're going to be a double agent for them and so will I. I'll tell my Government I took you with me and you got a lot of information for them. But your people will think we are working for them. You see they would have two good spies' out there and being you know how everything is done at the U.N. You could be a great help to them in finding out who is doing what."

"Good idea he said we go and tell them."

"Let's go." I said.

"No we wait till tomorrow. I need time to think. Good you do that. But we could be good together. Boy we could bring back all kind of information for them. And maybe we get promoted for this."

I know I had to use him in order to make him come with me. He wasn't that bright but he still was my brother. And I wasn't going to leave him. I don't know if it was the Vodka that did it to him or he was always that way. I couldn't remember him doing nothing but work with my father; and beating me up all the time. But that was part growing up. I had to get out of here I wanted to see my children again. I didn't care what it took. I wasn't going to end up like that old man that killed himself; No way.

When we got home I ask one thing and it bothered me. Where did all the food go the farmers grow? He smiled at me and said; "you don't remember what our father did with the food?"

"Yes I said for the soldiers, he smiled and said we got a big army to feed."

"I bet you do;" I said making him think I was proud of him and them. All the people going hungry; but the army was eating. Make sense to me I said and dropped it.

Well he got me into have a talk with the group of wise man I guess you would call them that. As I walked in I got the feeling they didn't want to hear what I had to say. Come Comrade;" the One that did all the talking said. I know sit next to me the same thing. Well my comrade has told me you have a plan?"

"Yes I said, as you know I have no good feelings for this General. And I feel being he is in with the CIA he could give a lot more information then he is. I can get that from him."

"Oh you can he said. Well comrade I think you have just answered our question."

"Oh and what is that"?

He smiled; it means all you want to do is get out of here. So you see we have no use for you."

"What;" my brother yelled standing up?

Comrade he pointed at my brother you know your place; now sit." Oh shit I guess they weren't as dumb as they looked. Now what? "I'm sorry sir I don't quite understand what you mean."

He looked at me and smiled. Oh I think you do. Let me put it to you this way; he said still smiling. You are no use to us and by us giving you back to the Vietnam we may help our course more. Do I make my self-clear; he said? Smiling still.

I could see my brother wanting to get up and start running but he know he couldn't run anywhere. The fat old man stood up and yelled for the guards to come and take me away. One stood over my brother so he wouldn't course any trouble. And two came and took me.

"You see the old man said we know what you did to your father. You love your country too much to just turn your back on it."

"That is not so if you read further you would have seen the thanks I got for loving it.

So here I sit. Me and the four walls; probable for the rest of my life. My brother couldn't even see me. I was kept away from everyone. I guess I was no better off then the rest of the Russian people you look at what they had and how they lived and put it all together and you got this. Four walls and a place to sleep, with someone else holding the key. I guess it was my own fault. I didn't us my head. I just wanted to get even. And not free I guess. The days went by and the nights were the same as the day. I didn't know what so I slept when I got tired and trough when I was awake. You see I had no window to see what was what. The guard that brought my food didn't say a word. He just slid it under my door and left.

I don't know if it was the tenth day or the fifteenth day but what ever it was it hit me. How could I be so stupid? What did people like them want? Power. And who had the Power. My father had it all. That was it. The good doctor. And his army. Why not; it was worth a shot. I had nothing to lose. I waited for the guard to bring me my food. I asked him if I could see the fat man. I had to tell him something that would make him want to see me. And the only word I could think of to get his attention was the word; Power. I got Power. I hope it works. I hope this ass tells him. There was no way of knowing if he did I just had to wait and see. Shit I guess he didn't. Another week went by and nothing.

Then one day I heard someone coming other then the guard. You got to know the sounds being here all by your self. The door opened and two guards looked at me. "Come;" one said. And picked my up. They took me to the small room at the end of the hall and left me. Then one of the fat men came in, not the one that did all the talking but I know he was one of them. He looked at me and said; "you got a good use of words; he said. I like this word you said. Power. My comrades don't think so but me I think you have something else in mind. So comrade you see you got me to come down to hear you."

"Good, that is all I want. My father as you know was about to take over the world with his army."

He just looked at me. "Yes we know that but he didn't." "No but he would off; he was real close to doing it."

"Ha he said but you saw to it he didn't." Yes but what would you say if I told you I know what he was planning to do."

"This is what you call power?" He said getting up. They were right you don't have anything."

"Oh but I do. I can continue where my father left off."

He just looked at me. And for some reason he didn't say anything. I remembered the look I use to try to imitate. The one Hitler and my father gave when they meant what they said. A dead stare and nothing on your face. He kept looking at me and didn't say a word. He turned and left. What the hell did that mean?" I yelled to him as he closed the door?

He was gone and the two guards came back and took me back to my cell. Did he think I was going out of my mind? Maybe my face did it. I don't know. Shit I hate that. He didn't even laugh at me or tell me I was full of shit. Nothing. That night I guess it was; I didn't sleep. I had to think of a way to get out of here. No way was I going to spend my while life down here. Then I trough about the old man that shot him self. Maybe he was right. I was just like them out there. And his way out was the only way. But how; I had no gun. Hang my self. With what?" Nothing to hang on. Elect cute myself. The light was so deep in the wall I couldn't get to it to give myself-a shock. Bang my head against the wall? No that would hurt. Ha listen to me. I was worried about hurting my self.

Then I heard them coming again. It must be the next day. Maybe he believed me. The door opened and the same two guards came. And put me in the same room. The same fat guy came in.

"Comrade; he said tell me more."

"No way I said, first I got to get out of here and then I talk."

"No," he said with that dumb smile. I can't do that." "Good; I said then you will never know will you."

He laughs and said." Look comrade. I'm the only one that thinks you're a master. The rest of my comrades don't think so. I got them thinking. I may self am going crazy like you. So I got to make them see what you have. If not I go and forget about it."

"No; I said.

"You can't do that?"

"I do have something."

"Then he said give it to me. I need something," he said. "The doctor, I said. My father's doctor I know where he is."

"The one with the spiders?" He asked.

"Yes him."

"Ha; he said getting up they said you would say that. I guess they were right you are going out of your mind."

"No I yelled. I can get him."

"Look comrade he said turning to me. We know everything that happened at your father's house. And the good doctor went up with your father. You my good man made sure of that. Nothing was left. No records nothing."

"Arr but that is where you're wrong. I took the doctor with me when I left."

"No; he said with that smile. We know you didn't you see we had someone there that said he died with the house. Don't you think we sent our own man to check it out? Your father was a genius and we all know it. But we also know what he was up to. He wanted the world for him self and we know that."

"Yes that is true but he didn't do it by him self-. The doctor did it for him."

"Yes; he said coming back to me. He took hold of me and looked right in my face. God his breath was bad.

"But the doctor is dead and you have nothing." He let me go and walked out.

"I do." I said.

He stopped and didn't turn. "What?" He asked.

"That is what I'm saving. I said. You go tell that to them."

"No Comrade; he said still not turning to me. They don't want to hear it."

"Look; what do they got to lose? You still got me; all I want to do is see their faces. I'll tell them how they could find out with out letting me go. They got nothing to lose but a little time."

He walked away again with out saying another word. Shit I hate that. The guards came and took me back. I know I had him on my side; he wasn't going to let it drop. He was too interested in me. He will talk them into it. I know he will. That night I was feeling good. I know it was going to work. I had time to plan it out and being the way they were I know I could convince them to see it my way.

I was right they did go for it. The next day I was out and standing in the big room now. No one was here but me and the two guards. Then the door opened and only two fat men came in. The one I was talking to at first and the one that came down to see me.

"Well comrade," the first one said, talk."

"First I would like to know what is in it for me."

"Ha the first one said. See he fooled you."

"No, the other one said let's hear him out."

"Look the second one said you talk and then we see."

I know I had to give them what I had. I was getting them mad. "All right but I don't want to go back to the cell."

"Talk;" he yelled.

I started with you have people all over the U.S. I know you do."

"So; he said you got people all over here; so what." "There is only one person I can get to prove the doctor is still alive."

"And who is that; the doctor?" They both laugh at me. "No I have someone that you could find him and not make anyone know what you are up to."

"Go on," he said.

"You have to understand if it, it is fouled up we all lose."

"Talk;" he yelled.

"When I left there I did have the doctor with me in the chopper the only other person from the house was this woman. One of my men took her."

"We got no record of her, he said. We just know your men and you got away and no one else."

"That is what I'm trying to tell you. My government covered it up. They didn't want anyone knowing of this. The doctor works for us now. And the woman Married one of my men and is still living."

"That should be easy to check," one said.

"No I said you can't do it. The first sign of anyone knowing. The doctor will go so far under ground no one will find him. You have to do it my way."

They both looked at me and laugh. "I guess you want to go and get her for us." They both laugh.

"Look I know you think I'm laying. But I mean it. The only way to do it is to have someone see this woman and talk to her with out letting anyone else know what you are up to. Remember one word and he is lost forever." They did it again. They turned and walked out.

"Hey," I yelled, what does that mean?' It didn't do any good; they closed the door and left. The two guards just came in and stood at the door. Now what? "Hey what the hell is going on?" They looked at me and didn't say anything. Oh hell I guess they will let me know. At least I wasn't going back down to the cell.

I walked around for hours then one of them came back. He had a file with him. "Come he said sit." He sat and opened it. Which man," he said.

Look at this; he had all of my men. "This is good what else you have?" I asked. I know he wouldn't tell me. And I know it was dumb of me to ask.

"Look," he said.

"This was no time to joke."

"Him I said. But you have to remember no one must know. Just asked her one question and make sure it is done with out her knowing what you're asking. That is the most importune thing if you fuck up;" I said.

He looked at me and said. "You go back to the Mafia."

"Right and you don't get the world." He didn't like that. I could see he was getting that look on his face. The one Power gives you.

"You know we can't let you go."

"I know that but you also have to know you fuck this up and we both lose."

He walked out again and left me standing there. Shit he did it again. This time I didn't yell back at him. I just got in a chair and sat. Hey look at this; food was coming in. I guess I got to them. Man did I eat. I didn't care what it was; it was better then Bread and water. When I finished, the guards took me to this other room. It was like a little bedroom, shower and all. Nothing I would pay for, but a castle compared to what I was in. I didn't have to ask if it was for me. I got undress and into the shower before they closed the door. I guess it would take some time for them to check it out and check it out they will. I was just hoping they did it right. Who know what she would do? I talked to her a couple of times when Snake had me over. She seemed to be like a normal person. But one would never know what she would do. If she knew something was up. She was a big woman and could break you in two if she wanted to.

Like they say; I was playing my last card and hope I win the pot. What did I have to lose? NOTHING REALLY I was right they took there time. I didn't see anyone for days. The food kept coming and I got a lot of sleep on a good bed for a change. Then the door opened and in the one came.

He looked at me and said," you were right."

"That was all?" I said.

"No, he said now we know your telling us the truth."

"So now what?'

"You tell me," he said.

"First I want to see my brother."

"What for?" he asked.

"Oh let's just say to see if you didn't kill him."

"Oh comrade we don't do that here."

"Oh no; then let me see him."

"Your brother is a good officer he is on a mission." "Good; I said then get him back from this so-called mission. I don't talk till I see him."

"But, he started to say.

I had the upper hand now. "But shit." I said. You still have nothing without me and without me the doctor will go no where. Now, my brother." I did what they did to me. I got on my bed and closed my eyes not bothering with him. As if he wasn't there.

He talked for a while but he knew I wouldn't answer him. So he left. Power, the feeling. That was the name of the game. The food kept coming and I kept sleeping. And that was all I could do. Again this room and no window; so nothing to see but four walls again. What seemed like two days went by when my door opened and my brother was standing there. I ran to him and hugged him. He returned my hug.

"You Joseph he said what are you doing now?"

I didn't know what he meant by that but after talking to him I found out why. They told him I was joining them and I was doing some intelligence work for them. Ha I was locked up in a cell all this time and nothing to eat; see what they tell you?" He didn't say a word he just looked at the walls.

"Hans I don't care if they can hear me. I run this place now." I said holding on to him.

"You have gone crazy; he said. Backing away from me. What have they done to you?" he asked the walls.

"Relax I said taking him again. Everything is going to be all right now. Believe me. I said looking at him.

"No, he said you got drugs in you."

"No Hans it is me and no drugs. I just found out something they want and I'm the only one that can give it to them. We have nothing to worry about."

"Then why you here?" he asked looking at the room.

"You have a good question there. I looked at the wall knowing they had some kind of camera hooked up to see us with. "Why am I still here?" I yelled.

The fat guy came right in and smiled he said. "You didn't ask to go."

"Funny; I said get me out of here and I want to go back to live with my brother."

"But you could live here."

"No I don't trust it here."

"Oh now comrade." He said.

"Comrade your ass I got what you want and by god I had better get what I want. Or there is no deal you get me comrade?" I said giving my look. It always worked before and no reason why it didn't work now.

It did; I was let out and giving all the freedom that they could give; big deal that wasn't much. One thing they did give me was a car. Good I said now where do I go with it?

"Ha he laughs no place."

"I know I said laughing with him.

"Well you take some time to rest .We will start the wheels going."

"Wait; you know I have to be the one to go back and find him."

"We know; that is what you have to do. We don't want you to run away from us." He said Looking at my brother.

I knew what he was talking about. They would hold my brother till I got back. I guess I made sure of that by asking for him the first thing. They know my love for him was deep. So they use it. Stupid me. Well you can't think of everything. I just had to play it as I went. So far so good but I know I couldn't let my guard down once.

We drove home and my brother kept asking what I was doing. I kept telling him he didn't have to know. Just trust me, I kept telling him and I loved him. That was all that he had to know for now. He didn't like it but he had to choose but to do so. The two girls were still there. I guess my brother didn't want to let her go. Why not she was pretty and what the hell the winters were long and if you couldn't have food the next best thing were sex. I don't have to tell you what I did for the next couple of days.

The fat guy sent all the food we could need. He wanted to make me happy and what better way was there, keep me full and pregnant; like they keep their woman. Plus a case of vodka of course. Hans was in his glory he had never seen so much food at once. And to him I was his brother; just like I was my father's son.

Then the time came when I guess they checked everything out, the only way for them to get anything was with me at the head. I was the one that could locate the doctor and being him back with me. They know I would be back because they weren't letting my brother come with me. They also had someone watching me in the U.S. Just in case. They didn't tell me who. But I know they weren't fooling. They had more people spying on us then we had over here but what the hell. Right now I had to worry about my self and my brother. They had it arranged as if I was captured for the reward but got away. That would explain my time gone. Nice. No one would question it being I know about the reward on my head would only make it look real? So back I went. My brother came to the airport to see me off.

He didn't say much but he did slip me a paper. I know he didn't want anyone to see him do it. So I didn't look at it till I was in the air. Shit all it said was the persons that were watching me back home knot of my family. I know what that meant. If I decided to run my wife and kids would pay. What was I getting my self into? Now my family was in danger. I know all along they would be but I didn't think of it that way. These people played for real. I couldn't go on with my life not knowing or not doing something about it so I guess it was up to me to finish it once and for all.

The first thing I had to do was to get back; then from there one step at a time. I had to move slow this time and make sure I made no mistakes. My family's life was on the line now. It was different when it was only mine. I didn't care. But now it is with Nancy and the two kids it made a big difference. Not for the better as you can see. I got back to the north and was taking to an out post along the boarder. I was let go and headed for our lines. My face still had scares, infect my while body was one big scare. That should work for me. It would prove I wasn't on vacation all this time. I had time on my side. They didn't expect me to do it over night so I had time to take it slow.

I walked down the road till I came across our look out. He didn't know what to make of me. I walked right up to him and said who I was.

"You got to be kidding you're a General"

I had changed into Vietcong black and with no I.D. he didn't fall for it. If I was him I wouldn't of either. He took his gun and put it to my head and told me not to move. I know he would shot if I did. He got his buddy to call it in; he just kept his gun on me with out saying a word. I guess I was making them pretty nervous. How many solders could say they held a gun to a Generals head?

It didn't take long for a chopper to come get me. It was here with in a half an hour. When it landed the soldier was glad to see it as much as I was. He didn't want to fuck up and also he didn't want to get me mad. Holding a gun on a General wasn't his Idea of making points. He was shaking all the time. He didn't say much and when he did it didn't make sense. So I just waited without making him nervous.

A Major came with the chopper, he know me. He ran to me and said.

"Sir glad to have you back." He had a medical team with him, they put me on a stretcher and took me away. I got back to the main base and into a hospital. There they worked me over checking me out. The doctor said it was too late to do anything about the scars. Maybe later they could do plastic sugary on them. But for now nothing. He did say I was in good health. I know what he was getting at. How come I wasn't under feed? I told him before he left I was getting feed to keep me alive for the reward money and that was the only reason.

I told him I couldn't go into detail over it. He knew what I was talking about and smiled.

"You're a lucky man you should be dead with all this on you."

"I know I said and left it at that. Then the Brass started coming in. I had to get back home. I did what I through was right. Look I told them someone here was a trader and I didn't want to talk till I got back to my home base. Those made them look at each other and wonder. Good I wanted it that way. It worked I was shipped out on the next flight. And was heading home. I had to get around people I could trust. The only one I felt I could was Greene. He didn't retire yet he was waiting for the war to end. He never liked to run out on something unfinished. Good thing for me he didn't. He wasn't in charge any more. But he still hung around taking up time.

I got a massage from him. He was going to meet me at the airport. I was hoping he would. Who know maybe the Mafia was still gunning for me. The Russians didn't say they talked to them. All they said was I didn't have anything to worry about. I didn't want to take that to the bank. That was for sure. So from now on I had to be on my toes. Who know who would go for two hundred thousand? They did say dead or alive. Well I got to D.C. in one piece. Now it was up to me to stay that way. When we landed I waited on the plane for the General. I wasn't going out there with no protection. He was on time like always and when he came aboard he just looked at me.

"My god they weren't kidding you did get fucked up."

"No thanks to you!"

"Me? He said sitting down.

"Yes you."

"Oh no he said you don't hang this on me."

"Then who?" Knowing he didn't like me calling him a rat. He was as honest as the day. And I know it. But someone set me up and he was the only one that could help me. "Who sent me over there and who gave the orders to have me find this drug dealer and who put a price on my head without no one knowing? You're the only one I could think of." I told him. I guess I hit home.

He took out his gun and handed it to me. "Here take it and uses it if that is what you think? Take it," he yelled.

"No, I said looking at him. That wouldn't answer any of my questions. I want answers. Not bodies. The bodies come later when I find out who and why."

"Let's get out of here," he said.

"No, you might have someone waiting for me out side."

That did it I guess I hurt him enough. He just stopped and said. "You really think it was me don't you?"

"I don't know what to think I said. Ripping my shirt off, you tell me."

He just looked at the whip marks. "God son he said you know I could never do that to you."

"Well someone did and I'm not rest till I find him or them out."

He took my hand and said holding on to it. "You're wrong. We won't rest," he said hugging me.

I knew it wasn't him. I had to make sure even if it hurt. Now I knew I could trust him. That was all I needed. I had to have him on my side. And I did. He back away from me and told me to wait, he would be right back. He went out and got on the phone. He called someone and came back into the plane.

"Let's go he said as he was watching out side. I got up and looked, he had a escort coming. He didn't trust it out there either. Now we will get to the bottom of this. We got in the limo and headed for his house.

"My place will be the best place to hide you I have guards all over the place. No one comes in or out with out being checked. We can do our investigating from there," he said.

"Good I would fell better knowing I still had one friend left.

"You do; he said. He took my hand and didn't let it go. We got to his place and he had a high fence around it with a guardhouse.

"Trouble?" I asked.

"I guess you could say that. We all got this protection when one of our men got blown out of his bed. You mean right here in D.C.?"

He looked at me and said, "Two blocks away."

"Who did it?" I asked?

He or they still didn't know. "But that was all he needed. Up went the fence."

We went inside and want right to his office. He had his command post set up already.

"I do most of my work out of here now. What the hell I was getting ready to get out anyway. This way they keep me a little while longer and I don't work to hard."

I agreed with him he did have 30 years in, may be more. He didn't tell me how long he was in. and I didn't ask. I know I had almost 20 in.

"Now you will sleep and work here along with me. No one will know where you are. That is till we get to the bottom of this."

"Good, but what about my family?"

He looked at me. "What about your family?"

"I was told they were watching them also." He picked up the phone and call who ever he was calling.

"Get his family to safety, and hung up. They should take care of them."

"How are they doing?" I asked.

He smiled and said;" your son is just like you and your daughter is just like Nancy."

"You think I could see them?"

"That is up to Nancy not me. You will be able to talk to her soon."

"Good I missed them." He smiled and said you got a right to miss them they are something. I don't know why you two broke up to begin with."

"That you will have to ask Nancy I didn't want it that way but your friend made sure he got back at me."

"He did didn't he. Well I guess you could say he got even. For what reason I still don't know."

"I do he said. It was what I did that got him pissed off. You see when you came to work for me it made him look like a fool; he could do nothing right in my eyes over you. He didn't like that so he transferred out and you became number one with me. Then when he heard I was retiring and you were moving into my place. He want out of his way to destroy you."

"Maybe as far as setting me up?' I asked.

"Maybe he said. I wouldn't put it past him. He had a lot of hate. You did know him and Nancy was going to be married before you came into the picture."

"No; I said. I did know she was seeing him."

"It was a lot more then that he said you not only took her away from him you took me to."

"I guess he would have reason to get even. I said. But why couldn't he be a man about it."

And do what?' He said. Have a shot out at high noon." "Something like that." I said.

"Not him, he is like a Fox he don't strike till he knows he got the upper hand. He just waits it out for his turn to come. And being you lied to me he found out the truth and use it. It would of worked if Seymour didn't get the lawyer he did. Any other lawyer would have blown the case for you. This guy knew his stuff."

"He sure did. Where is Seymour?" I asked.

"His is on his way. Once I told him you weren't dead. He has been calling me everyday asking when you were coming back. He should be here in a little while. Now can we get down to what you want to know? I'm just as excited to find out my self."

I guess he was right the sooner we found out the faster I could do what I came for and be back to get my brother and hopefully get him back home with me. That is what I wanted. So I had to clear things up first.

"Now do you want to tackle this?" He asked?

I told him we start back wards. From who gave the orders for me and her? Sue I meant.

"Oh by the way, he said we found her she lived for a couple of days and died. She told us something but she was too weak to go on."

"She was a good woman." I said.

"One of the best he said we didn't know what had happened to you, she said the last she saw was you getting whipped. For all she know you were dead. That is how we left it off as. You were missing in action."

"Case close." I said.

"No," he said. I was still looking for you and so were Snake and the Gunny."

"You're kidding?" I said the Gunny joined again."

"No, he said he would go over as a soldier of fortune once in a while. He would get reports about an American being held and he would go check it out."

"What, was he nuts?"

"I guess you could say that. Between him and Snake the both of them were driving me crazy. I had to fallow every little report that came over my desk. If I didn't he would get up and go find out him self. He was running out of money so he couldn't do it too much. Thank god for that. He said he would make a lot of trouble over there and I would have to pull rank to get him back home. You know the way he is."

"You know it and I can't wait to thank him."

Again He said, "We have work to do. He will be around soon enough. He always comes around him and Snake together. I don't know if it is to see my wife or what, but they come by."

"Hey, how is your wife?" I asked.

"She is having my baby." He said smiling.

"You old dog, I said congratulations."

"Yeah he said she isn't too happy about it. That is why she didn't come to meet us," he said.

"Why is that?"

"Oh she thinks she doesn't look good any more."

"Tell her for me I said it makes a woman look more beautiful when she is carrying a baby."

"Ha he said I tell her that all the time. It still does no good. She hide's now and doesn't come out."

"I'll go have a talk with her," I said.

"Your welcome to try; he said but I don't think it will do any good. But again let's start with you. You're in more trouble then anyone else."

"I guess you would say that."

"So let's see," he said. He took out file after file and put them on the desk. "We start here, he said.

We went right to it, him on one pile and me on the other. It was all reports from the office. Maybe we would find something that would help find out something anything to start with.

"Here we go, I said. I got the orders for me to go after this Drug dealer. But it was just giving from command nothing out of the ordinary. Wait, I said, maybe we were looking for the wrong thing."

He looked at me and asked, what then."

"The Vietnam file for the girl. She was working for them was she not?"

"She was, he said.

"So maybe it will show who assigned her to me."

"Good thinking, he said we may get some where with that. But I don't have the files."

"Can you get them?" I asked?

He said he could get anything, it just took time.

Just then the phone rang. It was the gate house calling. Nancy was on her way.

"Does she have the kids with her I asked?

No he shook his head she is by her self.

"Well, I guess the two of you will want to be by your self's," he said getting up. I'll fallow up on the other files while you two are talking. He said leaving the room."

I guess he didn't want to get in between us if we decided to have a fight. He let her in and when I turned around and saw her my heart stopped. God was she beautiful. I wanted to go and grab her but didn't want to make her mad so I just stood up and waited for her to make the first move. He closed the door behind her and she stood looking at me. At first she started to walk over to me and then stopped. The look that came over her face. I could see she just realized what my face looked like. The tears started coming down her face.

"Oh god," she yelled and came running at me.

Oh to feel her in my arms again. I don't know if I was going to pass out of what. All I know is my breath went away and I couldn't breath. My head was spinning around and I almost lost my balance. Did she do this to me or was it I didn't eat anything for a day?

What ever it was it help me. She came to me and didn't let me go, she was holding me up. She felt me go down but she wouldn't let me go.

"No, she said, your not going to pass out on me. She got my face in front of her and started kissing me. It was as if she was putting life back into me. The more we kissed the stronger I got. By the time she pulled away from me I was standing. My head was back to normal and my breath was back. My heart was racing but she always made it do that. She looked at me and said the words I was waiting to hear.

"I missed you," she said. And kissed me again.

I know I was forgiven from that point on.

"Hey, she said, wipe your eyes you're a big boy now."

I guess I was crying. Oh hell why not I deserved to. We talked and before we were finished the general knocked on the door.

He came in and said. "You were right it is here. It came from the CIA to her. That is why we didn't get it on yours. He went around the back way to get you. He left it up to the Vietnam to pick you. Even thou he recommended you for the job. He said here in the file that the two of you work together and it would be for the better if they contacted you to go with her. We didn't assign you they did but under his recommendation. Not his orders."

"Nice, I said looking at Nancy. Look I said I don't want to throw stones but I have to make you see what this friend of yours did."

"No she said holding my hand over the file. I know what he did. And believe me I wanted to call you back but it was too late, you had all ready ship out. Seymour kept telling me about him but at first I didn't believe him. Not until he kept coming around and trying to make me go back with him. I didn't suspect him until one day he was talking to your daughter. He didn't know I was listening to him. He was telling her now bad you were and that you were no good almost as if he was hypnotizing her. I stopped him and asked him what he was doing. When he said it was for the best we all forgot about you and he said he would even be willing to but my kids up for adoption if he married me. Well she said I don't know what came over me she said but he almost got his head knocked off. And till this day he keeps on calling trying to make a joke out of it. He said he didn't mean it, he was only fooling he would adopt them him self. To prove to me he meant it. The man is sick; she ended with.

"No I said he is dead."

"No, the General said not while you got me here. No one is going to kill anyone. He will get his day in court just the way you did. Do I make my self-clear?"

I know he was really on my side now. "Sir I said I know I lied to both of you in the past and I found out I shouldn't of, so what I'm going to tell you is coming from my heart. And I hope I'm doing the right thing. Like before I didn't know what was right and what was wrong. Just like now I still don't but I'm going to try it the other way for a change. I lived enough lies for one lifetime. Sit I told them. I started with what happened. I didn't stop till I got to the part where I got picked up by the out post. No one said anything. They just looked at me. Was this for real? I could see the look on their faces. hat was what they were thinking.

"So," I said snapping them out of it. Now what do we do?"

The general looked at me and said. "We go get them sons of a bitch. And I mean ever last one of them. From the Mafia to the Russians."

"What about my brother?" I asked.

"Him to he said I'll see to it that if he does get here he will have all the protection he will need."

"Thank you sir." I said.

"Don't thank me he said it is I who should be thanking you. You realize what this means?"

"No sir." I said.

"Well let me tell you. I head this investigation and get what you say. I go out in a blase of glory. My name will go down in the history book as one of the biggest shack up in the history of our government. And I mean it he said. Now we got to take a different approach to this. No one must know what we are doing until it is to late for any of them to run. Do I make my self-clear?" He said looking at the both of us?

"Don't look at me, Nancy said.

"Oh your going back to work he said I need a good staff and you're the best."

"What about my children?" She asked.

"They will be here for you to watch them. He said it would be better if we were all together under one roof for now. Lords knows we got the room. This house is to big for us and besides my wife could use the work out taking care of kids. Hell knows she had better get use to having them around. Once she has this one she is going to have a couple of more."

"Does she know this?" Nancy asked.

"No he said smiling she will find out one at a time." He said laughing.

"Your mean," she said to him.

"Oh he said I don't look at it that way. The way I see it she had her fun, now it was my turn." We all laugh it felt good holding on to her and laughing the way we use to.

It wasn't funny what we were laughing at but we did any way. The general must have had this planed a long time ago. And how he was following up on it. Let's hope his wife went along with him and had the babies. For some reason I didn't think so, but that was for him to find out. I only hope no one got hurt.

"Well he said come let's eat."

"Good I said I could use a good meal." It was month's since I had one."

Oh Nancy said holding on to me. You don't look undernourished."

"No I said, rice fools you that way."

"Rice," she said.

"And fish heads, I said. Morning noon and night.

"God how could you," she said.

"Easy, the general said. I went throw that once."

"I'm sorry sir I said. I didn't know your were prisoner."

"I wasn't he said when my wife died I had this gook cook and that was all she know how to cook."

"Why didn't you fire her?' Nancy asked?

He looked at her and said, "she was too good in bed."

Nancy was back to her self again She took a book from the shelf and throws it at him. "You dirty old man," she said. Reaching for another one.

"No, he said. I just love rice and fish head." She throws it. He was use to her by now and so was I. she liked to throw things.

"O.K. I said lead me to the food you two can fight it out. I'm hungry."

We walked into the dinning room and his wife was standing there looking as pretty as ever.

"Oh she said we got guest." She didn't even look to see who we were, she went back out and up to her room.

"Boy I said she has it bad."

Nancy said she will go and talk to her. As she walked by the table she said. "You still got the cook."

We didn't know what she meant by that till we both looked at what was for supper. Fish and rice. We both laugh till we couldn't laugh no more.

"Well at least you got vegetables with it." I sat down and started to eat. I didn't care what it was I was hungry. The General joined me.

"The hell with them, he said, dig in." He didn't have to tell me that twice. Nancy came down with out his wife and smiled. "She will join us later," she said.

"Hungry?" She asked me as I came up for air.

"No I said just picking." She smiled at me and said 'pick.'

I did one plate after another. I must have filled it three or four times before I stopped. Both her and the General watched me eat.

"God Nancy said where is he putting it?" She looked under the table to see if I was dropping any. Just them the phone rang.

The General came over and took it. "Good he said send them up. He turned to me and said. "The Gunny and Snake."

"Hey I said. I missed them two."

"Oh Nancy said she didn't. She saw the Gunny and Snake all the time."

"You see the general said they felt they were looking out after her till you came back."

"Yeah, she said they would catch my bag before it hit the ground, that is how close they watched me."

"Good men, the general said for her.

"Good she said, but a pain in the ass."

I just smiled.

When the door opened I got the surprise of my life. Mike was the first one to come in and he went right for me. "Good dog." I said holding him. Boy was he happy to see me.

Nancy said she gave him to the Gunny. "The dog would walk around the house all day long holding a picture of you in his mouth crying. I could just take so much of that and out he had to go. I know I missed you to but I didn't walk around with your picture in my mouth all day."

"Good dog." I said. Then the Gunny and Snake came in. Boy was they getting old looking. The Gunny said that was because of worrying about me.

"Ha I said you didn't have to you know I would make it."

"Ha Snake said he kept telling me that. But he would keep me up all night. Calling me if I heard anything. He would say the dog jumped and he know something was up." "No I would tell him and try to go back to bed. By this time my wife was a wake and you know her. She thinks you make love all night long, so I had to show her I was still her sitting bull and before you know it the sun was coming up. So I don't want to hear how old I look. You got me," he said looking at me.

I tried not to laugh but I couldn't help it. "How was your wife?" I asked.

"They all answered. "Getting bigger."

"You kidding." I said.

"How, Gunny said holding on to his stomach as if he was having a baby.

"You kidding I said, your wife to."

"Yes king mo savvy, he said, me sitting bull, don't sit.

"You Snake I said holding him.

"Snake he is, the Gunny said. Coming to join us. It felt good holding the ones you love. All I need was Seymour and guess who came in. He didn't need to have the guard call him in he knows all of them. He came right in. He didn't waste any time coming over he joined right in with the rest. Nancy was the one that broker it up. She said get all the shit over with how because from now on the only one going to be touching me was her.

"And the babies." Seymore said.

"And the babies she said looking at Seymore. I know she forgave us for what we did and she loved Seymore's and his wife's son just as much as she did ours. Even thou it was half mind.

"How is he doing?" I asked him.

"It was Nancy that said. He looked just like me. Seymore came back with, and am I glad he does. I hate to have my son look like me."

I know then we were all one again. When you can joke about something like that it was water under the bridge. And I was glad it was. Now maybe we could get on with our lives.

That was after I got my brother back home with me. "Seymore I got something to tell you. I told him about my brother and you know what he said. "Good I got nothing against him I never meet him." Again we all laugh Boy was it good. He would fit in just fine with our little family.

"Well, the General said, look what is here." His wife came in. We all turned and looked at her.

"Hey I said there is the pretty lady and I went over to her and held her.

"No I'm not." She said pulling away from me.

"Oh but you are I said holding on to her hand. There is something about you that makes me want you more and more. I know I said. Touching her stomach. This is what makes you different. You're carrying a baby."

"No she said, he is," pointing to the general. If I had anything to do with it. He would be carrying it."

"Now that I got to see. I said. He still would look as pretty as you are."

"Oh you, she said kissing me. It is good to have you back," she said. I guess they all missed me.

"Now can I see my children?"

"Nancy looked at me and said, you really want to."

"Oh do I ever." I said.

"Good she said because they are on their way. I didn't think I had any more tears left in me but I was wrong when the door opened and in came my daughter and my son. She was walking and Seymore's wife was carrying him. I guess it was too much for me my lags were getting weak. "Daddy," my daughter said coming over to me. She still remembered me. I went to grab her. She stopped dead in her tracks. Oh shit my face. I must have scared her she started screaming and Nancy came and picked her in.

"I forgot she said I should of known I'm sorry she said looking at me Knowing how I was feeling.

"No baby she told her daddy is all-right he just had a bad cut, she tried to clam her down. It didn't work I guess I scared the hell out of her. Look Seymore said take her in the other room and let her get use to it here first and later we will see. He knows. I guess he was expecting it. Well we were all here. "Now what?"

I guess we had to let everyone know that was going on. It would be for there own good. I couldn't tell them everything but all they needed to know was there lives could be in danger. The rest was up to the General and me. The General had a guesthouse by the pool so me and Nancy and the kids got settled there. Seymore and his family went back but had guards with them and the rest just had to be on the look out. Nothing was going to happen as long as I didn't foul up. We didn't know who was watching us so it was hard.

CHAPTER 20

The less people know what we were doing the better it was. For the sack of who was watching me we went to work on a dummy plan for the doctor. Just in case they were on the inside and know everything we were doing. The General and me went to work we know or objective and head straight for him. The faster we moved the better. It only took us three days to get all we needed on the general the rest was making sure we didn't blow it. We were working on files one day when Mike came in he came right up to me and put his paws on me. I didn't know what he was up to at first but he let me know. He had a note in his mouth.

How did he get this? I looked at it and it was from the person that was watching me for the Russians.

"Shit I said. He knows about us." The note said to meet him at a place alone. The General didn't like the idea of me going but I had to. I didn't tell Nancy when the note came she was with the kids. Good thing for that. I know what she would have done. So How I was to meet this so-called spy and make him believe I was doing what I said I was. That was going to be the hard part. You didn't have to be blind to see what we were doing. I left and went to the place and waited. I didn't know who I was to meet all it said was to wait for some one to contact me. So I waited. It was in a park and no one was around this wasn't such a good place to meet no one was around.

Then two kids came by on a bikes I didn't pay any attention to them but when they passed I looked on the ground and there was a bag. It wasn't there before the kids must have dropped it. I got up and picked it up. Inside was another note. For me to go someplace else. I followed it to the letter and ended at the other end of the park. It was more people around. I was to sit on this bench and wait. So I did. There was this old man sitting with me. I was hoping he would get up and leave I didn't want anyone getting hurt. Just in case of any trouble. I watched and waited for ten minutes. No one came. I guess they didn't want the man there. I had to make him move. But how, he looked as if he stayed there all day. He had his lunch and paper and coffee. As if he was relaxing.

"Sir I said to him do you sit here all the time." He looked over his paper at me and smiled. "All the time," he said and went back to reading his paper. Shit he wasn't going to move. I took out the note again to make sure I was on the right bench. The old man said something from behind his paper. "You got the right bench," he said. It was him I was to meet. How what. "Well I'm here I said now what?"

"Take your time he said we got all day. I'm in no rush."

"Oh but I am, I said.

"I know he said but your doing all the wrong things," he said. He knows something was up.

"And what do you mean by that?" I asked.

"Look he said you don't fool anyone."

"I'm not out to fool anyone I said. I am doing what I said I would."

"No comrade he said, you're playing games."

"That depends on what games you think I'm playing." I said to him.

Look I said I don't know who you are or even if I should be talking to you. Now if you got nothing else to say .I got to go."

"Sit," he said in a low voice but hard.

"Look I said I know your watching me so what makes you think I'm not doing what I said I was."

"You're spending time checking up on the General," he said.

"Oh, I laugh, is that it?"

"No he said and why did you move your family in with the General?"

"Look I said you got to give me something better then that. Anyone could find out what I did. I'm not hiding it."

"No he said but your not getting us the doctor like you said you would."

"Oh is that it? I said. You expected me to walk right in and pack his bag and come right back with him."

"No he said but you're up to something and we don't like it. Remember your brother is still in our hands." "Hey I said I told you what I was going to do and if you don't like the way I'm doing it then do it your self." I said getting up.

"Relax, the old man said. Sit back and hear me out, he said. Hungry," he said taking out a hot dog from his bag.

"No I said what else do you want?" I asked.

"Answers," he said.

"Look you know what I was going to do and I'm doing it. "But your also doing other things," he said.

"Oh so that is it. Look I don't know whom you answer to or what roll you play in this game. But I will tell you one thing your not to well informed on what I'm doing here."

"Eat comrade," he said handing me the hot dog. He handed it to fast. I didn't want it but it was in my hand before I could pull it away. "We know what you want, he said, but we come first."

"Look I said I told you I was going to get the General and he is on the head of my list."

I don't care if he is one of yours. I told you I was going to get him and believe me I'm not leaving till I do. That my comrade you can go and tell them for me." "You are disobeying orders," he said.

"No I said I take no orders. I told your people I would bring the doctor back with me and that is what I'm doing. I didn't promise anything else. If your people want me to join them then it is going to have to be on my terms.

"And your terms are," he asked.

"The general dies and so does the other people that but a price on my head."

"Ha he said that is what I'm talking about. You are fishing in a brook with no fish," he said.

"Oh you know this?' I said.

"You think we are stupid?' He said.

"But I got to do what I got to do." said.

"Very well he said and handed me a napkin. Here he said you will need this for your hot dog."

"No I said I don't want the hot dog."

"Read he said rising his voice. I looked at it and it was a print out of some kind. You Americans like everything on your hot dog. It gets messy. You need something to wipe your face with. Eat," he said.

"I looked at the hot dog and took a bit. He had unions and sauerkraut and sauce on it. I looked at the napkin and started to read. It was a report from some file. The Generals name was on top.

"You see he said he is the one that had the price put on your head. He is the only one you have to get. The Mafia was just going on what he asked them to do." As I read on I found out a lot about him.

"I see you're willing to give him up, I said.

"For you and your doctor he said we will. He started to get up.

"Hey I said how what?"

He looked at me and said. "We want you by the end of the week."

"I don't know." I said.

He smiled and said. "We do. On the other side of the report are instructions for you fallow," he said. I turned the paper over and it was when and where I was to meet them to get back out of the country and in to Russia.

"Oh he said by the way your brother sends his love."

"Oh have you talked to him?" I asked.

"Oh you would say that," he said and walked away. I sat and looked at the paper. When I looked up to see what way he went he was gone. No old man could move that fast. I stood up and looked for him. He was no where to be seen. Oh hell I guess I had to make my move. I looked at the hot dog and was going to throw it way. Hey that tasted pretty good. I took another bit. What the hell was this? Something hard was in it. I kept my mouth on it and pulled it out from under the sauce. Oh god it was a finger. I spit it out of my mouth. Oh shit I didn't have to even look at it I know what it was. My brother's finger. That mother fucker. He knew I would find it.

I don't know why but I started to run all over the park looking for him. Did this mean my brother was dead? No they wouldn't leave it like this. They know I wouldn't do anything for them if I knew he was dead. This was just a reminder they had him and what they could do to him if they wanted to. Mother fuckers. I went back and picked the finger up. If it was my brothers I didn't want anyone to go near it. "Them mother fuckers;" I yelled. People were looking at me as if I was going out of my mind. Maybe I was. Shit I got into my car and just drove. I didn't want to go back just yet. I had to get something out of my system.

I didn't know where I was driving to but when I stopped and looked up I know where I was. It was at the Generals place. The one Nancy drove to that day. Could he still be living here? Why not he wasn't married. He was still waiting for Nancy. The fool, I got out of the car and walked into the lobby. A doorman asked me if he could help me. No I said I was just interested in looking. I was getting stationed here and I was looking for a place to live.

"This place came highly recommended." I told him.

"Yes sir he said we do have quite a lot of Government officials living here," he said.

"I know I said some of my friends live here, he told me about it. You do have a place for sale."

"Yes sir he said we have a turn over all the time. You guys come and go."

"I know, I said but that is the life we chose to live."

He smiled and said he did it for a while but when he got married his wife didn't like it so he settled down and here he is.

"You sorry?" I asked him.

"In a way he said but I have two children now I guess it is better for them."

"Oh that is another question. I have; I asked taking out my children's pictures. Now are the schools around here."

"Oh he said boy and girl. That is nice he said I got two boys."

"No I said one two and quit.

"Ha he said that is what you say. But my wife wants two girls also."

"No I said two are just right for us. So I said; how are the schools?"

"Good he said they are use to you guys moving around so they understand what the child needs in the way of education."

"Good I said Oh by the way I had a friend that lived here a while back I was wondering if he still lived here."

"I'm sorry sir he said I'm not allowed to give out that kind of information. You understand, he said it is for the privacy of our tenants."

"I should know," I took out my old C.I.D. I.D. and had a twenty on top of it. You see I said secretes is my business."

"Yes sir he said he looked at the I.D. and at the twenty and smiled. The tenant's list is at my desk. I guess it is time for me to check the out side." He took the twenty and walked out the door. I went over to his list and there he was he was still living here. Good I said walking out.

"Have a nice day; the doorman said. Oh by the way he said if you want to see someone about a place she will be in around two."

"That was what I was just going to ask you my good man I said and her name would be?"

He said just ask for Mary. I should be on when you come he said I leave at four."

"Thanks I said I'll be seeing you."

O.K. he lived here and so now what? I had to see if he was at home our off some where trading secrets with the Russians. Now was I going to do that? I didn't have excess any more to the C.I.D. building and I didn't want to go ask the General. He made it clear what he was going to do with the general. I can't see letting him go on living. I had to do what I set out to do. Even if it meant losing a friend. He has destroyed my life enough. I wanted him dead. I know the Gunny he still had people he could get info from. I headed for his place. The bar was open so I went in.

"Hey." He yelled over the bar. He was talking to some guys at the other end. "Get over here," he said. He walked further to the back so we could talk with out anyone hearing us. "What brings you out?" He asked. "Oh I said holding my brother's finger in my pocket.

"Let's say I have a score to settle."

"You're not going to do what I think you're going to do, are you?"

"Let's just say you don't know anything." I said to him. You still have your contacts in the office?" I asked him.

"Some, he said what can I do for you?"

"I need the generals where abouts and home phone number."

"You are," he said smiling. He picked up the phone and dialed. He kept looking at me. "Want a drink?" He asked while he was waiting for some one to pick up. "I could use one?" I said. He told me to go back and get one. I went behind the bar and took a large glass of Vodka and poured my self-a full glass. I took a drink The Gunny was watching me. I down the whole glass straight.

"Woo he said that bad?" He said looking at me. The party came to the phone. He talked to them and as he hung up he wrote something down.

I took the bottle and poured it to the top again.

"Hold on; he said you keep that up and I'll have to carry you out." I put the glass on the bar and took out my brother's finger and placed it in the Vodka.

"Oh man, the Gunny said looking at it. What the fuck happened?' He couldn't take his eyes off of the finger. "You got it for me?" I asked.

"Here, he said handing me the paper with his phone number on it. He is here, he said. Did he do that?" he asked looking at my hand to see if one of my fingers was off.

"You could say he did." I said handing him the glass. Hold this for me." I said and walked out the door. The Gunny didn't have time to say anything; he kept looking at the finger.

"Hey; he finely said as I got to the door. Wait for me." I'm coming," he said going to the back of the bar.

"No I said, you're too old for this shit."

I know that would get to him.

"What; he yelled you got to be out of your mind. I can out do you any day."

"Good; I said, when I come back we will see." I left him standing there. I didn't need him. I knew he would only get in the way. I had to do it my self. I stopped at a phone and dialed his number.

"Hello," he said. He was home, how nice of him. I just hung up. It was a little past two so I headed back for his place. I got out and went to the doorman.

"Hey, he said she is here."

"Good; I said I looked at some other places this one is the best so far."

"Good, It would be nice having you here sir," he said. "Not so fast I said you know I can just look, my wife is the one that has to give the O.k."

"Don't I know; he said? Well she is waiting for you he said, I told her about you."

"Good; I said you don't waste any time."

"No sir, he said, that is what I get paid for."

"Good man, I said handing him another twenty.

"Thank you sir, he said and held the door open for me. "Down the hall the first door past the elevator."

"Got you." I said and went the way he told me. The door was open and this woman was sitting at a desk.

"Yes; she asked, can I help you?"

"I'm looking." I said. But my wife has final say so." "Don't we all," she said getting up. Your the one John said was looking.

"I guess so, I said.

"Well you're in luck," she said we have three that will be ready by the end of the month."

"Oh I said are you sure because that is when I would need it by."

"Oh yes; she said when you guys get your orders nothing stands in the way. That is why we like doing business with the Government. In out and in one day. I'm use to that; she said the moving company is also."

"Oh I asked; and how is that?"

She said when you're moving you get the same mover and he sends his truck to your place first and brings your things here. Then he unloads them and loads the other parties on. And this way one in and one out and only one crew doing it."

"You mean they take my things out and leave them on the street?"

"No we have a garage where they do it. You things will be safe she said. Come she said I'll show you." She got up and walked to the elevator and got in; down she went. When we reached the garage she went around the corner and showed me how it was done. The mover was they're doing someone else.

"See she said as they take your things up they bring down the other person's things and this way they don't go up empty handed."

"I wish the Government worked that way." I said.

"Oh, she said, from what you guys tell me it does."

"I don't know who you've have been talking to, I told her, but they lye."

She laughs at that.

"So how she said would you like to see what we will have for you?'

"That is what I came for." I told her. And up we went. The general lived on the tenth floor. She stopped at the seconded floor and went to this apartment and opened the door. We went in and looked around.

"No I said I need two bedrooms."

"Oh she said silly of me I didn't ask you have children."

"Yes two." I said.

"Oh then I got just the place for you." She got back in the elevator and headed for the ninth floor.

'This is two-bed room." She opened the door. I was looking at the apartment numbers. The General was facing the street. This one was facing the back.

"Nice I said I think this will do."

"Oh she said I have one more if you care to look?'

"No I think this one would be just fine." I said.

"Oh please she said the other one is just like this one but it is facing the street. A much better view," she said. Sorry I can't show it right now, how silly of me." "Oh and why not?'

"Oh the General is home, he isn't moving till the day after tomorrow."

"Oh what is his name?" I asked. It was him, he was moving. I started to sweat. It was now or never.

"Could I see it?" I asked.

"No; she said but if you come back tomorrow I'll be glad to show it to you. You see he is packing now and then he is going to his next duty station and his things well fallow."

"He lives by him self." I asked.

"Oh yes she said and the place is kept clean; he doesn't even have parties he is quite."

"But is it two bedrooms?" I asked.

"Oh yes he likes room, she said, he wanted it with two bed rooms."

I guess he was planing for Nancy to move in with him. Big surprise.

"I would like to see that one." I said.

"If you could come back the same time tomorrow," she said I could show it to you." He must have got the word I was back and looking for him. He was running. It was now or never. I went back in to the elevator with her. I had to get her keys. I need them to get in. She had one key that opened all the doors. It must be a master. Just then we stopped on the fifth floor this woman and man got on.

"Sorry." I said and moved over closer to the woman with the keys. Now if I could just take them from her pocket I would be home free. The elevator stopped at the next floor more people came on. Good it was better. I started to reach for them when it stopped again this time three kids and their mother came on; just what I needed. The two boys were playing and moving all over the elevator. Now was my chance.

I got them when one of the kids bunked into the woman. Thank you son; I said to my self. I got out and told the woman I would be back tomorrow and headed out the door. The doorman smiled and asked.

"See anything your wife would like?'

"I think so I said and left. Now I had to wait. The doorman left and another one took his place. I waited till it got dark and went around to the back the garage was my best place to get in with out anyone seeing me. It had a electric gate but it didn't close fast. I had my chance to get in before it closed when a car left. Now I was at the elevator. I press it and the door opened. I headed right for his floor. The tenth. It stopped and the door opened. No one here I went out fast and right to his door. Now key does your thing; I said and stuck it in.

"Hey," some one yelled.

Oh shit not now. I didn't turn around to see why was talking. I couldn't I was shacking too much.

"Hey he said again you coming?" Then I heard a woman yelled. "You go ahead I'll be right they."

Oh shit that was close. It was just this guy and his wife going out for the night. He wasn't talking to me. I got the door open and went in. This was crazy what if he was waiting for me. Well she did say the apartment was just like the one we saw. And I know it had a little hallway before you came into the living room. I was in and the door and closed behind me.

"Comrade is that you?" the general called.

Oh shit now what.

"Yea I said and waited for him to come around the corner.

"Well; he said come. I got what you wanted."

That fuck was meeting some Russian to give him some files before he left. I walked into the living room he had boxes all over the place getting ready to move. He was sitting on the couch with files in front of him looking at them and not at me.

"Come he said have a set."

"No thanks." I said. I'll stand if it is all right with you." He looked up and saw me.

"You; he yelled, how did you get in here?" He said jumping up.

"I wouldn't; I told him." I know what he was going after. His gun and I didn't want any noise. I said. "It is true you do work for the Russians?'

"Look; he said backing up, you have no right to be here."

"Cut the shit." I said walking over to him. Would you look at this, I said looking at the files on the table. How much will they bring?" I asked.

"I don't know what you're talking about," he said. I took these home to go over tonight. I don't know what you're talking about."

"Look ass hole everyone knows about you, so don't pull the shit with me."

"Oh he said and who is everyone?"

"Your Russian buddies know I'm going to get you. Did they tell you that?" I asked?

"They did he said but you have nothing on me."

"Maybe not, I said but, I bet if I stick around long enough I'll have all I need."

"Get your ass the hell out of here before I make a phone call."

"Oh and who would that be to? Mr. D." I said smiling.

"Who is this Mister D?" He asked.

"Man you still don't get it, your day has come ass hole. Now let's get your things together."

"You," he yelled and came at me. That was what I wanted him to do.

Man I beat him with all my heart and soul. I didn't even stop when he went out. I kept kicking him and hitting him. Blood was what I wanted to feel and blood was what I was getting. Man did he bleed. I was fucking up his face just the way mine was fucked up. As I was hitting him I started singing (all the kings' houses and all the kings' man couldn't put the general together again).

"Comrade," someone said.

"Oh shit here I go again. Not thinking. I was forgetting he had someone coming. Shit now what? I let the general drop to the floor. My gun was on the table. "Don't even think about it," he said. Just turn around and let me see your hands."

I did what else could I do. I turned slowly. Mother fucker it was him, the Russian that whipped me. All of a sudden I felt all my scars. The pain was real.

"Oh comrade, he said we meet again."

"You fucking piece of shit." I called him.

"Oh now comrade, he said you must not hold that against me. We are on the same side now." He said.

"Oh and what side is that?"

"Mother Russia, he said. Now comrade I don't think it was suppose to go this way."

"And what way was it to go?" I asked.

"Well, you were supposed to just lock him up. Not kill him."

"Oh I said and who said that?"

"Come now, he said we both know what the story is. We know you would get him before he left. All we want is the files he had for us and he is yours. But remember you got a date to keep at the end of the week."

"So you are willing to turn him over?' I asked.

"Him, he said he was only an ass hole as you called him. Man like him we got all over the place. Anything for money."

"I bet I said so now what?" I asked.

"Well I would put down my gun but like you I don't trust you; like you want to get at me. You see what we have here is you did what I did."

"Oh what is that?" I asked?

"Ha he said you know what. My comrades told you about me and why I did what I did."

"Oh yes, something about my father beating your father with a whip."

"Yes Comrade; he said the same way you beat the general. Yes," he said.

"I guess you could say that."

"Well my orders were to not do anything to you."

"So now what?" I asked him.

"So now Comrade it is up to you. I could just take the files and leave and we part friends or I could shot you if you wish."

"Look I don't blame you for what you did, I said but you did go a little over board with it; don't you think?" I said feeling my face.

"Oh no, he said. I was really trying to kill you. My comrades stopped me. I would have finished what I started."

"Oh I see then you still fell the same way?" I asked him.

"No, he said I got it out of me just like you got it out of you. You didn't kill him and I don't think you will; he said. Like me. You got stopped and how you feel better. You got your revenge and now you can go on with your life. For me, he said. I sleep well at night thanks to you."

"Oh I said. I'm glad to hear that. Now maybe it will do the same for me?"

"Yes Comrade, he said you will see no more nightmares." "Good sleep. Well thank you comrade." I said reaching for my gun.

"Go; he said you see. I don't hate you."

I guess he didn't, he let me pick it up and he put his away. Maybe he was right. We all had a lot of hate in side of us. But once it was out you did fell better. I felt that way once before; when I told the truth about my self.

"Well comrade; I said now what?"

"This is easy he said the hard part is over."

"Yes I said to him. Knowing it was my self.

"I go now he said reaching for the files.

"No I said you can't take them."

"Oh he said but I must. You see we paid him for them all ready."

"But I said what do I have to show?"

"Good question he said he looked at the files and said here you take this one we have it all ready."

"I can't believe it you mean he gave you the same file twice?"

"Oh no comrade; someone else gave it to us."

"Oh I see. You get them that easy?" I asked.

"Some times he said but as you can see what we got here isn't that importune."

"Oh I said mind if I see?"

"Here he said be my guest."

"What the hell is this?' I asked holding up a file that looked like a toilet bowl.

"What does it look like?" He asked.

"A toilet bowl." I said.

"That is what it is; he said you see we have had trouble with our toilets on our U-boats and yours work real good so why not pay for the plans. It is a lot cheaper then having our man find out something that works. We know yours works."

"Good point; I said and this?' I asked. Oh that he said we have trouble keeping the space food good. You have it down pat."

"So I said you copy the way we do it. Except for the food he said we Russians like Russian food Not Pizza.

"I can see your point." I said.

"Oh but one thing we do like, he said is the peanut butter and Jelly that we steal," he said laughing.

"You mean this is all this ass hole steals for you." Like we said he only does small thing. But we know we had him if we needed him for something big. He is an ass hole. Well comrade I shall be going now."

I couldn't shot him so I guess I had to let him go. Funny I didn't feel my scars any more. Well now what? Call the general and tell him I got him red handed. No I said I need time to think. This man fucked up my life and if I know the Government he will get maybe two years for what he did and kicked out of the service. Small price to pay for what he did. They were no way of telling what else he gave them; so all I had was this. I opened the file and looked at it. Shit this one was worse then the others. "Disposable Kotex for woman on space flights." Could you believe this? He wouldn't even get a year for this.

No, I can't just let him get off that easy; what the fuck was I going to do? I got up and went over to his bar and took a drink. Vodka of course. Shit it was beginning to taste like water. I went over to the patio door and opened them. Nice view of the White House. Nancy would have like it here. Ha I said but not with him. He was starting to come to. Well I guess I had to make up my mind. I put down my glass and went over and picked him up and put him on the couch. I went and got him a glass of Scotch. I know he wasn't a Vodka drinker. He looked up at me when I handed it to him.

"You change your mind?' He said.

"No, I said let's just say today is your lucky day.

He took the drink and downs it. I guess I would have done the same thing if I were him. Shit you get the shit kicked out of you and didn't expect to wake from it. And all of a sudden the one that kicked your ass is giving you a drink.

Something didn't make sense; to him or me as a matter of fact. "Want another one?" I asked reaching for the bottle. He held out his glass.

"No I said. I'm not going to pour it for you." I took the bottle and placed it on the table in front of him, you pour your own."

I went and got my glass and filled it up again. "Well I said holding my glass for a toast. Here is to the Russians." I said and drank it down. He did the same he drank it down. I took the bottle and poured my self-another one, he did the same.

"And here is to Nancy." He said. Holding his glass up. "I'll drink to that." I said. "A fine woman." I got my self another glass full and said. To the better man, and he did the same, he drank it down. I guess all the Vodka I drink with my brother In Russia it got me uses to it I wasn't feeling anything.

He was I could see it in his eyes. He was getting bombed. "And to the children," he said filling his glass up again. I did the same; what the hell I didn't want him to think he could out drinks me. Then he filled it up again and stood over by the patio door.

"And to the U.S.A." He said and downed it.

"To the U.S.A. I said.

He turned to me and said. "Now what?"

"Well I said we didn't drink to the ass hole?"

"Oh he said and who might that be?"

"You." I said and started to laugh.

"I'll drink to that," he said and came back and emptied his bottle in his glass. "To the ass hole." He held his glass up and I did the same. He downed it. Now he said I have to go."

"Oh I asked and where might that be?'

He didn't answer he just turned and ran out the door and over the ledge. You know I didn't even try to stop him, I just watched him go. I picked up the top-secret file and put my glass down and left.

I stopped at the hallway and went back in to the room I picked up the Vodka bottle and held it in the air. "And to me." I said and downed the rest of it. I didn't want him to thing he out drank me, he finished his bottle and so did I. But I was still walking. He wasn't. I closed the door and went down. When I got to the main entrance he was down all ready. He was all over the sidewalk and the doorman was just looking up in the air to see if any more were coming, I guess. I went out side and looked. "He did a good job." I said and stepped over him and get into my car. The doorman didn't know what to do, he just kept looking at him on the ground and then at me.

CHAPTER 21

I drove off and headed for the general's house and Nancy. Everyone was waiting for me when I got there. Even the Gunny, he must of came over and told them what I was up to.

"Well?" The general said looking at me.

"Case closed," I said and throw the file on his desk. Nancy came over to me and was checking my hand.

"What is up with you?" I asked.

"There all here," she said.

"What is all here?" I asked.

"Your fingers," she said.

"Oh that; I said coming back to life. That was my brother. I said, it was the Russians way of telling me to hurry up."

"Them fucks, the Gunny said, is he dead?"

"No I don't think so. They wouldn't do that. Not on less they know I wasn't keeping my end of the bargain. He is still alive. In a way I'm glad they did it to him." I said.

"You what?" she said?

"Yes, I said he didn't want to leave his Mother Russia now maybe this will teach him."

"That is one way of looking at it," the general said. Well I have till the weekend to follow their orders and then if I don't have the doctor I guess they will send his whole body to me."

The General came up to me and said we have it all worked out. We have a person that looks like the doctor ready to go."

"I don't think that is going to work." I said, they know what the doctor looked like, someone was at my father's house and knows about him and what he looks like."

"We know that, he said, so we trained this doctor to look and act like him. Come; he said and you will see."

The General went out and into another room. Two men were waiting for us. Oh shit it was two doctors. They both looked alike.

"Now; he said if you can't tell, they can't either. Pick out the real doctor." He said to me.

"You got to be kidding; I said. I can't tell."

"Good he said. Now ask them questions only the doctor will know the answer to."

"That is easy; I said. What was my dog's name?" I asked one of them?

"Mike but it isn't your dog."

"Good I said, but what do you mean it isn't my dog?" The other one answered. "The dog is his own master he only goes with you because he likes you. He has his own mind and listens to no one."

"Good; I said. Now what is the spider crossed bread with."

"Snakes and roach's."

"What did we just accomplish?' I asked one of them.

"To make the poison last longer in the spider."

"Good I said now one last question, who did my father have killed the night he had all the people for dinner." "The American from the K.K.K." They said.

"You satisfied?' He asked me.

"I guess so. There is only one way of knowing." I said and that is to go for it."

I guess it was now or never. I followed the plan to the tee. They said for me to be with the doctor out in front of where they know he was staying. Shit they even know where we had him. We had to act out the whole thing; we didn't know who was good and who was bad. I went over and meet the doctor and we were going to lunch, for old time sack, nothing wrong with that, the doctor comes and goes as he pleased, as long as a guard went with us. We got to the corner they said they would pick us up at. It looked as if no one was there. But was I surprised when a manhole cover came up and two guys shot the two guards right in broad daylight.

"Come comrade, one of them said to me. They also had chloroform for the doctor. They know he wouldn't come willingly. It was working with out any trouble. The sewer came out right in the back of the Russian embassy and a car was waiting for us. We got in and off to the airport. We went into a hanger and got out. They had a large box waiting for us and it was getting ready to be loaded on this plane that was warming up out side the hanger. "How nice I said it even had beds in the box.

"You lay down comrade," one said and we tire you in. I guess so we wouldn't bounce around on take off. I did and they did it to the doctor.

"Good Comrade one said; see you." They closed the box and I felt us being loaded on the plane. The general said he had made plans for me to return but I would have to wait a while before they came and got me. I didn't mind that. I know once that the Russians had the doctor I was headman. That is the way they worked, you get for us and we give you what you want. I was hoping it would go that way. If not the only thing they got was my brother and I. The doctor wasn't going to give them anything. But he was sure the General was going to keep his word and have us back in no time. I guess we had man over there that wanted money also. Anything for a buck.

Well we arrived and got let out of the box; it was a short trip. When we got out of the plane I looked around Oh shit I didn't like this. I don't remember ever hearing of Palm trees in Russia. I was right we were In Cuba.

"Do not worry Comrade," the guy from the plane said. This was the only way we could get a flight out; from the U.S. to Cuba."

"How did you arrange that?" I asked?

He smiled and says. "We fly here all the time. You see he said your Government allows us to bring medical supplies to Mr. Castro."

"Oh I said and where do you get them?"

"He said, your Government gives them to us."

"Oh that is nice of us."

"You might say it is for not putting our missiles here. Come he said Mr. Castro would like for you to have dinner with him. He said it would be an honor if you would."

"I bet, I said Look if it is all the same with you I would rather stay here."

"Oh Comrade; he said you have nothing to worry about Mr. Castro knows who you are and he wants to meet you in person. He said something about your father and him was a good friend."

I bet I said to snakes. I said to my self.

"Come," he said.

"What about the doctor?"

"On no he said he doesn't go no where, he is to vauliable to have walking around. He stays here under guard," he said.

Oh hell what do I have to lose? I got in the jeep that was waiting for us and off we went. I could see the base over on the other side of the water the bay was between the Marines and us. We came into town and drove down the main street. It looked like a city but something was missing. It just didn't look lived in; if you know what I mean? People were walking around but with no movement. Not like you would expect to see people moving. It was as if they didn't want to go where they were headed and took their time getting there.

We pulled into what was once a casino, It was a now Castro's palace. Guards all round it. No one came in or out with out going throw rows of barbwire, and troops; sand bags all over the place.

"Is he expecting some one?" I asked.

"Him; he said every day he calls and tells us the American's are coming and every day we tell him we check and not today. He knows we watch him from the settle light."

"I guess so." I said.

"Good for you. You got the same," he said to me. But ours is better."

"Of course, I said why not? You stole it from us?"

"Ha, he said, you make a joke," he said and kept on laughing.

"Well you did." I said.

"That is true but don't tell the Russians we do it. They think we make it first."

"Keeping the people in the blind." I said.

"Yes comrade, he said, what do they know?

"Nothing?" I said.

"Your right," he said and laughs again.

Castro was coming out to meet us.

CHAPTER 22

"Welcome General," he said coming up to me and kissing me. "Hey," I said remembering what they said about him being queer.

"A friendly kiss," he said.

"No, I said we shack hand where I come from. I held out my hand and he took it.

"You Americans are so cold; no warm hugs for love ones."

"No I said sorry we just shack hands. Sorry about that I said but we were doing it for a long time now and I don't see us changing."

"Come he said. I got food for you."

"Good I said. I could use a good meal." He put his arm around my shoulder and we walked into his palace. "How do you like?" He said holding out his hands for me to look at all.

Shit he still had the gambling tables set up and everything was working.

"For my Russian Friends, he said they like to bet."

"On I said that is why you still have them working."

"Of course; he said my big brothers come here to play." He was right I saw more Russians here then in Russia.

"Come," he said again and walked over to this big table. Food," he said.

He was right there was more food on this table then I saw all the time I was in Russia.

"Now; he said grab your self-a plate and dig in."

I did it looked good. He went over to one of the boys that were I guess a waiter and looked at him.

"You, you know you don't eat the food," he said and bang he bunched him in the stomach. He hit him again in the stomach. The kid throws up all over the place. "You see, he said to me. I know. He had some crumbs in his teeth," he said. They always try to take the food, you have to watch them, he said. We don't have enough food to feed our people and you get some pig like this that steals, then before you know it they all are doing it and then what do you have?" He said looking at me for the answer.

"Happy people." I said.

I guess he didn't like what I said.

"No he said looking at me. You got a rebellion on your hands." He told his guards to take the boy out and shot him.

Just like that he did it, like he was nothing. "Come he said you eat." Here was this ass hole-playing king and his people were walking around staving. I guess he was king for now. Like Hitler you keep your solders happy and feed you don't have anything to worry about. They will protect you to the death. Oh hell it was his problem not mines. I had my brother to worry about. He didn't stop talking, he was talking about how some day he would control this part of the world for Russia and how the Russians would give him the U.S. for sticking by them. This man was sick. No way was he going to run anything but what he had here and he was lucky they didn't take that away from him. I guess they didn't want to move just yet. So for now this bearded ass hole was king.

We eat and the Russian said we had to go. Castro said he was glad to meet me on this side of the fence. And if my father had lived he would be in the White House by now". "Yes I said you got that right." I told him if he lived. Some day; I started to say when the Russian came up to me.

"Let's go he said Mr. Castro has things to do." For some reason I didn't think the Russians wanted me to tell Castor about the doctor. Why should he know, he was only living on borrowed time anyway? They just used him just in case war between Russia and the U.S. broke out. Cuba had the airfield to land planes on and that way Russia could come for all angles. From the east from their motherland, from the west throw Vietnam the north from the Aloutaon Island and the south from Cuba. I guess you would say we were surrounded. But we had the bomb. I guess they were waiting to get something like that them self's.

We were back on the plane and off again. We unloaded all the supplies and headed for Russia. We landed in Moscow and had a convoy to meet us. When I got out of the plane the fat man was there to meet me.

"Comrade." He said.

"Hey fuck you and your comrade shit I want to see my brother.

"He is waiting for you back at his house," he said.

"I hope so; I said because if he isn't you got one hell of a fight on your hands."

"Come now Comrade; he said you must realize we had no choice but to do what we did."

"Look you fat fuck I told you I was going to deliver you didn't have to do what you did."

"But Comrade we did nothing."

"My brother's finger was nothing?"

"A small price to pay for the world," he said.

"Oh then let me cut your fat fucking finger off and see how you like it."

"Now comrade; he said your brother was well rewarded for his willingness to do so."

"I can't believe you, I said, it was nothing to you, was it?"

He just looked at me and gave me that look this time. "Knock the shit off; he said you have no room to talk. Look who your father was and remember you had fun your self."

"Fun; is that what you call it?"

"Don't you call it that? He asked. We know what makes you tick," he said.

"Oh and what is that?" I asked.

"Blood," he said and walked away from me.

Maybe he was right. I just didn't like it done to someone I know and loved. "Your right." I yelled back at him, the more the better."

He was gone. The other car was waiting for me. I had to make sure my brother was alive before I went any further. He drive drove me right to the house. My brother was in side drunk. The two girls were still there and he didn't seem to mind his finger missing. He said they got him drunk and the next thing he knows was waking up with out it. "It didn't hurt," he said.

"How do you know? I said have you been sober yet?"

"No; he said laughing we got case after case of Vodka what should I be?"

The girls pointed to four cases of it in the corner. They were drunk also.

Shit this wasn't going to be easy. I know once the Vodka wears off, he would be in pain.

"You do a good job?" He asked.

"A good job." I said.

"Good now we live happy ever after."

"I wish we could do that; I said, but we got to sober up." I told him.

"Tomorrow he said tonight we drink to your return," and he opened another bottle. I guess he was right; I couldn't do anything for a while. I had to wait for the General to give me a sign; when and how I didn't know.

He said something about knowing where they were doing the experiments and we had to take the doctor along with us. That was gong to take something to get all of us together. I saw the way they guarded the so-called doctor. This guy was good he could fool them for a long time. With the real doctors notes burnt up he used that as an excuse. He said he had to start from almost scratch.

So we got drunk day after day and I played with the girl when I was sober. What the hell I didn't have anything else to do and I got to like Vodka. I guess I was just like the rest of them. The fat man was right we did have more than enough; we got food delivered twice a week and along with Vodka; nothing to do but wait. One week went by and then two then three. Shit I was hoping it wouldn't take this long. I missed my kids and wife. It was different before when she didn't want me any more but now since she took me back I wanted to be with her.

A month went bye and nothing I was getting drunk ever day. Like I said it was the only thing to do. The drunker we got the faster the day went by. One day we passed out and woke up two days later. I think, I really didn't know it seemed as if we did. Shit what if they came for us and we were drunk? No way would they risk taking us out in this condition.

I had to stay sober. That did it from now on I wasn't going to drink. I took walks around the village and bike rides to pass the time away. What if they can't get us out of here, then what? Shit what the hell was I doing? I couldn't wait for them I had to get out of here by my self. "Brother I said I want to go into town."

He smiled and said. "Go."

"No; I said I went you to come with me."

"For what he said we got everything we need right here."

He was right from a Russians point of view what more could you want? Food, Vodka and woman. I guess anyone would settle for this. But I had my children waiting at home for me. My daughter was just getting use to me and my son didn't know any better. He loves me even thou my face were scared.

My brother told me to go to the soldier house and tell them to call for a car. They will come for me. I did and when I got back a car was coming for me. I went out side to meet it. It was one of the fat men.

"Hey comrade; he said what is wrong?"

"Nothing I said. I just want to get out of here for a while."

"What you don't like what we give you?"

"Look I said it maybe all right for my brother but for me I like to get out and walk around. You know what I mean?"

"Yes comrade, he said. "Come I will take you."

"Good;" I said and got my things.

"You want to stay long?" He said looking at my bag. "Just a couple of days." I said you must have something for me to do."

"Yes; he said we do. But we didn't want to rush you," he smiled and said.

On the way he was telling me what they had planed for me. Like my brother said the East Germans were acting up and someone like me could control them.

"How was the doctor doing?" I asked.

"Good; he said but you should have saved his papers. He has to start all over again. That will take time," he said.

"But he is doing his best." I asked.

"He said he could move a little faster."

"You want me to talk to him?" I asked. Not pushing my self on to him.

"And what do you think you could do?" He asked.

"I don't know I said maybe if I tell him we will give him a case of Vodka he will move faster."

"Ha; he said almost choking on his own laugh. You still make jokes."

"Not really I said but I can talk to him. He was a good man for my father, maybe he would listen to me."

"It is worth a try," he said. Good you come with me and we see."

Ha I got him. Now to see where he is and maybe I can get all of us out of here.

We drove back to the city and from what I remembered from the last time we were here he was heading in the other direction; on the other side if the city. More like the factory area. We pulled into this warehouse with guards all over the place; on the roofs around the fence. "Heavily guarded." I said.

"Comrade if you know what went on in here you wouldn't ask."

"Oh; I said I'm honored."

"Don't be," he said taking out a blind fold. You put this on," he said.

Shit that I didn't want. But I had to. Once he got it on me we drove for another hour. This place was big. We stopped and he got out. He opened my door and took me by the arm and said. "Don't worry I got you." And we walked. I know we went into this building and on to an elevator and down. How far I couldn't guess but I know we went down four or five floors. When the elevator stopped he took off my blind fold. The door opened and it was like another city under ground.

"The modern Russia, he said looking at me.

"You can say that again; I said, do we know about this?" I asked.

"You joke again; he said. I like that. Come we see the doctor. He got into this cart and we drove off. "You see he said we use your golf carts."

"Now nice; I said, did you at lease let the golfer get out before you took it."

"You very funny; he said it is good to laugh."

"I know what you mean I said I haven't seen anyone laughing here. Is it against the law to laugh in public?"

"No; he said but you get shot if you do." Ha, ha, ha, he said I make a joke like you," he said laughing.

"Oh; I said, that was a joke."

"What you think we do that?"

"I don't know I asked; do you?"

"Your T.V. does nothing for us; he said they tell you lies and you believe it."

"That depends on what they are lying about?" I said. "Everything, he yelled. They lye about everything." He was getting mad now I guess I should of laugh at his joke.

"Come he said we show you." Then we pulled in front of this door. He pressed something on the cart and the door opened. He drove in and got out. "Come," he said and you will see. See, he said pointing at some real large vegetables'. We make our own sun. Just like Alaska. They have six month of sun we have 12 month of sun and look how big things grow."

"Shit you could feed an army with just one apple."

"No he said that is a cherry."

"You're kidding."

"No he said taste."

He was right it was a cherry. "Do we know about this?" I asked?

"Oh yes he said who do you think we got it off of."

I guess I should have known.

"Well," he said looking at the other side of the room.

"The doctor is busy at work."

I looked at where he was looking and there he was. He was working with other doctors. "Could I talk to him alone?" I asked.

He looked at me as if I was going to kill him.

"No," he said, you think we are crazy?"

"I don't get you? I asked. I just figured if I talked to him alone I could make him understand what we are looking for and he will come out a master once again." "You don't want to kill him?" he asked.

"You got to be kidding I said I was the one that saved him remember. His brain is not for the dead."

"You know we trust you," he said.

"I do but how far?" I asked.

"Joke again," he said.

"No, I said, no Joke how far do you trust me?"

"Come he said you will see."

"Doctor, he called I got your friend here to see you."

The doc lifted his head and smiled. I guess he trough we left him here.

"You see; I said, he likes me."

"Good he said you talk to him. Maybe he will move faster."

"I'll see what I can do. I said but remember I'm not promising anything. He is his own man."

"That we know he said we yelled at him once and he sat for days doing nothing."

"See I said he knows you can't do with out him. That is what you have to make him think. My father did the same thing. And he was like a friend to him. You got to treat him like a comrade. Not a doctor."

"We will try; he said but you talk first."

"I'll see what I can do." I said and walked over to him. "Hey, I said putting my arms around him and hugging him. They got you working hard."

"Too hard; he said and took me over to a corner. What the hell is going on?" He asked.

"Look I just got them to show me where they had you; now we work on getting you out."

"Thanks he said I was beginning to worry. These doctors they got here are real smart and I can't go on fooling them much longer."

"Do you leave here at anytime?" I asked.

"Once a day I go for a walk out side. I use that to slow them down. I tell them I need it to think. So they let me out.

"Good I said what time is that?'

"Ten in the morning, But he said I got three guards that come with me."

That is nothing I said they got hundreds of guards all over the place. Three more doesn't make that much of a difference. Look this is what I want you to do. Just then the fat guy came over.

"You talk to him?" he said.

"Look I said it is hard to talk with everyone around. "That is his problem; he said too many people."

"He is use to working by himself."

"That is right fat boy; he said.

"You see, I said he don't like other people knowing what he is doing."

"But we have to have or doctors see what he is doing." "No he said I and I alone well do it."

I walked over to the fat guy and said with my arm around his shoulder. You're lucky I came when I did. Oh and why is that; he asked?

"You see the doctor?"

"Yes he said.

"Well he doesn't like anyone to know what he is doing. And for that he is getting even with you. Now he do that?" he asked.

I looked over at the doctor and whispered in his ear. He was planing to make some kind of drug to kill all of them. He was just about to give it to them when we came in."

"You kidding;" he said.

"Oh no I said he means it. Like I told you he is a funny guy. He and he alone will be the only one to know how the spider works. He told me my father trusted him but your people are going to be sorry they fool with him. The doctor kept smiling at us. And the fat guy was sweating.

"But we would know;" he said."

"No he said. The doctor said your doctors are ass holes they don't know anything.

What he said pulling away from me. They are the best in the world. That may be true I said but for what this doctor knows they don't. And the same with yours what they know he don't. He only knows what he was working on .so you can see it was luck that brought me here."

"So he said; what do we do?"

"Do what I say I told you he must work by him self and you will get it a lot faster? Look I said you know he can't go a where. So what have you to lose? If you don't you're going to lose a lot of good doctors. He means it. He is crazy enough to do it.'

"No he said you joke with me again. Shit I wasn't getting throw to him. Wait I said and went back over to the doctor. Shit I started something but I don't know how to get out of it I told him.

I told him what I told the fat guy and he smiled.

"Would a spider and bottle of the Lotion do?"

"You have one?' I asked backing away from him.

"The doc had one place in my shirt just in case."

"You mean he was making more of them?"

He looked at me and said. "I don't know what he was doing for Uncle Sam; all I know he said he may come in handy." He went to pull it out.

"No; I said I got to have time to think. Don't show it to anyone. He may be our way out of here. You have anything else the good doctor gave you?"

"Just this; he said taking out another bottle. He said this would make people go to sleep. Something about it going to there brain and numbs it."

"Now does it work?"

He said you had to get it on the tongue our in the eye to make it work; something about direct line to the brain."

"How much does it take?'

He smiled and said; "he gave me enough to take care of an army if I had to. One hundredth of a drop does it. See;" he said opening the bottle and showing me it took nothing.

The fat guy was looking at us and coming closer.

"Tongue or eye." I said.

"That was what he said."

"Good I said give me some." He put it on my finger and closed it back up and went into his pocket. This should do it. I walked back over to the fat man.

"Well; he said you have another joke for me?'

"No I said but could you call one of your guards over here."

"For what?' He asked.

"Just do it I said you're getting the doctor real mad. Now please before he does what he said he will do."

"What is that;" He asked?

"Look you fat motherfucker you want all of your doctor's dead?"

"No" he said

"Then god dam it do as I say."

He yelled for a guard to come over. He came and stood in the front of us at attention.

"What is this I said you got something on your face?" I went to wipe his cheek but put my finger into his eye. Lightly but I got it in.

"How what?" the fat man said.

"I don't know; I said looking at the soldier.

"How long did he say?"

He didn't shit. "You can tell him to go." I said.

The fat man yelled for him to go and looked at me.

"What was that all about?"

I didn't want to tell him just in case it didn't work.

I said; for some reason I trough I know him.

"Look he said you're playing games."

"No I said really No games he means it."

"But you show me nothing; he said just you and him smiling. I think you make big joke? he said. But I joke no more;" he said turning away from me. Guard; he said get him out of here."

He meant me. The same guard came over. I looked at the doctor and he didn't know what happened either. The guard took my arm and was about to walk me to the cart when he just fell. Oh shit thanks god for that. The fat man turned around and looked.

"What you do to him?' He asked.

"Not me I said the doctor did it. See that is what I was trying to tell you."

"You do joke again; he said you stab guard".

"No I said look at him." He went over and rolled him over and over again.

"Nothing; I said.

"You do trick;" he said.

"Look I said; get him up and you will see". He called another guard over to pick the first one up. I went over to make believe I was helping him. I got my finger as I got behind him and acted as if I slipped. My finger went into the other guard's mouth and on his tongue. "Sorry" I said and back off. The fat guy was getting real pissed now. "You he said I'll have you shot".

"No I said you're the one that will be shot if you don't listen to me. The doctor can kill all of you without you knowing it. Watch;" I said.

"Watch what?" he yelled. You joke no more."

"Look you fat mother; I said give me five minute's and if this soldier doesn't go down like the first you can shot me."

The doctor came up and smiled at the fat man; "you want to be next?' he said smiling like a crazy man.

The fat man backed way from him and said; "you have nothing. You just play game." He kept looking at the guard and us. The other doctors were watching us. I guess they couldn't understand what we were talking about. But they know something was wrong.

"Now he said you play enough I call and have you shot;" he said. He was going over to the phone he didn't take his eyes off of us. He walked back wards to the phone. He picked it up and was about to say something when the second guard just dropped. He went down hard. No stopping he just went down. The fat man looked at me and hung the phone up.

"You do that to me?' he asked.

"Did you doc?' I asked.

He just smiled.

"No the fat man yelled I can't dye;" he said running around the room.

Man did he move. He came back to said; "make him stop." he yelled.

"Stop what?" I said

"Stop him from killing me."

"You're going to have to talk to him." I said I don't know what he is doing. For all I know he did it to me." See you had to go fuck with him; I said. I told you he was weird."

"Please" he got on his knees and was bagging the doctor to stop. The doctor walked over to me and kept smiled. "Now what do we do?" he said under his breath.

"Leave it to me I told him just keep smiling." I told him. I went back to the fat man that was still on the floor. "Look he didn't do anything to you and the guards he just gave them enough to knock them out. He doesn't want to kill anyone he just wants to be alone. That is all he is asking. He can't go anywhere. So why don't you leave him by himself?"

"Anything he said you tell him he can have his own workshop."

I went over to the doc and smiled; "we got your way now you don't have to worry about them finding you out."

"No we have to find a way out of here".

"I'll be back tomorrow." I told him. I had to have time to see where we were and how we were going to get out of here. Oh I said stopping him; don't lose our friend." I said. Meaning the spider. I couldn't believe we were still working on it. In the wrong hands it could mean trouble. "Come; I said to the fat man the doctor would like to get on with his work. See I said that was easy. You should have the spider by the end of the week." "Really?" he said.

"I don't know I said but that is what he said. So I guess you'll just have to wait and see."

"You ready?" I asked him. I didn't have to say that twice. He was in the cart and starting it up before I got in. Now to see where the hell we are. "Look I said you had better let your comrades know what is going on here. I don't want them to think it was me that started him off. You tell them I was the one that saved your doctors. If it weren't for me they would be dead by now. And no one to thank but your self's if he did."

"That man is crazy;" he kept saying all the way to the front gate. Now let's hope he don't blind fold me again. I had to keep him think of now he almost died back there. It was working he got to the elevator and we went up.

When we got out some of the other fat man were waiting for us. They wanted to know what went on down there. It seems some of the doctors understood what was going on and didn't want to go near my doctor. "Good I said it was working.

I found out that the fat man were keeping the doctor to them self's. The Russians leaders didn't know anything about him. I guess they wanted to use him for them self's. Boy what Power could do to someone? They forgot to blindfold me. I was up and into the car heading for the main gate. Trying to remember everything I was looking at. I needed to find my way back here if I was to get him.

The fat man was still shacking and all he could ask was how did he do it? He didn't know I was the one that was doing it. It was better that way. So I kept telling him he would have done it to me to. Those made him trust me more.

"Look; I said maybe it would be better if I see him tomorrow to make sure he is happy."

"You go; he said I don't want to go near him ever again:" he said.

"Ha I said now you joke."

He looked at me and didn't know what I was talking about. "I don't joke anymore;" he said meaning it.

"No, I mean how I will get into the lab with all your guards around?"

"Oh he said I would leave you a pass you can pick it up at the main gate."

"Oh; so now you trust me." I said.

"You he said hugging me; you saved my life."

"No; I said while he was hugging me. You saved Russia's life. If you didn't bring me there they would all be dead by now. And what would you do?"

Ha; he said; "my leaders would have my comrade's shot and me."

"You mean they don't know about him?" I asked.

"No; he said we didn't want to tell them till we had the spider ready to go."

"Yea I bet; I said to my self. Well I guess they know about him now!"

"No; he said thanks to you we still could delay it. That is if you say he will have it by the end of the week." "That is what he said; he said he almost had it; but he didn't want the other doctors to find out. If they did then they would have no use for him. I could see his point; I said your people are not like my father; I said he was a wise man."

"You say we are not wise?" He looked at me.

"Well I said look what almost happened. That wasn't very wise. Was it?"

"No; he said I guess your right. One thing you have to understand. I said. This man can destroy thousands of people with out laying a hand on them. That was the whole Idea of the spider remembers."

"Yes; he said taking a deep breath. Scary;" he said.

"But it works." I said. I saw it work remember."

"Yes; he said and you will see it work again."

"To the world; I said holding my arm up like Hitler did. He followed and did the same thing. "To the world". I know I had him going. He would do anything I wanted him to.

Now to get back and work out a plan; I got out and he said he would send a car for me.

"Good I said Early; I said I didn't want him to start getting mad. I had to make sure he understood. He was to work alone from now on."

"Yes; he said you tell him that." And drove off. I felt something wrong as I started to go in the house. I don't know what it was but as I took hold of the doorknob I felt something in my hand. It was on the door. A flower. Now who the hell would leave a flower on the knob? Shit it was Snake. I know it could only be him. I opened the door and sure enough it was. Mike was ever with them. It was the Gunny and some of my old man, along with Snake.

"Mother fucker how in hell did you guys get here?" I said hugging all of them.

The Gunny was the one to talk; He always was the one. "Well you see the General didn't want to send just anyone so he called us back in and told us to come get you."

"You're kidding." I said.

"Your right; he said. We came here on our own. No one was coming for you." He said.

"You have to be kidding?"

"No; he said the general talked till he was blue in the face; no one wanted anything to do with it. They said to let you stay here and seeing the doctor was not here; the hell with the two of you. They said if they sent anyone here it would mean war. And that they didn't want."

"Nice; I said so when were they going to tell me?"

"They weren't;" he said.

"So Snake said. "We come to get you."

Yea; all of them said.

The big guy was here also. He was in the back of the room sitting on something.

"Hey the Gunny said. Talk to your brother he won't stop making noise".

The big guy was sitting on him. I laugh and told him to let him up. My brother didn't know what was going on and he still was half drunk. The girls were locked in the bedroom out of the way. I went over to him and took his head in my hands and said "friends". Hans you hear me Friends; I said they are here to help."

"Good; he said and passed out.

"I'll talk to him when he sobers up. I said. But now we have to talk."

"Come; the Gunny said this is how we did it thanks to Mike over here. He was great he would spot for us and we never even saw a Russian. We walked right here with no trouble. And that is the way we are going back; he said with no trouble. Mike over here will see to that."

"Mike baby." I said as he jumped on me.

This is great but one thing; I said the doctor.

"What about him?"

"We can't leave him." I said.

"Look if his own Government was willing to forget about him we should do the same."

"No; I said I can't do that. Look I know it was asking you guys a lot and God knows I never expected to see you. But I promised him I would be back for him. He can't keep fooling them forever and I feel I owe it to him."

"So we get him. Anyone disagrees? He looked at all of them. No, good; Now where is he?"

I know this would make them stop and think. "He is right in the heart of the Russians top secret base."

"Gunny said; you're joking."

"No; I said I don't joke any more that is where he is. "And you want us to march right in and thank the Russians for watching him and march right back out". "Something like that." I said.

"Man the Gunny said the Vodka has gone to your head.

No one could do that. Not even if we had every last Marine with us. You know how many men they would have down on us?"

"I know; I said I was just there."

"No; he said we changed our mind. We take you and your brother and that is it. And if you give us any trouble he said we knock you out and take you. Do I make my self-clear?" he said looking at me?

"No; I said. Man you are one fucking pain in the ass. I know you would say that. Look I have a plan worked out. "Oh here we go again; the guys said together; him and his plans."

"Hey, they got us out of thing before. Didn't they?" I asked.

"But Louie; the big guy said not the whole Russian army". What difference does a couple of more man make;" I said?

"Gunny Snake said. You were right the Vodka did do something to him."

"No, just listen. I'll go myself. I said but when I get back I want you ready to leave."

"And what if you don't make it?" he said.

"Then take my brother and go." I said.

"We heard that before; they all said. Now you know we aren't going to leave you."

"You have to. I said if I'm not back by sun down that means I'm dead. And it would be no use to try to come and get me."

I told them what I had planned and about the spider the doctor gave the other one and with me being the hero today I could do it. Just then Mike came with his paws on the table. I know what he was saying he wanted to come with me.

"Hey; the Big guy said with out Mike we don't stand a chance of getting out of here, you can't let him take him Gunny".

Mike turned around and growled at the big guy.

"What the hell; he said I lived long enough".

Everyone laugh. It wasn't a happy laugh they know he wasn't fooling. With out Mike they wouldn't make it.

"No Mike; I said you have to make sure they make it out. I'll be O.K."

No he didn't want to hear it. He just covered his ears as if not to hear me.

"You have to stay. I said. Now let's get some sleep. We have a big day ahead tomorrow."

Mike didn't leave my side. He slept with me. One guy kept watch;we didn't want the girls getting out or my brother waking up and going crazy. We didn't get much sleep that night. Mike kept nosing me. He wanted me to change my mind. But I couldn't; my men were more importune to me then my life. The sun came up and I told the Gunny to keep my brother drunk; the less he knows the better. I was waiting out side for the car when it came to pick me up. Snake was holding Mike. I know he would try to follow. I got in and headed for the base. The fat guy was waiting for me. He didn't look too happy.

"Anything wrong?" I asked him.

"My Comrades don't like the idea of you coming here by yourself."

"So, I said you come with me."

"No, he said I don't want to see that doctor ever again. He made me have bad dreams last night."

"So now what?"

He said; this man will come with you".

"So let's go. I said I don't want to keep the doctor waiting."

We drove to the warehouse and got in the cart and headed for the elevator. He didn't say anything I guess he had his orders. The only thing he was a long for was to make sure I didn't go into any other place I wasn't suppose to be in. That was fine with me I didn't want to go any other place. I just wanted to get doc ass and mine the hell out of here. We got to where the doctor was working and the guy left us alone. I guess the fat guy told him what had happened yesterday. He didn't want any part of the doctor.

"Look doc I said we have to go now." I said.

"Fine with me; he said. Let's go."

"Ha I said I wish it was that easy."

"First we have to go for your walk. And from there we have to get to the main gate and back to my brother's place."

"And how does you suppose we do that?" he asked. You have the spider?" I asked.

"He doesn't leave my pocket;" he said

"We would see when we go out. You have the Lotion?" I asked.

He took it out. "Good, give it to me". He took it out and asked; what are you going to do with it?"

I took out this little eyedropper and said; hopefully it makes him do his thing."

He didn't know what I meant but that was better that way.

"So; I said you ready?" It was getting that time. Ten we said ten on the nose." He smiled. "Guards he said my walk. They came and the other guy stopped them.

"No walk;" he said.

Oh shit now what. The doctor caught on. He went into his act.

"No walk?" he said you peoples keep fucking with me".

That was all he had to say. The guards opened the gate and let us out. I'll walk with him. I told them to claim down."

They felt better with that. As we went up in the elevator I took my lotion out and put some drops on the two guard's neck. They were to busy watching the floors. When we got outside I looked around two more guards were at the gate. I went over to them and was about to do the same thing to them when something came and hit me on the back and knocked me down. What the fuck was that? Oh no it was Mike how the hell did he get here? One of the guards was about to shot him.

"Stop; I yelled he was my dog. He isn't going to hurt me". I got up and he came over to me and sat. You ass I told him now what are you doing here?"

He went over and picked up the bottle of lotion. Shit I must have dropped it. He brought it over to me. Oh shit I broke the eyedropper. Now what? The guards came over to look at Mike. They were talking something in Russian. I told them how smart he was and they didn't believe me. Maybe this was what I needed.

"Mike I told him to go get the gun. He went over to the guard and took his gun out of his holster and brought it back over to me. I told the guard to tell him anything he would do it. As he did I was putting the lotion on them. Before you know it all the guards were coming over to play with Mike. I was putting the lotion on them one at a time making it look as if I was patting them on the back. "You like my dog?" I kept saying.

"Yaw they would say and tell Mike to do something else. He kept them busy. Then the office came up with his Jeep yelling. He wanted to know what the hell was going on?" The officer was a dog lover and fell in love with Mike right away. Mike knows he had to get to him in order for us to make our escape. Mike came over to me and took the lotion out of my hand and went over to the officer in the Jeep. He gave him the bottle and the officer opened it and put it on himself, he than did it to Mike.

"Oh shit I didn't know if the spider would go after Mike or not. But I couldn't wait around to find out I had to let the spider go. "Doc I said let him out and get ready to run for the jeep. I back away and tried to get Mike back with me. I know how fast the spider was and if he did bit Mike he would dye. I still had the Guards gun if I had to I would shot it. But I hope I didn't. One shot would be sure death for us.

The way was clear for us to get out. But it wouldn't be if a shot was fired. The base would close up tighter then a clam. And no way were we going to get out. Well here goes. Look at that mother he couldn't wait to get going. He jumped out of the doc hand and headed right for the first two guards. Man was he fast. He got the other two before the rest saw him; a lot of good that did them. The spider was fast. They tried to get away from it but they couldn't; this sucker jumped or I should say flew into the air. It was almost as if he knows what they were thinking.

"Let's go I yelled to the doc; we got to the jeep. The officer was running away from the spider. He was the last one. The first ones were dropping already.

"Shit let's go. I said Mike get in here." He jumped and made it in the back as we took off. "Oh shit the doc said the spider was coming after us. He had to get Mike Shit no way. I stopped the jeep and was about to shot the spider when he jumped at got Mike right on the side of the neck. Too late. God what did I do. I took Mike in the front with me and headed out the gate. No one was left to guard it. Now we had to make it back to my house before anyone knows what went on. The guards were all dead so they could talk; the only thing that would foul it up is if someone came by and saw all of them dead. I was counting on them not being discovered for hours.

I kept Mike close to me. I didn't want him to dye. Maybe he wouldn't Maybe the spider didn't hurt dogs; maybe this and Maybe that. Shit I really didn't know. I hated to lose him. Wait a minute. Now many men did the spider kill? I asked the doctor.

"I don't know; he said. You mean I carried him all the way here in my pocket and that mother killed all of them. Shit; he said shacking all over. God maybe he had babies;" he said taking his jacket off.

"How many man?" I asked.

"I don't know;" he yelled again.

I started to count them. If it was ten or more Mike may have a chance. I kept looking down at him. He didn't seem to be bothered by it. He just stayed next to me and wagged his tail. You O.K.? I asked him. He jumped up and licked my face. I guess he knows. He started putting his paw on me.

"Hey I said I have to drive."

"It looks as if he was counting them; doc said.

He was right he was. He shocks his head yes and started again. One up to ten; shit the spider did kill ten of them. That means his bit had no more poison left when he bit Mike.

Mike knows it all alone. He just barked at me as if to be laughing. Well we got back to the house and the Gunny was waiting. We all piled into the jeep. Way not it was faster.

The Gunny said let Mike tell you the way."

"How?" I said.

"Just follow his nose".

We did and before you know it we were coming up to the boarder. Mike jumped out and ran ahead.

"How watch this;" the Gunny said.

Mike got up on his back lags and started walking for the guard post. The guards were just watching Mike. Mike was walking away from where we were so the guards didn't see us coming.

"Now watch." Snake said looking at Mike. He did flips and roll ova's. I didn't blame the guards for wanting to catch him. He would make someone a good dog. He had the guards chasing him out in to the fields. He would stop just to let them catch up to him and then he would run a little more, just enough for them to think they could catch him the next time he stopped.

"See; the Gunny said he did it all the time. Now he said let's get out of here."

We took off and went over the border. "Mike will meet us on the other side. He said he always gets away from them.

We made it and as we got to the top of the hill we waited for Mike to come.

"There he is." Snake said pointing out in the field. "Come on Mike." I yelled the guards realized what Mike had done and was pretty mad. Oh shit they were shooting at us. "Everyone down". I pulled the jeep over the hill and got out. By the time I got to where I could see Mike they were shooting at him. Look at him go. He was running back and forth. No one could hit him.

"Good dog." I yelled. He was almost here. The Gunny started to shot back at the Russians. They didn't stop them. Mike was almost to me. He was getting ready to jump in to my arms when I saw the bullet hit him. "No" I yelled; it got him right in the head. He did a flip in the air and landed right in front of me dead; half his head was off.

For my country I yelled and bent down and picked him up.

The End.